The Van Helsing Murders

SAMUEL LIVELY

For Kelly

In 1963, the first vampire refugees arrived in America after fleeing Soviet oppression in their ancestral mountain ranges in Romanian Transylvania. These were not the undead monsters of European lore, but regular people carrying a genetic mutation that makes them dependent on the consumption of human red blood cells for survival. The great majority of these refugees settled in River City, then a minor metropolis overlooking one of the mighty rivers that run like arteries across the American heartland. In the three decades since, these vampire immigrants have overcome centuries' accumulation of libelous superstitions and violent prejudices to lay hold of the American dream. Their adopted city has risen with them, becoming a booming center of commerce and innovation, a beacon of American progress. But in 1993, on the eve of the vampires' 30th anniversary in the New World, River City witnessed a series of horrific events that transformed their dreams of progress into a new nightmare...

This is that story.

1

With every strike of his space age polymer soles against the pavement, Ion Dragescu felt more like a god. Not Zeus - soon! - but a young, upwardly mobile Hermes vaulting his way up the Olympian heights.

He had already run nearly ten miles. That would be a monumental feat for any of the obese onlookers staring at his long, lean body in drooling envy as they idled in the morning traffic. But for Ion, it was only a little more than his usual route. The burn in his calves had long ago ascended into a euphoric rush that made his whole body feel light.

The end was now in sight. He could see his apartment building ahead, its cylindrical head poking through the fog to join the surrounding skyscrapers above the fray. At twelve stories, it was only a dwarf, but Ion contented himself that he had reached its very top.

It was time for the final push. The morning sun had begun to crest, throwing the first of its piercing red rays across the river. Ion felt a primeval urge to get inside. He opened his gait and rocked himself forward onto the balls of his feet.

He felt himself racing the river. He too was unstoppable, incomprehensible, and eternal. The cars to his left were dinosaurs, rusting into obsolescence, their riders slowly petrifying as they sunk deeper into the asphalt. He left them in his dust, their idling engines receding into the past like so much cosmic background radiation.

Only the rumble of a motorcycle kept pace, its growls weaving in and out of traffic, a black panther stalking him in the river reeds. But Ion was the cheetah, his legs a blur, his eyes narrowed on his building. No one could catch him. His wind-chapped lips broke wide into a grin as the roar of the bike finally faded out behind him. He blew through the revolving doors of his building like a hurricane.

***

The elevator kicked upward with a jerk and Ion felt his head plunge. A little light-headedness after a run was normal, but not this. He grabbed desperately for the elevator's golden side rails to break his fall. He had pushed too far this time.

He resisted the urge to sink down to the floor and ride the wave out. The elevator walls were glass and he didn't want any of those schlubs in the courtyard to see him stumble. Nor was he sure he would be able to get to his feet again. The thought of bleating out pathetically for his 12th story neighbors to help him up sent a shiver up the lines of his track suit and up to the base of his skull. That little jolt was enough to push back against the encroaching fog.

He took a deep breath to steady himself and suddenly felt the ragged dryness of a parched throat. He closed his eyes and his mind leapt from the hum of the elevator to the thrum of his fridge. He felt himself reaching out towards that stainless steel monolith, its cool white light bathing his aching body. Emerging from its glowing mist was a bottle of red, its slender neck ascending gracefully to its open mouth, beckoning to his cracked lips.

A ding and his eyes opened on the hall. The dulled glimmer of wall sconces guided a still darkened path to his door. Ion staggered forward. There were no rails to lean on now. His eyes drooped again.

There was another ding. Ion's eyes snapped back open. It wouldn't do to let the neighbors see him like this. The sound of a step behind him filled him with renewed urgency, stiffening his back, straightening his gait. His hand stretched forward to meet his door handle and he felt the sweet tremble of relief. He was home.

***

Ion clicked on the lights and the red velvets of his apartment

2

came alive. He felt their old world decadence surround him like a comforter. For a moment his thirst subsided and all he wanted was a long, deep sleep.

It took the sharp steel grays of the kitchen, the only jagged edges of modernity left exposed by his mother's decorator, to slice through his reverie. He was again in front of his refrigerator. In less than a moment the red was on his lips, his neck arched backwards and the nectar of life coating his insides with velvet to match the drapes.

He deposited the bottle back in the fridge, half-empty. Looking down, he saw the red dripping down in two lines from his chin to his pale naked chest. In the gurgle of his stomach, he heard the echoes of his mother's voice chiding for gluttony. Sighing, he felt life returning, his head coming back from the clouds to rest on his shoulders.

Alert again, he traced back his steps, retrieving the track suit he had shed and closing the door he had left ajar. He glanced at his watch - only half an hour until work. He was cutting it close, again. Perhaps he could skip the shower.

He raised his arm and sniffed. A strange aroma greeted his nostrils. Not the usual rancid cocktail of B.O. and last night's vodka, but something pungent and acrid. His nose crinkled in distaste. The good news was it wasn't him. Fat Volya must have ordered takeout again.

Ion moved to the curtains, grabbing a velvet fold and pulling them back gingerly to get at the sliding door to the balcony. The bright heat of the morning sun poured through the gap, turning the red lines on his chest a dark crimson. He winced and yanked at the door, breathing in the rush of fresh air before letting the curtains fall back in place.

Shadows flitted at the corner of his eyes. He blinked, waiting for his eyes to adjust to the change in light. He sniffed again. The smell was still there. And it was stronger! *Damn that slob Volya.*

Another glance at his watch. No time, but he had no choice. He couldn't return home to this stench. He returned to the kitchen and opened the cabinet doors under the sink. There had to be some bleach in there somewhere. He dropped down on both knees for a closer look.

As his bare knees touched down on the cool porcelain tile, he felt something even colder snaking around his neck followed by a terrible sensation, like a thousand fire ants biting all at once.

His senses were ablaze - he could see, hear and feel nothing but the screaming burn of his neck, relentlessly tightening. He knew only that he was being dragged backwards. His arms flailed in every direction but his fingers grasped only air. His cries were trapped inside his exploding lungs.

It was up to his legs. Ion kicked with all his strength, his mighty calves pulsing with tremendous power. He could not see or feel but he knew he must be sprinting again, racing the sunrise, his chest pounding.

It was close now. The burn began to recede. His eyes flickered and he could see again though only faintly! He saw himself lying on the floor. But he was drifting away. He was fading, disappearing. He fixed his dimming eyes on the pale gleam of his chest and saw the two red lines again. He followed them, two streams trickling down, down into a crimson pool that spread until he could see nothing else.

2

Mandy awoke to an angry buzz. Her eyes blinked open with an ease her body could not match. She cast an arm to the nightstand where it landed with a thud, her insensate fingers clutching the vibrating pager.

Her eyes were clear - she hadn't been sleeping long enough for any mucus to settle - and her mind sharp enough to recognize Francis' number marching across the rectangular display.

She shifted onto her elbows, gingerly, hoping for the best. But it came, nevertheless. The vice squeezing at her temples, her body putting the old academy sleeper hold on her brain, forcing it into compliance. *You will sleep for your allotted eight hours or I will break you.*

Mandy slumped back down in momentary defeat. A wave of nausea swept over her as her nostrils picked up the unmistakable smell of chorizo on the morning breeze. Her eyes tracked wearily to her left. There was Angel's giant porcine head with his monster eyebrows glaring darkly over his closed eyes, daring her to reach out and pluck them. A wheeze pushed through his lips, propelling another blast of hot moist breakfast burrito into her face.

The gag reflex was enough to spring her out of bed. She tiptoed over Angel's patrol uniform, dumped in crumpled piles in a straight line from the door to the bed. She rolled back the closet door to see her own dress blues hanging crisply starched and pressed, their deep hues and sharp lines shimmering in the dark recesses of her wardrobe like a sapphire. She looked past them ruefully, her eyes joining her fingers to flick through the assembly line of beige and

5

cream pantsuits in front of her.

She settled on one in the mauve family, ripping off the JC Penney's tags on the way to the bathroom. The coffeemaker was ready and waiting on the vanity, and it was done percolating by the time she had wrapped her hair and makeup. She checked her watch and took a final assessment in the mirror: bland pant suit, lazy bun, dull cherry rouge. Shrug-worthy but sufficient.

The first gulp of black coffee woke her stomach but her fridge had nothing to offer. She popped the styrofoam to-go box next to the sink and eyed the crime scene underneath. A pair of black flies landed on the blood-red salsa caking the lingering entrails of the burrito. She closed the lid and collapsed onto the hard plastic chair in the breakfast nook that passed for her dining room.

She took another gulp, closing her eyes in a wince as the bitter twinge of the bargain bin "Supreme Roast" sledgehammered the back of her palate. Her eyes opened again and rested on the painting that hung where a window would have been in an apartment that wasn't a rat's nest.

Mandy didn't have the arts background to know what she was looking at - she assumed it was some kind of Picasso imitation with its bizarro abstract shapes. But from the first glance - at the mall kiosk! - it had mesmerized her, its black curves and impossible lines dancing in front of her like a pendulum. She sat transfixed, like one of the chickens her siblings would hypnotize and leave stricken and capsized on the dirt.

Angel had laughed when she bought it and complained about it on the few occasions they shared a meal under it. That used to bother her, but now it enhanced its appeal. It was a portal to a separate domain, cold and alien and aloof perhaps, but so alluring, in part because it was the one thing she did not share with the grunting boar under the bed sheets.

A squeal and a honk yanked her back from the portal and back into the grip of the half-nelson crushing her temples. She cracked the front door and spied the boxy gray Lincoln idling below. It was Francis, waiting, a Charon to chauffeur her into an underworld as dark and exotic and mysterious as the Supreme Roast in her hand.

***

Francis turned down the sports talk as Mandy plopped into the passenger seat. She didn't have to look to know he was staring at her. It was the same routine every call, day or night. He'd give her the once over behind his big black aviators, a Newport dangling from his lips. And always the awkward silence.

Finally, he spoke, his words heavy under the gravelly rasp of a chain smoker. "Can't believe you're still in the Pit. Should be moving up in the world now, detective." His thumb massaged the detective's badge on his hip.

"Yeah... Me and Angel might look for something better this weekend."

"Mmm," he grunted, breaking off his stare to shift the Lincoln into gear. Mandy exhaled. *I guess Angel's still good for a few things.*

She stole a glance at Francis as they waited to merge onto the interstate. He was probably good-looking back in his day - tall with broad shoulders and a strong chin. But he was haggard and drooping in all the wrong places now, his wrinkled skin hanging off his skinny neck like an old rooster.

Mandy turned her gaze ahead as the Lincoln carried them up and out of the choking ghetto bog. The map and the apartment leasing agents said Mitchell Heights but natives called it the Pit. Even the tallest buildings in the neighborhood looked up at the graffiti-streaked underbelly of the massive concrete overpass. But up at the top, if you could raise your eyes beyond the gridlock, the pretty facade of River City appeared on the horizon, the sun glistening off its sparkling glass towers and the river snaking below them.

Francis floored it, roaring onto the shoulder at 80, his face as placid as his aviator lenses as they flew inches past a thousand extending side mirrors. Mandy sucked in her breath. She couldn't help it. She hadn't spent enough time in the squad car to build her immunity to the lead foot of a true blue veteran.

"So where are we headed in such a hurry?" She hoped her voice didn't sound as breathless as it felt leaving her throat.

"Riverside. A jumper from one of the highrises."

A jumper. And not off the bridge. *That's a first. And a break from the OD's!* A month in at homicide and she'd yet to land a real murder. Not that a jumper counted, but it was better than another needle in the arm of a forgotten man.

There would be families and onlookers surrounding them. A chorus, full of weeping and gnashing of teeth. Behind them would be the tower, rising like a great Gothic spire. The body would be lying before them, crushed and contorted, its life force draining into the cracks of the crater it made in the earth. And she would be there for it, digging, poking, prodding. Reanimating the dead.

"HEY KID!"

There was Francis, out of the car leaning in. She saw her startled eyes staring back at her in his black lenses.

"You gonna work today or you just want to stay here and sleep?"

She turned away, hiding the flush warming her cheeks and pushing her way out of the Lincoln. There it was: the scene. The tower loomed over her, but only just. It wasn't the skyscraper of her daydreams, just one of those mid-sized glass cylinders developers were throwing up all along the waterfront.

A patrolman was heading toward them, dragging yellow crime scene tape as his eyes scanned the ground.

"Your perimeter's looking a little baggy, Officer." She cranked what little bass she had into her reedy voice.

He didn't look up. "We're still looking for the head."

Francis muttered something profane behind her. Mandy felt a shiver crawling up her spine.

She was moving now, bee-lining to the slouched shoulders of the crime scene photographer ahead. She cut a straight path through the tall swampy grass of the riverbank, paying no mind to her flats sinking into mud and shutting out the memories of her granny's warning whispers of deer ticks and Lyme disease.

Francis was way behind, tiptoeing through the muck in his penny loafers, when Mandy came up on Jenkins, the photographer. Before them in a narrow gully of the riverbank lay the body. A male white. His body was propped up like a grotesque sandwich board, his naked, headless torso and thighs folding together on a butt hinge. Dried blood streaks ran up the pale flesh of his back and up to his boxer briefs, themselves soaked in blood.

Francis appeared at her side, ignoring the body to glare at the mud on his shoes.

"This is no jumper. Look at the direction of flow and the saturation of the clothing. He wasn't in this position when he was decapitated. And that posture. He fell like a rag doll, not a diver. This is a murder!"

"Thanks for that, Sherlock." Francis took a drag off his Newport and then used it to gesture above them. "Now figure me which apartment he got tossed from."

She followed the cigarette up the high-rise, its hundreds of balconies jutting out like a huge Jenga tower. She chewed on a nail, her eyes flitting back and forth from the building to the body.

"It's got to be the top story."

"How'd you figure that; calculate the wind velocity?"

"He's wearing Hermès. A man wearing $300 drawers isn't settling for anything less than the penthouse."

Francis snorted through a drag on his Newport. "There's hope for you yet, Parker."

Mandy took another look at the body, but no amount of carnage could hold back her smile.

***

The first knock on the penthouse level opened on some politically connected schmuck in a bathrobe. He kept on asking if they knew who he was while they searched the apartment. *No, sir, we don't know who you are and we don't care, just like we don't care to know about that white powder residue on your coffee table. And of course he hadn't heard or seen anything and could you people just get out of my apartment so I can take my shower and you'll hear from my lawyer about this.*

The second was vacant. Beautifully empty with a spectacular view of the river and the dark forests beyond pouring through the naked windows. Mandy wondered how the rent compared to the rat's nest.

The third was the winner. Francis' nose wrinkled under his aviators in distaste as soon as the manager inserted his key and swung it open. Mandy smelled nothing.

"This is it," Francis declared but lingered at the threshold, unpocketing a fresh Newport. Mandy nodded and stepped in, slipping on a pair of latex gloves from her purse.

What she couldn't smell, she saw. The dusky light streaming in from the penthouse's half-drawn blinds dimly lit a path of blood from a great congealed pool of it on the kitchen floor to a streak like a painter's brush stretching across a massive oriental rug and out onto the balcony.

The manager, a slick-haired, pouty-lipped young man who had hovered around her like a gnat the entire way up, poked his head in and gave a loud whistle. Mandy turned on him.

"Do you think you could go down and get the name on the

lease for this apartment?"

He hesitated, looking for a reason to stay, but he couldn't find it, not in Mandy's cool expression at least, and so slunk off to do her bidding. She turned back to the crime scene.

There were only three rooms to clear - the main living area, a loft-style bedroom and its adjoining bath. Nothing was out of place. If it wasn't for the blood and the kitsch, this place could have been staged for a showing. *Maybe a fresh homicide would discount it down to my price range.*

As she came down the stairs from the loft, she felt... cozy. The crimson velvet drapes and the deep burgundies of the oriental rugs and the chocolate reds of the blood coagulating on the kitchen floor oozed a comforting warmth. *Like Gramma's little studio before she passed.*

"What you got, kid?" came Francis' jagged voice from outside.

"The blood's thickest over here in the kitchen. The smear marks are consistent with a struggle. No footprints. I think the attack happened here from behind. Maybe slit the throat. Then the perp dragged the body to the balcony and tossed it over."

"Point of entry?"

"No signs of forced entry. Guessing in and out through the front door."

"How about the head?"

A morbid thought sprang into her mind. She hopped over the blood trail and stretched over the tapestry of smeared blood on the floor to open the fridge with her gloved hand.

Nope. No head. Just a glass bottle half-full of... Mandy's heart skipped a beat.

"Francis!" A grunt from outside. "The vic's a vamp!"

A hacking cough spluttered from outside the door and Francis' head appeared in the doorway.

"Are you sure?"

The manager's head popped in next to Francis, looking for Mandy.

"I've got the name. Can't pronounce it." He held a piece of paper out for Mandy. Francis snatched it from his hand, replacing his aviators with a matronly pair of reading glasses.

"Ee-own Drag-eshkoo," he pronounced slowly, shaking his head. "F***. This is the last thing I need."

He combed a hand through his hair, disturbing the neatly

moussed silver waves into an angry maelstrom, swirling around an exposed bald spot. For a moment, Mandy saw what looked like panic radiating around his pale eyes before he sealed them off again behind the shades.

"Let's seal it off and leave the rest for crime scene. I'll get a uni up here and then you can handle the paperwork downtown."

Mandy's protest withered under Francis' sphinx stare. She took her time treading across the soft rug, her eyes lingering. *Goodnight room. Goodnight body. Goodnight penthouse with a beautiful view of the moon.*

3

The speed limit said 55 so Enoch Parker could not understand why the little city cars were buzzing around him like angry hornets. His '56 Ford pickup couldn't do much more than 50 uphill anyway so all their honking and swerving and glaring wouldn't do them a heap of good.

He sighed, doing his best to stretch his legs in the cramped cabin. Brother Frank had offered him his Buick, but Enoch had turned him down. Daddy's old pickup had always come through for him and he needed something sturdy and reliable and, you know, decent, to help him on this journey.

But going up this hill in the fourth hour of this trek was planting doubts. He shook them out of his head along with the sleep tugging at his eyelids and pressed down on the accelerator.

At the crest of the hill River City spilled out in front of him. The sight drove away all his fatigue. Just look at the place. He'd been born in a big city, but his mom and dad had whisked him out of there before he was ten. And he sure didn't remember it looking like this.

The night had seemed starless before, but no more. River City was its own galaxy, a billion glittering beams lighting up the skyline like it was midday. It filled the entire horizon, sprawling to cover the earth as far as he could see to the left and right, its glassy towers rising to pierce the heavens.

Enoch wondered if this was how the tower of Babel had appeared to farmers and hunters as they saw it rising before them on the plain of Shinar. This was how men could see themselves as gods, when they could see nothing else but the works of their hands.

His mind returned to the readings he had made in preparation for this trip. The Copper Springs library was tiny but it had one big book on River City and Enoch had devoured it. He had been fascinated to discover that its founding frontiersmen, having seen its rivers cutting through an arid plain like the old Ararat and Euphrates, had called it Babylon. Then came the rowdies and riverboat gamblers who built up the waterfront with saloons and brothels and made it worthy of the name.

Only when churchgoing families of good old American stock moved in did a new class of city fathers rise to clean up the waterfront and change the name to match. Enoch would have preferred something more stout and Biblical than the bland, anodyne River City, but he appreciated the sentiments behind the change.

He wondered what those good church folk would think of their city now. He had read that banking had transformed the city from "just another middle American bumpkin-burg into a bustling metropolis." The financial capital of the American heartland.

He guessed that it was the megabanks that had built all these skyscrapers. They looked like giant versions of the stacks he used to make of his nickels and dimes when he was a boy, saving up for that shiny bicycle in the general store window. Oh, how he had pined for that hunk of junk, spending every spare moment picking strawberries to sell at market instead of helping his mom take care of grandma in her last days.

It had been such moments of thoughtless greed that had fed the monstrous growth of these new Babels. The love of money was the root of all evil, and these were the tall trees that sprang from the well-watered seeds.

These thoughts took Enoch's wandering mind back to the orchard and the peach blight. With Emily helping out so much with the grandkids, it would be up to the boys to keep it at bay. Had it been a mistake to leave such a heavy weight in such young hands? No, he chided himself. *The Lord's hands.*

He forced his mind back onto the task at hand. He was not the farmer right now, but the shepherd after a precious lost sheep. His eyes flickered at a change in light. The glorious glare of the city was dipping out of sight as the road descended under an imposing array of earthworks and overpasses. He took the exit for Mitchell Heights, the road descending still further into a narrow gauntlet of grim concrete tenements and steel-sided warehouses.

Enoch instinctively leaned forward, his eyes searching for threats lurking in the shadows here away from the city lights. *Yea, though I walk through the valley of the shadow of death, I will fear no evil.* He gripped the wheel a little tighter. Of all the places for a man to have to look for his little girl.

***

The taxi stunk. Mandy couldn't tell if the driver needed a bath or had overindulged in some exotically spiced dinner, but it was enough to keep her awake.

She squeezed her right hand, trying to massage away the ache of the night's work. She had spilled a magnum opus' worth of ballpoint ink on a desk full of white sheets and their carbon copies. A computer would have made sense but she worked for Stone Age PD.

She glanced behind her to see the ugly rectangle of headquarters still looming. Could never really escape that place. It didn't help that Francis had disappeared shortly after they showed up. He had mumbled something about giving the brass a head's up and then vanished into one of the elevators.

That left Mandy stuck in the old hindquarters as her old Lieutenant liked to call it. There she joined the swampy churn of zombie-eyed detectives and civilian employees pushing paperwork through the intestinal labyrinth of the police bureaucracy. What didn't get shredded or absorbed through the walls of file cabinets on the way out would get dumped into the vast latrine of the county court.

Mandy's slow trek through the bowels of justice had left her feeling drained and dehydrated, and now she was soaking up the stench of whatever the a.c. was pumping into the backseat. It was almost midnight. Angel would be getting ready for his shift. If this cabbie could slow down a bit maybe she could take a nice long shower without him storming in like Norman Bates.

No such luck. The cabbie made great time and Mandy found herself leaning on the apartment gate, chipping off the cheap teal paint with her fingernails. Maybe she could sleep right here. Then the sound of a male voice swept down from above and blew her upright. *No, he couldn't be.*

She swung open the gate and crept up the stairs. As soon as her head cleared the second floor, she froze. Those cowboy boots. Those impossible daddy long legs. That stinky old leather jacket that mom could never get him to throw out. She didn't need him to turn around to know it was Dad. *How did he find me? He's right at my door.*

To her horror, she realized that her door was open and another voice was speaking from inside. He was talking to Angel. The realization dropped her heavily onto the stairs. Perhaps the cabbie was still outside the gates. If she snuck back out she could go back to work and wait him out. He couldn't wait around forever; he had the farm to attend to. She could outlast him.

Suddenly the gate creaked and in stepped the fat lady from next door. The grocery bags she carried in each arm added to her already imposing girth to completely block Mandy's escape.

When the lady's eyes alighted on Mandy, she dropped her groceries and thundered to her side.

"You okay, baby?"

Mandy made a show of grabbing her ankle. "Just a little twist. I'm alright."

There was more thunder from above and Mandy turned weakly to see her dad's silhouette framed at the top of the stairs. In one stride he was at her side and then somehow he had her in one arm and all the lady's grocery bags in the other until he deposited them all neatly on the doorstep.

She saw all their big heads pushing together to get a look at what they must have believed was her broken body. *I'm being fitted for a fainting couch.* She raised her hands in protest.

"I'm okay, it's okay, you can give me some space now." She pushed her way through her door and sat down heavily in front of her painting. Her cheeks were hot and she was breathless. Angel and her dad followed, Angel sitting across from her and dad staying at the threshold, leaning against the door frame.

"Hey, dad. What's the occasion?" She refused to look at him, returning to her masquerade with the ankle, intensely focusing on pushing out imaginary swelling.

"Your mother and I have been worried about you." His voice was so solemn, so quiet.

"You could sense me twisting my ankle, huh? When did you get into town? It's quite a drive."

"Got in a couple nights ago. Took me awhile to find you." She could feel those soft choir boy eyes boring into her neck. She couldn't look but she couldn't very well keep staring at her ankle. She raised her gaze to the hem of Angel's bathrobe and his big hairy naked body breaking out of every gap. The burn in her cheeks intensified. *Would a little shame kill you?*

"I see you've met Angel."

"Yes, I have." His voice was so heavy.

"I'd offer you a tour..." she said, freeing her eyes from the slipping knot holding in his bathrobe to flit around the room.

Over there's the den of iniquity. And if you look past the kitchen, you can see the living-in-sin room.

"... but it's getting late. You must be exhausted and Angel's got to get to work."

Angel glanced at his watch - *but you couldn't put on a pair of drawers?* - and a rumble started in that big barrel chest. He was about to say his shift didn't start for an hour so he'd be happy to talk for a little while longer. But her dagger eyes caught him just in time and all that came out was some mumbled nonsense and a "she's probably right."

"Of course. I'll be staying at the Garden Inn down the street. Maybe you could stop by tomorrow and see me."

"Definitely," Mandy said to the door frame next to him. She saw his shadow suddenly lurch forward and he was hugging her, pressing his scratchy cheek to hers. She felt a cool tear touch her burning skin and she knew it wasn't hers. He lurched away, his back turned, and he was gone.

4

Vladimir Paler sat uncomfortably in his captain's chair, staring at the giant painting across from him. He loved ships - not boats. A rowboat was a boat. He loved the big beauties like the one in the painting. *The Battle of Trafalgar!* When men were men! Oh how he loved this ship, the triple decker with cannons bristling like porcupine quills and sails as big as clouds and elegantly carved wooden accents at the fore and stern castles. So grand and so stately that you didn't even notice the mass of dead and dying sailors floating in its wake.

And to be the captain! King of the seas! To have the map of the world unfurled before you, the dragons and monsters lurking at the faded edges, fleeing before the advance of the great galleons, hopping from island paradise to island paradise. The sweet smells of rum and spices emanating from the holds below. And a crew of hearties ready to leap into action at the sound of his voice.

Vladimir's nautical obsession had the detectives surrounding his office - his captain's cabin - calling him the Vampirate. Never in his presence of course, but he didn't mind. A far better name than the ones he'd heard in hushed and sometimes not so hushed mutterings in the decade he'd been in the department. How far he had come. And yet he still sat so uncomfortably in his chair.

A captain's life in the River City Police Department lacked all the romance of the high seas. As a Lieutenant he had been mobile, riding his take-home vehicle through the streets like a British gunboat heading upriver. But now he was confined to his quarters

17

in the center of the eighth floor. His views? Detectives on every side, oarsmen in the galleys. But they were free to come and go and here he was chained to his desk, beating the bureaucratic drums to keep everything barely moving.

A true vampirate would be out delivering thundering broadsides, commandeering vessels, putting his enemies to the sword and ravishing high-born maidens on their way to foreign courts. Not vetoing vacation requests and performing crime stat analysis for corpulent colonels.

His door creaked and in poked Maggie's head. The darkened glass door made it too easy for her to hide that beautiful swan's neck of hers.

"I've got the Dragescus for your nine o'clock."

Vlad winced as he motioned her to send them in. He remembered his manners just in time to stand up and put on a pained expression before they stepped into his office. The Dragescus: a proud and noble name. One of the most esteemed houses of Leaota, the greatest of the vampire kingdoms. The mere mention of the name stirred Vlad's instinct as a lowborn Valley man to kneel. Vlad curbed the impulse, opting for a slight bow.

Mrs. Dragescu entered first. What a production she was, decked out in a gigantic black hat and a grim black dress, cinched together by what must have been a corset at her waist, while her skirt ballooned out over what he imagined was a bushel of petticoats.

Her husband came in behind in a similarly grim wool suit, a black armband on his sleeve. Their faces were dour, their motions stiff. Vlad gestured for them to sit down. The husband waited gentlemanly for his wife and then sat next to her, both of them fixing Vlad with the same lifeless gaze.

The dull, sexless fashions, the constipated gait, the emotionless countenance - it was the worst of the continental Old World staring him in the face. He hoped that his own face hid the disdain souring the back of his throat as he mouthed the usual bromides. *Condolences... Grievous Loss... Eternal Memory...* Et cetera, et cetera, et cetera.

The pair of them wallowed in the uncomfortable silence that followed while Vlad did his best to hide the squirming of his numbing butt cheeks. What was a New World buccaneer like him doing watching these fossils petrify in front of him? He should be out there pillaging and feasting on the fat of this virgin land instead of floating in this stagnant pool of suppressed grief.

He chided himself. They had lost their only son. And so what if they were unbearably stiff? These were the founding folk, as Dr. Duma used to say. The pillars of the old world on which the new would be built. And here they were shattered, no matter how stiff those upper lips remained.

Finally, the silence ended.

"We want to make sure that our son's case will be handled appropriately." It was the husband who spoke, slowly, deliberately, sucking in on every last syllable.

Of course he understood what they wanted. They wanted a countryman on the case. Not one of these vulgar American low lives. Someone who would ensure old country justice. Someone like Vladimir Paler.

"I've made it a personal priority of mine. And the department is behind me one-hundred and ten percent." He cringed as he heard his new world lingo land with a flop in the space between them. Their eyes narrowed. *Yes, yes, this is the same Vladimir Paler who came so highly recommended by your highborn friends. Yes, I may have picked up some American vernacular working in the trenches. So sue me.*

And Vlad wasn't bullsh***ing, to use another vulgar Americanism, about handling this case. He had no choice but to be neck-deep in it. As soon as the call had come down the line, the bigwigs had pulled him in for meetings. This was the first real vampire homicide in years.

"We trust the investigation will be handled with utmost discretion."

Vlad nodded. The department bigwigs were right there with them on that. Vlad's first thought on scanning the report had been jilted lover. And with the upper body strength involved in choking out a full-grown man and then cutting his head off, Vlad was guessing a homosexual relationship. But that notion wasn't what was putting discretion on everyone's lips.

The worry was this was a hate crime, which put as much fear in the hearts of River City's red-blooded American elite as it did in paranoid Old Worlders like the Dragescus. Remembering the panic he'd seen in the Colonel's eyes almost brought a smile to his lips. In the old days, the fat oligarchs of the upper floors had happily turned a blind eye to the most horrific acts of xenophobia. All of that had been excused in service of the greater good of making godforsaken vamp refugees think twice about settling in and around wholesome River City.

But now that vamp scientists and engineers and entrepreneurs were injecting new industries and tech and capital into River City, now they couldn't get enough of us. Who were the bloodsuckers now?

The couple was now looking at him expectantly. This was a silence he was supposed to break.

"I'm actively reviewing the case now. I'll make sure I have my best men working it and that everything is handled appropriately."

Their eyes lingered on him, still expectant, still unsatisfied. He wanted to tell them what they wanted to hear: that he'd put a countryman on the case. But there wasn't even any truth to stretch there.

"They'll be good men. Sensitive to the needs of the community." He paused to take a reading - still the piercing eyes.

"Ideally, yes, there'd be someone from within the community to take the lead on this, but I just don't have anyone in personnel yet. The old prejudices have ebbed somewhat, but it takes time for that change to trickle down to hiring practices."

Vlad gave a sad smile as that lament returned some of the dull to their eyes. All nonsense, but perfectly palatable to a pair of Old World cynics. The truth was the second generation of vamps wanted no part of being a cop, not when there were millions to be made in tech, medicine and banking. The Dragescus' own precious firstborn had been a prime example of the greedy little larva, forsaking drudgery and dirty work for the glitz and glamor of high finance.

Sensing their gloomy resignation, Vlad stood up with as much ceremony as he could muster. The Dragescus rose stiffly to their feet.

"Given the circumstances, I understand if you won't be attending tonight." That he was referring to the grand opening of the Duma Center for the Performing Arts went without saying. This was the pinnacle event of the social calendar for the vampire upper crust. They nodded morosely, politely requesting that he give their regards to Mr. and Mrs. So-and-so and Such-and-such and various other stuffed shirts whose company he was going to have to pretend to enjoy that evening.

At last, the niceties were over and they all gave their little bows and exited. Vlad plopped back down on his chair. He took one more look at his painting and then it was back to the piles of paperwork, sprawled out over his desk where a treasure map should have been.

***

Vlad tugged at the necktie squeezing in on his Adam's apple. For the first time, he missed the flimsy clip-on polyester tie that went with his dress blues. Tackiness was a small price to pay for comfort. But, no, the Mayor had insisted he put on a tux. *You don't show up to the opera in a costume.*

He directed his irritated sigh to the Mayor's back, rising bare from a tightly fitted black strapless dress. She looked as tall and imposing as her petite figure would allow, her posture perfect, her neck fully extended and her voluminous black and silver hair piled up in a spire like the Bride of Frankenstein.

It was all she could do not to look tiny in between the two towers she had chosen for her chaperones. Vlad glanced over at Simion Codrescu on her left. Like Vlad he was tall and elegant in bearing, though he had a painful looking curvature towards the top of his spine that pushed his head forward, giving him a certain goblin-like aspect. In their shimmering black tuxes, they looked like a pair of ebony chess pieces flanking the Mayor's queen. *Or doormen.*

Codrescu didn't return Vlad's glance, but he didn't need to; Vlad knew exactly what kind of disdainful look he'd get. Vladimir Paler, a Valley man, son of a drifter, a nobody, a mid-ranking flatfoot, sharing a platform with a Codrescu, scion of Leaota! And not just any Codrescu, but the first vampire city councilman, a beacon to his people! Vlad smirked.

They stood on the edge of the red carpet that stretched from the street up to the marble platform where they stood and then into the mouth of the monstrosity they called the Duma Center for the Performing Arts. Vlad kept his eyes locked ahead, avoiding the urge to glower at its ugliness. But it was irresistible.

The center was a sprawling behemoth with massive concrete beams shooting up from its foundation at impossible angles, supporting nothing, signifying nothing. Dense clusters of trapezoidal glass sprung at random from its darkly gray exterior like insectoid eyes. It crouched on the bluffs of the river, brooding like a grotesque spider.

He blamed Codrescu, whose planning committee had rammed this "design" through the city council. It was one thing to leave the suffocating fashions of the old country behind them, but to go this far in the other direction was embarrassing. A total surrender to the ridiculous pretensions of the American avant-garde. Vlad knew Dr. Duma would be rolling over in his mausoleum, a stately and tasteful neo-Gothic edifice in the foothills north of the city that Vlad visited every month.

The arrival of the VIP motorcade brought Vlad back to the present. The first of the black limos opened on billionaire Andy Ryan, the dapper pharmaceutical mogul that every ambitious young vamp in River City emulated. He strode up the red carpet in his flashy double-breasted suit - *no monkey suit for him* - with a supermodel on his arm and a pouty-lipped smirk on his sun-bronzed face. Vlad forced a smile in return while the Mayor and Codrescu gushed all over him.

How any self-respecting vamp could look up to this silver spoon sucking garlic-eater - *tsk tsk!* Vlad caught himself. Couldn't afford to even think in the old slurs. Of course the popular alternative terms had their own issues. "Normal" was obviously unfair to the vamps, as natural as it might seem to normal people. The technical label "hemotypical" was the most acceptable to polite society, but what a mouthful! Vlad usually settled on the least awkward of the bunch: "native."

Another bunch of native A-listers followed after Ryan, each stopping for continental face kisses with the Mayor and polite smiles at her two vamp escorts. *No kisses for us bloodsuckers! Don't want us too close to your necks!* The young councilman Garrick, as tall as any vamp, but with the sandy blonde hair and deep tan of a surfer, was at least willing to shake Vlad's hand. Though it was nothing compared to the heart-melting gaze he bestowed on Mayor Cohn before grabbing her up in a lingering embrace.

When the tide of natives ebbed and the vamp elite had their turn. The first wave was a grim procession of painfully self-serious dignitaries, a parade of Dragescu clones. Vlad gave them each deep bows, returning their richly accented Romanian greetings with mumbles to hide the badly pidginized state of his own mother tongue.

His back was beginning to ache when the caravan finally came to the younger vamps. Here came Alex Duma, the heir to the

Duma fortune and legacy, looking like a carbon copy of Andy Ryan, right down to the oversized double-breasted suit. He even had what looked to be a spray-on tan. But at least Duma gave Vlad a good firm handshake and a hearty greeting in English - he had his father's vitality if none of his good sense.

In Duma's wake came the roar of the "Bat Pack," Duma's posse of vamp playboys. Duma had at least matured enough to ride in a limo but his hangers-on were still fond of tearing around town in their Yamaha motorcycles, their faces hidden behind those alien helmets. Now they dismounted, tossing their keys and helmets to bewildered looking valets and grabbing onto the beautiful women emerging on cue from Duma's limo. They swaggered up the red carpet like the drunken reprobates they were.

Vlad saved his steeliest gaze for Adrian Dan, the most debauched of the bunch. Dan sauntered past them, leering as he went, his hands all over this barely-clad date. *Go ahead and strut you smug S.O.B. Someday soon that's gonna be a perp walk.*

The posse's last straggler was its strangest. Mikhail Andreanu came from a richer bloodline than any of those preening jerks but you would have never known it the way he slouched up the red carpet, hands tucked into the pockets of an all-black ensemble, his long black hair wild and hanging down over his downcast eyes. *It's an opera, not a punk rock show, kid.* Still the boy did have something that set him apart from the crowd, a sort of miserable charisma. If he would have looked up, he might have been the recipient of Vlad's first genuine greeting of the night. But alas.

Vlad glanced at his watch. Standing around and smiling like an idiot was bad, but it was all that was keeping him from sitting through three hours of Faust. He looked up. The caboose of the VIP train was trickling in. Here they came in their cheap suits and ill-fitting tuxedos, the stowaways and freebooters, the schmucks who couldn't or wouldn't pay the $10,000 for a box but had enough social gravity to merit an invite. *People like me!*

He recognized most of them. There was Charlie Grace, the tabloid journo in his trademark pink leisure suit, hot on the Bat Pack's trail as usual. Then his friend Big Mike Bouchard, the former gangbanger vamp-basher turned minister and vamp advocate. The old Reverend was looking absurd with his big frame bulging out of a rent-a-tux. Vlad shouted a greeting to him but the Reverend couldn't hear him, trudging zombie-like under the foyer.

And finally, Theresa Russell, the *artiste* who was always staging some shocking exhibit in the middle of big crowds to draw awareness to some obscure cause. Vlad would have to have a word with security to keep an eye on her tonight.

Just then the Mayor tugged on his sleeve. It was about to start.

***

The Mayor and Codrescu had filed into their box with assorted River City mucky mucks but Vlad lingered in the foyer, eyeballing the hors d'oeuvres tables that awaited intermission. It was always a production serving these mixed crowds. Where did you put the red without calling too much attention to it and yet still make it obvious enough that no careless or inebriated garlic-eater - *no, hemotypical person* - would accidentally take a swig?

It was a matter of considerable delicacy, but the past two decades of elite integration had established something like a groove for these occasions. Champagne flutes, the universal option, would go out amidst the mingling masses, while the red would remain at the far end of the table to be poured in tastefully opaque glasses.

A waitress was just beginning to stock that side of the table when Vlad heard the intensifying hee-haw of the orchestra warming up in the pit. He swooped down on the first pour, startling the poor waitress. The red was fashionably thin and chilled - neither to Vlad's preference - but no matter: he downed it in a single gulp. It was uncouth behavior, of course, but how else was he supposed to make it through this marathon?

Avoiding eye contact with the waitress, he deposited the glass and hurried to the booth, doing his best to open the door quietly. Other than an arched Codrescu eyebrow, his stealthy entrance went appropriately unnoticed and he took his spot behind the Mayor.

It was dark inside the theater and it took a moment for Vlad's eyes to adjust. As ugly as the building's outsides were, he had to admit it was breath-taking on the inside. The stadium seating went on forever, the packed house and the orchestra looking like ants beneath them. But the stage, still cloaked behind its great velvet curtains, was so vast and grand that it felt intimately close to the boxes studding the encircling walls.

That the view was already so good could not stop Vlad from reaching for the ornate silver opera glasses in front of him. He soon grew tired of inspecting the fibers of the huge curtains and

24

turned the lenses on the crowd in the cheap seats below. All of River City's strivers and social climbers gathered together to inaugurate the city's hot new venue. Dedicated to a man the same crowd would have hissed and jeered off the -

The sudden piercing soprano scream made Vlad bolt upright along with everyone in the crowd. Could it be some opening gimmick? He sat back again as the curtains shuddered and began to part. A little showmanship to launch the season would be a nice change of pace - maybe the next three hours wouldn't be so bad.

But then another scream sounded and this time Vlad realized it had come not from the stage but the foyer. Rising to his feet, Vlad leaned down to whisper something reassuring in the Mayor's cocked ear. Codrescu made a show of getting up but Vlad sat him back down with a hand on his shoulder. *This is police business. You sit down and watch the opera with the women.*

Feeling for the Beretta holstered over his waistcoat, Vlad headed towards the screams. As he stepped out into the foyer, he saw a small crowd of waiters huddling around the waitress - the same girl he had startled earlier. A growing throng of onlookers fanned out on either side of the girl, emitting shrieks and groans to match her hysteric sniffling. Vlad stopped to look around for Theresa Russell - this felt like one of her stunts.

The crowd had formed a rough semi-circle around the hors d'oeuvres table, kept back by some invisible perimeter. Vlad had acted too slowly; now he was caught in the churn and catching elbows from society women scratching and clawing their way to the front to get a view of the show. *Oh, to be in uniform!* He was forced to rely on a gruff bark and an officious glare to billy-club his way through the mob, resorting at last to knife hands to cut between the last line and break into the clear.

Vlad scanned the area. The same hors d'oeuvres table as before, just more heavily laden with food and drink. The wine flutes, the cheese plates, the fruit and vegetable medleys, the bruschetta spreads, all looking beautifully delicious. Then, in the center of the table, the main attraction, a silver platter topped with a bed of emerald-green lettuce and a severed human head.

5

Mandy liked to spend her rare nights off catching up on sleep, eating and reading ravenously and then unwinding with a solitary walk along the riverbank at daybreak. But the cold hand of dread that clutched and grabbed at her stomach had ruined all that. She slept in fits and starts. She couldn't keep her coffee down. Her fingers were twitching too much to hold a book and she felt an ache chewing at her lower back whenever she took a step.

So she had retired to her bed, rolling back and forth in search of some comfortable spot and never finding it. Her eyes refused to stay closed. First, they would glare at the buzzer, commanding it to come to life and pull her out of the Pit. And there it sat in silent defiance. Then her eyes would turn to the door and search for the slightest movement of the knob. *Francis shouting "get out of bed, we've got a call!" Angel returning home early from his shift! A homicidal sex fiend breaking down the door!*

But there was never any movement and her eyes would inevitably close again, and there would be the silhouette of her father in the doorway burning through the back of her eyelids. And then she would go rolling again and the whole cycle would start over.

There was a loud snap and Mandy jumped out of bed. The mouse trap under the sink had finally sprung its mortal coil. Mandy descended on the grisly little scene with feverish intensity. A perfect kill. The spine cleft right below the neck. No blood. The little beast's beady black eyes were still frozen in that moment of rapture when the month-old peanut butter lit up its gustatory cortex like the Fourth of July.

It was then that Mandy had felt the pull of the old dark art. Sure enough she still had the kit, tucked away in the trunk of keepsakes that her mother had insisted she take with her. What a flood of memories when she opened that trunk and pushed past those regrettable drawings and forgettable trinkets and diary after diary to finally reach it. Lo and behold, the teenage taxidermist was reborn.

The tiny scalpel fit neatly into the grooves of her hand which moved with the precision of undimmed memory. *It really was like riding a bicycle!* The hours dissolved under her little work lamp as she moved from prepping the hide to fashioning a new mouse body of clay and wire. The process required such intense focus and produced aromas so wonderfully foul that no thoughts or sensations but the ones at hand could penetrate the mind.

The mouse that resulted stood upright and unbroken, its tiny paws reaching upward to praise its creator, an act of worship marred by the creature's hideously misshapen face. *Oof, I'm rusty.* But still, she had done it! The old thrill had returned in force. But soon the fumes dissipated and with them the creative high. The thoughts seeped back in with the fresh air. *To Mandy, Love Dad.*

He had been so eager to indulge her morbid curiosity, letting her tag along on every fishing and hunting trip, immersing her in the gore of every kill, skinning and gutting. He had even taken to snatching critters from the cat's mouth to give her novice fingers specimens to practice on. He paid no mind to Esther and Hannah's loud exclamations of disgust. And he never had anything like the look on Mom's face when she saw her arranging her fiercest looking rats in a macabre dance around a fire made of tissue paper stained with red and orange food coloring. How they had argued when Mom told him her little creatures were demonic over that night's dinner. And how that had been the end of her taxidermy hobby. Or at least the one she let her parents see.

Mandy felt the hand around her stomach re-establish its cold grip. She pushed away from the table, not even bothering to clean up the little pile of mouse guts. They could take their place alongside Angel's leftovers in this hovel of an apartment. Once again, her father's figure in the doorway haunted her thoughts. *Why couldn't he stay where he belonged and look after Mom and the boys and the grandkids? Weren't my older sisters enough? Why not let the one little black sheep graze where she likes?*

Her eyes turned back to the grotesque face of the mouse staring up at her. Then with a burst of energy that had been missing all day, she picked it up and flung it at the flip top of the garbage can. It missed wide right. But no matter, she was up on her feet. Leave the cringing and the cowering in the past with taxidermy. She was a grown woman now, more than capable of standing up to her father.

She covered the ground in between the kitchen and the front door in three of the longest strides she could muster, steeling her chin. She could see Dad now, sitting in one of those roach-infested rooms at the Garden Inn, sitting in his faded blue jeans on a soiled mattress, speechless as she gave him both barrels. *Yes, I'm shacking up with some random guy. No, I have no intentions of letting him make an honest woman out of me. No, I don't believe in God anymore.*

Then she picked him off the imaginary floor, gave him a nice hug and kiss on the cheek and told him it would all be fine and she would see him for Thanksgiving. And then he drove off in the old Ford. Sad, yes, but the closer he got to the farm, the more the pain dissipated, and the more the unhappy thoughts of the black sheep were crowded out by the happy bleating of the many white sheep clamoring for his attention. *Yes, this was going to work.*

She opened the door and stepped out confidently. She felt tall and utterly calm. It was only a short bus ride to the Garden Inn. No way this liberated spirit could completely recede by then. A sudden vibration on her hip. The pager. Francis. A call! *Oh, thank God. Maybe you do exist after all.*

***

"The circus is in town," Francis uttered tonelessly. Even the most colorful police vernacular poured out of his mouth like dust.

But it still rang true. When half the police and fire departments and the media made a crime scene, the whole area had the look and feel of a psychedelic carnival. Nowhere more than the Duma Performing Arts Center, which looked like a giant version of one of those funhouses Mandy used to love at the county fair.

The blinding light show of a thousand red and blue strobes reflecting off the building's huge glass panels gave Mandy an instant headache, but she could barely feel it under the pulsing adrenaline.

Stepping under the DO NOT CROSS of the yellow crime scene tape, she saw red carpet under her foot. She flashed a look back at the crowd of beautifully dressed on-lookers pressing at the tape, staring at this beige pant-suited impostor with mismatched flats and knotted hair whipped up into a messy ponytail. A little homicide and the whole world goes topsy-turvy.

Francis dragged his feet by her side the whole way up the carpet, impressively unimpressed. Mandy hoped her face projected similar world-weariness - minus the saggy flesh under the chin of course - but she worried the flush burning up her cheeks told a different story. *Bright-eyed bushy-tailed rookie detective reporting for duty!*

She saw Jenkins clomping towards them with his gray trench coat and chunky camera, the beginnings of a yawn working around his jaw hinges.

"You two missed the party." He pointed behind them as the yawn finally escaped. Mandy turned to follow his finger, but shrank back, blinded by the sea of lights.

"Bomb squad's got the head back there."

She turned back to look through the glass into the interior of the lobby. It was swarming with River City PD, from patrolmen to the 12th story brass. Even the county sheriffs were there. Everyone is trampling around my crime scene but me!

She made a reluctant left and headed straight into the pulsing maelstrom of lights. Mandy wished again that she had a good pair of shades. She wanted to close her eyes and follow Francis and his aviators but no matter how slow she walked, he found a slower pace to keep just behind her.

At last they cleared the outer perimeter of squad cars and fire engines and Mandy blinked away the blindness to see the bomb unit's armored van in a clearing. A SWAT officer in full gear leaning on a makeshift barricade held up a hand for them to stop.

"Safety perimeter still in effect, folks."

"It's alright, this is our crime scene."

"Parker?"

He peeled off his big black goggles. It was Anderson, Angel's old academy buddy and fellow neanderthal. He gave her the once over, grinning like a fool.

"Haven't seen you since Academy! Dang, detective. And homicide! That was fast!"

She forced a smile. "Great to see you, Anderson. Could we just take a look?"

"Man, how is Mendoza? Still in patrol, right? Gotta burn him seeing both of us leaving him in the dust! Wait, you're still together, right?"

Mandy looked to Francis for help, but all she got was the usual Stygian gaze. Sighing, she succumbed to the demands of small talk for a few long minutes, even throwing in some half-hearted flirting, until Anderson at last circled back to business.

"Pretty wild stuff with this head."

"How'd you guys end up with it? Isn't that normally something for us detectives to handle?" He missed whatever she was suggesting with her eyebrows.

"There was a captain on scene when they found it. Went up for a closer look and saw the cheeks were bulging out like a chipmunk. He flipped out. Told everybody it was C4 and cleared the building. Turned out it was a bunch of garlic cloves."

Mandy exchanged looks with Francis, or rather, stared at her own musing reflection in his glasses. He was checked out.

"It gets weirder. One of the techs scrapes out all the garlic and finds a little crumpled up piece of paper in there. A page from a book…"

"And?"

"Had something about cutting off someone's head and filling their mouth with garlic." He nodded, his foolish grin returning. "We got ourselves a psycho!"

"I've got to see this," she said, taking a step towards the bomb van. Anderson extended a beefy arm to catch her, his hand lingering on her hip.

"Can't do it, Parker. The Captain was very specific on not letting anyone near this thing."

"But this is our case!" Mandy hated how much she sounded like a little girl in that instant. *It's my turn to ride the pony!*

Anderson shrugged and put his big goggles back on. Francis tugged at Mandy's arm, the first sign of a pulse he'd shown all day.

"Let's get out of here. You can buy me a coffee."

***

An hour later it was dawn and they were hunched over a diner counter, Mandy trying to sip away the headache pounding at her temples.

Bernhardt's was Francis' favorite spot in the city, a crummy holdout in rapidly yuppifying midtown, where the donuts were always stale, the coffee tasted like cigarette butts and Francis could smoke as much as he wanted. He usually watched baseball on the fuzzy TV screen over the counter, but today it was on the fritz, so he was just staring off into space.

Mandy tapped her fingers on the counter, her chipping French tips click-clacking for some attention. Francis didn't budge, but the fat guy behind the counter gave her an annoyed look and cranked up the volume on his radio. Annoying political talk radio... *weren't places like this supposed to play the oldies?*

Mandy savored another ashy gulp. *And wasn't coffee supposed to come with conversation?* Not that she usually minded the silence. But today she had a grievance and she needed an audience.

"I still don't understand why they would just take the case away from us like that. You're a vet. I know I'm new, but how else am I supposed to learn?"

Francis shifted on his stool, turning his thousand-yard stare on the flecks of breakfast clinging to the dormant griddle across from them.

"I told you not to take it personal. There will be other cases."

"More OD's and suicides and John Does?"

"Just give it time."

He reinserted his cigarette and shifted his stare back into empty space. Mandy receded back into her coffee. It was getting cold.

The sudden sizzle of hash browns and onions and the wonderful smell that came with it woke her appetite. She looked around and saw that they were still the only customers in the place. The fat guy must be cooking himself breakfast.

"Let me get some of that." The demand felt weak coming out of her lips but it worked.

A few minutes later and she had a huge plateful of deliciously greasy breakfast slop in front of her - fat cooks were always generous. *Unlike Dad.* She remembered how he would plop a few skinny pancakes on the table and turn his back and leave the five kids to sort it out. And of course the teenage girls were stuck competing to see who could eat less while the little boys stuffed their faces freely.

Look at me now, Dad, she thought as she shoveled in a steaming spoonful. *Ugh.* She pushed the plate away, half-eaten. The fat guy cast her another disapproving look and then turned to his own breakfast.

Bored, Mandy turned her detective gaze on him. She'd been coming here for weeks with Francis and he was always here, but she didn't know his name. He had an accent - Mandy guessed German. She wondered if he was *the* Bernhardt. Probably not. Didn't carry himself like a business owner - anyone who owned this place would look stressed out and anemic from all the bleeding profits. Must be the idiot nephew.

Oh and definitely a xenophobe too. Whenever the TV was off, that radio was always pumping out retrograde political commentary like carbon monoxide. Right now it was Dick Liggins, the worst of the bunch, particularly because he was so popular - she saw his big fat face and red nose on the back of every bus in town. Mercifully, he was on an extended commercial break, but soon he would be back and burbling about the case. *Those uppity vamps finally getting what was coming to them!*

Mandy wondered how a German immigrant could buy all that nativist bull****. He wasn't too well-off from the looks of him. Maybe he resented how the vamps had climbed the economic ladder while he was still working a counter. Maybe he was nursing some old country animus that came over on the boat.

Either way, she figured he traveled comfortably along the dark currents of unspoken but still seething hatred and bigotry that flowed through River City's working-class neighborhoods. Whether that was better or worse than the proud and open variety that men like her father preached from the street corners she didn't know.

She cracked a smile at the thought of her father bunking down that house of ill repute known as the Garden Inn. Not that he would ever indulge in the various forbidden delights on offer there. But of all the places he could have picked to stay, none could have done better at bringing his worst nightmares about the big city to life. *Your poor daughter suspended over this amoral abyss suspended only by a thin blue thread!*

The bumper music for Liggins kicked on, the usually grating rockabilly that these types loved. Then Liggins' velvety baritone rolled in, thick with sarcasm.

"We're still talking about last night's party crasher and naturally everyone wants to know who lost their head. My crew here has been pounding the pavement and we've got our listeners an exclusive inside scoop… Ham, have we got 'im on the line?"

There was a muffled sound of studio chatter and then the static of a phone line.

"Hello there," rumbled Liggins. "Welcome to the Dick Liggins Show. Can you tell us who you are?"

A strange voice piped in, alien and garbled. Mandy at first thought it was radio static, but as the voice continued, she realized it was the electronic distortion of a voice modulator.

"I am one who has seen a terrible truth."

"And just what truth have you seen?" came Liggins' reply.

"I have seen the face of demons behind a human mask."

"Demons? What sort of demons?"

"The demons who come from abroad to feed on the blood of our veins and the sweat of our brow."

Mandy could hear Liggins' suck in his breath and she felt herself leaning forward. She spied the fat cook and Francis cocking their ears to the radio. *Oh, the pot was churning now!*

"Those are strong words there. Very strong words. Words that can get you in trouble nowadays." Liggins waited for more. *Deliciously strong words to throw into the pot!*

But the alien voice was quiet.

"What do you have to tell us about this murder?" Liggins ventured.

"Is it murder to return the dead to the grave?"

"Whoo-wee!" Liggins squealed. "He said it, not me, folks."

Mandy's face soured. This was bad even for Liggins. He fostered these disgusting dialogues to give voice to the worst of the torch-and-pitchfork mob all while clinging to his plausible deniability. One big immorality play for his troglodyte following.

The electronic voice cut in again.

"No, it is a service to the dead and the living. No more will the plague afflict our heartland…" A building shrillness pierced through the distortion as the speaker's voice rose. "Harken to a voice crying in the wilderness: I will cut off their heads, stuff their mouths with garlic and drive a stake through their hearts!"

Mandy stood bolt upright, an arched finger pointing at the radio. Francis' watery eyes stared blankly at her over the rim of the aviators.

"Don't get so worked up. This is just one of his stunts."

The cook stared at her with an irritating smirk. She retracted her finger, feeling a blush come to her cheeks. But she wouldn't sit down. This wasn't an overreaction.

"That's what they found in the head! None of that is public information. Whoever's on that radio knows as much about the case as we do!"

"Cops will always blab. What are you gonna do about it?"

Mandy felt a shiver of anger as Francis and the fat guy swiveled away from her and went back to staring at nothing. She looked down to see a lump in Francis' jacket pocket. With a sudden lunge, she snaked her hand into the pocket and yanked out the keys to the Lincoln. She was at the door before he could get off his barstool.

***

Now it was Mandy's turn to go 80 on the shoulder. Her peripheral vision was creeping in on both sides as the adrenaline took hold of her body, but she could still make out Francis clutching the passenger seat arm support.

The New Harlem Radio Building was one of tallest buildings downtown, decked out from bottom to top with gold-tinted glass. It was the only media building in a city full of banks and tech and pharmacy companies and it had to stand out.

Mandy had never been inside, but now she was heading straight for the top. She pulled directly in front, hoping the magnet siren on the roof of the Lincoln would scare off any overzealous tow truck. A badge flash and she was past the doorman. The commanding tone in her voice got lobby security to cough up the floor for the Liggins studio without so much as a why. Francis had to break into a run to keep up. If he had any ideas of leashing her, he'd have to catch her first. The doors shut while he was still hacking.

The 80th floor. Mandy basked in the spectacular golden views and the warmth that came with them. This was what confidence felt like. She headed for the flashing sign that said recording in session and pounded on a glass window.

No security was there to stop her. Only a greasy producer with a bad combover.

He closed the door to the studio behind him and turned towards her, palms raised and pushing.

"For goodness sakes, lady. We're recording."

Another badge flash, but this one made no impression. Mandy

felt her breath catch. The wind at her back slacking.

"This is police business. I need to speak with your boss. Now." She felt her voice go up an octave or several on the "now." *No, down voice. Don't squeak!*

He shook his head, hairy arms crossing across his chest. The elevator dinged behind her and Francis lurched out, his mouth tight with irritation. His eyes, naked for once, were full of opprobrium. But, like a good partner, he took up a strong position on her left flank and turned those judgy beams at the producer.

The producer remained unflappable. Sparing only an irritated glance at Francis, he took a step forward towards her, planting his pungent aftershave and overpowering coffee breath squarely in her airspace. She took a humiliating step backward.

"It's ok, Bern. Let them in. This will be good." It was Liggins' unmistakable baritone, oozing out of a P.A. speaker above them.

With a hostile shrug, Bern pivoted out of their path and gestured to the door. Mandy took a deep breath to raise those flagging sails and stepped in.

The humidity inside the recording studio was immediate and intense. Her eyes darted immediately to the huge sweat spots welling underneath Liggins' massive arms.

Liggins was an enormous man. Even seated in his easy chair he seemed larger than life, bigger even than the huge pictures of his face plastered on buses and billboards. Though obese, and morbidly so, he didn't slouch, but leaned forward like a king looking down from his throne. He wore a dazzling red silk tie that pulled Mandy's eyes away from those big sweat puddles and up to his face. Nestled inside his oily complexion and bulbous features were a pair of sharp, unblinking eyes and the jutting chin, doubling and tripling into the folds of his neck, of a man in charge.

"Sit, please." He gestured magnanimously at the seats occupied by his attendants, a pair of goblin-like little men in short sleeves with chunky headsets hugging their ears. They stood up, their heads leaning slightly toward Liggins, tethered to the desk by the cords connecting their headsets to the sound bays at Liggins' fingertips.

Mandy felt herself sinking in the deep cushions of the chair. Liggins pulled forward, towering over her and Francis beside her from the other side of the desk.

"We've got five minutes of local news before we're back on the air. What can I do for you, detectives?"

Mandy leaned forward, struggling to sit upright and keep her gaze level with Liggins.

"I think you know why we're here."

"Let me guess: you think we crossed the line. I respect that, but I gotta tell you, miss, radio is a tough racket. We're riding a dinosaur into the space age. We're the chihuahua in a dog-eat-dog world. Pushing the envelope isn't a question of taste for us, it's a matter of survival."

"None of that excuses you interfering with a police investigation. Not fifteen minutes ago I heard you divulging privileged information on your show."

"You heard me doing that?"

"Don't be coy. Whoever you had as a guest."

The familiar distorted voice sounded beside her, low and foreboding.

"Who is this alabaster goddess that wishes to speak with me?" It was the same electronic voice she'd heard in Bernhardt's.

Mandy whipped her head to the goblin next to her, a taunting grin stretched across his face as he spoke into the mic.

"Got your vampire decapitations right here," he continued, a demonic glee quickening his rasping voice. "We're doing a buy one, get one free special this week and you know what they say, two heads are better than one!"

"What made you say that line about cutting off heads and garlic?"

With twinkling eyes, he spoke again into the mic. "I walk in the shadows of the night and the city whispers her secrets to me."

Mandy stood up from the chair, towering over the little man.

"Unless you want to catch an obstruction charge, I would drop the schtick. I need to know where you heard that from."

The twinkle left his eyes as they darted to Liggins. Away from the mic his voice sounded reedy and annoyed.

"She can't make us give up a source, right?"

"Detective…" Liggins eyes scanned the badge at her hip for a name.

"Parker."

"Miss Parker," his voice was a scratchy purr. "I understand where you're coming from, but badgering my staff isn't going to do anyone any good. Stop by the newsstand on your way home and you'll see the evening tabloids running with stuff juicier than anything you heard on our show. Now, we're willing to cooperate with our friends in law enforcement, but you've got to be reasonable."

She took a deep breath. "My main concern is whether the information you obtained came from someone with knowledge of the suspect in my case. The way I heard it... the way you presented it struck me as sympathetic to the perpetrator."

Liggins leaned forward. "I assure you: we are on the side of justice and we would not hesitate to come forward with any information that would help in the apprehension of this heinous criminal. As for our sources, we rely on whispers, little snatches of rumors and hearsay, from those on the good side of this fight. People such as yourselves."

Mandy sighed. Just as Francis had predicted and what she probably knew going in. Of course police talked to people like Liggins. She glanced at the door. Her righteous anger was ebbing, and the beginnings of the feeling floating in on the incoming tide felt like embarrassment. *Time for an exit.*

"Miss Parker, if you don't mind my saying, you strike me as a young woman of strong convictions." She was surprised to find Liggins staring at her intensely. "I don't believe you came up here just to see if we had a killer in the studio. There's something more, isn't there?"

"I'm just doing my due diligence. I wish that my colleagues had not been so cavalier with privileged information but I guess I can't blame you for taking advantage. Thanks for your time." She took a step to leave but Liggins eyes were still on her, so inquisitive that she turned back.

"That you would do so in a way that paints a hateful killer in a friendly light, I personally find grotesque, but you're entitled to your perspective. It's a dangerous perspective, rooted in ignorance and fear, or rather your willingness to exploit the ignorance and fears of others, but it's yours and it's protected by the first amendment so there's nothing I can do about it. I hope you and Leni Riefenstahl over there enjoy your ratings."

Mandy took another step towards the door. Francis stood up to join her, a look of blended surprise and amusement on his face. Mandy felt her cheeks burning. The words had just flowed. It was like she was 16 again and back in debate club.

"Now, just hold on a second, miss." Liggins was on his feet now, huge and imposing but with no trace of anger or offense on his face. On the contrary, his eyes were eager and his hands stretched out in entreaty. "I think you've struck on something important. You're right about our show. We do give a loud voice to fear and hatred; that's where we find the most passion and drama. But you're speaking a very different message with the same passionate voice... Here's a crazy idea: we're just about to come back from break... Would you be willing to address my listeners and give them a little bit of what you gave me just now?"

Mandy laughed. "You must have me mistaken for someone in PR. Detectives... we don't do media." She looked at Francis for support. He was staring at her blankly.

Liggins' hands went up again, supplicating. "I understand that. This would be perfectly anonymous. You've seen yourself how well we protect a source."

"But this is totally different. You want to put my voice out there."

"Exactly!" He snatched a headset from the sound bay and held it out to her.

She felt something tickling her throat, but it wasn't just another laugh. It was something like exhilaration. She stood paralyzed, tantalized by the headset in front of her and the eager eyes behind them. This was her chance. *Take the mic! Grab the megaphone! Let those bigots hear you roar!*

And then Francis' liver-spotted hand stole between them and broke the spell. He deposited a card into Liggins' outstretched hand.

"We gotta get back. Let us know if you hear anything useful, eh?"

Then, grabbing the crook of Mandy's arm, he led her back to the elevator.

When the elevator doors closed, she shook loose of his grip.

"You don't have to lead me around by the arm, you know."

Francis shrugged. "You looked like you were about to do something stupid."

Mandy looked away, flushed. She grabbed onto the railing as the elevator dropped. *Down, down, down to earth.*

6

The phone in the room didn't work and the clerk wouldn't let Enoch use the one at the front desk. "There's a perfectly good payphone on the street," she had said between puffs on her cigar. A *woman smoking a cigar!* Enoch almost exclaimed it as he headed out into the motel courtyard. He had never seen such a thing.

This seedy little place was full of firsts for Enoch. The first time he'd seen a prostitute, or at least such an obvious one. The first time he'd smelled that skunk-like odor that he later discovered was marijuana. The first time he'd had to call the police - that wasn't for the marijuana but to check on the next-door neighbor after her boyfriend put his fist through the wall. And, most galling of all, the first time he'd ever had to pay more than forty dollars for a room!

The clerk had told him she could give him a break on the nightly rate if he signed up for a week - two hundred she said. But he'd already spent half of his cash on gas and the first night here and this lady wouldn't take a check. Worse, the Ford had died on him last night on his way back from Mandy's. He felt a frustration almost like panic building in him. *Calm this storm, Lord.*

The payphone was under the Garden Inn sign next to the road. An Indian man was using it when Enoch reached it, arguing in animated tones, shouting to be heard over the roar of passing traffic. The hand that wasn't holding the phone was gesturing angrily in the air, the Ziploc bag it clutched clinking with its heavy load of quarters. This argument might continue for quite some time.

Enoch glanced at the bus stop behind them. A homeless man sprawled across the length of it, draped in a remarkably clean blanket; it was considerably nicer than the stained orange rags that covered his motel bed. Resenting Enoch's gaze, the homeless man rolled over to give him his back and tucked up his legs to expose his wrinkled buttocks to Enoch and the morning traffic.

Enoch's eyes darted to the bus stop advertisement uncovered by the man's retreating legs. A cheerful black font jaunted across a yellow background: "If you're in this neighborhood, you need Jesus." The rest of the text was obscured by the homeless man's stockinged feet.

Enoch politely asked the man to scoot over, placing a hand gently on his leg. The homeless man recoiled violently at Enoch's touch, rolling all the way off the bench onto the ground and then springing up to his feet. From his mouth proceeded an incomprehensible tirade of abuse and profanity that spattered saliva all over his bushy black beard. Having spit his piece, he turned sharply, gathered up a large gunny sack and stormed off, disappearing into the shadows of the overpass.

Enoch returned to the bus stop ad: "Take this bus to Rivers of Mercy Apostolic Church of Christ. Or tune in every morning to Channel 4 to hear Pastor Jim Haggerty."

Behind him, he heard a click and turned to see the Indian man leaving the payphone. Enoch eagerly took his place. Traffic was still roaring and he had to press the receiver firmly against his ear to hear the dial tone.

"Hello?" It was Emily's voice, quiet and calm as always, barely discernible over the din.

"Hello, sweetheart, it's me!" Enoch was bellowing.

"Why didn't you call last night?"

Enoch shouted through the list of his mishaps. He hoped Emily could hear him because he couldn't hear anything from her end. Finally, she spoke up.

"Have you seen Amanda yet?"

For such a little question it had a lot of force. Suddenly the traffic didn't feel so loud in his ears and he saw himself back in their kitchen, sitting across from her at the kitchen table, her hands reaching over the checkered cloth to grasp his, tears in her eyes as she shared what she had learned.

"Yes, for just a moment."

"Was she with… Brad?"

"No…" There was no sound but he could still hear her gasp in relief. He knew her hand was at her mouth and her eyes closed, her lips muttering a prayer.

Enoch wanted to ask about the new grandbaby's colic and the blight and the boys' Latin lessons. Such pleasant problems to pour over with coffee and eggs in the morning. But he couldn't bear this weight alone.

"She's living with a different man now."

There was only silence. The noise of traffic was building again. Enoch shifted, turning his back to the street to shield out the roar.

"So she's lost then." Her little voice had a terrible finality to it.

"Don't say that Emily! She's in a bad place. We've just got to get her out. The Lord will not let anyone snatch her from His hand."

"Who is this man?"

"His name is Angel. He's a police officer. He wore a cross. A Roman Catholic, I think." That sigh he could hear. "I'm going to get to know him and I'm going to bring her back, I promise you. I just need a little more time. I need you to wire some more money."

The details of the wire transfer and shifting funds from their savings and budgeting out the next month took some planning, but the logistics seemed to soothe Emily's mind. Their own savings would only hold out for another two weeks at these rates. But the closer Enoch saw their bank account moving to zero, the more he felt the Lord's hand and the more his panic began to subside. This was his chance to see Him work miracles.

An automated voice demanded payment for another three minutes. He fished in his pocket for another quarter. Empty. It was just then that he noticed a young woman standing a few feet from him. She looked cold and angry. Her arms were crossed impatiently over her barely covered breasts.

"I've got to go, sweetheart, there's someone waiting for the phone and I'm all out of change. Let's pray together quickly." He whispered the prayer and replaced the receiver, stepping back from the payphone with an apologetic nod to the woman.

She raised an eyebrow as she slipped in front of him.

"You some kind of priest?"

He laughed. "No, I'm a Baptist!"

"What the hell's that?"

"It just means that I love Jesus and do what he says!" The woman scrunched up her nose in curious confusion. It was just the sort of look Enoch's girls gave the cockroaches when they invaded the house that especially nasty summer. *What is it, Daddy?*

It was then that Enoch felt a prompting. He reached out and put a hand on the woman's bare shoulder. She flinched but remained still.

"Forgive me, miss, but I think the Lord wants me to tell you something. You may have lost your father here on earth, but know that you have a Father in heaven who loves you and sees you. God bless you."

With a squeeze of her shoulder Enoch released her, turned away and walked briskly down the sidewalk. He breathed hot moist air onto his chilled fingers - they had just about gone numb clutching that phone. He quickened his pace and tucked his hands into his pockets. His big, warm, empty pockets, filled only with his hands and the promises of the Lord.

***

Mandy's nervous fingers were making a mess of the polyester fibers in the cushion on the chair just outside the captain's office. There were magazines on the table next to her but she ignored them. *I'm waiting here to be disciplined, not have my teeth cleaned.*

She threw another glance at the secretary, hoping for some sign that her wait was over. She upped the intensity of her gaze, throwing all her psychic weight behind it. *Reach over and punch that intercom button. Get him out here and get this over with. Do it, do it now!* But no, she just sat there clacking her immaculate French tips on the desk as she perused the stationary in front of her. The girl glanced up at her and Mandy's eyes darted back to the pile of polyester tufts and her own chipped nails.

If the circumstances were different, she might have gone up and taken a stab at chatting. There weren't too many women in the department, and even though Mandy had never been the type to strike up free and easy conversations with other girls, even her sisters, she did occasionally seek the sound of a friendly female voice. It was nice every once in a while to have a casual interaction that didn't devolve into awkward flirtation.

But the circumstances of this office visit were not conducive to chatting. This had all the feel of the old "wait until dad gets home," though it had never taken dad this long to come in from the orchard. The secretary's appearance was also acutely irritating. Her pale almost translucent skin. The long, slender neck, which probably made her look like a gawky ostrich on bad days but was the picture of swan-like beauty from the right angle. And that unruly chestnut hair, vigorously flat-ironed into uneven submission. It was all too familiar. *A building full of cops and I'm a dead ringer for the secretary.*

"Miss Parker?" It was the secretary. Mandy noted with satisfaction that this girl's voice was several octaves higher and reedier than her own.

"Detective," Mandy corrected, rising from her chair and straightening her back.

"Detective. It looks like the Captain's 10 o'clock is a no show. You can go on in."

Mandy took a deep breath at the threshold of the darkened glass door. The blinds in the windows surrounding the Captain's center office were all drawn - she was stepping into the unknown. The door opened with a creak.

The Captain was slouched in his chair, a gangly sprawl of arms and legs, his eyes transfixed on some faraway vision or perhaps the giant painting of a ship on the wall opposite him. He did not stir as the door creaked shut behind her, but instead seemed to slouch further. Mandy realized as his eyelids drooped that he was on the verge of sleep.

She smiled and with the smile the grip of angst around her stomach loosened. This was the fearsome vampire Captain? He looked like a teenager napping in his father's office. His eyes had just completed their descent then and Mandy crept quietly to the seat in front of his desk, taking a seat without making a noise.

From so close, he didn't seem like a vampire at all. He had a ruddy complexion, unlike the precious few vampires Mandy had ever met in person, who had all been deathly pale. Though perhaps her most recent encounter with the blood-drained corpse of Ion Dragescu had skewed her perspective. His face was also half-hidden behind a full black beard, topped off by an elegant mustache, waxed at the tips; he looked nothing like the grim, uniformly clean-shaven vampire statesmen on TV.

And he was young! She had never heard of anyone making captain before 45, but this man could not have been a day over 35.

There wasn't a wrinkle on his face and even sleeping there was a youthful vitality about him.

Before him was a newspaper spread out on the desk over a messy array of papers. Circled in red pen was an article titled "Mountain Bloodbath Puzzles Sheriff's Department" accompanied with a picture of a giant charred heap of interlocked bodies and metal. Next to it was a single small picture frame, angled just out of sight. Mandy leaned over to get a closer look, the badge hanging from her neck slipping from her suit jacket lapel to swing out like a wrecking ball and hit the desk with a clang.

The captain snorted and jerked awake in his chair. His eyes, dark brown, blinked at a furious rate for several moments before resting dully on Mandy, now deposited back in her own chair. His eyes widened as they settled on her. Mandy smiled - she couldn't help it.

He sprung to his feet in a single motion and adjusted his suit, a brown tweed number with an explosion of color from the poofy tie slung loosely around his neck. *Pretty bohemian for a police captain.*

"Forgive me," he exclaimed, his voice too loud for the little office. His eyes had shed all signs of sleep and now fixed on her with a discomfiting intensity. He reached his hand, palm upward, towards Mandy. She rose awkwardly in her chair and gingerly placed her own hand on his. *Is he going to shake my hand or kiss it?*

"Vlad Paler," he announced, shaking her hand with an enthusiastic vigor surprising for his delicate grip.

She nodded, suppressing a wild notion to curtsy, but he didn't release her hand and took the moment to look at her, head to toe. As once-overs went, it was less leering than apprising, like a sculptor appraising a slab of marble.

"You are a strikingly beautiful woman, Detective," he declared at last, releasing her hand but remaining standing.

Mandy was long past blushing at compliments, but the awkwardness of them both standing across the desk from each other had put her in an uncomfortable state. She managed only a tight smile.

"Very striking. Do you think that's had anything to do with how quickly you made detective?"

Mandy reeled. This was the sort of surprise attack you wanted to handle sitting down but here she was still half standing, half squatting towards the chair, completely off-balance. She decided to straighten up and face it like a man.

"You're pretty striking yourself. Seems like it's worked out pretty well for you." She sucked in her breath. *The unbridled tongue!* But this was not an impulsive response. It was calculated, delivered without any anger or even mirth. In the years she'd spent working around the rough-and-tumble males of the police world, and away from the religiously enforced meekness back home, she'd learned that this kind of aggressive counter-punch was the preferred ritual response.

And it worked, just as it had so many times before. The Captain threw his head back and laughed. Not a real laugh so much as a shouted "HA!" but enough to puncture the ballooning tension and, finally, drop them both into their seats.

"There's my sugar daddy right there." He pivoted the picture frame towards her to reveal a faded black and white photograph of himself in academy fatigues, smiling as he slung an arm around a wizened old man.

"Is that Doctor Duma?" Mandy's eyes widened. Duma had been the most famous and celebrated vampire in River City, a vampire Mother Theresa, beloved by many and respected even by some of their bitterest foes.

"He was the only reason I was ever accepted into the Academy. He's been gone for ten years now, but I guess I'm still riding on his coattails."

He turned his eyes from the photo to Mandy, inquisitive.

"Word around the department is that you paid a visit to the radio building the other day."

So this is a disciplinary hearing after all. Mandy had fretted all through the weekend about this. She'd walked out of that golden tower feeling proud of her self-restraint only to come home to Angel spluttering incredulously and asking the same question over and over again. *Was it you? Was it you?*

Mandy exhaled and began her prepared defense.

"I went there to preserve the integrity of the investigation after hearing some privileged information go out over the radio. I admit it was a rash decision and I recognize we have a PR rep to handle these sorts of things. But I didn't do anything that could be reasonably construed as intimidation or any of those other things he talked about on his show."

The Captain grabbed a page from his desk and held it up.

"So you didn't 'blitzkrieg into the studio like a stormtrooper and trample Mr. Liggins' first amendment rights'?"

Mandy was surprised he hadn't gone with the Liggins' "jack-booted valkyrie" line. That one had been a real big hit with all the oldheads at her old precinct. And to think that two-faced, three-chinned orangutang had almost sweet-talked her into going on the air! He hadn't even waited for the elevator doors to close before he started spinning her visit into a deranged rant about "the axis of vamp money and a fascist city government conspiring to stamp out the last voices of dissent."

Mandy had more defense prepared, but she decided to eat it. Better to let him lecture and get to the negotiation over how many suspension days were coming her way. She assumed her best penitent posture - casting her head down ever so slightly, setting her lips tight with quiet regret and looking up at the Captain with vulnerable eyes.

"In a normal police department during normal times, this meeting would be on the twelfth floor and the brass would all be there and you'd be staring down a month without a badge and a gun and a paycheck." Mandy brightened at this open. A good "but" was on the way.

"But fortunately for both of us, these are extraordinary times. Nothing is going to happen to you."

Mandy couldn't hold back the sigh of relief. "Thank you" gushed out with it.

"Don't thank me. This is your doing. You couldn't have picked a better time to make ol' Piggins turn his guns on this police department."

Mandy looked at him in unfeigned confusion. He chuckled.

"I guess you are too young to know the reasons why, but you do know RCPD has a terrible credibility problem with my community."

"Are you talking about the Blood Moon Riot? I know the police turned a blind eye on the rioters." Mandy blurted the question out, eager to demonstrate her knowledge. As a teenager, she'd inhaled every whiff of vampire history that the dusty shelves of the Copper Springs library had on offer. That earned her a raised eyebrow from the Captain.

"That was what the good ones did. The bad ones were throwing the molotov cocktails." He paused and smiled, glancing out the windows surrounding him.

"That's ancient history as far as I'm concerned," he continued. "But it might as well be yesterday to some of the heavy hitters from the hills." Mandy guessed he was referring to the rich vampires that lived up in the nice houses in the hills just north of the city. "They've been making the brass upstairs sweat bullets since that disaster at the opera."

He paused again, fixing her anew with that intense stare. Mandy tried to hold his gaze but welched after only a moment and stared at the desk.

"All that to say that I've been given clearance to vacate this hothouse of an office and take personal control over the Dragescu case."

Mandy's gaze lowered further, sinking with her spirit. *So much for my big case.* "Oh. So I guess Francis and me will be back in the homicide rotation."

"Ideally, I'd be able to work this with another vampire. That's what the community was demanding, in fact. But the only one in CID besides me is that lazy SOB in Missing Persons. Fortunately, we have a detective who just made herself a name in the community for putting the fear of God into the king of the bigots."

Mandy looked up with her brightest eyes. "You mean me?" What a stupid question. But he nodded all the same, a smile curling under the waxed ends of his mustache.

"But what about Francis? I couldn't possibly work the case without him." It sounded weak coming from her lips, but she'd made a game attempt at earnestness.

"Yes, yes, your loyalty to your partner is commendable. Don't worry about him. He'll be plenty happy going back to ODs and John Does. An old dog like him just wants to hurry up and retire. Leave the glamor cases to ambitious ladder-climbers like yourself."

Now Mandy was blushing. Just then, the Captain's phone rang and he shooed her out of the office with a brisk wave. She floated out of his office, smiling down at her clone tied to the desk. *Don't wait up for me, stepsister. I'm off to the ball!*

***

Mandy's first assignment was a long time coming. It finally arrived via phone call from Maggie, the Captain's assistant. *No, Vlad's assistant. Can't go calling your partner Captain.* Of course, partners didn't usually communicate by routing commands through their assistants.

Maggie was pleasant enough about it. They'd spoken several times over the last several days as Mandy drifted in limbo. Francis was gone - the Cap... Vlad had been right about him. He had congratulated her so breezily, with such an unmistakable expression of relief, that she had started to worry anew about what she was walking into.

But, oh, the euphoria of that first afternoon on the case! Vlad had been so encouraging. The whole vamp community in her corner for her duel with Liggins! Why, if it hadn't been for Francis - that wet blanket! - she might have seized that microphone and sent that ogre whimpering back into his cave! With nowhere to go until Vlad emerged from his inner sanctum, she'd sat down at her desk and set her eyes onto the Underwood typewriter that glowered before her, a black metallic beast.

She fed the beast a whole heap of paper as her fingers went on the attack, Liggins' fat face floating above the keys the whole time, absorbing her blows. But it wasn't just Liggins. He was only one grotesque manifestation of the perverse spirits that hovered over the city... no... over the entire land... whispering the dark thoughts that gave rise to all the evils that had menaced the country since its hopeful inception.

The hateful legacy of their forefathers and the blood they had shed had not been washed away by the flood of modern technology and the belated acknowledgment of how wrong they had been. They had not remained buried in the ground but ascended to the sky. From above, they urged on their descendants to continue their bloody work: to uphold their old hierarchy no matter the cost, to rid the land of foreign people and ideas, to enforce their backward religion and punish all dissenters... They were a great cloud blanketing the city, their angry voices traveling over the airwaves, seeking among the mentally weak and aggrieved members of society vessels for their wrath...

The Great Cloud of Witnesses! The phrase had come whispering out of her past in Preacher's coolly menacing tones. The voice that used to torment her every Sunday morning. The Great Cloud of Witnesses, the ghosts of the old Biblical patriarchs surrounding the little congregation, blocking out the outside world, crowding out the sun, and bidding the faithful to regress deeper and deeper into a stifling past.

Enveloped by such a cloud, even the gentlest souls could be prodded into such cruelty. She'd seen it first hand a hundred times. Like Mister Thatcher... the smiling mechanic, the same man who never charged them a dime when times were hard, sent his own son to get electroshocked into repentance after Preacher caught him trying to kiss another boy behind the old church bus.

It was the same pattern playing out on a larger scale across the city. The same vicious intolerance, emanating from the past and diffusing across the entire community, transforming pliable individuals into its agents or its passive abettors. But how to address it? How could one person, even a whole department, make even a dent in such a cloud?

Here the words had gushed onto the page as her fingers tap-danced. At last, the chance to re-legislate her childhood, to cut through the veils of willful ignorance and blind fidelity to suffocating tradition! It was useless to argue, as much as she would have liked to put Liggins in his place. Like the battle with the chemical companies that had polluted the river, the only fight that mattered was at the source, not the already contaminated waters. Cut off the polluters' access to the mainstream and their toxins would build up in their own facilities, their own noxious fumes ultimately putting them out of business. Once the river was sealed off from the sources of contamination, the polluting sludge would be diluted and then finally washed away by its own natural course.

The same strategic approach should be considered with regard to River City's increasingly xenophobic atmosphere. Instead of limiting focus to the most viscerally disturbing products of this environment, like Dragescu's murder, the department and city government should expand its area of concern to include the outlets that frame such atrocities as inevitable or even desirable. Utilizing existing municipal codes regarding public safety, the city could bring the fight to the media entities that were pumping out all this filth. Pile up enough code violations and it would only be a matter of course to slap the tabloid rags or programs like the Liggins Show or that Haggerty televangelist on channel 4 with injunctions. Even the threat of one would go a long way to get them to self-police.

It was also so simple, so reasonable, so compelling... and she'd typed it up in just a few pages. She'd felt so good about herself that she'd left in the untranslated Latin quote she'd opened with in a fit of pretentiousness. Then she'd marched it up to Maggie and plopped it down with undisguised pride. "For Vlad," she'd said boldly. *Let's see if he still thinks I'm just a pretty face now.* Such euphoria!

All that was three days ago and there had not been a peep from him since. Sure, her little white paper had disappeared from Maggie's desk and Maggie had assured her several times that Vlad had the document and would be sure to read it. How quickly did all that soaring confidence transform into despondent second-guessing. What kind of idiot submits a lunatic manifesto on their first day on a new assignment! She pictured Vlad behind those glazed windows laughing at her imbecility as he browsed the paper before chucking it in the round file. Was probably interviewing other CID detectives to replace her as she stewed and waited.

After that first day of silence, her thoughts had turned hostile. *He probably thinks I'm just another secretary who has nothing to offer. Probably just threw my memo into a drawer unread. Or he did read it and now he feels threatened and that's why he's giving me the cold shoulder.* She took to glaring daggers at those glass walls as she paced restlessly around the office.

By that afternoon the stimulating qualities of self-pity and bitterness had lost their edge and the weird looks she got from the other detectives as she prowled around the building were taking their toll. Vlad... the Captain, whatever his reasons, was going to remain stubbornly incommunicado behind the Maggie wall, and she was just going to have to press on alone. She took to roaming the city in whatever she could sneak out of the motor pool. Better to be out pretending to follow leads then pouring over that embarrassingly skinny file in a homicide cubicle, waiting for him to call.

That roaming eventually brought her home - only after scoping the place to make sure Daddy wasn't lurking at the doorstep. Then - at last! - came a call from Maggie.

There was the small talk to get through first. Maggie was dating Angel's cousin, also in the police force, and had thus begun Mandy's initiation into the girlfriend circle. Mandy was too irritated to match her cheery tone. All she could manage was a phony "oooh" when Maggie brought up the possibility of a salsa dancing double date.

"So..." *At last, the point.* "The Captain asked if you could interview a Vladimir Dumitru for additional background on the Dragescu case."

The roommate. Chubby club promoter. "Francis and I already did. Notes are in the file."

"Yes, the Captain saw that. He wants you to speak to him again. He said this afternoon at the Red Velvet."

So he wants to micromanage me from the office, redo all my work and he can't even bother to speak to me on the phone?

Mandy forced out a pleasant "sure" and hung up. She dressed angrily, taking no care not to wake Angel. He groaned and rolled over, exposing a scrub forest of curly back hair. She glared at him.

She rode the pool car hard and rolled the windows down, letting the wind whip through her ponytail as she replayed the Vladimir Dumitru interview in her head. Known to his patrons and friends as Fat Volya. Rock-solid alibi. Quiet, polite. Nowhere near as sleazy as she had expected but no help either. Had roomed, or rather occasionally crashed after late-night parties, with Dragescu, a distant cousin and family friend. Knew no one who might want to kill him. No jilted lovers. Just a hard-working, ambitious young guy who was on the fast-track to success in banking.

The Red Velvet was on the outskirts of town, several miles removed from the swankier midtown clubs that Mandy had always associated with the vampire set. She was surprised to find it in a dilapidated strip mall whose only other tenants appeared to be a liquor store and a Chinese food place with several empty suites and "space for rent" signs filling the spaces between. The dusty parking lot was empty except for a fleet of work trucks and a cherry red Plymouth LeBaron parked in front of the lounge. She recognized Fat Volya sitting on the hood, stuffing his pale face from a steamy box of noodles as he watched Mexicans in paint-splattered coveralls flow in and out of his club.

Volya pushed the noodles to the side and stood up straight at Mandy's approach, slicking his gelled hair into place with both hands. He gave off the same chastened schoolboy air she had remembered from before, a vibe that jarred with the gaudiness of his suit, the garishness of the gold jewelry dangling from his thick wrists and beneath his double chin.

"Detective Parker," he intoned in stiff but unaccented English. "I apologize for not meeting you at the station. We're renovating and I had to be here to supervise... What else did you need from me?"

The question was politely offered, complete with a deferential tilt of the head, but it still made Mandy feel defensive and irritated. *I wish I knew.*

"Just circling back to tie up loose ends and see if there's anything we might have missed." She pulled a notepad from her purse and fumed at its blankness.

"We're still trying to figure out who might have had reason to hurt your roommate."

"I wish I could tell you more," he said, his eyes big and apologetic. "Ion was my friend from boyhood and I never knew him to have words with anyone. He was a man of joy and adventure, not violence."

Mandy was about to raise the politics angle again when she heard the grinding of gravel behind and turned to see a shiny black Mercedes with tinted windows pulling on the lot and park next to her shabby Ford. The door kicked open and out loped the Captain - Vladimir Paler, out of the smoke-filled rooms and onto the mean streets.

He stretched his lanky frame and yawned loudly, before descending on them in eager strides. Volya meanwhile shed the chastened schoolboy posture for the free and easy slouch of the school chum. He and Vlad shared a hearty embrace and Vlad clapped him loudly on the back.

Vlad kept a hold of his neck, presenting him to Mandy like a butcher showing off a prize duck.

"Parker: meet the best little halfback the foothills ever saw."

"You played football?"

Volya smiled sheepishly as Vlad continued to wring his neck.

"Real football, not your American version. And no ponies for this one either. Toeing the earth like a proper infantryman. Like his father."

Mandy held her smile, fighting the irritation that threatened to twist it into a snarl. Of course she knew vamps played soccer, not football. Just like she knew the ponies referred to polo. She even picked up on the class distinction Vlad was underlining - rich vamps played polo, poor vamps played soccer. *I didn't spend my teens obsessively reading about you all for you jerks to take me for just another ignorant garlic-eater. Yes, I even know your favorite slur!*

To make matters worse, Vlad yanked Volya off to the side,

pivoting away from her and launched into a conversation in half-English, half-Romanian pidgin. And no, Mandy's teen obsession had not extended to learning Romanian, though she had made an abortive attempt at learning it in community college.

Their conversation went on for what seemed like an hour as Mandy tapped her heels and stared at her notebook. From time to time she picked up on stray English fragments only to lose her footing in a rush of incomprehensible pidgin slang. In the many frustrated moments in between, she found herself staring at Vlad, as if her glaring eyes could compel him to include her. But no matter how much she glared or fidgeted or cleared her throat, the two of them never so much as looked her way.

At last the words slowed and Vlad turned to her, yawning again.

"I think we've got enough here don't you, Parker?"

Vlad suggested lunch to Volya who mercifully declined, gesturing to the workers with his half-empty noodle box.

Mandy turned to walk to her Ford.

"Parker," came Vlad's voice. She froze, struggling to push her glower back under a placid surface. "Ride with me. We'll have lunch."

"But my car…"

"We'll send someone for it. Hop in." He disappeared into his Mercedes before Mandy could respond. She wondered if he was staring at her behind the opaque tint of the glass. Like Francis all over again.

The interior was soft white leather and the AC ice cold. Vlad drove slowly, leisurely, like an old man, smoking like a chimney the whole way. Francis would at least roll the windows down, but Vlad seemed totally oblivious to the clouds building between them. And Vlad smoked rum-soaked cigarillos that produced a sickly sweet aroma.

Mandy remembered the tint and wondered for a moment whether he was allergic to sunlight and then chided herself for the thought. She adjusted the vent in front of her to blow the smoke from her face and suppress the cough tickling up and down her windpipe.

"So," began Vlad, extinguishing his cigarette in a brimming ashtray. "I'm taking you somewhere special for lunch. You're gonna get the insider's tour of Ruby City."

He gave her a grin and an eyebrow flourish. She turned to

cough and hide a smile. *So much for the suave European playboy in his Mercedes. He's like a cheesy dad.*

"Isn't that place just a tourist trap?"

"For you, maybe. You see only what they want you to see. With me, you'll see it as it is." He lit up again, eyeing her. "I'm sorry about that back there, by the way."

An apology?

"The language barrier… The customs… The history… There's a big wall in front of you and I just left you there staring at it."

"That's fine," Mandy stammered. "Part of the job, right? Just gotta lower my shoulder and break through."

He threw his head back for another shouted "HA!"

Ahead of them the street narrowed as they approached a little main street framed by an imposing steel archway. Dangling from its rusted H-beams was a cheerfully shiny red banner welcoming them to the Ruby City Vampire Festival that had concluded last week. Her first year in River City, Mandy had been one of the tourists that swarmed the place every winter. But that had been a Brad thing and she'd avoided it ever since the break-up.

A smorgasbord of cute little shops and streetside cafes and richly colored gypsy wagons and street vendor carts flanked them on each side. It was a double envelopment of chintzy old world charm, luring the tourists in and then pouncing on them from all sides.

"All this is a facade," burbled Vlad, suddenly a tour guide. "If you peeled off those fake bricks and plaster, you'd see the graffiti and cinder blocks of the old neighborhood. This place was a disaster area when they first dumped us here. They called it-"

"The Red Zone," blurted Mandy, unwilling to let another chance to let her vamp knowledge go unappreciated. "The military quarantined you all here."

"Yes! You know your history!" He beamed. "But it didn't matter. Put my people in any ghetto in the world and they will transform it into a shining metropolis in a single generation."

"Wasn't this place vice central only a few years ago?" Mandy felt a quiver in her voice. Cheekiness wasn't always the best idea, but it usually worked with men.

There was a flash in his eyes, but it was a mirthful one. "I didn't say how we'd do it, just that it would get done! But you're wrong. This strip hasn't been a hot spot for a long time. Even the worst of my countrymen were smart enough to do their business away from home. The really shady stuff they saved for the Pit. Your neck of the woods."

He threw her a grin with that last jab.

"Oh, I've only been there a few years. I'm looking for something better."

"You're originally from the sticks, right? Copper Springs. What is that, cow country?"

Mandy blushed. He'd done some snooping in the personnel file.

"My family grows peaches and keeps sheep, but, yeah, there's a few cows out there."

He had just pulled into a narrow alley behind Rosie's Cafe, squeezing past a dumpster into a back lot filled with shiny imports that made the Mercedes look like an economy car.

He guided her through the back door into a shadowy little dining room. Mandy blinked away the sunlight from outside and could just barely make out figures in the surrounding tables. Vlad grabbed the crook of her arm and pulled her gently to a corner booth dimly illuminated by a candle and the glow of the sunlight from behind the black-curtained window.

"This is the real old country back here, the part we don't let the tourists see."

"I still can't see anything." Mandy squinted to see Vlad's outline throw his head back for another laugh.

"Now I'm definitely going to order you the boiled leeches."

The food came remarkably quickly, deposited by a diminutive waiter that Vlad summoned and dismissed with a snap of his fingers. Mandy's eyes had adjusted enough to see what looked like a lamb chop on a bed of grains. She nibbled at it, sensing the gleam of Vlad's eyes on her. It was delicious and it took no small amount of self-control to resist the urge to grab it with both hands and scarf it down.

As she ate, the delicacy of her bites diminishing as the juices of the meat unleashed its rich blend of piquant spices, Vlad talked. He covered enormous swathes of territory, ranging from misty-eyed recollections of the humble peasant cooking of his father's plantation in the old country to excited recitations of the statistics on exciting patents generated by vamp-led university labs and biotech start-ups downtown.

Mandy did her best to keep up, not for lack of interest but

because of a nagging interrupting voice whispering that none of this stimulating conversation had anything to do with their case. *More like a date than a debrief.*

When a lull stretched on long enough, she stuck her foot in. "So what's next? Keep going back over the case file?"

"Ah, she wants to talk business." He sighed and shoveled the last chunk of whatever it was on his plate into his mouth, washing it down with a long gulp from a dark glass - Mandy had noticed the waiter didn't pour her any.

"No," he said, finally. "No more retreading old paths. You and Francis did commendable work. I only wanted to speak to Volya because of our past connection."

"And did you learn anything helpful to our case?" Mandy noticed she was leaning forward.

Vlad leaned back into the shadows, pushing his plate forward.

"Enough to puncture my first theory. Dragescu wasn't a homosexual."

"I could have told you that!" Mandy cringed at how loud her voice sounded in the dark little dining room. She felt the whole room's eyes on her. *So loud, so obnoxious.* She brought her voice down to almost a whisper. "Anything else?"

Vlad kept in the shadows, letting the silence linger. His eyes flickered in the darkness, watching her.

"Remains to be seen." He stood up abruptly from his chair. "I think that's enough for now. Let's pick this up tomorrow." She had to scramble to catch up with him before he was out the door, their bill unpaid.

The drive back to her car was long and uncomfortably silent. It was getting dark when they arrived, and the parking lot was packed. Mandy could feel the thumping bass from Fat Volya's club pounding her chest as she fingered the door handle.

A weak "see you tomorrow?" was all she could manage as the door popped open. Vlad responded with a click of his tongue, a wink and finger gun in her general direction. *Gee thanks, dad.*

Then he drove off, leaving Mandy standing awkwardly upright in her beige pantsuit, a stick in the mud, as girls streamed around her, heedless to the cold in their skimpy dresses, drawn towards the pulsing beats of the Red Velvet.

7

Angel Mendoza made an excellent second impression. The drafty bathrobe was out, replaced with a midnight blue uniform, a little wrinkled but still impressive with all those silver badges and buttons sparkling in the twilight. The badge-crested hat almost brought him up to Enoch's height.

Enoch smiled as Mendoza accepted his outstretched hand and gave it a good hard squeeze. Softer than a farmer's hand, but strong and firm all the same.

"My daughter in?"

"No sir." Mendoza's eyes held Enoch's gaze, but his lip curled in something like a wince.

"She was supposed to meet me for coffee this afternoon."

"I'm sorry sir. I'm sure she just forgot about it. She's working this huge case and she probably just couldn't get away. I know it's not like her to leave people hanging."

"How long have you two been living together?"

He took his hat off to run a hand through his curly black hair. His cheeks reddened. *He has the decency of shame.*

"About a year now... Would you like to come in for some coffee?"

He gestured inside, glancing at his watch on its way by. Enoch hesitated. The complimentary coffee thermos at the Garden Inn never had anything in it and he had stopped making the trek to the corner gas station to save money. But the man was clearly pressed for time.

"No, thanks all the same. But it would be nice to have a chat sometime when you're not busy."

"Man, that might be never," Mendoza said, chuckling ruefully. "We're short as a mother... um... we got a lot of mandatory overtime right now."

He closed and locked the door behind him, fumbling with his feet as he glanced down the corridor to the stairs exiting the apartments. *He's trying not to be rude. A good boy.*

"That's perfectly alright, son. It's very important work you're doing. I will be praying for you."

Mendoza nodded and accelerated down the corridor, its rotten floorboards groaning under the blows of his big black boots. He stopped one more time to look back at Enoch.

"You know, if you'd like, you could maybe do a ride along with me sometime. In my squad car."

Enoch couldn't hold back his smile. "I'd like that."

"Great," said Mendoza, grinning. "I'll set it up with my lieutenant."

And with a boyish wave, he was gone. Enoch heaved a sigh and leaned back against the teal railing, arching his aching feet. He stared blankly at her apartment door and its beady little peephole stared back at him. Such an ugly place in an ugly city. *This is a hideout, not a home.*

His thoughts drifted to Mandy's little hollow in the maple grove, at that spot near the creek where they'd buried mom and dad. Emily had been in hysterics that evening... How many years ago now? Dinner was served and everyone was at the table... except for Mandy. Her afternoon house chores undone, her favorite haunt in the attic empty, the hammerings of the porch dinner bell unanswered. A frenzied search followed, with Emily combing the orchard rows with baby Jake on her hip. Her shrill cries reached all the way to Enoch as he ventured into the still untamed shrub forest of the back forty. He'd seen her wandering back there a few days before and that memory punctured the panic rising from his gut and kept his feet on the ground. That and the prayers he muttered with each step into the brush, following the snaking line that he desperately hoped was her trail.

The trail led out of the thicket and into a meadow carpeted of fallen maple leaves, glowing red, orange and yellow in the dusk. A maple grove dead ahead. Beyond it the creek, dark and swollen with autumn rains, creeping over its banks and whispering terrible thoughts into his mind. She would be in the grove, he had told himself. It was just her sort of place: cool and dark, full of romance and dread. The roots of the giant maple in its center had long since sprung from the eroding soil, gnarling and twisting into an underground fortress. He had gone down on his hands and knees into the muck, into the undergrowth, into the underworld.

It was there, at the very bottom of the hollow, he had found her - oh, the sight of it still took his breath away! There she was, nestled under those roots, her head on her jacket, an open book flapping in the breeze at the edge of her pale fingers, her lips trembling ever so slightly under each sleeping breath. She couldn't have been older than seven or eight, she was so small. She hadn't even woken when he gathered her in his arms and carried her back, warding off every grasping branch, every tangling briar until they were in sight of the house and his joyous bellowing brought the whole family round, laughing and crying.

"Dad?"

He spun around and there she was, coming up the stairs. No more leaves in her hair, no more wrinkled pinafore dress with the red roses, no more muddy yellow rain boots, but the same sleepy eyes staring back at him. *What were you so worried about Daddy? I was only in my hiding place.*

***

Mandy sipped her coffee and watched her dad's eyes bulge incredulously as he beheld the Rimbaud's menu. She had already ordered her usual - a black truffle omelet with a plate of sugar-dusted beignets on the side - and was working on what she hoped would be the first of several mugs of Rimbaud's exquisite French press. Rimbaud's was always her favorite splurge - if you could call a weekly indulgence a splurge. It was an oasis in a desert of leftover fast food, discount coffee and greasy diner fare. A twenty-minute walk out of the Pit and she was there, warming herself in the glow and bustle of the teeming bakery, and casting cozy glances out over the river, clouded in the morning fog and smoke piping out of the chemical factory.

But Enoch couldn't see or feel any of that, lost as he was in the dollar signs on the menu, just as he had scarcely been there on the cab ride over, his eyes always darting to the spinning numbers on the meter. Of course when they were on her, they were so desperately intense and consuming that she was glad for the distraction. And when she tried to pay the fare!

It must be so overwhelming for him. She supposed that's why she picked Rimbaud's instead of Norm's across the street and why she'd opted for the cab instead of the usual walk. Her dad should get a proper taste of her city life. *Realize how much he doesn't belong.*

"Tell me about you and Angel," he broke in suddenly, discarding the menu to fix her with those terrifying eyes again. There was no small talk with him. He consumed her every response like it was his last meal. *I should have taken him somewhere he could afford a big plate of steak and eggs.*

"Really not much to tell. We met in the academy. We both needed a place to stay. It's worked out pretty well so far."

"You're roommates?"

"It's more than that but, yeah, basically." Mandy brought the coffee mug up even higher to hide her blushing cheeks. Enoch's eyes were bulging again.

"So you don't plan on marrying him?"

The coffee mug was starting to burn her knuckles. She set it down and turned her attention to color coordinating the sugar substitutes in front of her.

"Haven't given it much thought," she murmured to a packet of Sweet'n Low.

"Seems like the sort of thing you ought to be giving more thought to. Living with a man is no trifling thing, sweetheart. You know what the Lord-"

Mandy could feel where this was heading. That pocket New Testament would be flapping its dog-eared pages at her any second now. A bolt of nervous energy bucked her up in her seat and gave her vocal cords a sudden burst.

"I've been trying to focus on my career." That made Enoch blink, knocking out of his preaching rhythm. "I've never been happier than I've been doing this job."

More stunned blinking from Enoch. When his eyelids at last settled, a new curiosity burned and he prodded her for more. Grateful to have silenced the church bells, Mandy found herself rambling with schoolgirlish excitement through a recap of her first month on homicide, pausing occasionally for a breath and a gulp of coffee to let some extra lurid detail sink in.

She thought for sure he'd blanch when she recounted that suicide they found on the catwalk under the Babylon Bridge. How he'd been draped over the railing like a dishrag with both wrists slashed, his blood drained into the river below. But Enoch just nibbled away at his toast, shaking his head in quiet resignation, his eyes still eating her up.

So she dumped the Dragescu murder on him and all its gore, and with it spilled out her frustrations. The garlic-stuffed head migrated to the backburner, making way for simmering resentment towards Captain Vladimir Paler. An impossible boss. Cold and aloof for spells, then warm and encouraging, then back again. She'd always wondered what it would be like to work with a vampire, and she still did, but it was so infuriating…

"A vampire?" Again the bulging eyes. *I should have led with that!*

"Yes, dad, a vampire. We have them here in the big city. It's no big deal. You wouldn't even know it from looking at him."

"Sweetheart," he pushed away his plate of toast crumbs to focus every bit of his intensity on her. "They're a dangerous cult."

So were we! She wanted to scream it back at him, but instead she looked down at her omelet, cold and neglected.

"They reject the cross, they drink blood," Enoch continued, building his Sunday morning rhythm back. "It's a Satanic religion."

"It's not a religion, Dad," she blurted out, surprised at the volume of her voice. She brought it down a decibel, throwing an apologetic glance at the waiter coming to refill her coffee. "It's a genetic condition. We shouldn't even call them vampires, it's so misleading."

"Genetic? You're saying that everything they do is part of God's design? I don't accept that -"

"No, it's not design at all. It's a mitochondrial mutation."

"Then it's a curse."

"No!" She very nearly pounded the table, stopping just shy to grab a napkin and give it a fierce squeeze. "There's nothing supernatural about it. They need to metabolize hemoglobin for their cells to function, just like we need glucose or protein or whatever. There's nothing good or evil about, just a quirk of evolution that some backward peasants in eastern Europe spun into a big, scary mythology."

Enoch's eyes narrowed. "I see… But that doesn't explain their hatred for the cross."

"Actually, I think it does." Her eyes were flashing now. "Those same peasants and their priests tormented them for centuries, burning them alive, impaling them on stakes and cutting their heads off for sport. For you the cross is a symbol of salvation, for them it means terror and cruelty and death."

"And what does it mean to you?" His eyes were fine points of light now, piercing into her so sharply she could feel a sting. She returned to her omelet, stuffing a giant cold bite into her mouth.

"This has been great," she mumbled as she chewed, shoving in a chunk of beignet as soon as there was room. "But I should probably finish up and get a few hours of sleep before I have to go back to work."

Enoch scratched sadly at the wispy hairs drooping down onto his forehead. "Sure. We can pick this up later."

Mandy rose and fished in her purse for her wallet. Enoch shook his head and dropped a pair of twenties on the table. *That's not going to be enough*, she thought, cringing, but she only shrugged and leaned down to give him a quick hug. His big strong hand reached up to the center of her back and held her close, giving way only when she gave him an affectionate tap.

"Are you heading back soon?"

He was standing now, looming over her like a shadow.

"No, the truck's in the shop and there's still more for me to do here. I think I'll be staying for a little while."

"Oh, great." *Oh great.* She turned and walked towards the door, feeling his eyes on her with every step, even as she stepped out on the sidewalk, even as she turned the corner, until at last the cold wind coming off the river drove all feeling from her fingers and all thought from her restless mind.

***

Pink was not Charlie Grace's favorite color - he was a sucker for sheer and shimmering blacks of a gothic ballroom dress or a three-piece funeral suit. Nor was he especially fond of the leisure suits; indeed, he'd come to despise them. But when life has dealt you ugly, fat, short and bald, in that order, you have to improvise. And pink leisure suits helped Charlie stand out from the crowd on his own terms: not a freak but a provocateur, River City's leading arbiter of taste and cool.

What the suit didn't do was keep him warm in the brisk

morning air in the foothills. He tugged uncomfortably at the big flapping salmon lapels trying to close the chilly gap. He'd considered bringing the giant white mink, but lost his nerve at the thought of $5,000 coattails dragging in the mud of the polo grounds. Such irritations, coupled with his lifelong antipathy for all sporting events, were usually enough to keep him idling in the cafe with his typewriter until the big ball that followed the match.

But today he had a hot tip and that was enough to fight off the cold and muck and the stank of horse manure. Nor was he entirely immune to the enchantment of the spectacle playing out in front of him - it was like being in a Ralph Lauren commercial! Those young men in their tight white pants riding high on those huge stallions that made the ground tremble under his white leather moccasins. Back and forth they went, with none of the yipping and hooting of American cowboys but an austere, almost ominous silence, broken only by pounding of hooves.

There was a great scrum of them, jostling and stamping. Then a white ball flew upward from their midst, soaring gracefully through the air and coming to rest within a few yards of where Charlie was standing. Now all that cavalry was headed directly for him and all that stood between them was a slender wooden fence. At the head of the pack, coming straight for him, was a lovely ivory-skinned lad on a gigantic brown charger, his handsome face set with a long hawkish nose as he swooped down on Charlie like a bird of prey. *That rascal Adrian Dan, of course!*

Raised high in his right hand was a polo mallet that looked increasingly to Charlie like a saber as Dan bore down on him. For a moment, Charlie imagined himself as a rebellious medieval peasant - no, he was too portly for that - a medieval burgermeister out among the torches and pitchforks staring down the thundering charge of Cossacks. Thundering towards him was Dan, a feudal angel of death, leaning down to deliver the killing blow.

Then, so quickly that Charlie felt the rush of wind before he saw anything, another rider swept across Dan's path and sent the ball careening out of his reach. As Dan yanked on his reins, the other rider left off pursuit of the ball to turn and stare him down. The rider cut a dashing figure on his dazzling white mount, his long black hair whipping in the breeze under his glistening black helmet, his fiery eyes glowing with gleeful scorn. Charlie ought to have recognized this one too - he did look familiar, but he couldn't...

Mikhail Andreanu! The mopey kid and wannabe rock star with the perpetual hangdog scowl… But here he was transformed into a lion rampant.

Charlie knew nothing of the rules of polo but he had been told enough about these old world rivalries to get a general idea of what was going on. Adrian Dan and his compatriots wore red and yellow striped sleeves, representing the colors of the Bucegi noble families, while his opponents, including Andreanu, wore the black and gold of Leaota. It was all Greek to an outsider like Charlie, but he could still sense the extraordinary emotional power of the old tribal rivalries - enough to stir even a moon-eyed depressive Andreanu into violent and heroic action.

Charlie continued to watch the young men racing around so wildly on their ponies, a desire for a good hot toddy intensifying with every gust of wind. His eyes strayed round the pitch looking hopefully for a waiter with a platter of steaming delights. No such luck. The crowd was almost all vamp, standing tall and stiff, austere and emotionless, their only appetite for the spectacle. The only proper natives in attendance were the help, young people hustling to and fro making ready for the dinner and festivities to come. These were usually prep school larvae, willing to suffer the humiliation of manual labor to curry favor with River City's new elite. The best internships were earned on the polo grounds.

A little more than a decade ago, the situation had been reversed. It had been the vamps scurrying around at the beck and call of the natives, while the natives rode around on horses and gobbled up hors d'oeuvres in the stands - oh how Charlie's grumbling stomach longed for a return to those salad days! But the first generation of vamp players had driven them from the field in embarrassment. Now the native elites stuck to golf and pretended they'd never cared about polo.

By this time, Charlie had also ceased to care about polo. Only the shivers were keeping the yawns at bay. He thrust his chilled hands into his pockets and felt the folds of the typewritten note that had brought him here. He slipped it out and read it again surreptitiously:

Dear Mr. Grace:
Your presence is cordially requested at the 47th Annual Foothill Cup where the city's finest amateur   polo players will meet

together in a contest of horsemanship, chivalric spirit and will to victory. All of River City's best and brightest will be there and I am sure you will encounter much of interest. I know you don't have a sports section in your paper, but this promises to be a match for the ages. Don't worry if you don't know much about polo, just keep your eye on the ball!

Yours,
V.H.

Three things pushed this little note to the top of Charlie's mountain of daily mail, brimming with gossip and smears and naughty photos and all the muck he could rake. First, it was hand-delivered, slipped under his door during the night. This was not unusual in itself - he made no secret of the location of his midtown penthouse - but it was a strange way to drop a society invite. Second, for an invitation, it was awfully short on glitz: no embossed gold, no calligraphy, just the faded imprint of a cheap typewriter on an otherwise naked manila sheet.

Finally, there was the mysterious identity sender: "V.H.," scrawled in a cloudy, reddish ink. He didn't recognize the initials, but the sight of them gave him a tingling sensation. And so, as he always did his best to heed such feelings, he was here, bored and uncomfortable and impatient and increasingly remorseful that he hadn't chucked the invite in his assistant's bin with the rest of the junk.

But his last shred of hope and faith in V.H. bid him keep his eye on the ball and so he did. Back and forth across the pitch it went with a numbing monotony. A giant metronome of men and horses, stultifying Charlie into a trance... until at last *something happened*.

Dan and Andreanu were neck-and-neck, galloping in pursuit of the ball, Dan falling behind. Snarling, Dan extended his mallet, hooked it over Andreanu's shoulder and gave it a yank. Andreanu lost hold of his reins and for one wild moment appeared as if he would fall. Dan surged ahead. But then Andreanu was back, leaning forward in the saddle, his great white horse devouring the ground between them. As they both closed on the ball, Andreanu gave Dan a sharp blow across his jaw, clearing his path. Then with a shrill whoop - the first cry Charlie had heard for the entire match -

Andreanu slung himself sideways in the saddle and delivered a mighty strike.

The white ball soared skyward, flying over the goalposts, over the stands, and beyond even the vast stretch of perfectly manicured lawn before disappearing into the shrubby forest that climbed the foothills. For a moment, Charlie, the crowd, and the attendants stared dumbly at the spot the ball had disappeared. Even the riders lollygagged, their horses pawing the earth restlessly underneath them. At last the referee's whistle broke the silence - Charlie noticed with some surprise that the referee was no vamp, but a swarthy little man on top a gray pony - and a young attendant was sent scurrying off to fetch a new ball.

The crowd parted for the attendant, an impish sprout with a wild patch of blonde curls bouncing as he trotted toward an open utility trailer, his big blue eyes casting nervously left and right at the vamp dignitaries flanking him. Charlie couldn't help but smirk. *Better not screw it up, squirt, or you can kiss that rec letter to BankWest goodbye.*

The attendant disappeared into the trailer, the crowd idling as the sounds of rummaging emanated from within.

"Hurry up, Embry!" came the hoarse, accented cry of the little ref. Embry emerged a few seconds later tugging a great white duffle bag almost as big as himself. He pushed on doggedly, upping his pace, oblivious that the tail of the bag was dragging on the grass behind him. Nor did he seem to notice the gasps of the crowd in his wake. But Charlie did and his always active subconscious had already prompted him to liberate the tiny Instamatic camera from his jacket pocket.

He felt his breath suck in as he raised the viewfinder to his eye. SNAP! Embry's profile, his eyes fixed on the ref, his jaw set firmly. SNAP! A slice of the elegantly dressed vamp crowd just behind him, their mouths and eyes wide open, one woman in a gorgeous fox with a gloved finger outstretched. SNAP! A weird splotchy discoloration at the end of the bag. SNAP! A trail of thick dark liquid oozing behind in a jagged line over the grass.

Charlie had been on enough crime scenes as a stringer to recognize a blood trail when he saw one. Could it be a bottle of red broken inside the bag? Or something more interesting? Charlie took the first step into the still yawning gap in the crowd. He followed the young attendant, the Instamatic ready but inconspicuous at his side, his moccasined feet carefully dodging the line of ooze.

"What the hell you got in that bag?" It was the ref, casting a fiercely disapproving eye at the line stretching between the attendant and Charlie, still stalking his prey.

"It's the ball bag. I packed it this morning," replied the boy earnestly. He promptly dropped to one knee and worked the zipper with one smooth motion, keeping his eyes fixed on the ref as displayed the bag's contents.

Charlie saw the ref's eyes bug out and his lips curl but his viewfinder was pointing down towards the bag, towards the darkness inside. His feet quickened, his body hunkered down, his eyes tunneling toward the one image he needed to see. Closer now, the shadows were parting, but still so dark. A click and the flash was on and SNAP! A bolt of light and there it was, nestled among the polo balls, staring directly into his lens. Skin like marble, eyes like glass, a face that would launch a thousand – no, a hundred thousand subscriptions! A terrible, beautiful, severed head and it was his, all his!

8

It was Mandy's first time behind the one-way mirror in the homicide tank. Whatever itch she had to go in there was dull and easily ignored: it felt more important to be behind the glass. Even the sting from when Vlad grabbed her arm as she was about to go in after Big Eddie Moore, saying he wanted someone "more experienced in there," had faded. All she felt now was boredom as she sipped on her coffee watching Moore and Valentine sweat in the hotbox with poor little Embry.

The blonde urchin sat behind the metal desk, the picture of emptiness, his big blue eyes drained into the growing sweat patches underneath each of his arms. Why the two burly detectives kept at him was beyond her - she knew within a few minutes that the boy knew nothing and had done nothing wrong. He had loaded the trailer from the supply shed, opened it up next to the field and then left it open while he ran around doing a zillion errands for a huge crowd of stuck-up rich people. What was so hard to believe about that?

I guess we have nothing else to do but lean on this little guy. If it had been up to her, they would have swapped this kid for the greasy tabloid guy in the ridiculous pink suit. That guy knew more than he was letting on. But Vlad had been happy to take that typewritten note and send that smirking slimeball off into the afternoon sun. Then Vlad had disappeared with the note and left her to butt her head against this dead end.

"Mandy!" She turned around to see Maggie's long neck poking

in through the door, her eyes bright and cheerful. Mandy wished she had gone with "Detective" but she was grateful for a friendly face in this empty, barren little room.

"The Captain just phoned. He wants you to meet him right away." She waved a little piece of notepaper through the crack in the door, refusing to bring her civilian feet into this sacred police space. *At least there's one boundary she respects!*

The paper bore a single address that Mandy didn't recognize. When she got to the map book in her pool car, she realized why: it was in the Fens, the swampy southernmost outskirts of River City above the river bend. All that was down there were big gothic mansions and the meth huts deeper into the swamp. Fortunately, the rush hour traffic was already petering out by the time she got on the road. By the time the sun set, she was watching the last of the crimson horizon fading into the Spanish moss laden boughs of the bald cypress flanking the road on both sides.

The address took her to a private road that cut through the cypresses like a grand promenade and led to a stately old Southern gothic, glowing a spectral white in the twilight. She blinked and the rumbling chug-chug of the Crown Vic's V8 lowered into the clop-clop of a pair of horses and she was in a carriage riding up on an antebellum manor. To her left was a garden party, where children in frilly jumpers frolicked and hoop-skirted ladies floated under their lacy parasols, arm-in-arm with dashing cavaliers with their waxed mustaches and epauletted jackets. On her right, she saw the swamp drained and cleared for unending rows of sugar cane. In and out of the sharp green leaves, interlocked like crossed blades, surged the dark forms of black slaves, sickles in hand and songs on their lips, their eyes shining as they stared back at her through the green.

She blinked again and she was at a tall wrought-iron gate blocking the way to a courtyard centering on a giant fountain. She craned her neck out the window and saw Vlad's Mercedes parked behind the fountain and under a portico extending out from the house. But there was no one to be seen at the house or on the grounds. The only sound was the idling of her own engine - not even a cicada to welcome her. Her hand reached for the siren box - a good chirp should roust the house. Her finger hesitated at the knob. Wailing on the horn outside this great silent estate felt like the country bumpkin thing to do.

She sighed in relief as a mechanical click sounded and the gate began to roll open on its track. There was still no one to be seen as she parked next to the Mercedes. As she stepped out onto the glistening marble chips leading up to the house she noticed for the first time how shabby was the imitation leather of her flats and how cheap the fabric of her mauve pant leg. She was going to have to up her wardrobe budget if she was going to be making house calls like this.

At the door Mandy was relieved to at last see a human face: it was Vlad sweeping the giant oak doors open like a butler.

"What took you so long?" There was a sharp edge to his voice. He strode ahead of her, pushing through the foyer down a long hallway.

"I didn't realize it was urgent. I don't even know what we're doing here." She was panting between sentences, forced to jog to keep up with his long strides.

He stopped just before the hallway opened into a living area, snatching her by the elbow to pull her close. His voice was low and so close she could feel the warmth of his breath on her cheek.

"This is the house of the victim. I've been speaking to his wife and I want you to get a read on her."

Mandy's head was spinning. All she could get out was: "The victim?"

"Didn't Maggie give you the notes I sent over?" Mandy only stared. "That bubble-headed…" He shook his head in exasperation, pulling Mandy further back into the hallway to launch into a hurried briefing.

The victim was Pavel Petricean. Another vamp with noble bloodlines from the old country. Briefly famous for becoming the first vamp on the professional tennis circuit before an injury forced him into retirement. Part of Adrian Dan's notorious playboy "Bat Pack," but married and semi-respectable. Went out driving last night and never returned.

Mandy's brain was still doing laps, trying to catch up. "Don't you want crime scene out here to process? Should I get some more units out here?"

He waved her off impatiently. "No, no, there will be time for that later. This is our best chance to speak to her."

Mandy nodded as if she agreed when she didn't even understand.

"I will ask the questions. I just want you to watch her and then tell me what you think."

They stepped out of the hallway and into what looked like a gallery, the walls decked with Renaissance paintings dimly lit by a chandelier overhead. Some elegant but uncomfortable looking furniture beckoned them. In the center was a large wooden sofa, opening like a clam's mouth with Mrs. Petricean as its pearl. This lady was sitting stiffly upright on the sofa, staring vacantly at a portrait of a Mona Lisa-looking matron with her arms around a pair of children with disturbingly adult looking faces. She turned to face them when they sat across from her, her eyes blank, her mouth flat, her cheeks colorless.

Mandy thought she was a fine-looking lady, slender but shapely, with elegant posture and a beautiful face, unmarred by even a hint of wrinkles or a suggestion of asymmetry. She was a china doll, perfect and lifeless. Her voice snuck out through almost imperceptible movements of her lips, so soft and light and faraway that Mandy half-expected to find a ventriloquist somewhere else in the room.

Vlad was asking all about her husband. *In English, thank God!* Was he a friend or acquaintance of Ion Dragescu?

"Pavel was a very social person. I didn't know most of his friends." If she'd had a cigarette that would have been the perfect moment for her to blow a cloud of smoke into Vlad's face.

Did he have any enemies? Had he done anything to attract attention from a xenophobic zealot?

She shrugged. "Not for years. In Pavel's playing days, there were a few threats. A few nasty letters. But mostly just pictures and notes from garlic-eating women." Here she cast a brief glance at Mandy.

"So he was a lady's man?" Vlad's tone was surprisingly provocative. Mrs. Petricean smiled unpleasantly.

"He was a man that could frustrate any woman, including me." Again, she turned to Mandy. "Your captain has already confirmed my alibi, so you needn't look at me so suspiciously."

"Did he often go out driving by himself?"

"Yes. He was always looking for adrenaline and driving fast on empty roads at night was his favorite way to find it."

"And you said he took the Rolls-Royce last night?" She nodded.

Vlad took a new tack, probing the Petricean finances. Just how many fancy cars did he have? Many. Was the money still coming in from tennis endorsements? No. Did he have any other source of income? A shrug. Did she have any family income or money coming in?

On this last line of questioning, Mandy saw the beginnings of a grimace forming at the edges of Mrs. Petricean's flat mouth but it turned into the same unpleasant smile. "Not anymore," she said.

Vlad sat quietly, stroking his beard as he stared at Mrs. Petricean. She was completely unperturbed by his gaze and the awkward silence that lingered. Mandy wondered if she was the only one that felt the urge to squirm.

"Is there anything else you can tell us about your husband's whereabouts last night?"

There was a flicker in Mrs. Petricean's eyes, the closest thing to indecision Mandy had yet seen from her. She stood up suddenly and beckoned them to follow. Adjacent to the gallery was another smaller parlor. Instead of paintings, this one was decked with television monitors, attached to cords that spread up and down like clinging vines, connecting the monitors to a desk with a large computer terminal. The monitors on the wall displayed views from both the interior and exterior, including the gate that had so magically opened for Mandy.

Mrs. Petricean sat at the computer, bringing it to life with a push of a button. Mandy was struck by the confidence with which she navigated the system, her fingers working the keyboard expertly to generate long strings of indecipherable commands and codes. A distorted sound, like a pulse over a telephone line, chirped from somewhere in the innards of the computer.

"Are you connecting to some kind of computer network?" inquired Vlad, his eyes ablaze with curiosity. "Did your husband have this set up?"

"Yes and no," replied Mrs. Petricean, her fingers continuing to dance on the keyboard. "What you are looking at is the last of my inheritance from my father."

"Of course, Professor Gavril!" exclaimed Vlad. "The great computer scientist. I met him once."

Mrs. Petricean swung round in her chair, her gaze softened, a genuine smile on her lips.

"Yes. This equipment was his housewarming gift to me when we purchased the house last year. The modem in this computer is connected to a satellite array that we set up in the rear garden. Using it, I can send communications to my father or anyone else with satellite access." Here she paused, executing a command that summoned a brightly colored window onto the computer screen.

"I can also use satellite access to relay signals to other beacons. Pavel's car has such a beacon." With another click, the screen transitioned to a multicolored road map that bore a close resemblance to River City and its environs.

Mandy and Vlad exchanged glances, his face shining with childlike astonishment. He pointed at the map, his finger holding back timidly from the screen, as if he was worried he might dispel the magic.

"I can show you everywhere the car has been." She typed in another string of commands. A solid blue line appeared on the map, starting in an empty green slice labeled "The Fens" and snaking its way over the interstate into the labyrinthine grid of River City's east side. A small dot blinked at the end of the blue line.

"That's where his vehicle is currently located?"

Vlad turned to Mandy, grabbing her by the shoulder. "Get to your radio and get us some units to that car." His face was still lit up like a Christmas tree.

Mandy took off, feeling silly as her feet pounded against the old hardwoods. *Slow down, it's just a little errand.* But she couldn't help it. The electricity of Vlad's excited urgency was surging through her - she couldn't help but break into a run.

***

Mandy was in Vlad's car, her own car left behind again for some poor schlub to pick up later. Though the road was dark and unlit and a treacherous swamp hugged the edges of every sharp turn, Vlad drove so distractedly as to border on recklessness. His face was ever turned towards hers, his eyes on hers, flitting back to the road only fitfully. Mandy gripped her seatbelt but her anxiety was overcome by her own rising sense of elation. *We've got a real serial killer and we're on his trail!*

Vlad wanted her to recount her every impression of Mrs. Petricean and their house and he was devouring every word. Of course she was bizarrely cool for a woman who had just learned her husband had been murdered and decapitated - that wasn't just the famous vampire sangfroid, was it? Vlad assured her it was not. But Mandy thought she was not as cold as she appeared - her icy stares suggested more bitterness than apathy. And no woman who didn't care about her husband would go to all that trouble to track his car!

As for that house: so distant and remote, it made an unusual choice for a social animal like Pavel, but it fit Mrs. Petricean quite nicely. The kind of place you move to get away from bad influences or to get your husband away. But how could a retired tennis player and the daughter of a computer science professor afford such a mansion, not to mention that stable of motorcycles and sports cars?

Here Vlad turned his eyes back to the road. "I learned something from Volya the other day that I didn't share with you. It was a connection that I didn't know would be relevant until today." He looked back at her and paused, as if mulling whether to continue. Mandy put on her best trustworthy face.

"Dragescu was seeing a girl. Irina Nasturel. Part of Adrian Dan's circle."

"The Bat Pack!" Mandy exclaimed.

"I see you read your tabloids. And we know Pavel Petricean was a part of the same group."

Vlad paused again. He scratched at his cheek and threw her another look before continuing.

"Dan's money came from his father, a terrible gangster. A great embarrassment to our community from a chapter in our history that we have exerted tremendous efforts to keep closed..." He sighed. "I've long suspected that the apple didn't fall too far from the tree with young Adrian. My guess would be that Mrs. Petricean's plantation was purchased with drug money."

"And these two killings... some kind of turf war?"

"We used to see that a lot in the old days - not quite as theatrical as all this, but maybe that's just this new generation."

Mandy had been a little kid safely tucked away in the middle of nowhere when the gang wars raged in River City in the 70s but she had read about them and listened avidly to the old timers' accounts at choir practice. Vampire crime lords and native kingpins fighting for control over the booming underground markets of prostitution and drugs, with ordinary citizens caught in the crossfire. They'd gone by names like Two-bit Tony and the Scarlet Pimp with the outrageous outfits to match. What Mandy wouldn't give to have worked a beat in those days!

She looked at Vlad and was struck again by the ruddy, youthful glow of his skin, the total absence of gray from his beard and wavy black hair. Not even a hint of crow's feet around his eyes.

"Aren't you too young to have seen any old days?"

Vlad laughed, the intensity dissolving from his face, his shoulders loosening. "We vamps just have really good skin care regimens," he said with a grin. *A nice smile.*

By the time they got into the nightclubs had opened and the streets were crowded. The nicer clubs on Jefferson gave way to the seedier bars and strip clubs on 4th and then into River City's skid row by the recently demolished train station. A glow of blue lights emanating from the third floor of an ugly rectangle of dirty concrete and rusted metal beckoned them. It was a defunct parking facility, an illegal dumping grounds filled with garbage, junked cars and homeless tents. Vlad navigated carefully through a narrow corridor cutting through the mess.

They slowly made their way to the third floor, where the junk parted into a sort of clearing. There, in the center, surrounded by squad cars and department vehicles, a ghostly white Rolls-Royce Phantom reflected a thousand blinding lights of its immaculately smooth and contoured surface.

Jenkins the crime scene photographer and a herd of detectives were already there. No blood, no apparent crime scene, just a car that had been left idling until it ran out of gas.

Borman, who had just come over to Homicide from Vice, ambled over to share that this level was a favorite pick-up spot for hookers. "Girls and boys," he added.

Vlad stroked his beard. "My homosexual theory lives again."

"Couldn't he have been looking for a girl?" Mandy said, stifling a yawn.

"Very unlikely," said Vlad, throwing her a sidelong glance. "Unless he wasn't just looking for sex." Mandy nodded knowingly, her brain cloudy as she tried to guess what he meant. She knew sexual liaisons between vamps and natives were rare because of the health risks for natives exposed to vamp bodily fluids and the fatal prospect of pregnancy. That homosexual encounters were much less rare was chalked up to desperation among vamps and a generally higher risk tolerance among that segment of the population. But what else would a rich vamp jock like Pavel Petricean want with an escort other than sex?

The front page of a tabloid mag she'd spied at the old Stop-N-Go popped suddenly into her head - a cheerleader with her dress in shreds, her head thrown back and her throat ripped wide open. It was just that kind of shock-schlock that triggered the riots back in the day. All of it fabrications or distortions of gangland murders that had nothing to do with the "BLOODLUST!" those headlines screamed about.

She shook her head to fling the image from her brain. She felt a hand on her shoulder - Vlad's.

"You're looking tired. I've got a pillow and a blanket in the backseat - you should catch a nap while you can." Mandy nodded, feeling a sudden weight on her eyelids. She filed past the blue lights and abandoned cars and broken bottles and sleeping junkies to the beckoning soft leather of the Mercedes. She curled into a ball and rested her head on Vlad's pillow - it smelled smoky and sweet. *Like his breath*. Sleep came quickly.

9

Angel didn't usually pay much attention in roll call. Brannigan was a blowhard who loved the sound of his own voice, especially when it was employed in bellowing at the wide-eyed rookies. He had a whole row of them to preach at today, leaving Angel to nod off in the back.

He hadn't slept well. Mandy had been gone all night after being gone all day. No call, no page, no nothing. When she'd finally shown up, she'd barely said a word. She'd run past him without so much as a hello, hopped in the shower, and then came out in a new outfit - a skirt, she never wore skirts. He'd grabbed her by the arm before she could get back out the door. All he could get was a "gotta go" and a peck on the cheek and then she was off running down the stairs. *Man, she smelled good.*

He'd followed her. Couldn't help himself. At the edge of the railing, peering over onto the street below to see her get into the passenger side of a black Mercedes. He'd seen the driver's face in the mirror. He recognized him from the photos at the station. The pretty-boy vamp Captain who just got promoted to head CID. *They say you don't have to worry about vamp guys. But she was so... giddy.*

"Mendoza!"

Angel blinked and saw Brannigan's red face pointed in his direction. Everyone else was already filing out of the room.

"You've got some company today. Maybe try not to f*** up things as much as usual."

"Yes, sir."

He found Enoch Parker waiting for him outside the equipment room. Even in a hallway full of cops, the man stood half a head over the crowd. He was still wearing the same leather jacket, blue button-up, wrangler jeans and cowboy boots he had rode into town in. He turned to Angel with a huge grin, cranking a thumb towards the equipment racks.

"That's quite an arsenal in there!"

Angel shouldered his shotgun and gave Enoch one of those iron handshakes he seemed to enjoy so much. He'd never had a civilian ride along before, much less his girlfriend's dad. At least it would get him out of answering calls.

Enoch crammed his long legs into the cramped passenger seat but it didn't seem to bother him in the slightest. He was oohing and ahhing, pointing and gasping at every gizmo and glowing light on the dash, taking in Angel's absent-minded rundown with slack-jawed wonder.

"So what are we going to get into?" Enoch asked as they pulled off the lot. Angel yawned. What he really wanted to do was pull up to his spot behind the chemical factory and take a nap. But then a stray tidbit from roll call jolted his slouching brain.

"You know that big case Mandy's working on? The guy chopping the heads off of these rich vampires?"

Enoch nodded eagerly.

"They've got some kind of big break they're investigating downtown. We could head down there. Maybe get lucky and bump into Mandy."

"Or catch the killer!"

Angel chuckled. "Don't hold your breath. But if you want to see some action, there's plenty of dealers and hookers to mess with down there."

Enoch shook his head in astonishment - he sat forward in his seat, his head on a swivel, drinking it all in. Angel smiled. He watched Enoch as they got on the interstate. There wasn't much resemblance there. His hair was sandy blonde and thin where hers was dark and full. His skin was leathery and splotchy, hers smooth and soft, almost glowing. His nose long and straight, hers small and gently curving upwards. But the gray eyes and the freckles underneath them he recognized. He turned back to the road as Enoch suddenly swiveled back to face him.

"It means a lot to me, you bringing me out. Staying here this past week, the fights, the gunshots, the crashes... I never realized just how much the police had to deal with."

Angel gave the usual appreciative grunt but felt a flush of genuine warmth. It was a speech he'd heard a hundred times from awestruck out-of-towners but never with such burning sincerity.

"It makes me feel a little better about Mandy knowing she has someone like you looking out for her."

"You know Mandy. She can look after herself." *She didn't even look back at me on her way to that Mercedes.*

"She thinks she can. But there's going to come a time when she's going to need you. You just have to be ready."

The old man then launched himself on a sermon about how marriage and family were like taking care of a flock of sheep. That a man was not the shepherd - that was the Lord - but the sheepdog. As dumb and clueless as any of the sheep, but blessed with a nose for danger and the teeth to do something about it. In this day and age, it was getting much harder for a sheepdog to do his job; the fences were falling apart and the predators lurking the forest were growing in number, size and cunning. But the sheepdog must still do his job and be prepared to lay his life down for the flock.

All this farm stuff wasn't completely foreign to Angel, city boy that he was. When he'd become too much for his mom to handle that last year in middle school, she'd sent him to Tio Rigo in Texas to spend the summer working like a dog on a cattle ranch. It had been grueling, sometimes miserable work, but he'd loved the way he felt at the end of that summer: not a sullen, helpless boy but a hand, ready to tackle whatever they threw at him!

Listening to Enoch took him back to those days and filled him with that same urge to measure up. He spoke with such easy confidence and so much passion. Angel had heard plenty of men speak with authority in this job, but it had always been weighed down with weary cynicism. There was nothing cynical in Enoch. Angel listened so intently that he missed the Jefferson exit and the one after that and was almost into the foothills before he realized and doubled back.

"You think I can be a sheepdog?" he asked when Enoch paused.

Enoch turned a sharp gaze on him. "Yes. But you can't just hop the fence and be a part of the flock. What's a sheepdog without a collar?" He brandished his silver wedding ring, gleaming dully under a thousand scratches, giving it a twist with his thumb.

"A wolf?" Angel tugged at his collar ruefully. A glow of blue lights called his attention ahead. The road was blocked off. "Looks like we're coming up on the crime scene."

Angel looked for a familiar patrolman in the wall of cars and found one. It was Powell, his hillbilly classmate from the academy, fishing into a pouch of chewing tobacco as he leaned against the hood of his squad car. Angel pulled up alongside him. Powell flashed them with a juicy brown grin. "If it ain't Mendozer!"

It didn't take long to cut through the reminiscing and get to the meat. The victim's car was in a parking garage a block up the road, but a few hours ago a homeless guy had called in a body in a dumpster just up the street there. A headless corpse impaled through the chest with a sharp wood stick. No chance Angel and his guest could sneak a peek? Nope, Powell hadn't even seen it himself - they had that inner perimeter locked down tight. Best they could do is get out of the car and squint.

Placing one boot on the sideboard, Angel stood as tall as he could to peer down the road and past the lines of yellow tape to see *her*. Yes, Mandy! He felt a stupid thrill as he recognized everything from the bounce of her ponytail to the curve of her waist as her back was to him. Then came an equally stupid urge to call out to her. A tall dark figure emerged from the shadows to put a hand on her shoulder and stand just behind her, blocking Angel's view.

The vampire. His lips curled in disgust as the word echoed in his mind. He'd never had any problem with vampires. He used to talk about them when he went home just for kicks - just a mention was enough to get his mom making the sign of the cross and delivering some unhinged rant in Spanish. Angel didn't buy into all that superstition. Vampires had their rightful place in the world. But they should stay there, with their own kind. *Stop sniffing around where you don't belong.*

He glanced over to see Enoch's head peering in the same direction - he didn't need any boost from the sideboard to get the view. There was no snarl on his face but the thin line of his mouth suggested concern.

The toot of a horn turned them both around. A canteen truck painted a bright white had pulled up behind them. Angel recognized it as one of the blood drive trucks that used to frequent ghetto neighborhoods like this one, though he hadn't seen one in a few years. The driver was a gigantic black man in a red apron waving a muscled arm out the window at them. Powell shouted something at him and then muttered something into his radio. The wall of cars parted and the canteen truck rumbled on, pressing in towards the inner perimeter.

Angel shot Powell a look. He shrugged. "Beats me. The captain said to wave him on through." Angel sighed and sank back down into his seat, Enoch joining him.

"I guess we're stuck on the outside looking in," Angel muttered.

Enoch looked at him with a mischievous twinkle in his eye. "You give up too easily! Whenever a fox is after my hens, he doesn't stop at the door to the coop. He goes around the whole perimeter, looking for an opening." Angel shook his head and laughed as he put the car in gear, heading back towards the interstate. *This old man's got more stones than me.*

***

It was surreal seeing Vlad swallowed up in the big man's embrace. She'd never even seen a vampire hug a regular person before much less submit to the sort of full-bodied anaconda-squeeze the Reverend was putting on him. But there it was happening right in front of her and the crime scene guys and the handful of patrolmen milling about - all looking just as shocked as she was.

At last the Reverend released Vlad from his grip and Vlad turned to their onlookers with a big smile. He called Mandy over and ushered her closer.

"Parker, meet my good friend, the Reverend Bouchard."

The Reverend pulled her in with a leathery hand. "Please, my friends call me Mike and everyone is my friend."

She smiled at him. He was an enormously broad-shouldered black man with a bald head and a close-cropped silver beard. He had the muscles and posture of a young man, swaying side-to-side with restless energy, but he had such deep lines in his face around his clouded, watery eyes... He had to be at least 65. For all his physical power and restlessness, his face beamed gentleness.

"The Reverend is one of River City's greatest assets. No one has spent more time on Cotton Row working with the down and out. Whenever I've needed an ear to the ground on a case out here, he's been the first person I've turned to."

Bouchard lowered his head modestly. Mandy spied a large silver cross dangling from his neck. *Daddy would be surprised it hadn't burned a hole through Vlad's chest.*

A shout came from one of the unmarked cars parked behind the dumpster. It was Valentine, leaning out of the car clutching a radio.

"They're trying to raise you, Cap. The FBI's got the results back on that note. They want you downtown."

"You'll have to excuse me, Reverend." Vlad headed for Valentine, Mandy moving to follow. He turned on her.

"No, no. I need you to stay here with him. Give him the breakdown on the case. He can help us."

Mandy blinked away the flash of irritation she felt. *How long are you going to keep me at the kids' table?* Another flash as she watched Vlad hop in the Mercedes and take off. *And there goes my ride!* She turned back to Bouchard in no mood to be hospitable.

"What exactly did the Captain want you here for?"

"Well," his voice was slow, gravelly and thickened by a swampy Louisiana accent. "I know a lot of the people from this part of town. Maybe I can help you piece together a little of what might have happened."

Bouchard's soft eyes cooled Mandy's annoyance. They were utterly and eerily captivating, like pale gray mirrors, or dimmed headlights receding into the fog. *Must have glaucoma, poor guy.*

She glanced away when her stare began to cross over into rudeness, taking in his canteen truck. On its side was a slick black and red logo of little graphic blood drops forming the spokes of a wheel. The logo was unfamiliar and the glistening paint job smacked of fresh grant money, but the name - Full Circle Ministries - rung a bell from somewhere deep in her memory.

"You guys were the first ones to cross the barriers in the riots!" Mandy declared suddenly.

"It was Reverend Al's outfit back then. I was too busy beating on them vamp boys with bricks and chains to appreciate him at the time. It was putting the hurt on Reverend Al that finally sent me to jail." He smiled sadly as Mandy blinked in shock.

"I'm guessing there's more to this story."

"Oh, yes, but we can save that for another time. Suffice it to say that I did my time and then Reverend Al was waiting for me with open arms when I came out. He took me under his wing, taught me the ministry and I've been running it ever since he passed."

"Wow, I didn't know they still had blood charities on the streets. I mean, I see the commercials, but I thought it was all white collar now."

"There's still plenty of work to be done." He gestured at their surroundings. "So many people living on the streets with nothing between them and the cold but their crackpipes. We give them blankets, hot food, medical attention. And they give us their blood." There was an echo of passion in his voice, but it was faint and giving way to rote. *Must have given the fundraising pitch a few hundred times too many.*

"I remember now. There was an article about you a little while ago. And they get little accounts with the banks that get the blood, right?"

"That's right. Something for them to build with when they get clean. Our partners in the vampire community have been very generous in that way." He cast his cloudy gaze on the blight surrounding them. "But sometimes it seems like we haven't done much at all. Look at how many are trapped in this degradation... But that's enough from me, young lady. Let me help you with your case."

Mandy gave Bouchard a brief survey of their discoveries - the abandoned Phantom, the dumpster corpse, and the timeline they had sketched out. They figured the Phantom had stopped in the parking garage at midnight and the head couldn't have been deposited in the polo ball bag until around 8 a.m. And the body couldn't have been dumped until at least 5 a.m. because that was when the dumpster had been emptied.

"Do you have any contacts on the street that might help at least flesh out that timeline?"

The Reverend rubbed his silvery chin. "If anyone does, it would be me. I've taken blood from everyone on this street and on every level of that parking garage. But I might even be able to do you one better..." Mandy raised an eyebrow. He smiled. "I was in my truck here on this street at midnight. I even went in the parking garage."

Mandy shook her head, bewildered. "Did you see anything? Notice anything unusual? What were you doing there?"

"One at a time, please," he said chuckling. "I must say I can't remember seeing anything unusual, though I'm afraid my eyes ain't what they used to be - don't tell that to driver's services! I need to keep my license... But I can tell you the names of the people that were there. Just about everybody comes to my truck when I roll through. I'm like the ice cream man. Or the pied piper."

"Anyone that you think might cooperate with us?"

Mandy's heart raced and her pencil flew as Bouchard recited a laundry list of extraordinary street names from Boogers to Wonder Woman. "Do you have addresses or telephone numbers for any of these people?"

Bouchard scratched at his bald head. "I guess I don't - most don't have either." Mandy's heart sank. "But I tell you what I can do for you: when I make my rounds I can pick up all the ones I can find and bring them down to the station."

As Mandy thanked him profusely, Bouchard's misty eyes strayed to the dumpster behind them and the congealed blood that had formed a small pool beneath it. "That's where you found the body?" His voice dropped to a ragged whisper. Mandy nodded.

"There was a time in my life when I would've been your prime suspect. Lord knows I did some terrible things to those vamp boys." He looked down at his big hands, his broad shoulders drooping. When he looked back up at Mandy there were tears in his eyes. "It's a terrible world we live in, miss. We do such terrible things."

Such a big, powerful man yet he looked so completely weak and defeated in that moment. The flash of his silver cross caught Mandy's eye. A man of God, just like Enoch, but with almost none of that absolute confidence, that unthinking moral authority that her father possessed. Here was a man whose faith had taken a terrible beating, on the one side from his own checkered past and on the other from the ugly realities that constantly surrounded him. *Would this be what Daddy would end up like if he spent a decade on these streets?*

Mandy took Bouchard's open hand and gave it a reassuring squeeze. "I know it looks bleak from down here, but I think things are moving in the right direction. With the resources we have at our disposal now, the technologies... and with people like you helping us on the ground, we're gonna catch this guy soon. And once we've done that, what's gonna stop us from cleaning up a place like this?"

The old man smiled at her and returned the squeeze. Mandy saw another van pull up behind his - this one less cheerful. Body removal had arrived. She and Bouchard stood silently aside as a pair of pale, expressionless men emerged from the van and pushed a gurney towards the dumpster. The pint-sized medical examiner followed them, her feet prancing like a prize poodle to keep up with the long strides of the removers. As the trio passed, the rear man on the gurney stared at her. His pale, almost sallow complexion and patchy stubble reminded her of someone... *Brad.* She felt something like relief as he turned away and the absence of a ponytail reassured her that it could not be him. She'd never been able to convince him to cut that thing when they were together, why should he cut it when she left him?

She moved closer with Valentine and some of the others and they watched together as the men tugged and pulled from the rim of the dumpster, attacking from several angles until at last an arm cleared the rim and then a torso before it caught again. With a mighty yank from the pair, the torso sprang loose, the wooden stake protruding from its naked chest smacking the rim with a loud clang. They dropped the body onto a waiting tarp and then carefully untangled the legs.

Mandy suddenly felt a terrible ache traveling up her own legs. Hours of standing on concrete and asphalt in five-dollar-flats. She gazed wonderingly at the heels of the medical examiner as she stooped and teetered to poke and prod at the body. *But she gets to come and go... talking of Michelangelo.* She shook the old poem out of her head. *Another relic of Brad.*

"My feet are killing me. Maybe I can get body removal to throw me in the back with him and give me a ride home." She turned to grin at Valentine only to realize that it was Bouchard next to her - he apparently wanted to watch.

"Do you need a ride?" he asked plainly. A yawn and a nod later and she was riding shotgun in the canteen truck following the body removal van out of the blue light carnival and back towards the concrete horizon of the Pit. *Let us go then, you and I, when the evening is spread across the sky, like a cadaver upon a gurney.*

10

The FBI offices in River City were tucked away on the seventh floor of one of the many nondescript concrete ziggurats they'd thrown up before the 80's boom brought the flashy blue glass skyscrapers to downtown. The gray-flannel agents on the inside were similarly unglamorous - Vlad guessed River City was a dumping ground for the agency's deadweight. That was quite the change from the halcyon days when he first came on and the city was the nation's prime hotspot for human and drug trafficking. *But that's just what Mayor Cohn and Codrescu and the rest of those bloated moneybags on the city council want - a place where law enforcement has nothing to do but collect paychecks. No blood on the streets other than the vampire beverages transported in refrigerated trucks.*

The news from the FBI lab was just as unexciting as the office. The note had been printed on 20 lb. bond paper with standard toner - materials one would expect to find in an office supply room in the country. There was no trace of bodily fluids or fingerprints other than those that traced back to the oily Charlie Grace. The only element of real interest was that the "V.H." had been scrawled in blood, which came back as a close match for Pavel Petricean. There was also a comment from an unnamed handwriting analyst declaring with "75% confidence" that the writer was right-handed and male, with no further support or explanation provided.

Of far greater significance was RCPD's own vehicle unit's discovery of a hidden compartment in the Phantom containing multiple gallon bags of "peth-meth" aka "P.M." or "night-night," the potent and often deadly designer drug that had burst onto the narcotics scene a few years before. Vlad had never paid much attention to the chemistry side of the drug trade, but he knew enough to gather that this was high-end stuff, likely manufactured in a professional research lab or the equivalent. *Pavel's riches were getting more explicable by the moment.*

It was this discovery and its implications for an idea that had nipped at the corners of his mind for the last month that had prompted Vlad to call Maggie first thing in the morning to move up his monthly pilgrimage to the hills of Tigris County. But it was another disturbing notion that had him idling in his garage. *Enough of this - I need a drink.*

He cruised the streets, considering but passing each of the ubiquitous coin dispensaries. A vamp had to be desperately thirsty to get his red from those black metal boxes. It was an embarrassingly public display of thirst, like buying a porno mag from the gas station with a whole line of people behind you. Here in River City it also came with the added indignity of being assaulted by the headlines of the tabloids that inevitably shared space with the red at the street kiosk. Even in this more tolerant age, the lurid front pages bubbled with anti-vamp paranoia, blaming every missing person and DOA on some secret bloodthirsty vamp cabal. *Nothing like throwing back a pint of the red as the man beside you flips to A6 to read more about the bloodsucker who ravaged ten hookers in a single night of homicidal passion.*

Vlad settled on his new favorite haunt: the old Olympus Lounge on the edge of Mitchell Heights. Once the swankiest destination for the vamp nouveau riche, it was now a nearly-forgotten relic, its name a testament to the provincial thinking of that era. The fifteenth floor was the top of the world! The clientele wasn't even vamp anymore - mostly native sales reps for the big manufacturing outfits. But they still kept some red on tap for the rare occasion vamp bigwigs came to this part of town. The place also had a nice smoky corner, one that insulated Vlad from the prattle of the salesmen while offering him a gargoyle's eye view of the Pit.

This early in the morning Vlad was the only patron and found his way to his corner. The native waiter brought him a bottle - fortunately Vlad's novelty factor had worn off and the staff no longer ogled him in awkward fascination - and Vlad poured himself a tall glass as he peered down through the morning fog into the tenement. Her apartment was on the other side of the mist. He took a sip, feeling the red thick and cool as it traveled glacier-like towards his palate. The bitter hit of iron just before the swallow arrived with a disappointingly muted kick - the Olympus Lounge didn't have the freshest supply - but it was enough to take some of the edge off and send a burst of vitality to his extremities.

Vlad sighed. He knew none of this was healthy. A well-behaved vamp bachelor suffering the thirst was supposed to take his red in the privacy of his home, to clear his mind before the first gulp and then direct all that initial rush of energy to whatever pressing task was at hand. *I'm breaking all the old Constable's rules.*

But the curmudgeonly ghosts of mentors past could not hold his focus. Another sip and his mind's eye wandered through the mists. Out of the haze came soft waves of chestnut hair. Pale elegant fingers, like spider's legs, coursed through these waves, combing them neatly behind elfin ears. The waves parted to expose the gleaming porcelain skin of her perfect neck. Vlad emptied the glass.

***

Mandy answered the door in silk pajamas - the salmon-colored ones with the brown trim her mother had given her years ago. They didn't offer any place to tuck a pistol so she didn't have her gun either. This was not her usual practice, especially when Angel was gone. There were more than enough burglars, pervs and junkies in the Pit to keep a girl from coming to the door at all, much less answering it in bed clothes, however frumpy.

But Mandy had grown so accustomed to her father swinging by every morning that teenage muscle memory had taken over. *Here comes dad to chastise us for sleeping in until 7 on harvest day!* So it took a moment for her to register that it was not Enoch in the doorway but Vlad. When it finally hit, she felt a crimson warmth rush to her cheeks.

"Good morning." He stood there in the doorway, dressed in a blue jacket with gold buttons, looking like a sea captain just returned to shore. He locked eyes with her. "May I come in?"

She stammered a yes and opened the door wider for him. She felt the cold morning breeze hit her skin and looked down to see her stomach bare up to the curve of her ribs, the two ends of her pajama shirt flapping in the wind. Her cheeks got warmer as she hurried to button them back together.

Vlad strode inside and stood in the center of her untidy kitchen staring at her painting. He turned the stare on her as she closed the door.

"Coffee?" she offered weakly. He shook his head. His eyes fell on her pajamas.

"You should get dressed. I've decided to take you with me on a special field trip."

"Oh, okay," was all she could manage and she jogged behind him to the bathroom. He took a seat at the kitchen table and resumed his study of her painting.

She left the door open a crack and shed the pajamas, hunting for any kind of acceptable outfit in her barren closet. *Couldn't he have waited for my dry cleaning to come in?*

"So do I get an explanation for where you want me to go or is this one of those you say jump, I say how high kinda things?"

"You'll want something warm," he called out. "And pack a change of clothes. We may end up spending the night."

Do I get any say in this? She rolled her eyes in the mirror but her irritation dissolved as she spotted her beautiful black trench coat hiding in the back of her closet. A forgotten splurge from her last holiday check. She couldn't resist and slipped into it, feeling the caress of its fur-lining caressing her bare skin. She pulled it tight around her neck and arched for the mirror. Yes, that high-end Russian call-girl chic. *That will be ten thousand rubles, comrade.* She felt a smile coming on and squashed it.

She spied another forgotten item in the darkened recesses of her wardrobe - a scarlet v-neck tunic - and grabbed it. *Time to give the collared shirts a break.*

"Still no hint as to where we are going?""

"Tigris County. The sheriffs have something that might be big for our case."

Wow, thanks for being so specific. And I'm sure you won't get called away as soon as we get there and leave me to bum a ride from some stray hillbilly. She moved to the vanity and unearthed her one and only necklace - a small obsidian pendant dangling from a slender silver chain. She hovered at the vanity mirror, evaluating. *Might as well put on some mascara.*

"Where did you get this?"

She peeked out of the doorway to see him fixated back on her painting.

"Oh, I don't know. I saw it somewhere and liked it." It felt tacky to admit buying art from a mall kiosk.

"It's a Timcic print. Very famous in the old country. My father met him once."

Mandy stepped out and stared at the painting anew, its strange hypnotic pull feeling even stronger now that Vlad seemed similarly transfixed by it. She felt a thrill of vindication. *As if Angel knew anything about art anyway.*

"Do you like it?" she asked, her hand reaching self-consciously to play with the pendant dangling from her neck.

"Not particularly," he said flatly, sinking Mandy's shoulders like a deflated balloon. "But I don't think I've ever seen a Timcic print on the wall of anyone who wasn't a vampire."

He turned to her and his gaze widened, his head jerking back almost imperceptibly. *The art critic - impressed?* A tingle traveled up Mandy's spine, straightening her shoulders under that beautiful trench coat and sending her eyes running to safety - yes, the pile of dishes in the sink. *Aphrodite falling behind on her housekeeping.*

***

Mandy had never made it all that far beyond the foothills. As soon as the highway left the northernmost city limits, the road became steep, windy, narrow and treacherous. The one time she had tried to make a proper road trip out of it she'd stopped at the ramshackle biker bar with a gorgeous view of the city below and then insisted that they head back down. Of course she hadn't been in the mood to enjoy the view then, that being one of the final stops of the Brad farewell tour.

It was easier to enjoy the ride now; it helped when the driver wasn't taking his eyes off a road with sheer cliff drops to moon at her pathetically and grumble about how she didn't seem to be able to have a good time anymore. Not that Vlad didn't occasionally throw a stare her way, but the risk of a sudden detour into mopey murder-suicide seemed considerably less.

A long slow leftward curve and River City disappeared at last behind a huge gray rocky outcropping wreathed in green shrubs. The road climbed steeply again before dropping into a little grassy valley carpeted with purple rhododendron blossoms. Above a quaint little roadside rest stop an old wooden water tower was emblazoned with "Welcome to Tigris County."

"It's beautiful up here," Mandy said, breaking a pleasant silence that had lingered since they left the Pit.

"Yes. It's a dead ringer for the old country. That's why so many of us moved up here when we first came over."

She looked around and saw nothing but the little rest stop. "Where did they all go?"

"The call of the city! But there are still plenty of us up here. And every vampire eventually finds their way to higher ground even if only in death."

On cue, they rounded another corner where the valley widened into a broad flat expanse. Rising up against the background of snowy peaks in the distance was a sprawling complex of white marble buildings surrounded by gardens, statuary and gravestones.

"This was originally Doctor Duma's sanatorium. During his life it was a refuge for vampires in need. Since his death it has become one of the best hospitals in the world, as well as the final resting place for all of us here in the states. It's the closest thing to a sacred ground we have in this country."

"Dragescu and Petricean, will they be laid to rest here?" Vlad looked at her in surprise.

"I-I... uh... No. They will be cremated." It was the first time Mandy had heard him stammer.

"Forgive me," he continued, his voice smoothing. "It's a bit of a sensitive subject to talk about with an outsider..." He paused, looking at her as if to check whether she was still interested. She was. *It's nice that he's the one squirming for once.*

"It is our tradition that violent deaths are treated differently. It's a bit difficult to explain, but the general idea is that only by fire - complete destruction - can the soul be liberated from the suffering experienced by the body. Whereas in a natural death, the harmony between the soul and the body remains intact and they are interred together in the ground."

"Fascinating. You know I used to work in a funeral parlor."

He smiled. Not even an eyebrow raise. *Of course, he read my file.* She turned from him to look back at the marble metropolis that continued to sprawl out ahead of them. The funeral home and cemetery in Copper Springs couldn't have covered even a tenth of this and they had started burying people in the Civil War.

The burial grounds finally ended and gave way to a long row of houses. Shacks more like it. *Was this the hillbilly remnant of Tigris County, camping out on the outskirts of a vampire graveyard?* She wondered how these old-fashioned old country vamps got along with these rowdies - and vice versa. *Can't imagine those snake-handling preachers taking too kindly to cross-hating foreigners setting up in the middle of their territory.*

A ding sounded as the fuel gauge on the Mercedes entered the red. Vlad didn't strike Mandy as the type to let his gauge get so low. *He must be distracted.* He pulled into a seedy gas station, honking his horn and rolling down the window.

A couple emerged from the attached convenience store. Their dress surprised Mandy - it didn't come from the jumbled rural wardrobe of camo jackets, plaid shirts, overalls and floral print dresses she'd grown up around. The man wore a tunic over brown leather trousers, the woman a red cowl, a wool vest and a long skirt with tassels on the fringe. Both were short and stocky and approached the vehicle with downcast eyes. The woman operated the gas pump while the man raised the hood and examined the engine.

"Not used to this kind of service, huh?" Vlad said to Mandy. She shook her head. Vlad leaned out the window and barked something in Romanian. The woman curtseyed and scurried back to the store. She returned shortly, waiting outside Mandy's window with head bowed.

The woman curtsied again and held out a white rose as Mandy rolled the window down. As soon as Mandy took the rose, the woman produced a rag from the waist of her skirt and busied herself with wiping the dust and muck from the Mercedes' sideboards.

Mandy sat staring at the rose in confusion. Vlad laughed his usual "HA!"

"Are these two vampires? They don't look like any I've seen."

"No, no, these are *ţăranii*. Peasant folk from the old country that came over with us. Most of them melted away as soon as they got here. But these two and the people living in those shacks you saw back there are the few who remained. They still believe in keeping the old ways."

"Is that what this was about?" she asked, holding up the rose. Its almost sickly sweet aroma had already dispelled the memory of cigarette smoke.

"Yes, I told her there was a lady in the car. It is tradition to give every lady who visits your home a flower. A testament to the lady's beauty and grace. Of course, she would have given you that rose even if you looked like a dog."

Gee, thanks. She set the rose down on her lap. It was very pretty. As they drove off, the couple stood by the roadside, not watching them, but keeping their heads bowed to the road. Mandy wrinkled her nose in distaste.

"The old ways not to your liking?" Vlad was staring at her again.

"It's just… they seemed sort of miserable." *Say what you will about hillbillies but at least they look you in the eye and smile every once in a while.*

"They are!" exclaimed Vlad, brightening. "Terrified, groveling little buggers. They only stay in those hovels because they are scared of the outside world. They hate us vamps more than anything, but they cling to us because we're all they know. It's degrading for everyone involved."

"You don't like the old ways either?"

"I appreciate them, but that doesn't mean I have to like them. They're like moth balls: they preserve beautiful things, but only by sealing them away from the world and making them smell terrible." He got louder and his hands left the steering wheel to gesture as he continued. "We have this great, beautiful country that opened its arms to us when the rest of the world closed its doors and some of us just want to hide in a new set of mountains."

He flung a thumb backwards, in the direction of the city. "Even back there, we take refuge in our towers and clubs and exclusive neighborhoods and build walls around our lives."

"You don't think there's a reason for that? We do have a xenophobic maniac going around chopping heads off!"

Vlad dismissed her with a wave of his hand. "I'm not so sure it's not one of our own, but regardless, it's nonsense. We've got the whole city rallying in our defense. The FBI, even. There was a time when we were vulnerable to the zealots and the cross-wavers. But we won that battle. They're the outsiders now. So to continue to live like outcasts and refugees… it's absurd. Grotesque! We should be stepping out of the darkness and enjoying the fruits of our victory."

As he turned to look at her again, she lowered her eyes to see the white rose peeking back up at her. Its aroma had mellowed, fainter but more pleasant. She remembered then the old fruit and flower stand she would man with her sisters by the roadside. It was a quiet country highway with little traffic, but they never hurt for business - commuters in their suits, truck drivers in their baseball caps and dungarees. All of them surveying the harvest laid before them with hungry eyes - mommy's flowers, daddy's fruit. *Peaches, blushing peaches, soft to the touch, sweet to the taste, yours for the asking.*

She brought the rose to her nose and smiled.

***

They met the Tigris County deputies on a tiny little strip of an abandoned main street. It reminded Mandy of an old western ghost town, only if the gold rush had come and gone in the 1970s instead of the 1870s. There were garish signs with dead neon bulbs advertising motels with color TV and jacuzzi tubs and disco bars and strip clubs.

The old town square was roped off with weathered crime scene tape, its smooth yellow lines fraying into ragged plastic strips beaten by the mountain winds. The Sheriff was a big, broad-shouldered man, every inch the caricature of a Southern country deputy down to his brown leather cowboy boots. But when he spoke it was not with a low Southern drawl but a distinct if not quite thick Romanian accent. He was a vamp. So too were all the deputies who had shown out in force to meet this little River City delegation. *They must not have much else to do up here.*

"This is where it all happened," the big man said, gesturing at the empty square.

Prior to their arrival at the Sheriff's office, Vlad had finally relented and shared the reason for their field trip. A few days earlier, shortly after the Dragescu killing, Vlad had read of a biker bloodbath up in Tigris where a large but uncertain number had been killed and no one stuck around to say what went down. How that tied in to their case Vlad had left for Mandy to guess.

"Right in the middle is where we found the bodies. One big burn pile. You can still see the char marks on the ground." Mandy squinted and saw the faint outline of a great black circle under the swirling dust - it must have been 20 feet in diameter. Vlad was scanning the perimeter.

"We had to send out to outside agencies to do the testing on the bodies. So far they've got 15 positive IDs from dental records but we might not ever get a complete body count. Whoever did this threw some of the bikes onto the bonfire - it's been difficult to separate the man from the man-made."

"Have all the positive IDs come back to the same biker gang?" asked Vlad.

"Yes. All Cottonmouths so far as we've been able to tell."

"Could there have been a rival biker gang?" Mandy piped in.

The Sheriff eyed her curiously - it was more than a foot drop down to her eye level. "Not likely. The Cottonmouths are the last men standing in Tigris. We cleaned out the last of their rivals a few years ago with some help from RCPD's drug task force. My guess is this is some kind of power struggle within the group. These sorts of things happen from time to time."

"How have the Cottonmouths managed to stick around so long?"

"Well, in the words of my predecessor, they were some crafty sumbitches." Mandy smirked at the vamp imitation of one of the good ol' boys. He continued: "They were also smart enough to keep most of their dirty work out of the county. This shindig" - Mandy smiled again - "was an annual thing for them. It had never been more than a party before this happened so we usually left them alone. Not that we mind all this." He gestured at the charred ground. "They did us a favor."

"Did you find any narcotics or paraphernalia on the scene?" asked Vlad.

"Yes, as a matter of fact. We found some needles in the bathroom stalls of the old bar. They had some residue that they tested."

"What were the results?"

"I'll have to get back to you on that," the Sheriff's eyes narrowed on Vlad. He turned and lifted the tattered crime scene tape. "The crime scene's yours if you'd like to look around."

Mandy crouched to step under. Vlad's voice came from behind her: "I think we've got enough. Thanks for your time."

"Of course," the Sheriff's gaze narrowed still further, but Vlad had already turned away and returned to the car. Mandy scampered after him.

A few minutes later, Vlad pulled up to an old western style

tavern attached to a small motel. Its little yellow sign identified it as "The Wanderin' Inn." Tinny accordion music greeted them as they entered. The clientele seemed to be exclusively what Vlad had called *țăranii*. Almost all were male. And all parted for Vlad and Mandy when they took up seats by the bar.

The bartender was a heartier, less timid sort from the same peasant stock. He beamed at Vlad without making eye contact and smiled at Mandy as he poured her a glass of an amber liquid. He left the bottle and mumbled something cheerful at her in Romanian. "Plum brandy," said Vlad gulping at his own glass. Mandy sipped and felt a sweet warmth travel down her throat. She quickly followed it up with another.

The influx of liquid confidence loosened her tongue. "So did we come up here just to sightsee and bar hop? Because I don't see what you could have gotten from whatever that just was with the Sheriff."

Vlad threw a quick glance at the other patrons and the bartender - they had all retreated out of immediate earshot. "We came up here to confirm a hunch. I knew it wouldn't take long but it had to be in person." He took another drink and stared off into space. *That's it? That's all you're gonna give?*

Mandy took another sip. "Are you going to keep me in the dark about your little hunches and theories forever? Am I your partner or just another version of Maggie that you take on the road with you?" Her voice came out louder than she had wanted. Vlad looked at her in surprise.

"I know I've been keeping a lot from you. I'm sorry. But rest assured you are much more than another Maggie." Mandy felt another surge of warmth and looked down at her now empty glass. *Maybe I should cool it with this stuff.* She poured herself another glass.

"So much of this is still unformed in my mind and it's such a sensitive subject, I've been hesitant to speak to anyone about it. But there are a few things I ought to share with you." He leaned in closer and brought his voice lower, almost whispering into her ear.

"The theatrics with the bodies of the victims. The note in the mouth and to the press. I think they are distractions. I think the real reasons for the murders might have a lot more to do with what we just saw."

"Biker gangs?" A bitingly cold gust of wind hit her as one of the patrons left the bar and she took another drink.

"Drugs," said Vlad, shaking his head. "What the Sheriff didn't tell you was that the reason the Cottonmouths are still around when everyone else disappeared was that they were the only ones that paid their protection money."

"The County's crooked?"

"They used to be, at least before we got everything cleaned up. Wouldn't surprise me if they still were."

"I know you said Petricean was mixed up with drugs and maybe Dragescu too because they traveled in the same clique, but how does that lead here?" Mandy pushed the hair back, trying to open up real estate for warmth building up around her face and neck to escape.

"Narcotics has always had two pathways into River City: upriver and through the hills. The river route was controlled by Adrian Dan's father. We closed that when we cleaned up the port and closed the riverboat casinos. The hill route has always belonged to the bikers. We were never able to shut it down completely, but we at least got the County to help us make it expensive enough to keep the trade down."

"If the trade's down, why did we have... why have we had so many ODs this year?" Mandy had had the exact number ready, but it got lost in the tingling heat creeping upward from her throat to the back of her brain. She took another sip to throw on the fire.

"Imports are down but we've got a new domestic supplier. And I think the bodies here and back home are downstream from that. The bikers don't like the lost business so they go after their competition in the city. Then the competition from the city retaliates. It escalates from there." Vlad drained his glass.

"Wow," said Mandy. Her head was spinning and it was the best she could manage.

Vlad then leaned in again, so close she could feel the heat of his breath on her neck and smell the brandy on his lips.

"I'm telling you this in confidence and I hope you'll keep it between us. Even whispers of a new vamp-led drug ring could be explosive, especially if it gets tied to a body count."

"You can trust me. My lips are sealed," Mandy whispered back, bringing those sealed lips so close to Vlad that they brushed his cheek. Vlad didn't move and they sat cheek-to-cheek for several moments, Mandy listening to his breathing. Her head felt so heavy, she felt a terrible urge to nestle her chin into his neck. She blinked and realized she already had and further that she was nestling deeper and bringing her arms up to rest around his shoulders.

Then she felt his hands take a firm hold of her shoulder and gently set her back upright on her barstool. She raised her drooping eyelids to meet his gaze. She remembered again the hunger of the men at the fruit stand. *Farm fresh peaches. Would you like a taste?*

11

As soon as Enoch saw the big church bus stop in front of the Garden Inn, he knew he had to get on. He'd avoided the stop since nightmarish earlier treks on the River City transit buses. It wasn't that they were covered inside and out with sleazy, full-color advertisements for cigarettes, hard liquor and strip clubs, though that was enough to rankle Enoch's spirit. It was that they were populated so heavily with mental cases. A passenger could scarcely travel a few blocks without being approached by one of them, demanding money or screaming abuse. And the drivers, sullen and rude to a man, drove with a reckless disregard for safety, desperate to discharge their miserable cargo at the final stop. *A legion of unclean spirits headed for the river.*

But this bus - the Rivers of Mercy Shuttle - was something entirely different and refreshing. Its sides were painted with a gorgeous mural of Jesus and John the Baptist in the Jordan river, the Holy Spirit descending on them in the form of a dove. Cheerful hymns boomed from loudspeakers attached to its roof. Inside, waiting with coffee and hot cocoas in thermoses, was the smiling bus captain and his wife, both dressed in their Sunday best. They greeted Enoch warmly and the lady escorted him to a nice, clean and comfortably plush seat.

Then the bus was off, blaring its cheerful music into the most miserable ghettos, stopping at every city bus stop It encountered to give people a chance to get on. Most declined - including the babbling schizophrenics, who seemed to be repelled by the church music - but gradually the bus filled, and every rider, even the filthiest street person, received the same warm welcome from the captain and his wife.

When the bus had been filled, they were off to the church, which was a surprisingly long trip along the freeways, well beyond the skyscrapers and slums. But it passed like a happy blur to Enoch, who felt ecstatic to be in the presence of so many believers again. They arrived at the church, one of at least a dozen buses to spill their contents under a vast awning that led into the church. To Enoch, the place seemed less like any church he'd ever seen than the Plaza Hotel in New York City, which he'd only ever seen in a coffee table book.

An army of smiling ushers surrounded him as soon as stepped off, greeting and guiding him and the thousands of others streaming out of buses and the endless stretch of parking lot jammed with private vehicles. This river of humanity was channeled across a broad entryway that split in the middle for a spectacular fountain that doubled as a baptismal pool. Overhead a huge banner welcomed them to River of Mercy and asked if they'd been washed in the blood.

As they drew closer to the entrance, Enoch felt the pulse of music thrumming in his chest. Beyond the doors were the walls of the sanctuary, walls that were not thick enough to contain the explosion of gospel music within. Enoch braced in anticipation; he liked to belt hymns as much as the next Baptist, but he'd never experienced something quite like this.

The herd thinned as ushers split off groups this way and that. Enoch's guide directed his bus troop off from the main body and up a hidden stairway that took them to the upper decks of the sanctuary. The pulse of the music pounded ever more intensely in his chest until the usher opened the door at the top of the stairway and a sonic flood burst through, drowning them in the exultant noise.

As Enoch staggered out onto the upper deck, the vastness of the sanctuary struck him as suddenly and forcefully as the music. Rows upon rows of people, all standing and singing and waving their hands spilled out in front of him until they reached the stage, itself enormous. A choir of hundreds, wearing beautiful red robes, were arrayed in bleachers on the stage. Leading them in their deafening chorus was a red-headed young woman. She was too far away to be anything but a dot to Enoch's naked eye, but she was blown up to giant size on the humongous projector screens that flanked the choir on both sides. And her voice - a powerful soprano that ululated between angelic and piercing - rose above the clamor of choir and crowd to shatter Enoch's ear drums and leave him quivering with an unknown emotion.

When the song was over, it still rang in Enoch's ears, so much so that it took him several moments to realize that the preacher had mounted the stage and replaced the pretty redhead on the big screens. Enoch recognized him immediately from the program the usher had handed him: Pastor Jim Haggerty. He was an average looking man, on the shorter side, with a fleshy face and portly bearing that suggested an overindulgence in soul food. His only remarkable features, other than a shock of thinning red hair in the same shade as the singer's, were a big, broad chest and a mouth to match. As soon as he spoke, Enoch understood immediately how such an ordinary looking man had drawn a flock of thousands.

His sermon rang from his mouth like his lungs were a pair of church bells, clanging forth in deep, sonorous tones that went out in waves to the furthest reaches of the crowd, causing every man's heart to vibrate in his chest. He preached from the second chapter of Daniel, directing the congregation to follow along in their own Bibles as an attendant wheeled out a podium. Chained to it was the biggest Bible Enoch had ever seen and Haggerty flipped through its ancient pages with a painstaking care that suggested its fragility. When at last he arrived at the passage he looked up at the crowd and never again returned his gaze to the book, reciting the words entirely from memory.

Haggerty's magical voice carried the whole congregation off to ancient Babylon, to the court of old King Nebuchadnezzar and his dream of a magnificent statue constructed in descending layers of gold, silver, bronze, iron and clay. In the dream, a boulder, unhewn by human hands, rolls in to crush the statue's feet, made from an unstable admixture of iron and clay, bringing the entire statue, including its glittering golden crown, to ruin, to be swept away to nothingness by the wind. Meanwhile this boulder grew into a mountain that ruled the earth forever after.

Haggerty let his audience stew in the imagery for a moment, pumping up his big barrel chest like a bellows before speaking again.

"Here's where you're thinking, and I know it's what you're thinking because it's what I was thinking when the Lord put this story on my heart last night: what's a pretty old fairy tale got to do with modern life? I confess: I pushed the good book away in frustration and I moved to the balcony for some fresh air and a clear line to heaven. And I shouted to the Lord: I don't need mystical visions, I need something real to give my people. And he told me to lower my eyes to the horizon. And I saw the towers of the city skyline sparkling in front of me, dazzling me just like they did when the architects first raised them and put our city on the map...

"Then I heard that still, small voice say to me: Behold. Here is your vision. Is it not real enough? And that's when I fell on my knees on my balcony, just like old Nebuchadnezzar did before Daniel. And just like Jesus before Jerusalem, I wept for my city." Here the preacher wiped the tears that began to stream down his cheeks, along with the sweat from his brow - and if any in the congregation doubted, the cameras zoomed in so close on his face that they could see the tear drops spilling from the corners of his eyes.

"But the Lord wasn't done opening my eyes!" Haggerty went on to explain that the statue was no mere object of beauty but a gigantic idol in the image of the Babylonian god Marduk, a terrible demon with the symbol of a serpent who fed on sacrificial human flesh and blood and held the Babylonians in a state of abject slavery while Marduk and his demonic brethren lived in leisure. The destruction brought on by the unhewn boulder was no tragedy, but a blessed measure of divine justice meted out on a symbol of hellish evil.

"When I gazed out at our towers, I realized then that it was the image of Marduk - no, of Satan! - leering back at me, taunting me with his great power and demanding I give my blood to his unholy priests as a tribute... I ask you saints, have we not all paid his tribute? Have we not built these towers with sacrificial offerings of our blood? Have we not bowed before its twisted beauty and offered it our worship?" He fell quiet, watching the crowd as his words shook them in their seats.

"I will speak plainly now, even with all principalities and powers of this town listening over the radio and television broadcasts, speaking the words they do not wish you to hear. We've been told to be tolerant, to broaden our minds and be receptive to new ways of living, that our moral misgivings are a form of ignorance and bigotry, to be cast off and discarded like a soiled garment. In many ways, we've already done so, and in doing so have commingled our human clay with the iron of this hard-hearted people that have settled among us. Doubt you that they are iron? Daniel tells us as that iron 'breaketh in pieces' and 'subdueth all things.' In thirty years, have they not broken and subdued us?"

"Saints, can you not see that together with this foreign people we have become the feet of this statue? We, who were called to be set apart from the world, to be a holy people, have instead formed this abominable alloy with darkness, so eager were we to add their strength and power to our dusty frames. And what is our reward for this: we have become the first target of our Father's wrath, the first ones who will bear the crushing weight of his judgment. We along with the lost souls of iron, those we flatter unto damnation with our silent acceptance."

"Consider, however, that despite the false friendship we have offered these people, they still view us, the body of Christ, with fear and loathing, and in this they are closer to the truth than we! For all that we paint smiles on our faces and seek to appease them with empty words, they see in our eyes, in our souls, the reflection of the One in whose image we have been made. And in their eyes, that is the image of the Rock of offense, the stone unhewn by man, coming to grind them and their great works down to dust."

"Do not believe, brethren, that this means we are to reject them, to cast them down so that we might raise ourselves in their places. God forbid! We should seek their destruction in the same sense in which we seek the mortification of our own flesh. In their folly is every part of us that yearns for the forbidden fruit, to exalt ourselves in the face of the Most High, to set ourselves up as a Marduk over the earth. Happy is the proud soul crushed into dust by the Merciful Maker, and then fashioned into new life and form, to take a place of service in his Holy House... I tell you, brethren, there is such a soul with us today!"

Whispers rippled through the crowd. At a gesture from Haggerty, a squadron of broad-shouldered men in dark suits emerged from the edge of the stage and formed a corridor down the center of the crowd. The whispers rose to chatter as a door opened at the other end of the auditorium and out stepped a tall figure in an elegant gray suit. Clutching his hand and leading him down the aisle was the red-headed young soprano. Enoch squinted to make out the man's face, which seemed strangely dark and blurry, realizing as he drew closer to the stage that he wore a black shroud over his head.

"Coming before you today is one of the iron men we have referenced. But unlike so many of his fellows, and so many of us, he is not running from the hard, unhewn face of the Cornerstone. No, he is running toward it, ready to lay himself down before it... Bring him up Pete." Haggerty gestured again, and another of the dark-suited men emerged, this time from the shadows behind Haggerty. Enoch didn't need to see him on the big screens to see that he was double the size of any of the others, a walking refrigerator.

The giant stooped at the edge of the state where there were no stairs and pulled the shrouded man up next to him with one hand, bringing him before Haggerty. The preacher clapped his hand on the mystery man's shoulder.

"Many of you would recognize this young man if we were to remove this shroud, but to do so would put him at a terrible risk. For there are many among his own people who would seek to destroy him if they knew he was denouncing the devil's birthright they hold so dear." Haggerty grabbed a hold of the shroud and gave it a tug. "This fabric may hide his face, but it won't stop the Holy Spirit, will it?" The crowd roared "no!"

"Are you ready now, son?" Haggerty, his voice soft and intimate even as it boomed over the loudspeakers. The shrouded head nodded. Haggerty bowed his head solemnly and cupped the man's face with both hands. From somewhere Enoch could not see, an organist began to play, filling the whole auditorium with the thrumming sound of the vibrating brass pipes.

"Heavenly Father," Haggerty bellowed. "You are a God of miracles and we are asking for a miracle today. Take the curse from off of this young man. Free him from the terrible lust that haunts his every thought. Cast out the unclean spirit, oh Lord and fill him with your own!" Then Haggerty's whole body began to shake violently, his hands slipping down to the shrouded man's neck, so that it looked like he was strangling him.

Then Haggerty threw back his head, his eyes turned heavenward and a strange sound proceeded from his lips, slow and guttural at first but picking up in speed and volume as he went on, until he was shouting at the top of his powerful lungs. His words were not English, nor did they sound like any human language, but Enoch was sure it was not gibberish. He felt a twist of discomfort in his gut as all around him the same sounds poured forth: the whole congregation was joining in, speaking their own strange tongues.

Then, just as Haggerty reached fever pitch, his voice crackling through the air like an electrical storm, his body shaking like a jackhammer, the shrouded man throttled like a crash dummy in his grip, he stopped suddenly, falling silent and motionless. With him stopped the organ and echoes of the crowd. Everyone in the building waited with bated breath as Haggerty brought his hand off the man's neck and held his open palm out, just in front of his shrouded face.

Then, with an unintelligible cry, Haggerty struck the man's forehead with his palm. The young man flew backwards as if he'd been struck by lightning and fell flat on his back, motionless. Haggerty immediately raised his hands in the air and stepped back, grinning at the crowd like a prizefighter announcing his victory.

An energy swept from the stage over the crowd and with it spontaneous paroxysms of emotion. Enoch saw people springing up from the pews and rolling in the aisles. Others produced brightly colored banners and ran through the crowd, holding them aloft like kites. Others reached beneath the pews and stood up with enormous ram's horns which they proceeded to blow, the otherworldly wailing sounds adding to the bedlam.

Enoch sensed the wave reaching the upper decks as the strange cries and outbursts exploded around him. He startled when the woman to his left, a large woman wearing a capacious floral dress, sprang upward suddenly, uttered a wild ululation and then collapsed where she stood, her head landing like a cannonball on Enoch's foot.

He stood too, not by any command of the Spirit, but out of an instinct to escape. It was not that he looked down on these people and their outlandish behavior - a part of him wished that he might find some way to join in their experience. He was certain they were sincere. But he could not shake the feeling that he had when he was trapped on the city bus, surrounded by people under the control of wild, unpredictable, perhaps even dangerous spiritual powers. With the woman's head still weighing heavily on his foot, he looked longingly at the EXIT sign gleaming red in the shadows behind him. Oh, how he wished to be home again!

***

Mandy woke to a pounding at the door that was immediately joined by pounding at her temples. She was in a bed. Or rather on top of its sheets. She was wrapped in her beautiful trench coat, now wrinkled and crumpled underneath her.

She pushed herself up. This place didn't look like a motel room. The bed itself was an old-fashioned four-poster, complete with curtains pulled back behind a sash. The walls were all wood paneling. The dresser across from her was a weathered-looking antique, topped with ornate candlesticks and piles of old books. She slipped off the bed and her stockinged feet disappeared in a rug that felt like some kind of animal fur. Her boots were set neatly at the foot of the bed.

There was another knock at the door. This one sounded gentler than the one that woke her, but still her head throbbed with each sound. She ran her hands quickly through her tangled hair and opened the door. On the other side was a dark-haired young woman wearing a maid's uniform.

"Sorry to wake you, miss, but Mr. Paler asked that I get you up before it got too late."

"Mr. Paler? This is his house?" Mandy felt a blush in her cheeks that momentarily dulled the ringing in her ears.

"Yes, miss. There's breakfast for you downstairs if you'll follow me."

Mandy followed her out of the room onto a loft that looked down onto some sort of sitting room or library. They took a wrought-iron spiral staircase down, Mandy holding on tightly to the railing to steady her wobbling legs. They bypassed the sitting room to enter a hallway leading into a big kitchen. Mandy felt a soothing blast of air radiating from a huge kitchen stove, its interior glowing from a crackling woodfire. Waiting for her on a little picnic-style table was a steaming plate of eggs and toast spread with a crimson jam.

Mandy sat down and the maid filled a mug with black coffee right off the stove. Her hangover stood no chance against this onslaught of comforting sights, smells and tastes. She couldn't hold back a heaving sigh. The maid glanced up at her from the stove with a raised eyebrow and Mandy blushed again.

"Thank you so much for this. You work for... Mr. Paler?" Mandy asked, fortified by a bite of toast and a sip of coffee.

"Yes, I'm his housekeeper..." She paused and then stretched her hand out awkwardly to shake Mandy's. "My name's Maria."

"I'm Mandy. Yeah, he's kinda my boss too." They both smiled and Maria sat down opposite her with her own cup of coffee. Mandy took a deep breath and continued: "Were you here when I... arrived last night?"

Maria hid a smile behind her coffee. "Yes. You were... uh... asleep."

"Ugh," Mandy groaned, hiding her face in her palm. "How did I manage to get in bed?"

"Mr. Paler carried you."

"Oh goodness." Mandy brought both hands to her face and felt her face burning underneath them. "Then he came back down?"

"Yes, right away. He made his bed on a sofa in the sitting room and asked me to go up and help make you more comfortable. I'm sorry I only managed to get your boots off."

Mandy sighed heavily and impulsively reached both hands out to grab Maria's, giving them a grateful squeeze. "Thank you. I can't believe I got myself into this situation."

"I can. Wearing a beautiful coat like that... having Mr. Paler carry me up the stairs like Scarlett O'Hara. Sounds like a dream to me!"

Mandy looked up at her in surprise and as soon as their eyes met they both burst out giggling. *Giggling!* Suddenly, Mandy was 15 again at the church masquerade ball when Esther's beau had shown up in a welder's mask. How they had laughed!

When their laughter receded, Mandy felt her spirits and her appetite soar. She devoured the eggs. Maria sat back and contemplated her coffee.

"It's a shame," she said with a sigh.

"What?" came Mandy's reply through a mouthful of toast.

"He's got it all. So handsome, so smart... He's got this beautiful house... why did he have to be a vamp?" She laughed again. This time Mandy didn't join in. Her headache was coming back.

"I almost forgot!" Maria exclaimed, springing to her feet and leaving the kitchen. She came back with a bundle that she deposited in front of Mandy. It was a folded-up newspaper with a hand-written note attached to it, all tied up by a pretty little red ribbon.

Mandy read the note first:

> Read this and come to the office as soon as you wake. Take the Cadillac in the garage. My sincerest apologies for abandoning you in a strange place yet again, though I hope you did not find my home too strange. I trust you will allow me to find some way of making it up to you.
> V.P.

He had remarkably delicate penmanship for a man. Mandy detached the note, slipping it into her jacket pocket. She unfolded the paper and out sprang the screaming headlines of the Daily Manifest: LETTER FROM A MADMAN! Underneath, the subscript: *River City Ripper spills all in exclusive letter. Signed Van Helsing.*

Van Helsing! She remembered the first time she had spied Dracula on the shelves of the Copper Springs Library with its garish cover of the black cloaked anti-hero feasting on the neck of a half-naked woman, her head thrown back, her eyes wide with terror or ecstasy. It had somehow made it through the censorship gauntlet, sliding past both the ever-vigilant eyes of Copper Springs prudes and the enlightened mandates banning the book for stoking xenophobic hate. Mandy also had to sneak it past the watchful eyes of mom and dad; a Pilgrim's Progress dust jacket had done the trick and she'd devoured the book in a single sitting.

The echoing chime of an old grandfather clock brought her back to earth. "I've got to go," she said, standing. "He says I can take the Cadillac?"

Maria guided her out of a side door leading from the kitchen into an immaculately landscaped courtyard. A red brick pathway wound round a fountain-ringed brass statue of a maiden embracing a swan and then continued on to a red brick carriage house with green trim. Mandy stopped at the door to look back at the house and saw it rising like a castle above her, its smooth gray stone siding traveling up and up to a gothic spire. *That Captain pay bump must be pretty special!*

Inside the carriage house was the Cadillac, a shiny black

behemoth gleaming in the dim light. It looked like something out of a black and white gangster movie. Even Daddy's Ford truck, beat up as it was, seemed more modern.

"Does it run?" Maria nodded and handed Mandy the keys from a hook near the door.

Mandy felt like she was piloting a boat, spending the first leg of the interstate terrified she might drift into another vehicle and put a dent in this shining relic. Gradually, the terror subsided and she even began to enjoy the experience, even the ogling of the surrounding traffic in their cheap Japanese imports. *Like leading a parade.*

Then the thought of pulling up to the apartment in the Pit spoiled her mood. This was not the right vehicle to pull off a stealthy wardrobe change. The thought of answering all of the inevitable questions from Angel, spoken and unspoken, brought some of her waking nausea back. Her hand toyed with the steering wheel. *A walk of shame right back into the office?* No, those gossipy detectives would be as bad or worse than Angel.

As she drifted forward, the sign for the Chinese laundry pushed into her peripheral vision and the solution presented itself. She collected her pantsuits and snuck past the service counter into a supply closet to change. She emerged to find a little Chinese girl in pigtails staring at her. Mandy handed her last night's outfit with an apology and made her escape.

She arrived at hindquarters having stashed the Cadillac in a dark corner of the garage. She glanced at herself in the reflection of the garage elevator's steel doors: normal. Hair a mess but that was normal too.

There was a crowd outside the interview rooms when she made it to homicide. She pushed through to the slot window to see. It was Charlie Grace in yet another pink leisure suit. Mandy wondered for a moment if there was another Chinese laundry out there with racks and racks of these hideous ensembles to keep the Grace look going.

"Whoa, Parker, make-up today!" It was Valentine next to her, grinning like an idiot. "Is this the day you finally get up the courage to ask me out?"

"You're available now, Val? That's great. All this time I thought you went with that tranny hooker from central booking." Valentine turned red as the detectives broke up laughing.

"I never said she was hot!" he declared.

"She?" came the chorus around him and the derisive howls mounted. Mandy turned away from the group and snuck a peek at her face with the compact in her purse. She cursed under her breath. *The mascara!*

"Shut up, all of you!" came Vlad's bark as he swung open the interview room door. He spied Mandy at the other end of the crowd. "Parker, get in here."

The gaggle of detectives went quiet and parted for her. She walked down the aisle and Vlad placed his palm at the small of her back, herding her in and closing the door behind them.

It was just Mandy and Vlad behind the one-way mirror. Grace was on the other side, looking sweaty but smug. Vlad opened her hand and placed a sheet of white copy paper in it. "Read it."

In her hand was a photocopy of another typed note, but this one considerably longer.

Citizens of Babylon

This is my third letter to you. I had hoped the first two would have made my message clear enough, but everything I have seen and heard on television, the radio and the newspapers tells me otherwise. They say I am a monster, a sadist, a bigot, a xenophobe. They call me the River City Ripper and declare me insane, killing to satisfy some psychotic thirst for deviant sexual thrills.

I am writing to you now in a more conventional medium to set the record straight. None of these accusations are true. My work is not motivated by any prurient fixations or uncontrollable violent urges. If you must characterize me with an epithet, which I suppose the extremity of my acts demands, call me a terrorist. For what is a terrorist but an artist using the medium of horror and violence to fashion his message?

In a civilized society such terrorism is indistinguishable from the sort of evil of which I have been accused. But this is no civilized society. We live in a grotesquerie, a parody of civilization so degraded and deluded that the only means it offers to communicate hard truth is its own perverse language. If I speak in the tongues of men and angels but have not blood, I am become as sounding brass, or a tinkling cymbal.

A society stricken with plague turns to leeches and

bloodletters for their healing. Can you reason with such a people? No! You must minister to them in the debased traditions of their chosen physicians. So I have chosen as my pen a scalpel. I have slit open the gangrenous veins of the city to purge the toxic humors from the body politic. I have severed the sucking heads of the leeches to empty the contents of their bottomless stomachs. Is this your medicine? Is this your salvation?

I suspect that even now you are stopping your ears and closing your eyes to prevent these earnest words from taking root in your mind. Only a madman could write such things, you say. Yet it is only to reach those precious few still capable of hearing that I even write at all. Perhaps that will soon change as the tide of blood washes away the illusions of a prevailing civility and the ears and eyes of the people will heed plain-spoken truths again. Until then, however, I will continue to say what must be said in the only language you will understand.

Yours,

Van Helsing.

"Grace says it arrived yesterday the same way the first one did: slipped under his door. The camera we put in his hallway didn't pick up anything but there were some technical issues and it wasn't working."

Mandy wrinkled her nose. "Grace could have messed with it. Are we sure he didn't write this himself? Something about the tone just feels... *off*. And Van Helsing? It reminds me of the pranks Liggins pulls on the radio."

"The original's with the FBI again, but everything matches so far." Vlad turned to watch Grace. "As for him, he probably knows more than he's saying, but he's been pretty cooperative. We're about to cut him loose."

Mandy turned back to the letter. Vlad moved closer to read it over her shoulder. "If this is legit, doesn't it sink your drug turf war idea? This doesn't sound much like your usual biker crank dealer." She shot a teasing glance over her shoulder.

He smiled at her. "Ah, she remembers! I was worried the whole night might be a blur." Mandy looked for a place to hide her reddening cheeks - the black folds of his jacket were inviting.

The door behind them swung open and Valentine burst in. Vlad was suddenly two steps away, staring at Grace again. "Rev Bouchard's downstairs, Cap. He's got a bus-full of junkies ready to talk."

Valentine turned to Mandy and squinted at her. "Are you wearing rouge too, Parker? You really don't have to glam up for me, you know."

Vlad broke in before Mandy could get in a withering response. "Take her down with you, Val. We need IDs and written statements from every one of them."

Mandy followed Valentine to the door, dragging her feet as her stomach see-sawed. *Still just a grunt, a flunky, a -*

"Wait." Vlad caught her by the arm and pulled her back towards him, his voice dropping. "Show the letter to Bouchard and tell him our theories. He might have a good read on it." He paused, his hand lingering at her arm. "Come back when you're done so we can discuss."

Mandy floated off towards Valentine and the elevators. Valentine turned to her as the elevators closed. "Word to the wise, Parker. Might want to do some rethinking on this schoolgirl crush you're nursing for the Cap."

She turned on him in a flash, her fists balling at her sides.

"Easy!" He yelped. She saw he wasn't grinning or teasing any more, his face having softened with what looked like genuine concern. *Still, a very slappable face.*

"I'm not trying to be mean... it's just getting kinda obvious, you know, the way you're always staring at him and jumping when he calls your name."

Mandy hardened her angry glare into something icier. "I'm not trying to mean either, but whenever you open your mouth all I hear is a chauvinist pig. Maybe you should try shutting up about something you know nothing about."

He raised his hands in surrender. "I get it, I get it. I'll stop..." But he didn't. "Really I'm just trying to look out for you. Don't want people talking about you around the office, calling you stuff like 'vamp tramp.' - OW!"

The doors opened finally and Mandy left him nursing the sore spot where her knuckles had jabbed between his ribs.

By the time they made it to Bouchard's canteen at the entrance of the canteen, Valentine was well behind her, trotting to keep up. There was no one in the cab but the muffled sound of church music emanated from the back. The back doors were open and Mandy poked her head in to see more than a dozen people crowded into the little space. They had the distinct look and smell of street people, but the way they clustered around each other, hands on each other's shoulders, their chins lifted in song... *Wednesday night youth choir.* They were even singing "Great is Thy Faithfulness." *Deacon Leroy's favorite. Not up to his standards, though.*

Bouchard stood in their center, his voice, so soft and quiet when they had spoken before, booming loud and strong in song, clear above the caterwauling of his junkie choir. He saw Mandy and his foggy gray eyes twinkled in recognition but he did not stop. When the chorus at last wrapped up, he slipped through his flock and clutched her hand.

"Miss Parker! You see: I kept my promise." He gestured around him.

Valentine arrived at her side, panting.

"Great. My partner here is going to take their statements." Before Valentine could protest, Mandy whisked Bouchard away from the canteen.

"Do you have a few minutes to spare? Captain Paler thought you might be able to help us a little more."

"Of course. Let's walk while we talk. These old legs been cramped up for too long. If they don't get to moving, they might stop working altogether."

Together they walked towards the square of light where the garage opened onto the street. She cast a look back at Valentine and smiled when she saw him glaring at her.

As they walked, Mandy spilled the details of the case. When she arrived at the massacre in the County and summarized Vlad's turf war theory, Bouchard sighed.

"The Cottonmouths. I remember them. The Highlanders used to tangle with them. We always got the better of 'em, though."

"You were in a biker gang?"

He unbuttoned his cuff and rolled up his sleeve to expose a blob of a tattoo, faded so badly that Mandy could only guess it was some kind of biker insignia. "From my bad days. Got into all kinds of mischief."

She gave him the copy of the Van Helsing letter and he stared at it blankly, his glassy eyes running to and fro over the page. Mandy apologized and took it back, reading it to him as they emerged from the garage and stepped out into the glass forest of skyscrapers. It felt odd reading the letter aloud. She had to suppress the instinct to read it in character, a lingering habit from the old days of staging scenes from Shakespeare with her sisters. But she found herself doing it anyways, delivering the closing lines with a dripping menace worthy of Iago.

"Sure doesn't sound like any biker I ever knew. Don't have time to learn to talk like that when you're spending everyday busting heads or getting wasted," Bouchard mused. "But I wouldn't rule it out. There's nothing like the pen to teach a man to appreciate the finer things in life. I just devoured that library. Was ignorant when I went in, left with a master of divinity!"

"Do you know if this kind of xenophobia is still pervasive among bikers or street gangs or was it more of an artifact of the general culture of the time?"

He looked at her with eyebrows raised. "I can only speak for myself and say there was a lot of hate in my heart... You know, come to think of it, you don't sound like any cop I ever knew, other than maybe Mister Vlad. Don't hear too many of those big words out here on the street."

"I guess I read too many books as a kid," Mandy blushed. "I try to talk like a normal person, but sometimes I forget and the encyclopedia slips out."

Bouchard laughed - a deep rumbling laugh that made Mandy smile - and shook his head. "Don't you go getting embarrassed now. It's a good thing to be so smart. You remind me of my daughter. Beauty and brains!"

"Did your daughter end up as a cop too?"

"Oh, no..." His voice dropped suddenly, the booming rumble of his laughter fading into a tremulous quiver. "I lost her a few months ago."

"I'm sorry to hear that. What were the circumstances if you don't mind my asking?"

"You really are a detective... Well, she had a need for the needle, as they say. I kept her with me after she dropped out of college. We had some good months together. But she couldn't stay off it for long. Then one day she just up and disappeared."

"So sorry," Mandy said quietly, feeling a sharper pang of empathy than she'd become accustomed to after hearing the near identical story so many times from shell-shocked parents and siblings during her first weeks on homicide. *A few weeks away from the OD assembly line and I'm getting soft.*

"There you go being sorry again," he boomed, his vivacity returning and light twinkling back into his misty gray eyes. "It makes this old man smile to see a young woman like yourself, so put together, serving the community, going after the bad guys, making something worthwhile of your life. Your daddy must be awful proud of you."

Mandy felt a derisive snort coming on like a sneeze, but it dissolved under Bouchard's kindly gaze. For a few moments, thoughts of the case drifted from her mind and they walked together in a comfortable silence under the shadows of the surrounding towers.

12

Vlad dithered at the threshold of the exhibit on the pretense of smoking a cigarette. The jazz orchestration of Grieg's *Hall of the Mountain King* burbled out from under the closed double doors, serving as a constant reminder of the obnoxiousness waiting for him on the other side.

He exhaled a thick cloud of smoke and watched it disappear in the bright daylight. These Gleaner's Club functions had been so much more bearable when Duma was running things. They would meet in some capacious Elks Lodge meeting hall and sit at plastic fold-out tables, while homely retirees served them scrambled eggs and coffee on styrofoam and the good doctor would go up on stage to hand a big cheesy check for a few grand to somebody like Big Mike Bouchard. Real people eating real food, helping real charities. *Not this bull****.*

As soon as Duma passed, and his son decided to party instead of carrying on the legacy, the Gleaners had fallen to Slim Codrescu and his people, along with all the other prestige vamp organizations. Since then, the Gleaners had become just another vehicle for showcasing avant-garde absurdities to separate the elites from their inferiors. Vlad looked down at the program in his hand, a giant laminated sheet fashioned after a 1950's diner menu. Garish red and yellow lettering at the top announced "The Hall of the Burger King, a Theresa Russell Production." A woman wearing a comically oversized Grace Kelly mask had thrust it into his hand when he entered, prompting his speedy retreat to the porch.

Vlad stepped off the porch and doused his cigarette as the door swung open behind him and the music came pouring out.

"Oh, there you are!" Posing in the doorway, with one arm reaching diagonally to the corner of the door frame and the other sharply akimbo on a jutting hip, was the unmistakable Theresa Russell. Unusually tall for a woman, she was also wearing treacherously high heels, adding to the step of the porch to make her tower over Vlad.

"Do come in. Mr. Codrescu is waiting for you." She gave her graying hair a flip and thrust out her chest as if to shout "come hither!" Vlad noticed that she appeared to be wearing nothing under her frilly pink baking apron, but he felt nothing but revulsion for her. *A disgusting old spider, scrambling madly toward any man with a pulse and a society calendar.*

He combined a reluctant nod with a poorly disguised sneer of disgust, but Russell only smiled more wickedly and grabbed at his wrist with her long spidery arm. This was not their first encounter, and she seemed to enjoy provoking him, along with everybody else. He turned his eyes away as she exposed her naked backside and pulled him after.

But there was nowhere to hide them inside. Joining the incessant pounding of the music, playing on an endless loop from unseen speakers, was an unrelenting assault on his eyes. The exhibition hall, only recently the stately home of a traveling Rembrandt collection, was now stuffed to the brim with performance artists and oversized stage settings, organized into a giant parody of a fast food restaurant.

Flanking Vlad on either side were dining room tables arranged in a semicircular array towards the entrance. At the head of every table sat men in identical gray flannel suits, hiding their faces behind open newspapers. Patrons would take seats at the table and give their dining orders to masked waitresses exactly like the one that gave Vlad his menu. Apparently, no matter what the patron ordered, the food was delivered to the man at the table, each of whom were now surrounded by heaps of uneaten hamburgers.

The center of the hall held the service counter and kitchen, elevated above the rest done up to look like a church. The cooks wore sparkling vestments and bishop hats as they crowded around a sizzling "altar" to flip burgers. Suspended above them was a stained-glass window, softly diffusing the ugly neon glow of a

Burger King sign.

Russell led Vlad behind the chef-priests to a black-paneled wall, a section of which gave way before her searching hand and brought them into a perfectly normal little bar and dining area, where men and women sat being served by an unadorned wait staff and that terrible music stopped as soon as Russell pulled the panel closed behind her. Vlad breathed an audible sigh of relief.

"Ahh, the sound of another satisfied patron," purred Russell, uncomfortably close to Vlad's ear. He recoiled, bringing on another one of her vicious smiles.

"Where is Codrescu? You said he was looking for me."

"He'll be along shortly, I'm sure. In the meantime I have some questions I've been dying to ask you." She sat down at the end of the bar and beckoned for Vlad to join. He hesitated but his eyes flitted to the beautiful display of reds behind the bartender and he took a seat.

"Is it true..." Russell asked, her voice a husky whisper. "Does the killer really stuff the victims' mouths with garlic?"

Vlad avoided her gaze as he gulped down a fine red - warm and thick just as he liked. His irritation dissolved immediately. "Why don't you read about it in the Manifest? These days the tabloids know more than us cops."

"You shouldn't be bitter. It's so unattractive." Vlad grunted and held out his glass to the bartender for a refill. "And you shouldn't be so rough on Charlie Grace. I heard you had the poor man interrogated for twelve hours."

"A friend of yours?"

"No. No journalist can truly be a friend to an artist. But they are a necessary means to an end, and one should not treat the means so meanly."

"I'm sure he'll find solace in the millions in advertising this killer is bringing him."

"Who is bringing the millions, Van Helsing to Charlie or Charlie to Van Helsing? The success of the journalist is the price the artist must pay to find his audience."

Vlad turned to her, finally. She beamed. "So you believe Van Helsing when he says he's an artist? You accept him as one of your own?"

"It's not a question of acceptance. An artist is whomever you cannot ignore, anyone with the power to compel your gaze, to captivate your mind, to direct your conversation…" She paused languorously. "In the middle of the grand opening of my new exhibition, what are we talking about? Whose words and images dominate our thoughts?"

Vlad's eyes narrowed on her. "Sounds like you're quite the admirer."

"I am only recognizing his power. As for admiration, I think it may be the other way round."

Vlad raised an eyebrow and she continued: "There are unmistakable traces of my work in his."

"Do you have a pile of decapitated vampire heads in your studio?"

"Now who is the journalist?" she frowned. "Study my earlier work. You will see the influence. It might even help your case."

Vlad leaned in to ask another question but she stood up suddenly, putting on another horrible smile for someone behind him.

"Mr. Codrescu: look who I found!"

Vlad turned to find the spindly Codrescu hovering behind him, his thin lips pursed in their usual sneer.

"If you'll excuse me gentlemen, I've got an exhibition to get back to." She turned to walk away with a parting shake of her sagging buttocks.

"I don't know how you deal with these people," said Vlad, blinking and shaking his head to dislodge that last image.

"I thought you were the great advocate for native culture, Paler," said Codrescu coldly, adjusting his round-frame glasses, which along with his perpetual sneer, gave him the air of a Prussian aristocrat.

"This isn't culture, it's a dressed-up freak show."

"Russell is the rare hemotypical individual honest enough to depict it in such terms. I, for one, appreciate her boldness."

Vlad shrugged. Codrescu was always tendentious and would have happily dragged out the debate but Vlad was already feeling his own feet tapping impatiently.

"The board would like to speak to you," breathed Codrescu finally after a disappointed silence.

The Gleaner's Board. Vlad used to be on it, albeit a junior member, when Dr. Duma ran it and they were focused on bridge-building with native institutions. He had been one of the first of

Codrescu's purges. Following Codrescu into yet another backroom, he saw them sitting around a coffee table loaded with expensive-looking bonbons. There was Dragan the banker, Ungurelu, the chemist and native billionaire Andy Ryan's right hand man, and Stelian the university don all clustered together. Then there was young Alex Duma, sitting uncomfortably apart, chomping on an unlit cigarette, his foot tapping even more briskly than Vlad's.

Codrescu sat at the head of the group and motioned for Vlad to sit opposite in what looked suspiciously like an interrogation chair. Vlad stood obstinately, staring coolly at his waiting inquisitors.

Codrescu eyed the empty chair, his brows twitching in irritation. "You might want to get more comfortable. We have a lot to talk about."

"I'm curious what a charity board has to urgently discuss with a police captain." He pushed away the chair to aggravate Codrescu and was satisfied to see the eyebrow twitch intensify.

"You can drop the pretense, Paler." It was Dragan, leaning forward. Like Vlad he was a lowborn Valley man, an interloper in the high society circles dominated by the Bucegi and Leaota families. Unlike those aristocrats, he didn't mince his words. "You know perfectly well we represent interests broader than this charity. And I hope you're not so dense not to realize it was these interests that are responsible for you being assigned to this case."

"Ah, so I owe my demotion back to field duty to you. Much obliged."

"This personal rancor is unseemly," hissed Stelian, an unsightly man behind coke-bottle lenses. "We are all on the same side here. Our goals are the same: we all want to see this killer stopped."

"Good. Then you should have no problem letting me get back to the work which you arranged for me to do."

"We asked you to come before us because we have concerns about your handling of the case," Codrescu piped up now, his gaze finally liberated from the forsaken chair. "We feel that you aren't exercising proper control of crucial matters. Or perhaps the whole undertaking has outgrown your capacity."

"I'm afraid you'll have to be more specific than that. If you don't think much of my detective work, I don't see how you can expect me to guess what you're driving at."

"No one here believes you're anything less than a fine detective," came Dragan again, oozing snake oil. "It's the secondary aspects that are worrying the community, particularly the press."

"Yes," chimed in Strelian. "The atmosphere of hatred has become palpable. Our community is in the midst of a crisis of terror and yet the papers and the TV preachers would have the public believing that this some sort of divine judgment visited on us!"

"I don't like it either, but what would you have me do? Muzzle the press? Close the churches? I think the community may be overestimating the municipality's police powers."

"We understand there are constraints you must be working under," it was apparently Ungurelu's turn to talk. "But we believe a change in posture might produce an indirect change in the situation. A shift from the current languid stance to a more muscular and aggressive pose."

"Perhaps a return to the approach your junior colleague took with Rich Liggins," translated Dragan. "It seems inconsistent that the department could bring such pressure on him only to leave Charlie Grace a free hand to spew his filth in print every morning."

"The best way to stop Charlie Grace is to catch the killer who has been hand-feeding him, a task to which I have devoted the entirety of my effort and attention. You will be glad to know he is currently under surveillance, at my request, in hopes that we can locate whoever is supplying him with information. But, if it would please the community, I would happily set Detective Parker loose on him and the other tabloids in hopes of intimidating them into greater propriety."

Codrescu perked up at the sound of her name, his sneer becoming more pronounced. "Speaking of your partner, I've heard a few troubling reports regarding the two of you. You say you've been devoting all of your attention to the case: if so, why are the two of you making a weekend getaway to the foothills in the middle of the investigation?"

Vlad felt the gathering tension in his jaw tighten into clenched anger. "For one so concerned about libels in the press, you seem awfully comfortable trading in malicious gossip. My trip to the foothills was strictly investigative in nature as any close examination will bear out."

Alex Duma, who had become increasingly uncomfortable during the course of the inquisition, finally stopped fidgeting and spoke up. "I don't think Slim meant to offend you Vlad. We all have a high opinion of you, just as my father did. I think all we're trying to do here is give voice to some concerns and, you know, get some reassurances that you have everything under control, which I'm sure you do."

Vlad turned to him, his anger cooling into scorn. *If only your father could see you now: kowtowing to this highborn coven of second-rate conspirators, gossips and crones!* "Thanks for speaking up," he said, through still clenched teeth. "Perhaps with a little more muscular and aggressive pose you can return Gleaners to what it was under your father and take it back from these meddling old women."

Vlad enjoyed the start that sent each of the board members back in their seats. Codrescu, though, did not sit back but stood up, his sneer deepening into a snarl. He looked disdainfully at Vlad before turning to his colleagues: "He has always suffered from such emotional outbursts and lapses in judgment, especially when it involves a garlic-eater woman."

"Don't..." Vlad tried to continue but his voice was swallowed into a gurgle as his throat tightened like a vise and a dark cloud spread across his brain and filled his eyes.

"It is unpleasant to bring up personal histories," Codrescu said, turning on him. "But you apparently refuse to learn from yours. Come now, don't lose your temper. It was the community that pulled you from the burning wreckage of that gypsy girl's funeral pyre."

Vlad did not remember if any more of this shameful speech made it out of the odious councilman's mouth, only that Codrescu was sprawled on the floor, with his glasses broken in half as the rest of the board stood and gestured indignantly. The young Duma had a strong arm wrapped around Vlad's chest and was pulling him back, back, back. Out of the black-paneled rooms and back to the chaos of the exhibit hall

The horrible pulse of the *Mountain King* pounded in his head again. The masked waitresses clustered around them, their painted faces smiling, mocking him. He felt again the scorching heat. The flames licking at his cloak. The smoke filling his lungs. And then her screams. *Oh those terrible screams.*

At last they were outside and Vlad escaped from Duma's grip, a cough racking his body, his hands bracing his pounding temples. He heard Duma saying something, but he ignored him and staggered to his car. He pressed down hard on the accelerator, rolling the windows down. The exhibit hall shrank from his rear-view mirror and the cold fresh air swept through his hacking lungs and drove the clouds from his mind.

***

Enoch had felt good as he deposited the cash in the woman's outstretched hand, even if his shoulders ached as he did. "A laborer is worthy of his reward," he declared cheerfully as she counted it, puffing on her cigar. He didn't quite know if he was saying it for her benefit - she didn't even look up - or his own, but he had long before cultivated the habit of sharing whatever scripture popped into his mind.

And Enoch did feel worthy. The previous day marked his third consecutive day with Tom Layman's construction crew and he'd hung in after a rough start. Three days ago had marked the crossing of a threshold and the arrival of a difficult decision: to stay or go home. The decision itself wasn't that difficult - he meant to stay and Emily supported him. Rather it was the means to stay after running out of cash and approaching the red line on their emergency savings that had vexed him.

Looking for work among the men he'd seen clustering in front of the lumber yard near Mandy's favorite breakfast spot had been his first instinct and it turned out to have been a good one. Tom Layman's outfit had been one of the first to pull up with several trucks. It had taken Enoch a few minutes to convince the foreman that he wasn't a junkie after which he was ferried to the worksite. The ride had reminded him of the shuttle to Rivers of Mercy, packed in as he was with so many strangers, but it was rock and roll, not gospel, that filtered back from the cab of the truck.

The worksite was a sprawling estate with a huge manor-house rising in the distance like a medieval castle. The foreman had put Enoch and the others to work on a stone wall that was to stretch around the entire perimeter of the estate.

Enoch's muscle memory had served him well at first; for the first few hours he'd worked with the speed, determination and skill of the young Enoch who had worked so hard to repair the stone wall to please his new bride. Around lunch time however, his back had given out, and he'd only been able to groan and grimace as the younger, inexperienced men ran laps around him. *How the Lord humbles the proud!* But the Lord had also granted him the grace to overcome his desperate soreness the next morning to get out of bed and rejoin the Layman crew. He'd also given him favor with the same foreman who had called him a junkie; that vessel of the Lord's kindness had put Enoch in charge of his own little crew to spare him some of the lifting!

His motel room still smelled of urine and skunk but he hardly noticed, nor did he feel the hard springs of the mattress pushing through the paper-thin cushion. He fell instantly to sleep and dreamed of Emily. He woke to his arms reaching for her on the empty side of the bed and a knock at his door. Staggering out of bed, he groped his way to the door. He felt a sudden shiver of fear, remembering a few nights earlier when an angry pimp had almost broken his door down in the mistaken belief that Enoch was harboring one of his girls. But it wasn't an angry pimp. It was Angel, grinning in his uniform.

"Rise and shine, Enoch!" He laughed. "Did you forget about our ride-along today?"

Enoch had not forgotten. He'd even set the alarm. He'd just slept through it. *One more dose of humility from this weakened flesh; I accept it Lord!* He joined Angel in laughter and excused himself to get dressed. His rising excitement soon dispelled the sleep from his eyes and tempered the screams from his lower back. In a few minutes they were both in the squad car and back on the open road.

Enoch was greatly enjoying this addition to his daily routine and he was encouraged to see that Angel was warming to him. After that first ride-along, Angel had come to him, telling him of a policy that allowed any patrolman to have a chaplain ride with him for four hours of any shift. It had only taken a few minutes of conversation for the Lieutenant to accept Enoch as a chaplain and ever since Enoch and Angel had been thick as thieves.

Angel would regale Enoch with stories of the many wild and dangerous encounters he'd had on the job and then fall quiet to listen hungrily to Enoch's accounts of life on the farm and off-the-cuff sermonettes. He was even interested in Enoch's new job. In between conversations, they would respond to calls for police that came piping in through Angel's car radio. The bewildering blend of numbers, codes and jargon was indecipherable to Enoch, but Angel swam through it all like a fish, responding back in his own gibberish and then expertly navigating the labyrinthine streets without so much as consulting a map.

Enoch was similarly impressed with how Angel handled himself on these calls. Hysterical women clutching their babies as they traded screams with tattoo-covered boyfriends, shopkeepers with blood gushing from their heads after strong-arm robberies, the smoking, twisted metal of high-speed wrecks… Angel strode calmly through them all. He absorbed the abuse, comforted the wounded, took command of the chaos and then returned to the car, unfazed and unshaken, a rock in the storm.

"You're very good at this," Enoch had told him at the end of the previous night, probably not for the first time, after Angel had just defused a potentially deadly fight from breaking out between armed security and a belligerent gang of drunken young men at a nightclub. Angel had laughed boyishly and shaken his head. *Here is a man for Mandy.*

"Got some new orders out of roll call today," Angel said after returning from a gas station convenience store with coffee and candy bars in hand. He slipped a paper from his clipboard and handed it to Enoch. It was a map with an area outlined in red. "We're on serial killer duty tonight."

Enoch brightened. "Is there a new lead? Are we closing in on him?" *We! I've made myself a deputy already!*

"I don't think so. My Lieutenant said the vamps are in a panic and they're putting the squeeze on the Mayor's office for more protection. So the brass is pulling from every precinct to increase patrols on the vamp side of town."

Do you think there's any chance we bump into the killer?"

"I wouldn't count on it. The neighborhood they're sending us to is pretty nice, so we're probably not going to get into much of anything tonight."

Enoch nodded and leaned back against the headrest, watching the city fly by as Angel accelerated onto the interstate. Angel was talking but Enoch was having a hard time focusing on his words. The sun was setting and casting spectacular pinks and purples behind the glittering obsidian spires of the surrounding skyscrapers. It couldn't compare to the beauty of the silhouettes of his oaks and elms against the twilight horizon back home, but Enoch had come to a grudging respect for the dark charms of the city skyline. Stretching up like hands raised to the Lord in defiance, these obelisks couldn't help but reflect back the glory of God's designs.

Enoch's drooping eyes fixed on the highest building, shimmering gold in the distance. He remembered Pastor Haggerty's dark vision and it brought on one of his own. *O, Jezebel, wicked and beautiful, haughty and cruel, seducer of men and ruler of eunuchs, aloft in your regal tower. You paint your face to set it against the sun and the coming of God's wrath. Foolish Jezebel! Descend from your lofty place and abase yourself before you fall and your body is thrown to the dogs!*

It was with visions of Jezebel's swirling descent that Enoch finally succumbed to the weights over his eyes and fell to sleep.

***

Angel's mind drifted as he cruised the hilly streets of the Citadelle District. The high-brow jewelry and fashion boutiques had been closed for a while now and the few people he saw milling about were retail employees preparing to head back to the working-class neighborhoods on the other side of the interstate. There was even less life to be found as he ventured into the lower foothills - whatever was happening in these mansions was well out of view behind the brass gates and stone walls.

He nursed his cold coffee, taking sips to keep his darker thoughts at bay. A good conversation would help. He considered shaking Enoch awake - the old man had barely made it five minutes before drifting off. Old man... Enoch had one of those craggy, weathered country faces like his uncles in Texas. Made it hard to tell whether he was 50 or 70.

He certainly seemed to be too old to be slinging boulders around for 10 hours a day. And then crashing in a roach motel like the Garden Inn. Angel wouldn't wish that place on his worst enemy. Of course, his own place in the Pit wasn't all that great either but at least it was clean and everything didn't smell like piss. He looked at Enoch again. *All this just to get closer to your daughter?* A powerful surge of admiration overcame him. I should be such a man.

He'd been trying - *why couldn't she see that?* The night she'd left without saying a thing and stayed out until late the next night had been the worst. They'd had a big fight. He'd tried to make her feel guilty about being gone so much but that had backfired - she just got quiet and sullen and stopped talking to him. So he resolved to fix things the way he knew how: *Angel Mendoza is a man of action!*

First, he'd decided to do something about their living situation. Their little apartment had been fun when they were fresh out of the academy, making nothing but pocket-change. But he'd gotten too comfortable while she'd been growing. So he'd taken out his savings, plus some cash on loan from his uncles, to put in an offer on a nice little house on the edge of the city. No traffic, no junkies, lots of grass and trees. The kind of place you could see your kids playing.

He'd been waiting for the right time to spring it on her - a break from the never-ending work when she'd have more than a few minutes - and that's when the other notion had wormed into his brain. *Marry the girl.* He blamed Enoch for that. The man had heaped a lifetime's worth of church into just a few rides together. Marriage was what God wanted. Of course it's what Mama had always wanted. According to her, it's what all women wanted, Mandy included. So Angel had maxed out his credit card and bought a ring. He was already stretched too thin with the impending mortgage to get her anything too fancy - certainly no ring from a Citadelle jeweler - but he got the biggest diamond he could find.

The ring was tucked away now in his pocket, but it was the slip of paper folded up next to it that he couldn't drive from his brain. He'd tried to make the occasion right by driving away the clouds of their last fight. Cleaned the house. Washed the dishes. Gathered up all his clothes to take them to the cleaners. Why not pick hers up while he was at it? She liked gestures like that. Then the Chinese lady had handed him a note from her jacket pocket and it hit him like a Mack truck.

He felt a shiver of anger travel up his spine. He shook it away looking for something, anything on the street. And that's when he saw it, at the edge of his peripheral vision, a black motorcycle, its rider wearing all black, riding parallel to them. Nothing particularly unusual about a motorcycle in this neighborhood - lots of vamp riders, especially of those futuristic Japanese bikes - but he'd seen this one before when he first pulled into the Citadelle. It was cruising.

Hadn't the Lieutenant mentioned something about bikes when he was reading out Van Helsing suspect information? Angel's mind had been elsewhere, but the notion clicked and he hung a right as he killed his lights. Tonight would have been a good night to be plain-clothes, but these dusty old squad cars could still disappear in dark alleys. He crept forward softly through the alley, emerging onto a boulevard that wound its way up into the hills. The bike was a block ahead.

Angel squinted. He couldn't be totally sure at the distance with so little lighting, but it looked like one of the new Hondas and a nice one too. The rider was weaving in and out of his lane, crawling along slowly as a red light approached. Angel treaded gently on the accelerator to follow, keeping the engine to a low purr.

The rider started suddenly in his seat - could he have spotted Angel? - and, with a roar, the bike blazed forward through the red. A panicked horn blast sounded from an oncoming panel truck, then the horrible screech of its tires. The bike continued forward, the rider not even turning his head. It disappeared as the panel truck came barreling through the intersection. Angel's whole body tensed in a sympathetic brace for impact, but there was no sound of a crash. As soon as the truck hurtled out of his vision, he saw the bike speeding up the hill.

He reached over to shake Enoch awake. He bolted upright just as Angel floored it and suctioned him back to the seat.

"What is it?" Enoch asked, groggy.

"We got something." He raised the radio mic to his lips. "Five-fifty-alpha, I'm at Benoit and Lafayette. We've got a suspicious vehicle heading northbound on Benoit driving reckless…"

As he continued, the rider turned his helmeted head round and spotted them accelerating on the bike's tail. The bike turned suddenly across oncoming traffic, riding up a grass embankment and then disappearing over a ridge.

Angel dropped the mic to flip on the siren and put both hands on the wheel. "You're gonna want to hold onto something," he shouted. He swung the wheel and the squad car careened left, straightening just in time to hit the embankment at 60 miles per hour.

Angel heard Enoch gasp as they soared over the ridge and landed with a jolt on the debris-laden floor of a drainage canal that wound southwest back down the hillside. Angel accelerated slowly forward, waiting for the wheels to find their traction, throwing a glance at the gray walls of the canal, uncomfortably close on either side.

Enoch was upright and fully awake, his face sparkling with the thrill of the chase. He pointed excitedly ahead of them. "There he is!"

Angel saw the black figure ahead through a cloud of dust. He stomped the pedal and the squad car peeled off in pursuit. While his left hand at the wheel jerked back and forth to keep those walls at bay, his right groped blindly for the fallen radio. Enoch snaked an arm down into the foot space and snagged it for him, the bumps of the canal floor bouncing him around the cabin like a rag doll. He deposited it in Angel's grasping hand.

"Five-fifty-alpha, we're in pursuit. Going to be a black motorcycle, possibly a Honda. Heading westbound in a drainage ditch off Fayette. Send some units to Culver - I think that's where this ditch is heading."

He threw a glance at Enoch - the old man was still getting the popcorn machine treatment as the canal floor only got rougher. "Sorry for getting you into this!"

Enoch looked back at him, grinning like a dog with his head out the window. "This is the most fun I've had in my life," he shouted back.

The bike was slowing down ahead, weaving between the bumps and branches that the squad car was plowing through. As the gap between them closed, Angel could feel his breath coming faster and shallower, his muscles tensing, his ears shutting out Enoch's excited chattering, his gaze tightening until all he could see was the rider. Tunnel vision - he'd been warned about it, he recognized it, and still he couldn't stop it from coming on. *I'm gonna get you, you son of a bitch.*

Angel leaned on the gas, the rider growing in his eyes as the distance narrowed. He was long limbed and tall, with black hair spiking out from under the shiny black helmet. The helmet twitched back and forth between Angel and the road hazards. An alien. A big black praying mantis. And Angel was going to squash the bugger under his boot.

The bug was getting antsy - Angel was so close now! The bike jerked from a sudden boost of gas and zipped ahead. Angel felt a wave of anger as the bike pulled out of reach. He stomped his right foot to the floor but it was already there. *It's too goddam fast!*

Then the bike swerved and wobbled, for a moment sliding forward at an impossible angle. And then it was down and the rider was rolling, insect limbs flailing in the hair, giant shiny head striking the cement wall with a sickening - no, satisfying! - impact.

Angel stomped on the brakes and brought the squad car swerving to a sudden halt. He told Enoch to stay in the car and then he was out. His legs instantly shed the stiffness of the cabin and he was flying, his boots darting between the puddles of mud and the chunks of broken cement that had brought down his insect foe.

There it was, lying flat on its back in a little gully of mud, arms splayed to both sides, the visor of the alien helmet shattered and behind it a pale face. Not a bug, but a man. A young face, with mouth ajar and eyes wide open, staring blankly at the night sky. Angel slowed, his breath catching up. *Is he dead?*

Angel started as the wide eyes suddenly flicked towards him and grew even wider. His heart accelerated as the rider pushed himself onto his hands and began to scrabble backwards.

"Don't you f***ing move, cockroach," Angel heard himself roaring. The rider ignored him, scrambling to his feet. Angel charged, but the rider dodged him with surprising quickness and took off running. The canal ended in a dark tunnel ahead, the walls disappearing into a grassy slope leading up to another road.

Angel sprinted after him, but lost ground with every stride. His chest on fire, his lungs stretched to the sensation of tearing, incapable even of giving him the breath to scream at his escaping enemy. But then he heard it. The sound of sirens, like angelic trumpets! Angel felt hope like oxygen in his lungs and blazed forward.

The glow of blue lights lit up the ridge ahead of them and the rider froze in his tracks. His pale face turned to see Angel charging at him. Too late he tried to sidestep. Angel was #55 again, middle linebacker for the Conquistadors and designated punisher of any lanky receiver dumb enough to get caught coming across the middle. He wrapped the gangly rider and pile-drove him into the pavement.

Angel leaned in with his shoulder as they headed for the ground, anticipating the crunch of the impact and that amazing "oof" when a perp smacked concrete and all the air left his lungs. Instead he felt himself twisting in the air and it was his own shoulder striking the pavement with bone-jarring force. Then it was the rider's spindly arms swimming out of his hold, an elbow striking his chin and breaking his grasp entirely. For a moment he lay sprawled on his back, tingling in pain.

A surge of fear coursed through him, snapping him out of his daze. He rolled onto all fours to see the rider sprinting back towards the squad car. Angel staggered to his feet and gave chase, his brain lurching. *He's getting away.* The rider was almost at the car now, his long legs carrying him further and further from Angel.

It was then that Enoch sprang from the squad car, his door flying out to strike the rider with a loud *thud* and send him spinning to the ground. Then Enoch was on him, his knee in his back and both arms pressing down on his shoulder blades. Angel felt elation and adrenaline pulsing through him as he came alongside them, his booted foot joining Enoch's knee to pin the rider to the ground, his hand sliding to his cuffs. The rider writhed on the ground with unsettling power, dislodging Enoch and knocking Angel off balance.

Not again. He's not going to get away again. Angel brought his fist crashing down on the rider's face like a hammer. He felt the rider sag and struck him again and again and again until he wasn't writhing anymore. Angel felt Enoch's arms grabbing him from behind, but still he swung.

"Come off him now, son," he heard Enoch saying in his ear. With one final lurch, Angel slapped cuffs on the limp wrists beneath him and fell backward heavily against the car.

"Are you alright?" Enoch asked. Angel could barely hear him over the pounding in his chest. He felt a tingling race from the sting in his right hand to the ache in his shoulder to the throbbing pain in his head. He stood up, towering over the motionless rider.

"I've never felt better."

13

There were few places Mandy hated worse than the trauma ward at St. Anthony's. The cattle car chorus of groans and pleas for pain meds. The unsettling hum and shrill beeping of a hundred medical monitors. The mess of gurney beds, crowded into every nook and hallway like some nightmare Tetris game. The nurses, running back and forth in a simulation of hyperactivity, deaf to every question and request. And, worst of all, nowhere to sit!

She eyed one of the passing nurses, glaring enviously at her comfortable-looking sneakers. She had a half-serious notion to flag her down. *If you can't get me a chair could you get me an orthopedist? Or at least some cushioned soles for these flats?*

Her mind strayed from her aching feet to the floor-to-ceiling translucent plastic paneling that separated the small rectangle of the "V wing" from the rest of trauma. It was usually dark, but that morning it was glowing a bright white, with dark blurry shapes bustling back and forth inside. It had been several hours since the subject had been upgraded to stable condition and still she was outside looking in. *Sorry, miss, our blood contamination protocols are strict. It's for your own safety!*

Of course, Vlad had been able to go in as soon as he had arrived. He'd been in there for only a few minutes, but the screams of her feet made them feel like hours. The excitement she'd felt when Vlad sent her to St. Anthony's to ID a possible person of interest had worn as thin as her soles. Most of it had drained the moment she'd found out the subject was a vamp - Vlad's insistence that the killer might be preying on his own still rang false in her mind. The sanctimonious hate soaking through that letter and oozing from the atmosphere had felt too familiar, too local to have come from any vamp. This monster had grown up close to home.

It still remained to be determined just who this vamp was; he hadn't had any ID on him, though his face did look familiar. But that was secondary. Her gut told her that this was just another case of uni patrol getting over-excited after getting too much pressure from the higher-ups. She felt bad for whatever poor idiot was about to get bent over for putting a vamp in the hospital when cops were supposed to be out there protecting them.

Mandy turned at the sound of commotion behind her. A pair of gray-shirted security guards were struggling to contain a red-headed young woman, who writhed in their arms like a ball of fire.

"Let me go!" Her voice rang out high and strong, a piercing cry over the clamor of the emergency room. Then from behind her, a huge figure barreled forward, lowering his shoulder into one of the guards and stiff-arming the other. Both of them tumbled to the ground like bowling pins, leaving the rectangular monolith of a man holding the red-headed siren, glaring at all around as if daring them to approach. Mandy's hand sought the handle of her duty pistol.

The girl broke from her protector's grasp and ran towards the plastic walls. Mandy side-stepped into her path, still keeping her grip on the gun and a weather eye on the looming gorilla. The girl stopped short of a collision, less willing to tangle with Mandy than she had been the guards, both of whom were slow to get up. Perhaps she'd seen Mandy's badge.

"Stop right there," Mandy barked, feeling more chihuahua than K-9.

The girl's bodyguard took a menacing step towards Mandy, but the girl stopped him with a look. She turned to Mandy with a pleading expression.

"Please, officer, I've got to get in there. I need to know if Andy's alright."

Seeing those green eyes staring at her, big emeralds moist with tears, Mandy was struck by the beauty of this girl and knew at once that she'd seen her before. She had the look and aura of a pop star, and it radiated from her so powerfully it was intimidating. *This girl isn't used to being told no.* But Mandy stood her ground.

"That's the V wing you're trying to get into. They won't even let me in there. It's not safe for us." Those big green eyes were unfazed, undeterred.

"I need to see him."

"Tell you what… You tell me who you are and what your relationship is to… Andy in there, and I'll see what I can do." The giant took another step forward, the thunderclap of his footfall shaking Mandy's bargaining position. "And you're gonna wanna restrain your friend there before he gets people hurt."

"Let me handle this one, Uncle Pete," she said without even looking back at him. "My name is Christina Haggerty. Andy is a dear friend of mine." *Haggerty.* Mandy knew the name. The fire-breathing televangelist with the megachurch on the outskirts of town. Notorious vamp-hater. This fire-nymph must be his daughter. Mandy remembered where she'd seen her: on a billboard ad for the church, next to her dad, microphone in hand, mouth open in song. Did Jim Haggerty, Pastor Xenophobe himself, know his daughter was out chasing handsome young vamps?

"He was supposed to meet me tonight and he never showed up," Christina continued. "Then I heard about the accident and I rushed over."

"How do you know Andy?"

Before Christina could answer, the plastic panel doors swung open behind them. Mandy turned to see Vlad walking towards them, looking irritated. Another vampire was walking closely alongside him, a shark-eyed creature in a silver-suit attached to his side like a lamprey. Mandy chided herself. *Can't even think that!* But if ever there was a vamp to invite slurs it was Dacian Popa, the most obnoxious criminal defense attorney in the city. Mandy had heard vamps didn't like going into law - too coarse and undignified - but the one who did had apparently decided to embrace and amplify all of the worst stereotypes of the profession.

There he was hissing into Vlad's ear. "The day of reckoning is here, Captain. This atrocity here is where the city is going to pay for a generation of savage cruelty."

Vlad looked at Mandy, rolling his eyes. "Parker, this is Dacian Popa. The suspect's family has retained his services as an attorney." His eyes turned to Christina in curiosity and then widened in recognition when they landed on "Uncle Pete" behind them. But Popa burst in before he could say anything.

"Suspect? Mikhail is a victim!"

Vlad looked at Mandy again, fatigued, looking for someone to tag him out of the cage match.

"Mr. Andreanu is a suspect because he's in custody for evading arrest and driving while under the influence," Mandy chimed in.

Popa turned and looked down on her like a child interrupting the grown-ups. "Have you tested his blood?"

"The results are pending. But for our immediate purposes, it's irrelevant. From the paperwork, he met all the field criteria for an arrest."

He smiled scornfully. "Irrelevant? Captain, your young detective here, undoubtedly speaking from her immense knowledge and experience, has declared the contents of a blood screen to be irrelevant in a DWI investigation."

"That's not what I said," Mandy protested.

"When the results do come back, assuming they haven't already and you have ignored them, they will show no intoxicants in Mikhail's system. They will however show every sign that he was suffering from acute vampiric hypovolemia. Do you think you can that condition to your hemotypical detective, Captain?"

He didn't wait for Vlad to explain and turned on Mandy again.

"You see, detective, when a vampire abstains for an extended period of time, he begins to metabolize his own blood. The resulting hypovolemia produces symptoms that are easily confused with intoxication."

"It's true!" They all turned in surprise to Christina Haggerty, whose voice rose above them all. "He'd been fasting for weeks."

"I know what vampiric hypovolemia is," declared Mandy, exasperated at the redhead butting in where she didn't belong. "But you can't expect an officer in the field to make that kind of diagnosis."

Popa sneered. "And I guess you can't expect them not to beat a vampire into critical condition for manifesting symptoms of a medical crisis, can you?"

"Critical condition?" burst in Christina again and she tried to push her way past them. This time it was Vlad who grabbed her with both arms. Mandy felt a flash of irritation.

Popa stared at the redhead, bug-eyed. "What do you think you're doing here?"

"He needs me!" was all Christina would say.

"Dykstra, get her out of here," shouted Vlad as she squirmed in his hold. "She's gonna get herself hurt."

The giant stepped forward to wrest the girl from Vlad's grip, staring daggers at Vlad as he did. Then he said something quiet in the girl's ear and she calmed down and the two of them made for the exit. This time the guards gave them a wide berth.

Popa started up again. "Peter Dykstra! It's lucky I was here, or you probably would have let him and that bigot's spawn in to finish the job your patrolman started. Some things never change at RCPD."

Vlad sighed. "That man hasn't worked for us in more than a decade. Save your slander for whatever bogus lawsuit you've got planned for us. Now, if you'll excuse us, we have some questions for your client that pertain to a completely different investigation."

"You know it's perfectly within his rights to tell you to follow your man Dykstra out the door," he said through pursed lips. "But against my advice, Mikhail has decided he would like to speak to you without an attorney present. I will be standing by."

Vlad detached from him, taking Mandy by the arm and leading her over to a medical tent protruding from the side of the translucent walls of the vamp ward. He pulled the curtain behind them.

"Who was that Dykstra guy?" Mandy asked.

"Ex-cop. He quit before you came on."

"What, does private security for a guy like Haggerty pay so much better than the Department?"

"Who knows? But he always had a reputation. He was on the frontlines during the riots... Didn't win himself any fans in the community. And I heard he threw a fit when I came out of the academy. Haggerty's outfit is more his style."

Vlad gestured at a stack of folded blue plastic sheets on a table in front of them. Mandy guessed them to be some kind of hazmat suit. "You're going to have to put one of those body gloves on before they let us in to talk to him."

She lifted one of the suits off the table - an inner lining of vinyl surrounded by a billowy secondary layer of transparent plastic. Vlad just stood there, peeking out beyond the curtain, as if worried that Popa might change his mind.

"Is all this really necessary?" she grumbled, struggling to find an opening in the plastic. "I've been wading through swimming pools of vampire blood lately and the Department never asked me to cover up in one of these."

"That's because we're surrounded by ugliness all day. We're not going to cover up any reminders that there is still beauty out there."

Mandy hid her reddening face behind the plastic.

"Still," Vlad continued. "You can't be too careful in here. All the syringes and scalpels, you don't want any part of us getting into your bloodstream."

"I've seen the PSAs." Mandy had missed out on education in River City schools, but it had only taken a few weeks in the city before she'd been baptized by the flood of television sermonettes that filled every gap in programming on the local networks. When faced with possible contamination, you were to CISS: cover up, irrigate, sanitize, seek help.

Of course, Mandy had already received a much broader education on the subject from the trashy romances she'd devoured so hungrily as a teenager. How many shy maidens had lost their virginity and their lives to the lusty vampire lords between the stacks at the Copper Springs Library!

"Funny though, I got the impression that Christina girl has swapped a few fluids with our vamp in there."

Vlad shot her a look. "I doubt that."

"You think that girl was too Christian for him? She seemed pretty crazy about him."

"She may be. There's a certain type that can't get enough of us." Mandy caught a sidelong glance. *Was he looking at me when he said that?* "But not Mikhail Andreanu. He's... sensitive about these sorts of things."

"You know him pretty well?"

"Every vamp knows of him. His family is the closest thing we have to royalty."

Andreanu... Mandy was pretty sure that was the name of a big shot during the war.

"Is he related to the dictator?"

"I'd be careful about calling him a dictator," said Vlad, chuckling. "There are many in the community who still look at Ion Andreanu as a god. He's still known as the Great Liberator in some circles... Mikhail is his only surviving grandson."

"He's a big deal, then." Mandy again cringed sympathetically for whatever hapless patrolman put the hurt on him.

"Yes and no... He's become a black sheep among those that still revere his father. Seeing the scion of vamp royalty throw away his birthright to slum as an American punk rocker was bad enough. But then to fail at it, too? Unconscionable... Nor do they like to see a son of Leaota riding with Adrian Dan's Bat Pack."

"The Bat Pack! He couldn't actually be our guy, could he?"

"That I doubt. There's nothing all that unusual about Mikhail Andreanu creeping around at night. That kid's always been a moody recluse. But with the right prompting I do think he might have something useful to share about his comrades. He's always struck me as the ugly duckling of that bunch..."

"Ok, I'm ready," she said, slipping the second layer of plastic over her head and disappearing behind its billowy frumpiness. Vlad turned and smiled at her ensemble as he pulled the curtain of the tent open for her.

They entered through the plastic panel doors and the background of beeps and moans and shouts was extinguished. Inside all was quiet, almost serene, so still that Mandy could hear the swish of her plastic shroud as she walked. *World's ugliest wedding dress.*

Mikhail Andreanu was the only patient in the ward, sitting upright in his hospital bed, watching their approach. His long black hair framed a badly swollen face, with a line of fresh stitches stretching from his left eye around the pronounced curve of his cheek to his jutting chin. Even in this condition and seated on the bed, he looked regal. He grimaced as a nurse adjusted an IV line pumping red into his left arm. The nurse was dressed identically to Mandy. *Greetings, fellow vestal virgin.*

At Andreanu's other arm stood a tall woman of similarly regal bearing. Her cream-colored dress, white gloves and pearl necklace reminded Mandy of Jackie Kennedy. Her face was not attractive but it was striking, with sharply protruding features and harsh blues eyes set under an imposing brow.

"Alina Andreanu," Vlad whispered into Mandy's ear. "His mother."

"Please keep this brief, detectives," boomed the lady Andreanu, her voice deep and powerfully resonant. "My son is not well and needs to rest."

Andreanu's eyes were on the red tube attached to his arm, his grimace deepening into a fierce scowl. "Will you get this thing out of me?" His voice was strong and commanding, like his mother's, but with none of her accent.

His mother placed a stern hand on his shoulder. "That's enough of that, Mikhail."

Mikhail flinched at her touch, his bare shoulders recoiling to crowd his neck.

"Mrs. Andreanu," started Vlad, his voice oozing with deference. "If you could excuse us briefly, we would like to speak to your son privately."

"Leave him alone with the police, after what you've done?" she thundered, her jaw tensing.

"Go, mother!" commanded Mikhail, his voice reaching an imperious depth that exceeded her own.

"Very well." She snatched up her purse and moved angrily towards the door, stopping to grab hold of Vlad's arm as she passed. "Can I at least be assured that the officer who did this to my son is in custody?"

"That officer is standing by for questioning. You can rest assured that we will act with utmost impartiality and resolution if it is determined that any wrongdoing was committed."

She frowned in dissatisfaction but released him and left. Vlad turned to Mikhail who had wrenched the IV from his arm as soon as the door closed behind his mother. He leaned back against his bed with a sigh. "You've made it past the dragon and the ice queen. Now what do you want from me?"

"You could start by telling us what you were doing tonight."

"I get restless at night and taking a ride helps me take my mind off things."

"You take anything else to… take your mind off things?"

Andreanu snorted, shaking his long black hair from his face. "I get high off homo sapiens, just like you. Never wanted any other drug." He scratched his arm where the IV had been. *Junkie's itch.*

"Then why hadn't you partaken? Your lawyer says you were on the verge of hypovolemic shock."

"A little abstinence does the body good every now and again."

"If you're so concerned about your health, why are you driving recklessly, blowing stop signs and running from the police?"

Andreanu winced, dabbing at his stitches. "You're very aggressive. Can't good cop over here have a turn for a while?" He glanced over at Mandy. "Or are you just another nurse?"

"Just answer the question," said Mandy.

"I guess I was a little jumpy. It was dark. I saw a car following me. We all know there's a psycho hunting people like me. So I got spooked."

"You saw a squad car and thought it was Van Helsing? Sure you weren't on something?" asked Mandy snidely. *I'm not gonna be your good cop!*

"Who's to say he isn't a cop? And was I wrong to be afraid?" He gestured at his bloodied face and smirked at her.

"When you say 'people like me' are you talking about vampires in general or friends of Adrian Dan?" Vlad interjected. Andreanu twitched, his smirk disappearing as he turned back to Vlad.

"Whoever said I was his friend?"

"You've certainly spent a lot of time together. You and Pavel Petricean and Ion Dragescu and the rest of the Bat Pack."

Andreanu twitched again, scratching at his neck.

"There are only so many social options for people with names like mine. I wouldn't call them friends just because we happened to be in the same places at the same time."

"Did you happen to be in the same place at the same time with Dragescu and Petricean when they were brutally murdered?"

Andreanu's eyes widened in incredulity as he gave a surprised laugh. "First you beat me into unconsciousness then you accuse me of murder?"

"It's an easy question. Where were you last Tuesday night?"

Andreanu's eyes flashed at Vlad but he said nothing.

Mandy jumped in, sensing it was her turn. "We're not accusing you. We're just trying to put the pieces together. You say you knew these two, traveled in the same circles and that these circles were not very big. You said you were afraid you might be the next victim. Can you help us understand why this killer's targets all seem to belong to such a small group?"

Andreanu's scratching intensified and he squirmed in his bed.

"I don't understand why you expect me to explain this killer's motivations. Isn't that your job, detectives?" He looked at them sullenly. They stared back. He continued, reluctant: "I don't know... He's a bigot... perhaps he sees young, successful vampires with their pictures in all the papers. Maybe this makes him angry..."

Mandy's eyes narrowed as Andreanu continued to shift

uncomfortably. "Are you sure you would describe yourself as successful, Mikhail? I know your grandfather is a legend in the community, but is there anything that you personally have done?"

He stared at her, eyes baleful behind the swelling. "I don't understand what you're asking."

"What I'm asking is what you and Petricean and Dragescu and your buddies have in common because it certainly isn't greatness." Mandy felt a thrill travel up from her stomach to catch the breath in her throat. She heard her mother's chiding voice from the recesses of her memory. *Tongue like a sword, bitter words like arrows.*

Andreanu cast his eyes downward, his hair descending to cover his face. "I've changed my mind," came his voice, growling behind the forest of black lines. "I don't want to talk anymore. Send in my lawyer."

Mandy felt a pang of regret. She opened her mouth to speak but it only hung open foolishly. Vlad took hold of her arm and led her away and through a back door that opened into a darkened hallway.

"Did I screw that up?" she blurted as soon as the door closed behind them. She searched for his eyes but could not see them in the darkness. The stupid plastic veil wasn't helping. She ripped it off in irritation.

He stood silent in the darkness and her heart sank. *I did. I messed it up.*

Then Vlad's voice broke the silence with a warm chuckle. "No, you didn't."

She felt the thrill returning like a surge and she started to babble as they walked toward the light at the end of the hallway. "That whole time I thought he knew something and he was hiding it. And he was giving me such strong addict vibes and I know you can never be nice with an addict if you want them to tell you something. You've got to push them 'til they break. So I was mean. But it didn't work! He kicked us out..."

"No, you wounded his pride. In a way I never could - for a vamp like him, a native woman's scorn cuts sharper, deeper. He won't be able to rest until that wound is healed. He will reach out to us in some form or other, I'm sure of it."

They had reached the light at the end of the hallway but Mandy stopped. "So I did okay?" Mandy hated sounding so needy but she couldn't help it - her lips were loose and she was almost twitching with nervous energy.

"You were magnificent," Vlad declared, and Mandy could see him now, staring at her with an intensity that shocked her. She felt a tightening pressure on her elbow and realized he still had a hold of her arm. He pulled her closer now, his hand slipping from her arm to her waist. She looked up at him, her mouth parted in surprise and she felt his lips on hers, his hot breath coursing into her mouth, his arms wrapping around her, pulling her tight.

As fast as it had begun it was over and Mandy was slumping against nothing, her lips still parted. Vlad was gone, his back turned, pushing through the door, leaving her gaping in the darkness.

***

The bench in the lobby of Internal Affairs looked like it had been modeled on one of those ugly hunks of meshed blue steel they put in parks to keep the homeless people from sleeping on them. Angel had been sitting in this one for hours now and it had long since started to take its toll on his aching lower back.

He hadn't exactly had the perfect police career. His score on the detective's exam - the same one Mandy had aced - had been so embarrassing he'd used the gas burner to torch it right there in the kitchen and set off the smoke alarm. There was also the time he'd caught a few days suspension for wrecking a squad car after falling asleep at the wheel on his first week working midnights.

But for the most part he'd avoided the bad stuff. Cocaine-powered bachelor parties, using a police transport van to kidnap an ex-girlfriend, collecting get-out-of-jail free services from hookers… he'd already sidestepped these and other pitfalls that had gotten old classmates and partners the ax, or worse, a trip down to the basement level the county jail kept reserved for bad apple cops. He'd never even gotten a civilian complaint, at least one serious enough that they'd let him know about.

Nevertheless, here he was, his back groaning, his eyes drawn incessantly to the closed door leading to the Internal Affairs detectives' offices, hoping for someone to come out and tell him it was nothing serious and he could go home. He'd only seen one detective coming and going, a lady who'd told him to sit there in the first place but didn't even make eye contact each time she passed him on her way to the vending machine. He wished they hadn't shooed Enoch away at the scene. It would have been nice to have the old man sitting next to him, spouting Bible verses and patting him on the shoulder.

Angel would have to settle for his union rep, but whoever that was sure was taking his time getting here. He heard a ding of the elevator and breathed a sigh - maybe that was finally him. The door to the lobby opened and in came... Mandy! Angel jumped to his feet, a gush of happiness loosening the angry knots in his back and pushing back the gloom of what was waiting behind the other door.

"Hey there, good-looking," he grinned. She turned to him with a blank, uncomprehending look.

"Angel? What are you doing here?"

He came in close, kissing her warmly on the cheek, unable to shake his idiotic smile. It just felt so good to see her, to have her standing here with him.

"Just the usual I.A. bull****," he said, waving a hand at the door behind them. "Had a traffic stop that went a little haywire but I don't think it will be too big of a deal."

She pulled away from him, her jaw dropping. "That was *you?*"

Angel knew something was wrong, but the sensation was dull and slow coming. Maybe he'd been sitting on that bench too long and all the blood had drained from his brain.

"I get it, I might catch a few days for one punch too many, but I don't think it's all that serious."

Her eyes grew wild. "Not that serious? You just put a vamp VIP in the hospital for running a red light. He's already got Dacian Popa representing him."

"What are you talking about? The guy was stoned out of his mind and resisting."

"No, he wasn't. I just saw the blood screens. Not a trace of controlled substances. No alcohol. Nothing."

Angel felt himself dropping back to the bench. "I don't get it. He had to be. He wasn't acting right!"

"He had hypovolemia. It's like with diabetics when their blood sugar gets messed up and they start acting drunk. Don't you remember them hammering that into us at the academy?"

Angel dropped his head into both hands, replaying the scene in his mind, willing himself not to throw those punches. He felt Mandy's hand on his shoulder and suddenly Enoch's face popped into his mind. *What did I get the old man into?*

"Don't freak out on me now," she said. "It's not like you were acting out of malice. You were just trying to do your job... This is what we pay the union for. And maybe I can get Vlad to help."

The sound of his name on her lips sent an involuntary shiver up Angel's back and into his shoulders.

"What is it?" she asked.

"Nothing. I'll be fine. The union will be enough, you don't have to go calling in any favors." But he couldn't shake Enoch's face out of his mind. "I'm just worried about your dad. I really hope this lawyer doesn't go after him too."

Mandy's hand tightened on his shoulder. "What are you talking about?"

He looked up at her, wincing to see anger working in at the edges of her eyes. "He was with me on a ride-along. He helped me detain the guy."

Angel felt her shove him back, her face now white-hot, her lips quivering. "You put my family at risk? You're a f***ing idiot, you know that right?"

She spun on her heel and stormed off towards the elevator. Angel called after her, but she was already gone. He sank deeper into the bench, begging for the ache in his back to drown out the echoes of her voice in his ears.

14

Harbor Patrol had always been the job Vlad really wanted. Setting out in the thick, sooty fog that carpeted the river every morning... The dazzling city towers glittering in the mist on the west bank and a swampy jungle of vegetation on the east bank... The great torrents of brown water coiling and tumbling and slithering underneath him like spawning water moccasins, his little power boat skimming the roiling surface, hoping not to be noticed and consumed by the writhing sea serpents...

But alas the conventional career path had been decreed for Vlad, and that meant ceding the river to the crusty pairs of quasi-retirees that manned each of the cruisers in the department's little fleet. The duo he had drawn for this morning's excursion had seemed especially disgruntled by his appearance on the dock. He guessed it was because it meant keeping the beer cooler and fishing poles below deck for longer than usual. But it could also be these two codgers were of the old-school, vamp-hating variety.

Vlad sighed through his envy and reminded himself of his tasks. First in importance, and the only one he had cited when petitioning the Colonel for the use of the boat: to rendezvous with the Coast Guard and the giant dredger they had digging up the sand bars near the west bank. Word was they had found some bodies. On the way there, if his ferrymen could be persuaded to make an unscheduled stop, his second task was to pay a visit to Alex Duma on his yacht. Vlad wasn't sure how much of this visit would be useful for the investigation, but he still needed it to shore up his support after the incident with Codrescu.

This being an official investigative trip, there was every reason Mandy should be at his side now. He could see her... that black coat pulled tightly about her as the boat rumbled from the dock, her chestnut hair whipping in the wind... Vlad shook his head and focused his eyes on the turgid water foaming beneath him. Being on the river was supposed to clear his head of such thoughts.

Perhaps Codrescu was right. He shuddered. He felt the same currents surging around him that had led him to disaster before. But this was different. This wasn't the fetid Danube, exhausted from millennia spent carrying the sewers of Europe into the Black Sea. This was a wild, dynamic river. Old yes, but untamed by man, still flush with energy and power to unmake and reshape the fledgling civilization on its banks. Just one downpour and this river could chart an entirely new path, claim new tributaries, usher in a new landscape... But none of that would be necessary. He would abide by the rules. He would keep his distance. *Let the next generation be the trailblazers, I will heed the old ways.*

The fog was lifting now, pierced through by a surprising warm morning sun. Vlad spied the unmistakable outline of Duma's yacht on the horizon. It used to be Andy Ryan's yacht, a giant floating monument to his billions and a recurring source of scandalous parties and liaisons for the River City tabloids. But since Ryan had pulled back on his jet-setting, Duma had taken his playboy mantle and the yacht with it. Vlad curled his lips at the ugliness of the thing. He couldn't expect a return to the clipper ship, as much as he might desire it, but they could have at least stuck to the pleasing aesthetics of the old paddle steamers. That would be much better than littering the surface of the river with these fiberglass behemoths.

Vlad cajoled the grumpy Harbor Patrolmen into hailing the yacht and after a few minutes of maneuvering he was onboard. The deck was abuzz with workmen, mostly painters in spattered overalls. Vlad heard a "HALLO!" from above him and there was Alex Duma waving from the flybridge. "Come on up, Paler," he shouted. *That's fine, no need to come to me. Would you like me to bring you a breakfast tray on my way up?*

Vlad navigated the stairs leading up to the flybridge, his irritation flagging as he climbed higher. The ship might have been gruesome to look at but at 60 feet above the water with a commanding view of the whole river spilling out in front of him, aesthetics ceased to matter. He pulled himself onto the flybridge to see Duma sprawled on a deck chair, shirtless, his eyes hiding behind black sunglasses. Vlad had half a mind to toss the sunning sybarite overboard and commandeer the ship.

"That's a lot of sun for a vampire," he said.

Duma didn't look up, sinking more comfortably into the deck chair. "Strip down and join me. It's great. I saw the weather forecast this morning and I knew I had to get out on the open water. Figured I'd give the guys a treat and let 'em see this baby in action."

The bustle of the workers below was barely audible all the way up in the flybridge. "Yeah, I saw them on the way up. Must be very relaxing for them." If Duma noticed the sarcasm, he didn't show it. "What kind of work are you getting done?"

"I'm giving the whole yacht a makeover," Duma said, finally sitting up. "Got to transform her from a party boat into something more statesmanlike. You know, give her some class. In a week, she's going to be taking me and my bride on our honeymoon."

"Congratulations. Who is she?"

Duma looked at him in surprise and a little irritation.

"Who else? I thought you would at least read the tabloids." He snatched a *Daily Manifest* from under a paperweight on a little table next to him and tossed it to Vlad. *Just the sort of intellectually stimulating reading material the heir apparent should be reading.*

"I do, but your love life has been pushed off the front page for a while now," said Vlad, flipping past the grainy photos that the paper insisted were photos of Van Helsing to find the wedding spread nestled next to an ad for a miracle longevity drug.

"That damn Van Helsing," Duma said, shaking his head. Vlad perused the announcement, double taking at the picture of the bride. The caption underneath: Irina Nasturel.

"Irina?" Vlad could not hide his surprise. "I didn't realize you were still seeing her."

"We've been off and on for a few years, but we've always been friends. And we've been through a lot together."

"She wasn't dating Ion Dragescu?"

Duma snorted. "That little ankle-biter? He followed her around like a lost puppy, but no, Irina could never love a man like him..." Duma trailed off. His face twitched in momentary self-awareness.

"I mean no disrespect to the dead. He was a fine young man with a good future," he added without sincerity.

He stood up now, placing his hands on the guardrail and looking out over the river ahead of them. "I've been thinking about what you said at Gleaners. What my father always expected of me. I think it's finally time I took on his mantle. And Irina's the woman to help me do it."

Yes, a wild party girl who helped you waste the last decade in debauchery - that's exactly who your father would want you to turn the page with. "She's a beautiful woman, no doubt. But I'm not sure she fits anyone's idea of settling down."

"That's just it," he exclaimed, turning to Vlad, his face lighting up. "I'm not settling. We're going to expand the horizon together. The community is so wrapped up in recreating the dynamics of the Old World. They are still fixated on the old plantation, even if they get Theresa Russell to redecorate."

Vlad rustled the tabloid in his hands, pointing at the blurb under the wedding announcement. "Says the man who just hired Russell to do his wedding."

"That's different. Those stuffed shirts at Gleaners… you were right to punch Codrescu in the face! They think she's just a provocateur. They wear her like a fashion statement. But I see her vision," he said, looking back out on the river. "It's a New World out there. It's not something to be conquered or domesticated. It's a Goddess to be seduced, and seduced by!"

"It's a nice vision, but a man of your responsibilities needs to be grounded. You can't go losing your head," he added, placing the tabloid back in Duma's hand, Van Helsing headline face-up.

"That's in poor taste," Duma grimaced.

"It doesn't concern you that both of his victims have been your… associates? We ran into your old friend Mikhail Andreanu the other night and he seemed to think he was being hunted."

Another snort. "Mikhail has always been too sensitive for this world. Van Helsing is nothing more than the desperate clawing of the old order, lashing out wildly as it slips further and further towards the abyss. He is targeting my friends because we represent everything that he cannot prevent from happening. The only thing he can do about it is pick off the younger and weaker ones who stray too far from the pack."

"And you have nothing to fear, because you're the pack

leader?"

Duma shot him a glance.

"The only leadership I'm interested in going forward is at Dumatech. I'm happy to leave the social scene to Adrian Dan and the rest of the bachelors."

"So you won't be doing any more business with Dan?"

Duma's eyes narrowed on Vlad, warily. "I'm not aware of having done any business with Dan. Our relationship has been strictly social."

"Good to hear," said Vlad, cordially. "Because there are some signs that Dan is getting back into the old family business."

"I don't know what you're referring to."

"Forgive me if I'm overstepping my bounds here, but even to an outsider like me, there would seem to be some tempting synergy between a medication manufacturer like Dumatech and a drug dealer like Dan. You should see the new product: it's professional-grade stuff."

"If you have some information that Adrian has gotten mixed up in something criminal, that is truly unfortunate, but it's not something I have any familiarity with." Duma drew himself up, looking at Vlad with cold hostility. "I've always made it a point not to mix business with friendship. I wish you could have done the same."

Standing so straight with his nose raised disdainfully in the air, Duma looked to Vlad like a sun-bronzed Slim Codrescu. With some obligatory clucking about needing to get back to supervising his workers, Duma dismissed him and Vlad could do nothing but return to his ornery companions on the cruiser.

Vlad watched the yacht shrink into the distance as his boat sped off. *Nice work there, Vlad. Now you've got one less friend in the community.* He turned to look at his shipmates at the helm. They had their backs to him, continuing the sullen silence they'd sustained ever since he climbed aboard at the dock. *These two wouldn't even notice if I slipped and tumbled overboard. They might even give me a push.*

He sat down gloomily, the brisk wind in his face doing little to alleviate his spirits. By the time the hulking form of the dredger appeared before him, and behind it, the soaring steel curves of the gigantic suspension bridge that spanned the river, he had sunken into a sulky lethargy. He mounted the rope ladder the Coast Guard had dropped for him and began the long climb up.

It was a dizzying ascent, made all the rougher by gusts of wind that slammed him against the hull like a bug on a windshield. The jarring impact shook the clouds from his mind and he scrambled up the rest of the ladder at a breakneck pace. At the top he accepted the proffered hand of a guardsman and swung aboard. The resounding clap of his feet against the deck sent an invigorating jolt up his whole body and he breathed in deeply, feeling the laziness seeping out of his bones.

He was immediately greeted by a grisly scene of bodies laid out on a tarp on the deck. They were laid out snugly next to each other like sardines, so closely intertwined and so badly bloated and decomposed that Vlad couldn't tell how many there were. He guessed about ten, his eyes narrowing on a cadaver at the end missing its head.

A diver stood next to the pile shedding his gear, starting with a sleek yellow helmet. Vlad felt a twinge of boyish disappointment that it looked nothing like the antiques of his imagination. Many a time, he'd stared into the murky waters beneath and dreamed of donning one of those colossal brass helmets to hunt for shipwrecks at the bottom of the trench. He sighed and looked back at the spread of corpses. *No romance in these seas, just bodies.*

"Find any to your liking? It's buy one get one free," came a voice from behind him.

Vlad turned to see a grinning man in white Coast Guard uniform. Surprisingly long white hair pushed out from under the brim of his captain's hat. "Captain Kendrick," he declared, offering his hand.

"Captain Paler," said Vlad, returning the handshake.

"I haven't seen you out here before. Usually it's that other vamp detective… Rooskie."

Rusu. Vlad didn't bother to correct him. He was surprised to hear that sloth had ever left the office, much less climbed the rope ladder to get up here. The man had been hiding out in Missing Persons for as long as Vlad had been a detective.

"You must pull a lot of bodies out of the river?"

"We only dredge this area once or twice a year. We get some all over the river but your fine city generates more than just about everyone else combined. We always try to bring one of you folks out here when we bring in a haul."

"You ever seen one missing its head before?"

Kendrick shoved his cap up to scratch at his bushy white hair. "None that I recall, but they are usually missing something. The currents are fierce and the fish are hungry."

Vlad knelt down for a closer look at the headless body. It certainly wasn't a clean cleft like Dragescu and Petricean. Muscle and flesh still clung in ragged bits to the jutting spinal column. The skin was badly discolored and distended but from what Vlad could tell, it was far too dark to be a vamp. He glanced down the naked torso. Female. No signs of any puncture wounds.

"Doesn't quite fit my guy's M.O. But I am still curious. How long do you think this one was down there?"

"Hard to say... The water's been real cold and all these bodies have been trapped in the sand bar so they haven't been exposed to the birds or the sun. Could be anywhere from a couple weeks to a couple months."

"And where are you taking it from here?"

"We dump all these on your coroner." Kendrick gave Vlad a mischievous look. "You know you and Rooskie could save yourselves a lot of hassle by just waiting 'til we bring these hauls to shore like everybody else. I'm happy to have you aboard anytime, but why go to all the trouble?"

"We're vampires," came back Vlad. "We like 'em as fresh and juicy as we can get."

Kendrick threw his head back and laughed uproariously, giving Vlad a friendly shove as he did. Vlad couldn't help but join him in laughter, throwing his own head back and feeling the breeze pour into him like an intoxicating spirit. *Oh to be with such shipmates sailing on a stormy sea!*

He handed his fellow captain his card, asking for a heads up if they found another with its head off - more raucous laughter - and descended the rope ladder. A powerful feeling of warmth kept the cold wind and all sense of panic at bay as the ladder was buffeted back and forth and the churning brown waters waited so far beneath him. He skipped the last several rungs and leapt down, landing like a coiled spring between the two shocked Harbor Patrolmen. He clapped both of them heartily on the back. *Run up the Jolly Roger, boys. The Vampirate is back!*

***

The most challenging part of Theresa Russell's design to

151

convert from the sketchbook to the canvas had been the inverted steeple, and like all of her great ideas, remained fluid until the moment of its completion. She had decided in the end to erect a proper steeple and then remove the key supports so the entire thing collapsed in on itself. It had descended with such a wonderful billowy grace that she had then decided to put the thing back upright to save the effect for the ceremony.

Naturally, her buzzing hive of worker interns was not happy about all the extra work and were beginning to grumble. Not with their mouths, of course - they knew better than that - but utilizing the arsenal of passive aggression kept by every good artist. The clipped breaths, the sidelong glances, the wincing nods, the jutting hips: these were just the beginnings of the great portfolio they would assemble before they left her service. She took a moment to smile at their busy irritation. *No, they will never truly leave the service of their Queen.*

She walked back down the aisle, feeling the pokes and stings of the burs and nettles along with soft caresses of the fine fescue grass on her bare feet. She made a mental note to insist on the removal of all shoes prior to entrance. She sat again in the pews that had arrived last night from the factory. It had arrived in a distastefully rough white plastic. But a night of sanding and polishing from the interns and it was gleaming like ivory. She slid down the voluptuous arch of the seat, the angle allowing her bare feet to dangle just above the grass as the slope put a devilish pinch on her lower back and forced her to lean forward in a half-bow. *Perfect!*

From there it was back down the aisle and through the flapping canvas doors to get a look at the whole structure. She brought her long, spidery fingers to her chin and studied it - *the artist as her own critic!* The bride had asked for "an old-fashioned American church wedding that's not an old-fashioned American church wedding" as her groom smirked behind her. Quite the pair, those two. Irina, the athletic fake blonde with extraordinarily pronounced cheekbones striking enough to make up for her drawn, almost haggard face. Her eyes were almost feverish at the prospect of this wedding. Alex, sun-bronzed and self-satisfied, so eager to pass off the fragments he remembered from his freshman art appreciation course as his credentials as a discriminating patron of the arts. So desperate to impress.

As unimpressed as she was with the couple, Russell was still pleased with the project. A canvas, cellophane, and cardboard cathedral reaching 100 feet in the air! The very likeness of the mighty brick and mortar monolith that was the old Methodist church downtown transformed into a giant disposable pop-up tent. The great monuments of the ages condensed, distilled and recycled into a huge plastic bag, which, should she free it of its flimsy tethers, would lift off with even a mild gust of wind, taking flight to find its home in the nearest landfill. Such an achievement! And all slapped together by her little army in a few days.

She looked again at her swarm as they hovered around this, her latest and greatest hive. River City's best brightest, vamp and native, stripped of all outward signals of their pedigree, blanketed in the bland homogeneity of Russell's special ordered brown plastic smocks and meshed hairnets. They had had their opportunity to share the spotlight in the Hall of the Burger King. Now they were again an anonymous mass of fingers and toes, mere extensions of her own, making manifest the thoughts of her own hive mind.

Her smile faded as she noticed a particular worker bee detached from the swarm. There was nothing off about its appearance - it wore the same shapeless smock as its fellows - but it was not where it belonged, halfway up the scaffolds that led up to the top of the steeple. She'd asked them to mount an enormous cross she'd constructed of corrugated cardboard but she'd told them to take it down after the epiphany of the collapsing inverted steeple had struck her so forcefully. However this rebellious drone was not disassembling the scaffolding but climbing to its top. She noticed too it was lugging a heavy garbage bag behind it, bouncing against the rungs in the slow ascent. She scowled; she'd given specific instructions not to bring anything heavier than a few pounds beyond the upper level.

Her long strides brought her quickly to the base of the scaffolding. "You there!" she shouted, her voice losing its pleasing husky quality and taking on a piercing shrillness in the cold air. "Come down this instant before you do any damage."

From what must have been fifty feet below, she saw the intern flinch, shoulders hunkering down like a wild rabbit caught out in the open. It pleased her that she could strike fear into a worker's heart even at this range. Now, for the long slow descent and meek submission at the feet of the mistress. But this intern did not descend, but rather ascended all the more quickly, dragging the garbage bag behind.

Russell felt a terrible wave of anger and shouted again at the rebel. But he ignored her. *Yes, he.* Only a male intern would show such callous disregard to the risks of gallivanting around with heavy weights atop her creation, ignoring her commands. But what if he was not an intern at all? Could he be one of those Pentecostal nuts who had vandalized her Seduction of Eve sculpture at the children's museum? *A saboteur!*

Her next shout was for "security!" They were at her elbows in a minute, already out of breath from running when they first heard her shout. Those big, broad shoulders heaving under their black security jackets. Those granite chins jutting out as they looked up to follow her long pointing finger and see the figure climbing ever higher. *Such men!*

And now they were vaulting up the scaffolding at her bidding, swinging like gorillas with those powerful arms. Soon they would be on the delinquent intern, the snake-handling saboteur. She pictured the struggle. A violent see-saw on the scaffolding as the arms grasped and ripped and clung. A desperate final leap from the fugitive, hurling himself bodily from the summit to land with a splat at her feet. It would be her greatest show yet!

The guards were gaining, the saboteur a comparative snail with his garbage sack trailing behind him. He lurched onward in haste, the bag slipping from his grasp and tumbling down, bouncing with clangs and gongs against the metal piping of the scaffolds until it struck the damp ground at the base of the church with a squelch. Russell ignored it, craning her neck for a view of the top.

Now the saboteur was cornered. He had reached the top and there was nowhere to go. The guards were only a few swings away. His moment had come. Russell braced herself on the precipice of euphoria. He leapt! But not into the air, to the steeple!

She screamed. The coward! Treating her creation as if it was just an extension of the scaffolding. The PVC pipes holding up the steeple were so thin, so fragile, so unequal to the task of supporting the unwelcome weight of this intruder, this vandal! The steeple swayed precariously under him, like an inverted pendulum. With each yaw, the saboteur swung between the scaffolding and empty space.

The guards had reached the summit of the scaffolding and made violent snatching motions from their perch, but he was always just out of reach. There was a snap - Russell screamed again - as one of the pipes broke, but the steeple did not collapse, the arc of its teetering only growing wider. Then one of her men, one of her glorious gorillas, angry from yet another empty snatch, sprung from the scaffolding in mad pursuit. *King Kong astride the Empire State building.*

The big guard caught hold of the steeple several feet below where it connected to the rest of the canvas and even further below the saboteur. There was an ominous groan from the canvas as he clung to it, and the whole church joined the steeple in its teeter. Then another terrible sound - a snap so loud Russell felt it in her own bones.

First slowly, like a phantasmic cruise liner sinking under the ocean surface, the top of the structure began to topple. Then the snaps and tears accelerated - popcorn in the microwave - and the entire building gave up the ghost, collapsing straight downward in a cloud of torn canvas, cardboard dust and floating cellophane.

The panic and rage that had been welling up inside her subsided in an instant. Yes, it was all gone. But such a collapse! To witness a moment of such ephemeral beauty from the perfect vantage point. A moment that was all hers, shared only by the workers. And even they were, fundamentally, just an extension of herself. The sigh that finally escaped her gaping mouth was one of rapturous ecstasy, not despair. *I have become Death, destroyer of worlds!*

Her workers descended on the carcass of the fallen cathedral, pulling and tugging manically at the ruins. *Poor fools! Were they trying to put Humpty Dumpty back together?* Then she realized that they must be looking for the guard and the saboteur and perhaps the workers who had been inside when it fell.

A shriek sounded from in front of her. One of her smocked interns was bent over something in the wreckage. The intern spun round as Russell approached. Russell recognized her as one of the fresh batch of recruits. She was staring aghast at her hands, both coated with blood.

"Do you think... they're dead?" The girl was whimpering now. Russell grabbed her by both arms and slid her out of the way. On the ground where the intern had stood was a black plastic bag - she recognized it as the one the saboteur had dropped. Underneath it was a pool of blood.

Russell knelt down and pulled back the black plastic. The girl behind her exploded at once into screaming hysterics.

"Somebody call the police!" she wailed, running.

Russell only stared, her face allowing only the slightest of grimaces. She knew immediately that the grisly display staring back up at her was no accident. It was art. Gruesome, yes, but that was primarily because the work had been aborted. Exposed before its time.

She stood up and scanned the scene for any sign of the man who had brought down her church. There was no sign of him. He had not been a saboteur, but an unauthorized collaborator, swooping in to spray paint his signature over her work. She sighed and looked back down. A pair of severed heads. A man and a woman. Alex Duma and Irina Nasturel, she was sure of it. Lifeless eyes gazing at each other, mouths bulging with words they could not speak, thoughts they could not share. *Another partnership that wasn't meant to be!*

15

Mandy kept glancing back at the elevator doors. Borman, Moore and Valentine stood beside her, shooting the breeze, watching as the buses continued to roll into the dungeon of the parking level.

"Jeez, how many interns does she have? What a waste!" exclaimed Borman. He hadn't stopped spewing disbelief over Theresa Russell's popularity since she had glided into the interrogation room hours before.

The hiss of the bus door sounded and another dozen smocked interns stumbled out, herded by a patrolman into the throng of their fellows. Just like the ones that had come before them they all craned their necks and gaped in horror at the low concrete ceilings, hovering over them like an anvil.

"I bet you there's a couple of them right now dreaming up a comparison to Auschwitz or some sh**," snorted Big Eddie Moore. "We're all gonna be in their next exhibition with Hitler mustaches and jackboots."

"You know they're just fantasizing about us when they come up with that stuff, right?" chimed in Valentine, looking for curves behind the wall of shapeless smocks. "It's like a kink to them."

Mandy resisted another urge to glance toward the elevator and smiled. None of these guys had any kind of comfort level dealing with Russell and her art freaks. Not that it was her scene either, but she'd at least been to River City's Modern Art Museum a few times. She'd probably even met a few of these interns or their predecessors at the college parties in her pre-Academy days. *In my*

Brad phase.

That passing familiarity was the reason why it was Mandy taking the lead in the interview room with Theresa Russell for the last few hours. Well, that, and Vlad being a no-show. She cast another glance at the elevator. It would have gone so much better if he had been there. He was so cultured - he would have understood so much more of what Russell was referencing, or seen through whatever smoke screens she was throwing up.

Mandy supposed she did okay without him. This Russell lady didn't seem to like talking to women - she had felt like she was transparent the entire time, like Russell was waiting for a man to walk in behind her. But she'd at least gotten past enough of her schtick to discover that Russell truly believed she knew the killer. She had no specific identity, at least not one she would disclose, but she was thoroughly convinced that whoever it was had worked for her at some point and snuck into her organization. She'd brought a hefty leather-bound tome of her work for them to peruse, asserting with total confidence that the killer has taken his inspiration from within.

Mandy was not so sure. Not quite so much of the world revolved around Theresa Russell as she supposed. She smiled again as she remembered her describing the early vandalism of another exhibit. That saboteur hadn't gone into deep cover. He'd just purchased a ticket to the Children's Museum, walked right up to that statue of Eve getting pleasured by a giant snake and started hacking away with a hammer. Mandy remembered that story when it first came out. It had sounded like something her dad would have done.

"Hey, kid." Mandy turned at the sound and a poke between her shoulder blades. It was Francis, a sheepish smile on his lips. She felt a cozy warmth at the sight of him. A blast of warm air from the distant past of three weeks ago when all she had to worry about was toe tagging John Does. She had an impulse to hug him that died when she remembered the hint of a leer at the edge of that smile.

"Francis! What are you doing down here? Did you come to help us with interviews?" She gestured at the waiting horde of interns. "We're looking for a serial killer in a haystack."

Valentine perked up. "Yes. Anyone else coming down to help? I'm for damn sure not handling a whole group by myself again.

Processed that entire busload of Bouchard's bums all by my lonesome and for what? Not even a single description of the suspect."

"I wish I could help," Francis replied. "But I've got an O.D. on the northside to get to. Maybe if you guys are still at it when I get back in five or six hours I can chip in."

Francis gave Valentine a malicious grin and turned back to Mandy, his face turning serious as he pulled her away from the group.

"I was just up on the roof having a smoke," he said, his voice low. "I saw the Captain up there. He asked me to send you up to see him."

Mandy felt her body tense, ready to bolt for the elevator without so much as another word to Francis. But Francis kept a hand on her arm.

"Not so fast, kid. You've got to be careful."

"Of what?" She felt a flush rising to her cheeks and the retort came out sharper than she had intended.

"Of him. And this case. If the body count keeps on piling up they're going to be looking for a fall guy. I just don't want to see anyone pin anything on you."

Mandy smiled. *I guess the old lech does care about me.* "Thanks for looking out for me, Francis, but I think I'm good. And don't you go counting us out. We're this close to catching this bastard."

"Still," continued Francis as she escaped his grasp and took a step toward the elevators. "Watch yourself. The man had a desperate look to him."

Mandy broke free and skipped to the waiting steel doors, keeping herself from running. *Desperate?*

"Hey, where do you think you're going?" It was Valentine. "Don't think you're gonna -" The elevator closed on his whining voice and yanked her upward.

Reaching the top, Mandy realized she'd never been on the roof and didn't know how to get up there. She poked and prodded at the closed doors surrounding her, feeling like Jane Eyre searching for a secret passage in her master's medieval manor. This was the thirteenth floor! Everything was behind buzzer activated locks. Every door hid some new and more intimidating department VIP. What was she doing up here? *What was he doing up here?*

At last, one of her pushing hands met a door that gave. Instead of a battle-ax secretary there was a staircase leading upward. She vaulted them two at a time, bursting out onto the rooftop out of breath. The sky, glowing white through a gray haze, came at her from all sides, a breeze sweeping from between the shoulders of the surrounding skyscrapers. She felt dizzy and light-headed. A strong enough wind and she'd be swept away.

She grabbed onto the rusted bulk of one of the gigantic vents protruding from the floor of the roof, steadying herself. Then she saw him. A gargoyle crouched at the edge of the roof, his back to her, his shoulders hunched under a dark gray overcoat that hung like a cape behind him. If she spoke, would she startle him? Would he fall? Would he jump? *Would he fly?*

"You asked for me?" Her voice sounded so thin and frail all the way up here.

He spun round at the sound of her, standing upright, cutting a jagged black outline against the towers studding the horizon behind him. His face was taut, his eyes sharp and searching. He said nothing.

She stepped closer. "Why are you up here?" Still no answer. Another step closer. "I could have used your help today."

"I'm sorry. I had to think," he said quietly and turned back towards the edge.

"Is something wrong?" she asked his shoulder, angled high to hide his face.

She saw his shoulders rise as he sighed. "There's always something wrong."

Mandy felt a sudden flash of irritation. *You asked me up here! Just come out with it.* She took a final step, coming right alongside him, trying to get around that forbidding shoulder to read his face. As she sidled next to him, the corner of her eye caught the sudden drop spilling out underneath her. Her legs quaked and she gasped. *Straight down.*

Vlad whipped round to catch her with both arms. "Careful!" he shouted, his face suddenly close to hers. *Got you!*

"I'm not going to fall," she snapped, but her shoulders relaxed comfortably into his grip. "I just want to know what's going on with you."

A sadness crept over his face as he stared at her. "The case..." he began. "I think it might need someone else."

Mandy sucked in her breath and it plunged down into a void in her gut. Francis had been right! She was the fall guy! She had slipped over the edge. She was falling. And he was pushing her! She could feel her cheeks turning crimson and her eyes welling up. She turned her head.

"Get someone else then," she muttered and tried to pull away. A tear had just escaped and she needed to get to the door before any others followed. But Vlad did not release her. Instead he brought one hand to her chin and pulled her face back to his, softly brushing away the tear with his thumb.

"No, no," he said, his voice suddenly tender. "I don't want anyone else…" He trailed off, the words searing into Mandy. The falling sensation lingered, but this time she clung tighter to him, staring back.

"I'm the one who has failed. I'm the one who should be replaced."

"That's ridiculous," Mandy spluttered. "There's no one in the whole department who could do a better job."

"You don't understand," said Vlad, bitterness in his voice. "I failed him. The old man trusted me to look after him and now he's gone, lost forever.

"Alex Duma? You can't blame yourself for that. We offered him police protection after Petricean and he turned it down. He didn't take it seriously."

"That is why it's my fault!" Vlad cried, closing his eyes and shaking his head. "He's always been like that. Reckless, foolish, childish. So desperate to be liked. If he had been capable of looking after himself, his father would have never asked me to do it. But he did and now look where he is… A head in a trash bag."

"His father must have thought a lot of you to have asked that of you," said Mandy softly. Vlad looked away. "Don't you think he would have also asked for you to be the one to catch his son's killer?"

He turned back to her, an ember of curiosity smoldering behind the veil of bitterness over his eyes.

"If I couldn't accomplish the first task, why would he give me another?"

"Because nothing has ultimately changed. You're still the best man for the job."

"You think so?" The ember glowed brighter.

"I know I haven't been on the department that long, but I've been around enough to know that just about everyone here is an idiot. And the few that aren't are selfish a**holes who won't lift a finger unless it's to climb the career ladder. You're the only one I've ever met who is smart enough to catch this guy and cares enough to try."

"So you're saying you think a lot of me too?" Now the embers were fires that brought a rush of warmth to her cheeks. She tried to turn away but his hand caught her chin again, this time to pull her into a kiss.

Another kiss! And this time her arms snaked around his neck and she pulled him closer and she felt her hot tear extinguished against the coolness of his cheek.

***

They had the call and they were on the road together. The street lights on the highway stood at attention on either side of them, their glowing salutes lighting the path through the fog for them. Behold the captain and his lady. *Make way!*

He glanced at Mandy beside him. *Mandy. Amanda.* She sat there like an unpinned hand grenade. If he let go of her hand, this dream would explode and the cutting shrapnel of wise counsel would once again pierce his mind and destroy his fragile rationalizations. The solution was simple: don't let go.

But they had arrived and the prying eyes of the crowd of patrolmen lit up by the flashes of the crime scene cameras disentangled their fingers with alarming speed. Now they were apart. They had come to a narrow road that led through wooded wetlands towards a dock that pushed out onto the river. Vlad remembered the spot from his first stint on patrol in the western district. The area used to be a local favorite - a lovers' lane - before a city committee had shut the place off as an ecological preserve. No one was supposed to use the dock either, but that hadn't stopped the likes of Duma. *Rule breakers the two of us! Convention defiers! Taboo breakers!*

There was a Range Rover ahead of them, gleaming in the dim light, posed at an angle against the foggy, moonlit landscape like it was starring in a commercial. *Escape with your lover! Leave the beaten path! Ignore the boundaries!* Only the crime scene tape spoiled the visual.

Bulging in on his peripheral vision was a Lieutenant, beckoning towards the two of them from his spot atop a stony ridge. They walked towards him - just beyond arm's reach - in parallel lines. *Parallel lines never meet.*

"You're going to want to see this," said the Lieutenant. Vlad didn't recognize him. He pointed his hand down the stony ridge into the thick shrubs of a slope leading into a marsh. A pair of unhappy patrolmen stood at the edge of the marsh, ankle deep in mud, grabbing onto branches to keep themselves from sliding further in. Jenkins the crime scene photographer was crouched next to them, oblivious to the surrounding sludge, his bulb clicking and flashing in a staccato rhythm.

Vlad spied Mandy eyeing the muddy ridge and broke his parallel track to offer his hand. He felt a thrill as she took it and with it gave him a furtive glance and a smile - *a secret smile!* He guided her down, his own feet sure.

At the end of the slope, following the nod of the patrolman, he saw the entangled feet of the corpses, poking out from under the shrubs. Four legs twisted together under a blanket of mud and leaves. The naked torsos rested on their sides in the underbrush, cleaving together, chest to chest, man to woman. But instead of a lover's embrace, their arms were bent backwards at cruel and impossible angles, shoulders dislocated. A slender wooden spike punctured and pinned them to each other, protruding from both their backs. *The beast with two backs...*

"I'm thinking he decapitates them up there, stacks them on top of each other, female on top of the male, stakes them and then rolls them down the ridge." Mandy's eyes gleamed as she pantomimed kicking the bodies down the slope. He nodded grimly.

"If Van Helsing's sticking to his methods, he would have approached from behind and strangled them first," she continued. "But how does that work with two people? Perhaps he took the man first. Then the woman. Maybe she ran and then he caught her in the woods, killed her and then dragged her back?"

Vlad shook his head. A vampire woman would be unlikely to run. Too aggressive, too strong for that. He glanced at Irina's corpse. Such a long, sinewy body, tortured into leanness by constant activity and diet, her curves straightened and sharpened into cutting edges. A man-eater who ate nothing else. No, she was a fighter, not a runner. She would leave an attacker with scars unless she was caught completely off-guard.

He turned from Irina to Mandy, his eyes tracing the suggestion of the lines underneath her blouse. Slender, yes, but soft and supple, not hard and taut. She might fight - he saw the fire in those eyes that looked back at him above those blushing cheeks - but she would lose. She would succumb as soon as he took her into his arms.

"I don't think he would have moved on them when they were together," Vlad said at last, clearing his throat. "Too risky, too difficult for someone working alone."

"What if he's not working alone?" she said, brightening. "He could have a partner."

"Possible," mused Vlad, but the notion found nothing to cling to in his mind. These killings had the familiar stink of desperation and obsession, the telltale emotions of a man alone and despised. A man with a partner would not be reduced to such acts. The emptiness that would yield to such anger would be filled.

"A partner complicates things, though… Seems more likely that he killed Duma first. Maybe as he came off the boat. Then waited for Nasturel to pull up and got her."

"She gets out thinking it's her fiancé and then it's Van Helsing…" Mandy shivered. "That's a terrible thought." She sidled closer to him, her head tilting up towards his, her eyes soft as they glanced up at him. "You knew them pretty well, didn't you?"

"I knew him." Duma the delinquent! *How often did you consume your father's waking thoughts. How thoughtlessly did you steal the last of his vitality.* Vlad winced as memories of the old man, dwindled to nothing on his deathbed, rushed back. Nothing but the signal fires in his eyes, burning with inextinguishable hope that his son would eventually see the light and follow in the wisdom of his father.

A little guidance and a good woman is all a man needs, Vlad remembered the elder Duma whispering. And now the younger Duma lay at his feet, without a head and trapped in an eternal embrace with this whore. He looked back at Mandy, still looking up at him. *This was the kind of girl you wanted for Alex.* Beautiful, but no temptress. Smart, but not worldly. Tough, but still clinging to the shreds of innocence. *But we can't always have what we need.*

Vlad sighed and looked back up the muddy slope. The fog had grown thicker and descended all the way to the edge of the ridge, obscuring everything beyond. He reached back for Mandy's hand and she grasped his own again. He helped her tread through the muck, pulling her forward as the ground slid beneath them.

***

Look, Mendoza! It's your family reunion! That was what Majewski, his training officer, had always hollered when they drove by the lumber yard on the way back to the precinct. Mendoza had yukked it up like he was supposed to and then, if he was feeling his oats that day, fired back with the best dumb Pollack joke he could muster.

But the dumb Pollack had the last laugh because here was Mendoza blending in with the crowd of migrant laborers, rubbing their weathered hands and stamping their cowboy-booted feet to ward off the cold. He stared down at his still pristine Nikes, the one signal that he didn't belong here.

Angel Mendoza with his spotless white sneakers was not just another pair of brown hands grasping for whatever work the white man would offer him. He was a child of America with all the perks that came with it. He had a down payment on a house with a white picket fence. He had a beautiful white girlfriend and a beautiful diamond engagement ring in a white gold setting waiting in his pocket for her. And on top of all that, he was a cop, a badge-carrying member of the great brotherhood. All these things were still technically true!

Thirty days. Thirty days relieved of duty pending further results of the Internal Affairs investigation. Thirty days without a paycheck. Thirty days until that big fat first mortgage payment was due. Thirty days to figure out why Mandy hardly even came home anymore. Thirty days to keep the dream alive.

He cast around looking, irritation growing, as he saw only faces like his own. *Where was Enoch?* This had been his idea. Did he stand him up? Mendoza's anger dissolved as he saw the familiar wisp-tufted head bobbing a full head above the crowd like a buoy floated above the tide. He threw up his hand to wave and Enoch grinned in recognition.

Enoch clamped Mendoza's hand in that iron grip of his and clapped him on the back hard enough to leave a mark. "At last some muscle to take over the heavy lifting," he declared cheerfully. Mendoza noticed the curious glances of the men around them.

"What exactly am I signing up for here?" Mendoza asked, pulling his jacket tighter to keep the icy breeze at bay.

"That's the beauty of it. We don't know. We just finished the stone wall yesterday."

"There will be something, though, right? If I don't come up with a couple grand by the end of the month, I'm... I'm screwed."

"What did I tell you about all that worrying? The Lord has your back, and so do I."

Mendoza managed a nod and a smile. The Lord and an old man breaking his back to afford a dive motel on the hoe track. *Friends in high places!* But he felt comforted all the same.

"See - here they come." There was a murmur in the crowd and then some jostling as the men pushed to get close to a caravan of pick-ups approaching. The leader was a shiny white Ford with TOM LAYMAN CONSTRUCTION emblazoned on the side in big, important-looking orange letters. A big white man hopped out of the passenger seat and surveyed the scene. He looked past the first line of men, all babbling in broken English, and brightened as he spotted the Enoch buoy.

"Preacher man!" he shouted enthusiastically, waving him over. The crowd parted and Enoch gamboled forward, pulling Mendoza along with him. "I've got another pair of strong arms for you, Mr. Layman. This is Angel Mendoza."

Layman nodded absently, staring right through Mendoza. "Hop in back, we got a long ride ahead of us today and we need to get moving."

He stepped up on the sideboard of his truck to address the crowd. "Necesito veinte hombres," he bellowed to the crowd in confident but accent-less Spanish, flashing his big hands twice to signal 20. "Solo los mas fuertes," he added, patting his own hefty bicep. The crowd surged in on him and soon all three pick-up beds were full, Angel and Enoch squished into the leader just behind the cab.

The caravan took off, the crowd still grasping and shouting their gibberish. Mendoza shook his head in disbelief. It felt like they were leaving a refugee camp. Behind him, the sliding glass to the cab pulled back with a screech and Layman's face appeared in the gap. He had big bristly jowls, like a bulldog.

"You feeling up to running another crew for me today, preacher?"

"Absolutely! What are we doing today?"

"Earth mover's transmission blew so we're going full manual.

Need as much trench as your guys can dig for me - we've got a short timeline before the city comes in to lay down the new wires."

"Sure thing!" Enoch seemed totally unfazed. Angel shook his head again. *Ditch digging!* Why not slap an orange jumpsuit on if he was going to do convict labor. He brooded in sullen silence as the vibration of the truck bed lulled him back into unhappy thoughts.

What good will the pocket change from this gig be if that vamp lawyer takes me to the cleaners? He tried to stretch his legs out without starting up a game of footsie with the laborer across from him. The ring was digging uncomfortably into his thigh. Maybe he should hock it to help him pay for a better lawyer than that frazzled guy with the wrinkled suit the union was trying to foist off on him. Not like he was going to get a chance to use this ring anyways. Mandy hadn't even talked to him since that day at IA.

Even if Mandy thawed, could there be a worse time to pop the question? *I know I'm a tardy slip away from getting sh**-canned by RCPD - oh, and you'll probably be a chief before I make sergeant - but how about you and me tying the knot? After I default on the tiny house I bought for us and my wages get garnished to pay that vamp VIP, maybe we can live off your salary in the apartment you hate. Or we could move back to the country with your parents - at least your dad seems to like me.*

He threw a glance at Enoch and saw him staring happily out at the blur of the river behind the old cotton warehouses. He had the look of a dog sticking his head out of the window. *How does he do it? Broker than me, two hundred miles away from his wife and kids, out here on some mission to save a daughter that won't give him the time of day... and he's smiling like a fool.* Enoch must have sensed his thoughts because he turned to find Mendoza staring.

"What's on your mind, son?"

Mendoza sighed and looked away. "This just isn't where I hoped to be about now... Honestly, I don't see how you can be so cheerful."

"Did I ever tell you why I came out here?"

Mendoza shrugged. "You were worried about Mandy?"

"That's a part of it, but I've always been worried about Mandy. That's just being a parent," Enoch said with a chuckle. "No, the reason I came out here is because I kept having this dream."

Mendoza saw the smile leave Enoch's face as his eyes drifted to the horizon and his brow furrowed.

"Back on the farm, we've got this creek that snakes onto the property in the back of the woods. Most of the year, it's just a lazy little thing, almost a pond. My dad used to let me go fishing there by myself in the summers. But after a good rain that little creek turns into a monster that'll grab up everything near it and drag it down to the bottom." Enoch took a deep breath before continuing.

"In this dream, it's been storming like crazy. Just buckets and buckets of rain and wind and thunder and I'm in bed with Emily and there's this crack of thunder that wakes up the whole house. And all the kids - they're little again, none of 'em more than this high-" he held up his hand to his belly button. "They all come running in scared from the lightning like they used to. All of them but Mandy."

"So next thing in the dream, I'm already outside and it's pouring and I'm looking everywhere for her. And I can't see anything except for when the lightning strikes, but I still can't find her... But then I hear her... And she's screaming 'Daddy' but it's so far away..."

Enoch took another deep breath to compose himself. "Finally, I find her. She's in the middle of the creek and the water's all around her and she keeps going under. So I run to her... But the bank is so muddy, my boots just sink all the way down. I can't move and I can't get my feet out and I still hear her, calling for me..." He brought his sleeve to his eyes and looked away.

"I had that terrible dream every night for two weeks. Got to be so I'd dread even closing my eyes. Couldn't hardly sleep. Couldn't even think. The Lord just wouldn't take it up off of me until I did something about it..." He looked back at Mendoza with a smile. "But as soon as I set out on that road, I felt the weight lifted off my shoulders and I felt His peace flooding through me again. And I tell you, there's not a pain or worry that can get me down when I've got His peace..."

Mendoza stared down at his sneakers, gleaming white amidst the muddy browns of the surrounding cowboy boots. Whatever was twisting his insides into knots wasn't peace, but it wasn't a dream either. He'd stumbled into a waking nightmare with no end in sight. Why he was following this crazy old man who seemed perfectly happy to fall ever deeper into the suck he didn't know. But he could use some of that peace.

The caravan pulled up at the work site and Mendoza felt his

legs quiver as he vaulted over the bed and landed on the grass. *No more squad car for you two. Time for you to tread the paths of your ancestors.* The grass stretched on for what looked like forever, expanding out from the road to cover the rising foothills. Atop the closest one was what looked in the distance like a grove of cypress trees surrounding what must have been a truly huge mansion to look so big from afar.

A vamp plantation. Supposedly every vamp built one of these castles as soon as they made it big enough. A place so remote it would always be safe from the torch and pitchfork mob. *Or maybe a place so remote no one can hear the screams of your victims.* Mendoza didn't know if that was cop cynicism or more of his newfound hostility to vamps bleeding out. He could still feel Mandy's disapproval over such forbidden thoughts - the way she arched her eyebrows and cut him with a look. But the further she pulled back from him and the closer she clung to that vamp - *that bloodsucker, oh it felt good to think it* - the less he cared. Yesterday he'd even let the Dick Liggins Show blare at max volume throughout the apartment. Let her come in and see him nodding and laughing along to that garbage. Let her come in at all.

He felt something in his palm. It was the wooden shaft of a pickaxe that Enoch thrust into his hand. "Cursed is the ground for thy sake," he declared. Then, softly into Mendoza's ear: "Nothing better for a troubled mind than some good hard labor. I'm putting you on point. We don't stop until we reach the house."

Mendoza gripped the pickaxe - he liked the way it balanced in his hand. His eyes settled on the ground at his feet, kicking at it with the white toe of his sneaker. It was hard clay under the thin carpet of grass. He gave the pick a test swing, feeling a pleasing tug of its weighted end on the knotted muscles of his shoulder and back and then a satisfying slice as the curved spike penetrated deep under the clay. He gave it a yank and the ground came up in big broken chunks beneath him.

He swung again and he felt the impact echoed in the blows of his *compadres* lining up next to him. The earth was already crumbling and they were only just getting started. He felt the pick becoming a part of him as he swung again and brought it down with pulverizing force. Deadlier than any pitchfork. He eyed the curve of the slope leading up to that big, beautiful mansion so high up the hill. A long way, yes, but within reach.

16

Sally Cohn pulled at the curtains - the obscenely rich kind that Scarlett O'Hara would have had - to get a better look below. The crowd was just rounding the corner of city hall. This must be their fourth circuit. Only three more and the walls - these ostentatious faux-stones that just screamed French Chateau - would come crumbling down under their righteous fury.

Yes, righteous! I thought it! She had half-a-mind to open these gilded windows and shout it. *Can't you see I'm with you? Look at these red cords dangling from my window. I'm Rahab!* Hadn't she done all in her power to let two of them onto the city council? Had she not vociferously and courageously condemned the bigotry of the likes of Liggins and Haggerty and the million votes they represented?

All this sacrifice and service for what? And for whom? *Look at the pathetic size of that "crowd!"*

Nothing but a few meager rows of upper crusty old vamps, marching silently in their dour gray suits and starched dresses and their... She squinted. These ladies were wearing heels to a protest? They didn't even have proper signs, just a big banner across their first row that read "END THE BLOODSHED." If it wasn't for their money and their conniving yuppie children, they might as well be a nursing home out on a field trip. *One more circuit around the track and then off to the glue factory with you!*

She glanced back at the sheaf of paper grinning wickedly at her from her desk. Her own ticket to the glue factory. They had all signed it, even Garrick, her erstwhile protege! The mayoral boytoy!

But the ink had the unctuous blackness of Codrescu's pen. A state of emergency! Special emergency powers to a committee of three! Over four measly dead bodies. How many multiples more had died in the Blood Moon Riots? And no one had dared force through any committee of three on that scion of the old WASP establishment, Mayor Jim Pierce.

But Pierce had never had to contend with the likes of Van Helsing. Her eyes shifted to the newspaper with its screaming headline "VAN HELSING SPEAKS AGAIN" beside Codrescu's hateful little ultimatum. She was surrounded by terrorists! She ground her teeth in frustration. There had been far more ink than blood spilled. Four bodies? Scarcely enough to be a rounding error in any major metro's monthly homicide stats. And they wanted her head for that? The fifth victim, that's what she was.

She closed her eyes and the taunting words from Van Helsing's new letter danced on her eyelids. "The city gallops after me in a blind rage, trampling its own in its senseless quest for vengeance, a headless horseman running amok." The headless horseman! Oh how the press had loved tying that albatross around her neck. And how swiftly had Codrescu slipped in for the kill. Terrorists on both sides!

She turned back to the crowd as they filed under the statue of Andrew Jackson rampant, his cavalry saber raised to strike their unprotected rear. Did they not recognize that she was all that stood between them and nativist fury? Why must they treat her, a Reform Jew, as if she was just a braying congregant in one of Haggerty's revival tents? *I am your sister in oppression!* Hadn't her people suffered along with them? *And to a much greater extent if one were really to dig into the details...* Hadn't they borne the same vicious blood libels? *Only one set of which, if one were being really honest, had any basis in fact...*

And yet here they were, ready to throw Rahab out the window as if she were Jezebel. A Madame DeFarge and they trot me out like Marie Antoinette. She rubbed at her long neck, feeling where the guillotine had struck. This beautiful neck, that had held out so inspiringly against the spots and wrinkles that were already overtaking her face and arms. This elegant bough that had so often and so patiently borne the lascivious gaze of that backstabber Codrescu. Now he was sinking his teeth in. Sucking her dry. And there was nothing she could do about it.

She turned from the window finally and approached the

loathsome paper. She plucked the mayoral quill from its stand and dipped it in the golden inkwell. Of all the baroque relics in this tomb of antiquity, she liked this one the best. If she had to sign her own death warrant, at least it would be done in a pretty stroke.

***

"Among all the threats that can face a city... natural disaster, economic collapse, civil unrest... none is ultimately more poisonous to the body politic than the fear and hatred towards one's fellow man. Whether that hatred takes the form of racism, misogyny, anti-semitism, homophobia, or, sadly, the virulent xenophobia we've become all too familiar with in our fair city..."

Slim Codrescu's attention faded as the pressure on his thoracic vertebrae became unbearable. He tried to readjust without giving the appearance of any kind of squirming restlessness. Impeccable posture and a bad back: both were gifts from his mother. He felt confident that she too would be groaning inwardly as this insufferable woman droned on. *Blacks, women, Jews and gays! Why must she always insist on surrounding the community in such ridiculous company?* And still she continued.

"... and we cannot afford to take such threats lightly, nor can we ignore the cry for justice that springs up from the ground where innocent blood has been spilt. We must listen to these four voices as they now join the terrible chorus of the aggrieved in a song that goes back centuries... all the way back to the dirges of the Quapaw natives who were driven from this land, or under it, by the cruelty of our predecessors..."

The Indians too! Codrescu stifled the exasperated sigh that now gathered under the ball of thoracic pain. How long could she keep this up? She didn't even have notes and he knew they had ambushed her with this diktat: from what spring flowed this fountain of pretty nonsense? He allowed himself a begrudging admiration for her improvisational skills even at this stage, the unquestionable nadir of her mayoral career. This knack for smoothly spinning every occurrence into an opportunity for grandstanding was distinct to the natives; he knew of no vampire who could sink so comfortably to this occasion. Perhaps this was an example of that jazz streak they were always bragging about.

Still... however artfully she might toot her own horn, however interminable this jazz riff, she had no choice but to play his tune.

She would retain the title and she would continue to have chances to spread herself all over the public stage, but the true organs of city power would finally pass to abler hands. Not just his own. There would be his fellow vamp and protege Councilman Vinea and Councilmen Garrick - a native yes, but one of the most realistic and pragmatic he'd ever encountered - to help steer the city through this critical phase in its metamorphosis.

No more "controlled chaos." No more "symphony via cacophony." Yes, there had been some advantages to marinating in the primordial soup of frontier-style American governance. The cheerful war of all against all had trained up and sharpened a dynamic class of institutional leaders. But now that they had matured, it was time to face the fact that the same petri dish that had nurtured them had also spawned pathogens like Haggerty and Liggins and... Codrescu shuddered... Van Helsing. It was past time to drain this cesspool of its toxic elements and transition the city into its new phase.

Cohn had just started outlining the mandate of the Committee of Three. Codrescu gazed out over the crowd to gauge their reaction. He saw nothing but the impenetrably stony faces of his countrymen, all first generation from the looks of them. So proper, so dignified, so stiff! If they shared any of the degenerative scoliosis genes with his matrilineage, they would never show it, no matter how long Cohn blathered on. Such people! The true constituency for a civilized polis. Turning out in force even on this cold morning.

Still, their numbers seemed so terribly sparse in comparison to those raucous hordes that would turn out whenever Haggerty so much as snapped his fingers. And where were their children? Where were his fellow Olympians - the generation that had soared to the heights of finance and medicine and technology as he had to this roost of municipal power? He frowned. Did they not realize they were the ones being targeted by Van Helsing and the seething underworld of hatred and bigotry that had produced him? Did they not recognize that their very lives depended on his governance?

Codrescu blinked at the sudden realization that Cohn had finally stopped speaking and was now gesturing to him. He cleared his throat, ignoring her as stepped to the podium, using both hands to push his sloping back as straight as it would go.

"Fellow citizens," he declared, producing a handful of index cards. He attempted to raise his chin along with his posture, but he had to lower it again to keep the cards in view. "Our city has undergone an extraordinary and explosive burst of evolutionary growth, and with it economic, social, and moral progress. Such change has brought enormous benefits, but it has also provoked a terrible reaction from the societal forces that would cling to the past at any cost. For the last several years, our city has attempted to promote growth and progress while accommodating those sectors that have grown increasingly resistant to any kind of change…" He tilted his head here towards Cohn.

"The hope was, given enough time and space, these elements would adapt to the changing environment, and that a mutual tolerance would prevail. But, as the tragic events of the past month have made only too clear, 'time and space' have only allowed the old prejudices to fester into something even more wretchedly evil. Today we face a raging current of bigotry that grows in intensity by the day. Far from enticing them into a civic accord, the immense prosperity brought on by our evolution only feeds their reactionary fury. With each day their toxicity pollutes our beautiful city, their hatred streaming over the airwaves, pouring out from the newsstands and overflowing from the pulpits…"

He raised his hands to the crowd, leaving the cards still in sight on the podium. "The time has come to turn back these dismal tides, to build the dams and levees we need to keep these backwaters from submerging the enlightened civilization our ancestors worked so hard to lift from the swamp. This work will not require any transformation of our laws and values. The tools for addressing these threats are already at our disposal; all that is required is the will to use them, fully and effectively."

Codrescu now lifted his gaze beyond the cards and the silver-fringed crowd to the teeming streets and illuminated towers above them. *It's alright. Go about your busy lives. We'll have your attention soon enough.* "It is the solemn pledge of this committee to bring all of the powers designated to us to bear on the emergency before us. Let the citizens of our community rest in the confidence that they will be protected at any cost; it is the hatemongers' turn to tremble in fear at the coming judgment."

Pocketing his cards, he waited for applause that never came. Of course it didn't. These were the founders. They would never be reduced to the crude American practice of senseless noisemaking, the vulgar mashing of hand against hand. This was all good and proper, and only Codrescu's corruption by the undignified excess of popular politics - *the noise at Cohn's re-election party! Deafening! Exhilarating!* - could have made him expect anything else. Nevertheless, it was alright. Soon the rest of the city would be ushered into their serene silence. That was all the tribute any true vamp statesman could ask for.

***

A view that somebody else had to die for! Mandy wished for a moment she had the usual crowd to bounce sick jokes off of for a few cheap sniggers. But the desire passed as soon she took another drink of that vista. The river to one side with the bridge on the horizon and skyscrapers everywhere else. She'd done it! Goodbye to the Pit. All that remained was to sever a few more of its grasping tentacles.

That shouldn't be too hard. Her name wasn't even on that lease. Angel had fallen on that sword back in his days as a shining knight, galloping in to rescue her from Brad and the ruin he'd made of her credit. As for Angel himself... well, that was a conversation for another day. But she could at least soften the blow with the proceeds of that magnificent check!

Such a check! She'd scooped it out of the inbox like so many others, her hands oblivious to its new and spectacular dimensions. So many months of toiling at the piddling patrolman wages, she'd known that some kind of bump was coming with the detective badge. When there'd been no difference on that first check, she'd still been riding high enough on the new title not to care. But then the raise arrived in force, reinforced by a deluge of overtime and backpay to flood her eyes with dollar signs. A windfall! Fort Knox in her pocket.

Spend it! The impulse had run wild as soon as she had opened the check and gaped at the extra digit. Gone were the still small voices of her parents whispering save, save, save. They were trampled senseless under the pounding hooves of unbridled prosperity. No more scrimping and saving to live in the Pit. No more pathetic waiting for rides. No more ugly flats!

She looked down from the railing - the same railing that saw Ion Dragescu's headless swan dive to the riverfront below - and felt the spinning sensation of vertigo coming on. Had she moved too fast? A penthouse with a river view? *No!* Her mother would have been proud of how low she had arm-wrestled the rent. Of course, she would have been horrified to find that she had immediately spent the entirety of the serial killer crime scene discount on a downpayment for the BMW waiting for her in the parking garage. And if she discovered the shopping spree that followed, which had bled Mandy's savings back down to zero and maxed out the first of a shiny new deck of credit cards... That would have sent her over the edge with Dragescu.

Mandy shook off the guilt, feeling the silk of her new blouse caress her shoulders as the weight left them. She was free to fly. The chains to the past were slipping off, leaving only the sounds of their clinking as fading memories. The old boundaries had once seemed like impassable cliffs on every side, bidding her wallow in the murky depths by sheer intimidation. But after so many years of struggle, and so many attacks of fear and anxiety that nearly drove her back to the bottom, she had crested the summit and she could see clearly in every direction. All paths were open except for the one that tumbled back into the bondage of the past.

New apartment, new car, new shoes... new man! Her legs quivered and she pulled back from the ledge, her heart pounding as she pulled back the glass door and re-entered the apartment. There was no furniture, nothing to hide the sharp lines and naked edges of the space. The sole concession to comfort, and connection to home, was waiting in the loft above in the form of the mattress. She'd extended her shopping spree and her credit limit to get that bare necessity. It would be her and that mattress alone tonight. *Or would it?*

A translucent cord stretched from the wall to the only other possession, outside her new wardrobe resting in shopping bags in the closet, that had made it across the threshold. It was an ugly old phone, a pale maroon colored thing that had been hiding in the storage closet at the old apartment, but she had been willing to suffer this little contagion of the past to maintain her connection to the outside world... to him.

That connection had felt so thin, so tenuous for the last few days. That second Van Helsing letter had brought the brass squeezing in on them like a vise. Killing was one thing, but mocking the city for its inability to catch him was apparently the bridge too far. They'd had a city councilman, the chief and every colonel in the building sitting in on the briefing yesterday! The room had been so crowded, she could barely make eye contact with Vlad and then for only a few seconds before he was whisked off into an endless series of conferences and closed door meetings. But they couldn't hold onto him forever. Just before that councilman had pulled him away she'd slipped her new number into his hand and the touch of his fingertips had made the hair stand up on the back of her neck.

The phone rang and she jumped. She was breathless when she picked up the receiver.

"Detective Parker?" Her shoulders sank. It was not his voice.

"Yes..."

"This is Colonel Ivy. Sorry to bother you on your day off. Captain Paler said this was the best way to get a hold of you."

"Okay..." A feeling of trepidation began to crawl up her spine.

"If you wouldn't mind coming down to headquarters, there's a few of us that would like to talk to you. Shouldn't take too long."

A few of us? Was this some sort of hearing?

"Sure, I'll be right over." A terrible feeling landed in her stomach as soon as the phone clicked. *Someone reported us.* Valentine - that red-faced creep - might have gone and said something. No, he didn't really know anything and he wouldn't stoop that low, no matter how pissed he was about getting stuck with the grunt work. Could someone have seen them on the roof? She knew guys liked to go up there to smoke and the brass were right there on the floor below. No, they were only there for a few moments, and it was just a kiss!

Just a kiss, who am I kidding? A kiss with a supervisor. A kiss that crossed the red line. *A kiss your career goodbye.* She felt the sharp corners of the naked apartment point accusingly at her. Not even any furniture to hock if she missed a payment on suspension. And if she got canned? Might as well tie the lease and the car note around her neck and throw her into the river. Maybe she'd find another Angel at the bottom and start back over in the Pit. Or maybe Vlad would fish her out and carry her back to his midtown castle and that beautiful garden and that amazing bed...

Vlad. Weren't the male supervisors always at fault in forbidden office romances? Was she actually the victim? *No, don't even think it...* Though perhaps she could sue the city for sexual harassment and split the damages with him.

Am I that ruthless? She stared at her reflection of the silver fridge door, the lone holdover from the ill-fated Ion Dragescu administration and the closest thing to a mirror in the cold emptiness of this apartment. She looked so put together in this creamy silk blouse and the black pencil shirt. And her face! So calm and collected, not even a trace of the panic racking her brain. Even her hair was playing the part today. She was looking at a cold-blooded assassin, a black widow capable of spinning any web and devouring any mate. But inside was she still the same little girl whose every conspiracy - *the boys left the barn door open, I swear!* - collapsed in tears at the first hint of doubt in Mom's voice?

Enough of this nonsense! She set off for the elevators with a determined step. Once she felt the reassuring embrace of that heated seat, the hum of the engine riding up her leg from the accelerator, the rush of the wind in her face... all this paranoia would melt away. And it did. The drive - 80 mph at the gentlest pressure of her feet against her Italian leather insole - went by in an exhilarating flash and she had arrived at headquarters. Ready for what was sure to be a completely mundane sit-down with the higher-ups with no crushingly negative implications for her career - or secret love life - whatsoever. No one saw them. Impossible. *Nonsense.*

Then, with a ding, the elevator doors opened, and she saw the firing squad again. There he was! Walking right at her, his eyes staring down at his brown shoes, one hand thrust into his pocket, the other stroking absently at his beard. He had the air of a man carrying the burden of freshly delivered bad news. *This is really it.*

And then Vlad looked up at her and smiled. There was a little sadness in it but it lit her up all the same. He didn't stop as they brushed shoulders, but leaned over and whispered in her ear. "Knock 'em dead." His free hand snuck down to give her hand a squeeze and then he was past her, still smiling his sad little smile as the doors closed between them.

"Detective Parker?"

She turned to see a fat man with a crown of white hair leaning out of an open door and fixing her with a pair of beady blue eyes. A colonel, but she couldn't remember which one. He gestured her in, holding the door open with one arm. She obeyed. *I'm ready for the chopping block.*

Inside was a spacious conference room with oversized photo

portraits of the higher ups plastering the walls like a gothic org chart. The fat colonel took a seat at the end of a long conference table, completing a row of brass that extended into the shadows at the other end of the room. *The last supper*. He directed her to the hot seat across from them, the only chair on that side of the table. She sat down.

"Thanks for coming in," continued the fat colonel, who then sped through an introduction of the gold collars... Colonel What's-His-Face, Colonel Combover, Colonel Coffee-Breath... and so on until he finally reached the Chief - that crypt keeper looked half-asleep already - and three men in suits, all city councilmen. Two were vamps. The one called Codrescu was staring at her disdainfully. The native, Councilman Garrick, a good-looking man with a presidential sweep of hair, was giving her a big cheesy grin.

Their presence unsettled her - what kind of disciplinary hearing had city councilmen sitting in? Did they have to bring out the big guns when you crossed the red line? She sat upright and put on her best poker face. The silence that followed was finally broken by Garrick, charm dripping off his grin and down his big all-American chin.

"We just finished talking with your partner, Captain Paler." *Supervisor*, something inside her wanted to shout in correction. *I didn't have the power to consent!* "He spoke very highly of you."

Mandy readjusted in her chair. *Not a firing squad after all?* Garrick picked up a slender manilla folder. "You wrote this white paper correct? 'The Great Cloud of Witnesses?'"

She nodded, her eyes growing bigger.

"I gotta say, this is great stuff. I think I can speak for my colleagues on the committee and the leadership at this table when I say this is exactly the kind of direction we're looking to go in with this case."

She opened her mouth, but no words came out. All the righteous denials, all the pleas for mercy, all the repentant hand-wringing her mind had prepared for left her with nothing appropriate for *this*. So she just gaped and nodded like an idiot.

"Quick question before we get started - this opening quote. 'Tantum religio...' - I'm not gonna even bother trying to pronounce the rest of it... Is that Greek or something?"

"It's Latin," interjected Codrescu, his face still twisted in scorn. "From Lucretius."

"'Tantum religio potuit suadere malorum,'" Mandy recited mechanically, finally finding her voice. "It means something along the lines of 'religion has so much power to drive men to do evil.' It's an old saying I had to memorize back when I was learning Latin."

Garrick grinned again and turned from Mandy to the line of brass to his right. "No offense to you all, but I never thought I'd hear the words 'back when I was learning Latin' from a cop." The table laughed, except for the still sneering Codrescu. Mandy blushed.

"Seriously, though, this is very close to the blueprint we want to follow. The steps you lay out for using existing city ordinances and state laws to dissipate this 'atmosphere of hate' fit our situation to a T. The papers, the radio, this televangelist: the filth that these people are pumping out has got to be checked..." He looked up from the manila folder to stare at her with twinkling eyes. "We asked you here because we'd like you to be a part of spearheading the effort."

"That sounds like important work," she replied, her voice breathless in her own ears. "But the Captain and I still have a lot to do on Van Helsing, and I don't want to short-change that. Did he share his... theory on the case?"

Garrick shrugged. "Yes, he did. An interesting idea, but we're not sure it fits the facts-"

Codrescu leaned forward to interrupt, wincing through his sneer as he did. "Captain Paler suffers from a sense of self-deprecation that is prevalent in our community... We have a reflex to view every calamity that befalls us through whatever lens places the greatest blame on ourselves... In this case, I think it may be clouding his professional judgment..." The way he stared at her so balefully on that last aside made Mandy's paranoia surge upwards like an acid reflux attack.

But Garrick cut back in, his pearly white grin and gushing praise extinguishing all fear and insecurities. "Of course we're not here to criticize or micromanage. We love the job you all are doing here. We just want to help focus your energies in the most constructive direction..." Here he glanced towards the Chief, who was staring blankly at the wall behind them. *The man must be over 80!* The colonel beside him jerked upright and began to chatter.

"Yes! And the Chief is totally on board with your input

councilman. That's why we're gonna be creating a task force to carry out a lot of what's in this plan and naturally Miss… uh… Detective Parker's gonna be involved in that in a big way." This declaration prompted a lot of head-nodding from the brass, some more grinning from Garrick, but no change to the sneer of Codrescu. The other vamp councilman seemed happy to sit back in the shadows.

Then the fat colonel at the end stood up and Mandy took it as her cue to get up from the hot seat. Garrick sprang up and leaned all the way across the table to grasp her hand warmly, beaming another huge smile at her. And then the colonel's meaty hand tugged at her elbow and she was headed back out the door.

"What just happened in there?" she asked the colonel as they cleared the threshold. It was an awfully casual question to lob so carelessly across the rank barrier, but his doughy, grandfatherly air discouraged formalities.

"Beats me," he whispered back, good naturedly. "They sprung this little paper of yours on us and I don't think any of us have had a chance to read it."

"They said something about a task force? Does that mean I'm off Van Helsing?"

The colonel chuckled. "You just continue to work with the Captain for now, detective, and let the jaws of the bureaucracy chew on this for a while. We'll let you know as soon as we've got some new responsibilities for you."

"Oh." They were at the elevator now and the colonel gestured her in. She clung to the side rail, her head still spinning.

"Don't look so worried about it, kiddo," the colonel's voice continued as the doors closed. "It's nowhere but up for you from here on out."

17

The Battle of Trafalgar was offering Vlad less and less inspiration as the days went by. The ship, that beautiful ship, was receding further and further into the clouds and with it his place at the helm. The half-naked man at the bottom of the frame was coming to dominate the foreground, his head, almost detached from the torso, dangling upside down over the water, the vacant eyes staring at him.

Vlad had retreated here to the quiet cove of his office hoping the serenity of the space would help him focus. But all he saw on the desk in front of him was a hopeless mess. Valentine was such a worthless hack - a hundred witness interviews and he'd turned in a few skimpy pages of notes, most of them illegible. The biggest item on any of them was a phone number, which Vlad guessed came from a voluptuous art intern based on the gigantic pair of breasts Valentine had doodled underneath it.

Not that his own notes were of any more help. A thousand leads were as good as none. His probes into the narcotics unit to trace the source of the designer drugs in Petricean's car had only yielded more questions. Forensics from the crime scenes had generated an enormous amount of reports, but thus far none of them had led anywhere. Even the Andreanu angle he'd had such hopes for had dead-ended. In a hushed confession over the phone, Andreanu had revealed that he'd spent the nights in question in the company of the lovely Christina Haggerty, an alibi that the preacher's daughter had later confirmed in similarly whispered tones. So caught up was Andreanu in this forbidden romance, that he had little of pertinence to share regarding his erstwhile companions in the Bat Pack. Vlad was initially skeptical of that last claim, but who knew better than he the distracting power of native beauty?

He felt like sweeping all his papers into the garbage and starting over. But there was no time! After that inquisition on the 12th floor, he was surprised he still even had this office. Codrescu was out for blood! If it hadn't been for that Garrick guy smiling and preaching moderation, that goblin-necked creep probably would have demanded Vlad's removal from the case effective immediately. Even so, his presentation on the Bat Pack's drug affiliations and the possibility that the Van Helsing killings might be a dressed-up outbreak of old-fashioned gang violence had landed like a belly flop off the high dive board.

He had tried to convince them that the psychopathic bigot that they were reading in the papers was almost unquestionably a bit, a sick prank. He had no doubt that there were religious fanatics that would have loved to brutalize the young vamps of the Bat Pack - their gleeful debauchery and ostentatious wealth made them natural targets for hatred and envy. But what random nut was going to have the intimate knowledge of each of their routines and their homes that each of these killings demonstrated? And even if such knowledge could be obtained by obsessive stalking over a long period of time, where would such a would-be killer obtain all the skills and experience to complete these killings and execute all these grotesque set-pieces without ever being caught?

The strength to strangle and decapitate young, vigorous men like Dragescu, Petricean and Duma... The cunning to sneak bleeding heads into crowded social venues brimming with security... The wit and sensibility to stage these gruesome spectacles and write these letters... This killer was a renaissance man, a virtuoso. He couldn't be some demented loser listening to the radio... he had to be a vampire. It was not self-loathing to think so, whatever Codrescu said. No, it was the opposite. No native could be capable of reaching such depths of depravity, just as they could not reach the same heights of achievement and virtue. Only a vampire could tread so closely to the realm of angels or demons. Only a vampire could raise murder into an art form.

For once he found himself agreeing with Theresa Russell. There was an art to this devilish work. Casting over the spread of note paper again, his eyes stopped on a glimpse of brown leather poking out from under a yellow legal pad. It was the gigantic portfolio Russell had left for him when he had been too busy brooding on the rooftops to talk to her. *Too lovesick to interview a key witness!* Pathetic! No wonder he was this close to being shuttered back into administrative oblivion.

He flipped angrily through the portfolio. A bunch of tasteless, pornographic arthouse smut meant to shock the rubes. Anything for a reaction. She did have that in common with Van Helsing. He continued to flip pages, his curiosity ebbing, his eyes glazing over. Then, just as he was about to slam it shut, a single image leapt from his peripheral vision and lit up his brain. He flipped back, looking for it and there it was staring back at him. A black and white photo of a sculpture. A bald eagle in brass with wings outspread its beak bending downwards to feed its young. Beneath it however, were not hatchlings, but a row of severed human heads tilted upwards toward the eagle, their eyes open in wide vacant stares, their mouths swollen with food...

It was right there! For Russell, this was probably just her vulgar, self-important way of criticizing America's "cultural imperialism" or some other radical bugbear. But for the killer this was a portal to the Gothic horror sensationalism of Bram Stoker and his Dracula. Vlad grabbed up the portfolio with both hands, electric excitement pulsing from his fingertips through his whole body.

He felt the urge to bust out of this office, find Mandy, snatch her up from wherever she was and share this lightning that danced across his nerves. He sprung from his desk as the door opened and she was there! Her perfect silhouette behind the glass! But then the door opened and it was not her face, but Maggie's, with her plastic smile and shallow eyes and tightly-wrapped bun blocking the path of his lightning like so much rubber.

"The coroner's office is on line one," Maggie chirped. "They've got an ID on that Jane Doe they got out of the river."

"Okay." Vlad looked down at his phone, its wiry coils coated in ugly plastic stretching from the desk to the wall, pulling him back to the ground. He could feel his epiphany escaping, seeking a more suitable conductor for its kinetic energy. "Could you find Parker and send her over?" he added, still clinging to the spark.

He recognized the coroner's voice over the phone. He had an

overwhelmingly nasal voice that gave the impression of a man with glasses so thick and heavy that they pinched his nostrils shut.

"Finally cracked this Jane Doe you asked about last week, Paler," came the voice, pausing to take a wheezing breath. "You sure do like to send us some tough ones! No head for dental records! Fingerprints chewed off by ocean critters!"

Vlad sighed. This guy fancied himself as the Sherlock Holmes of the profession and insisted on setting up every positive identification as an extraordinary feat.

"You'll never guess how we finally got her..." Vlad sighed and waited for the incredible reveal. Finally: "Intra-uterine device! Most people don't know but some of latest of these devices have serial numbers now. Can track them back to the doctors that stocked 'em and the patients where they stuck 'em!"

"Wow," obliged Vlad.

"Yep! Fortunately, we didn't have to go very far. The procedure was done right here in town at the university clinic. The patient was a student by the name of Patricia Currington."

Vlad stared at the door, hoping for Mandy to appear and give him a reason to plug this guy's nose once and for all.

"Here's where it gets more interesting. We pulled her records to determine next of kin. Mother is deceased. No siblings. But her birth father's name rang a bell: Michael Bouchard. Isn't that the guy always on the radio stumping for donations and blood drives?"

Bouchard! So the coroner did have something to knock him back down into his chair after all. A memory jarred his brain as he hit the seat. A few months ago the Reverend had come to him in tears. That huge man broken in front of him, begging for help to find his daughter. And what had he offered? A "warm hand-off" to the pit of despair known as the missing persons office topped off with some false assurances that he'd check back in on it, personally. It wasn't that he didn't feel badly about it - he felt terrible for the old Reverend - but there had been so much else to do and he'd forgotten about the old man's predicament soon after.

Patricia... No, Trish - he'd met her once. Some vamp function he couldn't remember. She'd looked tiny, as almost anyone did next to her father, with the waif-like countenance of a young junkie. He'd figured her for one of Bouchard's recovering street people, dressed up to thank her benefactors, and had been surprised almost to the point of rudeness when Bouchard had introduced her as his daughter. A pretty thing if she could have lost that thousand-needle stare and put a little more flesh on her emaciated frame. And now she was driftwood, dead and decapitated, whether by the hand of a psychotic man or the maniac currents of the homicidal river. *Who was gonna tell the poor Reverend?*

His door opened and this time it was Mandy.

"You wanted me?" She was smiling and her eyes were twinkling. Her porcelain cheeks had that lovely blush of red, not from any embarrassment but from elation. *Still riding that high from the meeting with the councilmen.*

He sighed. The electric epiphany had fizzled from his fingertips, its energy shrouded by the horrible images of the dead girl. This beautiful woman so close to him, so inviting, so full of life, so eager for him, and the coroner has to go and ruin it all. He hung up the receiver, cutting off the nasal voice in mid-drone.

"Yes!" he tried jump-starting the enthusiasm and pushed the portfolio across his desk towards her. Her eyes widened as she followed his finger to the photo.

"I guess she wasn't kidding when she said she was Van Helsing's muse!" Her brows furrowed. "You don't think we should look into her possibly being involved in this, do you?"

Vlad shook his head. "I checked her out after the Dragescu stunt at the opera. She wasn't even in the country when he was killed. Besides, she's never been the type to get her hands dirty. I doubt she even did these sculptures; probably just slapped her brand on one of her intern's hard work."

"And maybe one of those interns decided to continue his work in a new medium... Did we get anything from the intern interviews?"

"No..." He gave her a reproachful eye. "You've got to stop saddling Valentine with all the grunt work. I don't care how much the city council loves your ideas, you're not above the job, Detective."

"Of course. I'm sorry." She looked wounded.

"Also, he did a terrible job. Sometimes I feel like you're the only one around here who actually knows what they're doing." A smile. The wound healed. A warmth came into her eyes and she slid her hands across the desk to take a hold of his.

"I appreciate your confidence in me... I know it was you who gave the council my memo. You didn't have to do that."

He fought back an urge to pull her all the way across the desk, settling for a caress of his thumbs across her fingers. Of course, he could never tell her that he had hated her little memo. As a glimpse of the elegant mind behind those bewitching eyes, he couldn't help but appreciate the keenness of its rhetoric, but the ideas were just the sort of fuel for vamp paranoia that he detested. But he wasn't going to let his opinions stand in her way, not when the political tides were turning and the community was looking for a champion like her. Nor would it hurt him to have his wagon hitched to such a star. *Such a beautiful star.*

He realized that they had just been staring at each other, holding hands. Feeling his own quiver of paranoia he detached and made a show of flipping back through the portfolio, his eyes darting to the windows to see if anyone was looking in.

"I'm going to go do some digging on this," he said, clearing his throat. "Meanwhile, I was hoping you'd take care of another job for me. It's an unpleasant one unfortunately. We need to do next of kin notification on a Jane Doe that got fished out of the river a little while back."

She shot him a quizzical look. "Does this have to do with Van Helsing?"

"Probably not. Her head was gone, but 90% of the bodies we get out of there are suicides and accidents, and a lot can happen to a body in the water. But we just found out she was Reverend Bouchard's daughter."

"Oh, that poor man."

"Yes. It's a very tough situation. And I was really dreading to be the one to tell him. I'm sorry to even ask this of you - it's a rotten assignment. But you'd be doing me a big favor."

She smiled at that. An "I'd do anything for you" smile that made his heart race. She stood up to leave and then leaned over the table to stare down at him. She was wearing a chiffon blouse - almost transparent from up close - and the sweet scent of her hair as it fell in locks that cascaded down around her neck. *Intoxicating!*

"You got it, boss. But you're gonna have to pay me back." She looked down shyly. "I'm working on a project paper for this task force they're talking about - on my off-hours, at home, I promise! If you could swing by later, I could really use your input."

Vlad nodded, feeling a foolish grin break across his face against his better judgment. Remembering his manners, he rose to his feet as she left. He reached down to steady himself on the desk. The electricity of his epiphany had gone, but who could notice it from inside such a cloud of euphoria?

***

The Reverend Bouchard's church was an unassuming rectangle of concrete plopped down on the old drug corner of Washington and 5th like a bunker. It had none of the usual features of a church: no cross, no steeple, hardly even a slope to the roof. All that distinguished it from the fractured stretches of asphalt and sidewalk from which it rose was a small circle of stained glass and a colorful mural coating its sides with pretty, yellow flowers atop bright fields of green. And even this had only its childlike strokes of innocence to separate from the garish graffiti adorning the nearby traffic signal box. Only the little shingle hanging next to the front door that read "Lilies of the Field Community Church" assured Mandy that she had the right place.

She hunted for a good spot for her BMW - there was no church parking lot and she wanted no part of the alley behind the church. She finally settled on the space behind the surprisingly nice black motorcycle parked right in front of the church. Sure, she was blocking the fire hydrant, but she knew a guy at court who would shred any ticket. And besides, what was the chance of anything in this hellish concrete landscape catching fire?

As she walked through the door, the overpowering smell of mildew almost pushed her back out. But she pressed on, her eyes adjusting to the dim light. Past the little foyer, double doors opened on a tiny sanctuary. There was room only for two sets of pews with a tiny corridor running in between. Two dark figures sat just beyond the pews at the foot of an altar, huddled together in prayer. On the back wall behind them, the circular panel of stained glass depicting Jesus carrying the cross cast a reddish glow over their bent heads.

The floor, scarcely covered by a faded red carpet thinned almost to nothing, creaked under Mandy's step. The figures stirred and a voice called out to her.

"Is that you, Miss Mandy?" It was Bouchard's unmistakable baritone. "Go ahead and flick on the lights. The switch is right behind you."

A row of long fluorescent bulbs on the ceiling flickered on, flooding the little space with painfully bright light. Mandy blinked away the brightness and saw Bouchard rising to his feet, followed by his companion. Mandy squinted at him. He had the gaunt figure ubiquitous among the junkies in this neighborhood, but his long, neatly-kept black hair and the expensive-looking sheen to his black leather jacket did not fit the profile. As he turned to her, she recognized the long pale face of Mikhail Andreanu, still bearing the bruises of his beating.

A vampire in church! Kneeling in front of a cross! She could tell from his wide eyes that he was as shocked to see her as she was him. He was no longer the petulant prince in the hospital bed. No, he seemed more like one of the painfully pious boys from back home that had dogged her dad's footsteps on Sundays after church, desperately seeking to pull him away from his family so they could tearfully confess their latest transgressions.

"Andy, meet Mandy," said Bouchard with a smile.

"We've met," said Andreanu, gazing at her with pained eyes, moist around the edges. *Had he been crying?* "She's one of the detectives who came to check on me at the hospital. Any breaks in the case, detective?"

His eyes flashed at her, taunting, the petulance returning in force. Vlad had been so sure that they had rattled him in the hospital, that he'd come forward with some of whatever he was hiding. But he'd kept his distance after making his embarrassing admission about Christina Haggerty. Perhaps he was made of sterner stuff than Vlad thought. Or maybe he was more intimidated by a Bible than a badge.

"Any day now. We just keep poking." She allowed a smirk to curl the edge of her lip. "Not used to seeing a vampire in the house of God... you must have something pretty big to confess."

Bouchard stepped in close, his gentle face hardened, his massive jaw tight. Mandy suddenly felt tiny between the two of them and stepped back instinctively.

"That'll be enough of that now, Miss Mandy," his voice was cool but commanding. "I understand you've got a job to do, but I won't let anyone be interrogated in this sanctuary."

Mandy dropped her head like a chastened little girl. How had she been so easily distracted? How was she supposed to deliver the bad news to him now? It would come out like the worst kind of spite.

"I apologize. I didn't come here to interrogate anyone and I'm sorry if I overstepped."

Bouchard's face softened again. "Don't you worry about it, Miss Mandy. It's good to see you."

"I wish I came under happier circumstances. I've got something I need to share with you, Reverend." She glanced at Andreanu. "It's of a sensitive nature, if you've got somewhere private."

"Don't worry about Andy," Bouchard declared, clapping the vampire on the back. "This man is my brother and we keep no secrets from each other."

Mandy hesitated. Andreanu shifted. "It's alright, Mike," he said. "I've got a lot of work to do and I should get going anyways." He turned to Bouchard and the two shared a hearty embrace.

She watched Andreanu leave, his shoulders slumping, his hands digging into the pockets of his leather jacket, and then turned back to Bouchard. "How do you two know each other?" she asked, eager to postpone the conversation ahead.

"That's a long story," rumbled Bouchard, scratching at his silver beard. "I guess you already know vamps and the church haven't had the best relationship over the years. I've spent most of my years behind a turned-around collar trying to change that. And Andy... he's always been so interested, but he hasn't always had the easiest time. When he found me, he'd just started going to Rivers of Mercy."

"Haggerty's mega-church? I thought they hated vampires." That man's congregation could always be counted on to show up at any vamp function, hollering their bigoted chants and waving their signs. But Andreanu had to have met Christina somewhere.

"I'm not sure hate's how I'd put it. But they've sure put poor Andy through the ringer. Hooked him up to wires and tried to shock the bloodlust out of him. And when that didn't work, they got him starving himself."

The bloodfast. Mandy had read about certain vampires in the old country so overcome with guilt and shame that they would starve themselves to death rather than feed again. No matter how much the vampires pulled away from the hyper-religious communities that always seemed to surround them, a few would inevitably succumb to the pull of the cross. It had never ended well.

"I've met Haggerty a few times and I don't think he's a bad man. It's just his crowd is convinced that these vampires are sinners that can change their ways if we just preach enough fire and brimstone at them."

"And what do you preach at them? Peace and rainbows?" Mandy regretted her snotty tone immediately. Being back in church brought it out of her. But Bouchard didn't seem to mind.

"I dunno about that. I just think there ain't no use trying to change what can't be changed. Vampires are still gonna need blood no matter what we tell them. The only thing that can be changed is what people believe about vampires. And that's what I'm trying to do, in my own way. And Andy's been helping me. He's got a real big heart."

Mandy nodded and a silence fell between them. There was no putting it off.

"The reason I came over here, Reverend, is that I have something very difficult to tell you..." She paused, wincing as she waited for his reaction.

"Oh," he said quietly. "I'm guessing this has to do with Trish."

"Yes. I'm afraid she's passed away. Her body was found in the river last week. It's possible she was... she's been gone for a few months now."

"I see." The big man's voice was deathly quiet but his face was placid and unchanged. "Do you think it's a suicide... or something else?"

"The coroner's autopsy was inconclusive. It can be difficult to tell after someone's been in the water for a while."

"When can I see her?"

"The morgue is ready to release her to any funeral home you wish to use. They can also do cremation right there."

"I don't care about all that right now. I just want to see her." There was a trace of anger in his voice but he remained stone-faced, his glassy eyes vacant.

"You can do that right away then," she said, continuing cautiously. "I should warn you though. I used to work in a funeral home, and it can be very traumatic to see a loved one in this state. There's been a lot of damage and decay. The body is not intact."

Bouchard slumped down to his knees so quietly and so suddenly that Mandy thought the old man might have had a heart attack. Then she heard a rumble in his chest and saw him throw his head back, his cloudy eyes staring wildly up at the little circle of stained glass ahead of them.

"God in Heaven!" The words came out as a roar and then he collapsed prostrate on the ground, his enormous back quivering as he mumbled prayers into the threadbare carpet.

Mandy stood helplessly as Bouchard lay at her feet, babbling incoherently into the ground. She hated seeing people do this. Stuff like this was why she'd always left the next of kin notifications to her partners. Why she always kept to the back room of the funeral parlor when the families came. *Why does he have to be so... pathetic?* She tried to chase the word out of her head. This was totally legitimate grief! A man losing his daughter in a terrible way! Would this be how her father would respond if she were found in pieces in the river? *Shutting his eyes and begging for his imaginary friend to come make everything better?*

She knelt down and gingerly placed a hand on Bouchard's heaving shoulder. Her hand looked miniscule against his frame, like a toddler petting a huge St. Bernard. She patted him awkwardly. How long were they supposed to stay like this? Could she just walk out and leave him grief stricken on the floor?

Then Bouchard reached one of his powerful hands up and took hold of hers. He grasped it so desperately that Mandy could feel the man's heartache, streaming through his clinging fingers and pouring into her. It traveled up her arms and into her chest. She felt it choking at her throat, spinning round her head, filling her eyes. *How was he doing this?* How was he making her *feel*, against her will?

And then he spoke. A single word. Almost a gasp. "Patricia!" He was calling out to her. *She's gone and all you've got is another man's prodigal daughter to comfort you.* She looked up at the stained glass as her own tears began their escape. The expressionless face of Jesus stared back at her, the sun's muted radiance glowing in his eyes.

18

Enoch smiled as he stared up at the popcorn ceiling and let the pain seep out of his back and into the jabbing coils of the mattress. The little white tufts of plaster had taken on a sickly yellow tinge from the slow drip of water from above, stretching out above him like a parody of the beautiful sunset he had just left. *How feeble and corruptible are the works of man when compared to your handiwork, oh Lord!*

Still, there was a certain beauty in even so inferior and accidental an imitation. Had his childlike hand not just completed his own canvas? And now he held it up to the Lord, closing his eyes to project it up through moldy old ceiling and into the heavens. *Look at my work, Father. Bless it. Delight in it. See in it the love of your humble servant!*

They had come to those hills as a rocky wilderness and they had left them as a happy highland of pleasant civilization. They had wrestled with the earth, toiled with the dust, cutting channels through which to send the miraculous power of electricity and life-sustaining waters. They had ripped stones from the clutches of the ground to surround the estate with a wall sturdy enough to last a millennium. And they had done it all by the sweat of their brow.

But Enoch was no mere stonemason. He was a mason of men! And such men! When he had first seen them, he had assumed them to be countrymen, maybe even kinsmen. How wrong he had been! They had shared nothing but skin turned copper by generations spent under the sun. They were a panoply of nations: Mexico, Guatemala, Honduras, El Salvador, Nicaragua, Colombia,

Venezuela... He thought they shared the same tongue, but they could hardly understand each other. Each was his own rough stone, a rock separated from the maternal earth by violent and traumatic disruption, to be gathered and thrown into the back of a truck bed and carted miles away from its origin.

And yet after only a week of struggle against the elements, they fit together as surely and seamlessly as a slab of granite. They worked together, ate together, sang together, prayed together! Layman had marveled at them. "Never seen a crew like this!" The words still rang in Enoch's ears. And Angel Mendoza! The cornerstone!

The first day Angel had been so full of anger and despair, attacking the ground like a man digging his own grave. He'd driven himself to a state of total exhaustion, scorning food and drink to hack wildly at the ground until he nearly passed out and had to spend the rest of the day watching the others work from the meager shade of the truck. It had not been a good showing and Enoch had worried that Angel would not return the next day. It was too easy for a young man to sulk in his bitterness.

But the next morning, he'd shown up with a pair of proper work boots in place of those shiny white sneakers, and not even a trace of sullenness. And he'd worked himself like a pack mule. Not in a frenzy like before but at a steady pace, following the lead of the strongest and picking up the lead when that man tired. And he'd listened to Enoch's every word, obeying without grumbling and then translating to the other men. Layman, who had been so disgusted to see Angel collapsed beside his truck the first day, now beamed whenever Angel showed up by Enoch's side.

And after a hard day's work, the rides back into the city had transformed from the silent sojourn of strangers into a boisterous fellowship of friends, shouting to make themselves heard over the chug of the engine and the rush of the wind. Enoch had even managed to talk a few of them out of the usual late night drinking sessions around the convenience store to join him around a corner table of their second-favorite spot: a seedy Mexican restaurant. Whenever the mariachi band took a break, Enoch pulled out his Bible and began to share, leaning on Angel to translate. The men seemed to like Exodus the best, so that's where they had stayed. Then, when the others had left, full of *frijoles* and the Word but perhaps a little thirsty, Angel had lingered, hungry for more.

195

This evening had been the breakthrough. The others had already left the cantina and the two of them had just come out on the other end of the Red Sea when Angel's head drooped to the table. Enoch had thought for a moment he had fallen asleep, finally out of juice, but when Angel lifted his head, his eyes were heavy with tears. Then the words had poured out of him. He'd had a dream.

In the dream, Angel was in his squad car at the tail of a police pursuit. There was such a mess of blue lights in front of him that he couldn't see where they were going, only that they were chasing somebody at reckless speeds. They were coming up to the bridge but it had been closed off, so they all veered right. Angel almost lost them and was driving around desperately looking for them until he saw a faint blue light disappearing down a great black tunnel that burrowed under the riverbank. He sped desperately to catch up and before he knew it the tunnel had swallowed him up too.

There was only a trace of the blue glow as he accelerated into the blackness of the tunnel. But as he raced towards it, he saw that it was not another squad car but water gushing towards him. As he looked around, he saw the support beams of the tunnel splintering and giving way as geysers of water were shooting all around him. He threw the car in reverse, but the water was coming in from behind him too. Then the whole tunnel collapsed and he had woken up.

From the squad car of his dream to Pharaoh's chariot washed away by the Red Sea was a small jump and Angel had made it as they'd read over the chapter again. The Lord had him by the tail and wasn't letting him go! Did he want to join the chosen people on their path to God or perish in the wrath to come? And, sure enough, right then and there, with the mariachi music blazing so loud neither of them could hear themselves talk, Enoch had pulled Angel out of that flood of darkness and into the marvelous saving light of the Gospel.

Enoch yawned and stretched as the ecstasy of the moment washed over him again. Another soul in Jesus' hand, never to be snatched away. Mandy would be next! Try as she might to run from his grace, the Lord was surrounding her. There would be no escape from his mercy! Enoch smiled. The popcorn ceiling's imitation sunset exuded no warmth, but he was basking in it all the same.

***

Vlad had sounded so excited over the phone. Maybe the malaise that had enveloped him since the Duma killing was finally peeling away. Maybe he really did have a big break this time. He must have gotten a lot more out of Theresa Russell than she did. But he didn't elaborate. Just a "Meet me at Mazzini's" and a click. Was this a celebration or a strategy session? *Or a date?*

Mazzini's was an upscale restaurant on the north end of downtown that Mandy knew by reputation only. It was a favorite of the bigwigs and Mandy feared for her bank account if Vlad, for whatever reason, forgot to pick up the tab. But a swanky place like that at least gave her a chance to wear that black sequin dress she'd tossed on the pile at the end of her shopping spree. *Take it for at least one spin before I have to return it.*

It was valet parking, of course. Dreading that tip, she circled back to one of the rougher parking garages and hoofed it to Mazzini's. That was a mistake in the heels that she'd chosen for this ensemble and she was wincing by the time she walked through the restaurant's big mahogany doors. Dazzled by the enormous chandeliers sparkling above her head, she didn't even see Vlad waving at her from the bar and only turned to him when he shouted her name.

"Well, aren't you a sight to see," he declared, a glass of red in his hand, as he gazed at her admiringly. She noticed with horror that he was wearing a polo shirt and slacks.

"We're not eating here, are we?"

"I was thinking we'd rendezvous here before we headed up to Dan's place," he said, smiling guiltily. "The bartender here always takes care of cops."

Mandy looked down at her dress and the sequins glittered obnoxiously back at her. She felt her cheeks burning.

"I should go home and change. I can't do a person of interest interview in this get-up."

"No!" Vlad caught her hand as she tried to turn away and pulled her closer. "You look perfect. And this will work in our favor. Nothing disarms Adrian Dan like a beautiful woman."

That didn't do anything to stop the blushing, but the urge to get away subsided. Vlad kept a hold of her hand and, leaving the bar, pulled her along after him. She still felt comically overdressed next to him, but the feeling lessened as they walked. He had such a cool elegance in the way he moved that he made even a polo shirt seem classy. And it didn't hurt when the valet pulled up in that gleaming Mercedes and held the door open for her. *Like stepping off the red carpet.*

"You're not going to tell me what's got you all excited?" she asked as he drove.

"You mean besides you in that dress?"

"I'm being serious," she chided, but squeezed his hand anyway.

"I'm not going to tell you just yet. Want you to keep an open mind. I'll take the lead on this one. You just keep his eyes busy and watch his reactions."

They ascended the foothills, mansions flanking them on both sides. Each driveway climbed at a steep angle from the road leading up to forbidding stone walls with wrought-iron gates that block from view all but the peaks and spires of the houses beyond them.

"Dan lives in one of these? He must be worth a fortune."

Vlad shook his head. "These are peasant hovels compared to the Dan estate." He gestured ahead to a hill rising above them. A dense phalanx of cypress trees formed a crown along the broad crest of the hill. Above the tips of these green spears rose two white towers, their surface so smooth that they almost shimmered. From this distance, they looked as if they had been built of porcelain.

As the road curled round the base of this hill, Mandy saw the private drive leading up to the estate. At the base of the hill was a cluster of cottages with the thatched roofs of a European village. Adding to the effect was yet another stonewall encircling this little village of outbuildings and then ascending the hill to surround the porcelain castle in a motte and bailey style. The gate to the outer wall was adjoined by a small stone gatehouse.

A short, stocky man in a chauffeur's uniform stepped out of this gatehouse as they pulled up in front of the gate. He kept his eyes towards the ground, raising his head only slightly to get a look at them. His posture and the sallow complexion of his lowered face reminded Mandy of the gas station attendant from their trip up into the county. She guessed they were not so far away here at the base of the foothills.

"Is he one of the *țăranii?*" she whispered to Vlad. He nodded and barked something at the man in Romanian. The man returned to the gatehouse and there was a sound of a motor engaging as the gate began to roll open.

"Dan must have brought some down from the county. Living out his old world fantasies."

Vlad pulled through the gate and sped past the cottages to begin the climb uphill. He seemed impatient and agitated, and generally unimpressed with the view. But Mandy was spellbound as they drew closer to the house. House... It was closer to a cathedral! She could just imagine on a misty morning, those two towers shimmering like ghostly apparitions. And the wings that stretched for what seemed like a mile on both sides. This place could house an army of servants and still have room to host every VIP in town.

The driveway curled in front of a broad stairway leading up to a beautiful stone archway over the entrance. At the stop of the stairway stood a man in extraordinarily tight white pants and a sharp blue jacket - riding gear, Mandy guessed, after seeing the riding crop in his hand. The outfit, along with the hawkish features that stared down imperiously at them as they exited the vehicle, gave the man an overwhelming aristocratic air. The Lord of the Manor.

"Adrian Dan," Vlad muttered contemptuously as he came alongside her. Dan waited for them to trek up the stairs before speaking.

"I wish you would have called ahead. I was about to go for a ride."

He frowned at Vlad, not bothering to shake his hand and then turned to Mandy. Vlad had been right about the dress - Dan didn't so much look at her as drink her in.

"I can only assume you've come to accuse me of something... I'd invite you in but the house is in complete disarray. We're in the midst of renovation." Mandy guessed Dan was using the royal "we" as she didn't see anyone but servants around and there was no ring on his finger.

"We don't mind," said Vlad. "We'd be very interested in a tour." Dan avoided his gaze to continue to stare at Mandy.

"I have an idea. Unless you've come to execute a search warrant, spare me the embarrassment of entering the house and join me on a ride."

Mandy almost snorted. "I'm not sure I'm dressed for it."

"Nonsense," declared Dan, giving her another once-over. "I

have lady's riding gear in the stables that's sure to fit you. Come."

He strode off without waiting for a "yes," heading towards a large outbuilding beyond the Manor's east wing. Mandy looked over to Vlad, who had already begun to follow. She trotted to keep up.

The stables themselves were as big as a mansion, and nearly as beautiful as the manor, constructed from the same gleaming white material. A pair of *țăranii* opened the giant wooden doors for them. They opened onto a broad hall with a vaulted ceiling that rose at least twenty feet above them. *An awfully grand set-up for a few horses.*

Dan directed her to a little room off the hall where she found a closet full of riding clothes, mostly men's but with a single ensemble pushed off to the edge. She held it up - it was clean at least and it looked to be her size, though there were no labels. She tried on the pants, the soft white fabric clinging to her leg. She glanced at herself in the full-length mirror as she slipped on the blue jacket and tied her hair into a tight bun to fit under the black velvet cap. *Not bad, just need a British accent and a fox to hunt.*

She stepped out to find Vlad speaking to Dan with hushed intensity. Dan seemed to be ignoring him to gaze admiringly at the white stallion his attendant was leading towards them. Dan turned to Mandy as she approached, his expression unchanged as he took in the wardrobe change.

"I knew it. You and Irina must have sprung from the same mold."

"Irina Nasturel?" The vision of those two pale bodies staked together near the riverbank flashed back into Mandy's mind, her stomach surging in revulsion.

"The one and only," he said with a leering smile as he admired the exposed shape of her legs. "They're yours to keep. She won't be needing them anymore."

Mandy fought off an urge to run back to the dressing room to strip the dead woman's clothes off of her. Her eyes darted to Vlad. *Can you believe this creep? Let's get out of here! But he only shook his head.*

Dan mounted the white stallion gracefully, towering over them as his attendants slunk away and returned leading a pair of brown mares, both notably smaller than the big charger. Vlad struggled to pull himself up, hopping on one leg with one foot in the stirrup as the attendant held the horse by the bridle. Mandy mounted her mare with ease before the attendant could come around to help.

The advantages of being a country girl.

She looked down at Vlad's desperate little dance and couldn't help but smile, thoughts of Irina Nasturel subsiding. At last he made it up, his face flustered and his lips twisted in irritation. Dan was already gone, his stallion setting a quick pace out of the stables.

"Try and keep up," Mandy told Vlad with a mocking smile and she sped off after Dan, leaving Vlad to struggle behind her.

She brought her horse alongside Dan as they curled round the east wing of the manor.

"You ride pretty well for a garlic-eater," Dan said, glancing at her as she kept to his brisk pace. "Where did you learn?"

"Growing up in the sticks.""

"You're making my countryman look foolish," he said throwing a smirk back at Vlad, falling ever farther behind. "And I'm very grateful to you for it. What a disgrace that man is."

She rode on in expectant silence.

"Do you realize he's waged a personal vendetta against my family? Locked up my father and my brother, destroyed our family businesses…"

"Aren't those just the risks that come with dealing in vice?"

"That was trumped-up nonsense. No one can run a casino without running into a criminal element. But only my family's business was targeted and punished. It was personal. The petty jealousy of a little man, trying to raise his station at our expense." Dan glowered, shaking his head bitterly. "He ruined us."

Mandy raised her eyebrows. They had just swung round the east wing and an immaculately landscaped garden stretched out in front of them, protected by a low stone wall. Studded with statues and gushing with more fountains than she could count, it reminded her of the pictures she'd seen of the Sun King's garden at Versailles.

"Looks pretty good for ruins."

"It was a ruin!" Dan declared. "All this used to be an abbey, but it had been abandoned for years. He didn't even get a chance to work on it. Your partner back there threw him in jail. This was the only piece of property the state didn't confiscate because they didn't want to deal with it. Before we started back working on it a few years ago, it all looked like that." He pointed to the wilderness of closely clustered trees that spilled out around and behind the gardens, filling the broad valley that sloped down from the manor and between the surrounding foothills.

"It's very impressive work." Mandy's admiration was genuine. "I take it the family business has recovered somewhat, then?"

He shot her a sharp glance. "I see Paler has been filling your head with his ideas about me. As if a man can't make a success in investments without launching some vast criminal conspiracy. It's small-minded, plebeian thinking like this that holds us back, detective. These money-grubbing men see a man above their station and they can't imagine how he got there other than by their own habits of clutching and grasping and stealing."

"Maybe you could broaden this pleb's perspective, because I'm having trouble imagining it, too."

Dan brought his horse to a stop and contemplated the dark forest rolling below them. "Then you've been spending too much time scrounging in the dirt. It is among men just as it is in nature: resources flow upward from the very bottom and downward through the very top. The great families have their roots deep in the earth, reaching the hidden underground springs and feeding on the minerals laid down for centuries. At the same time our branches stretch high above the rest and absorb the sun's purest light. The beasts that slink on the surface, fighting tooth and claw over a few grubs and mushrooms cannot comprehend how we grow so tall and strong."

"Maybe we need to trim a few of those branches to let some of that light shine down on the beasts."

He turned to stare at her. "You must give me the chance to elevate your perspective sometime…" He paused, mulling and then spoke again. "It's my birthday this weekend. We're going to have a fox hunt here at the estate to celebrate. I'd love to have you here, if you're free."

A fox hunt? What century was this? A laugh tickled Mandy's throat. But before she could respond, Dan's eyes darted away from her to narrow on something behind them.

"The fool!" he cried suddenly. "What does he think he's doing?"

Mandy turned to see Vlad some distance behind them, riding his mare under a trellis arch over a footpath leading back to the house.

Dan clicked at his horse and the stallion took off at a gallop towards Vlad. Mandy followed at a slower pace at first, but feeling the wind in her face and hearing the wonderful sound of hooves striking at the earth, she gave her a squeeze of her knees to see how fast she could go. What a rush!

Dan reared to a halt at the arched entrance. Vlad had hitched his horse to the post outside the entrance and proceeded in. Dan did likewise and called out angrily to Vlad. "Where do you think you're going! Get out of there this instant! "

"Just a minute," called Vlad. "I need to use the restroom." He disappeared into the house.

Dan took off after him at a furious pace that Mandy, now dismounted with the rest of them, struggled to match.

The door they entered was an exit off the back of the kitchen. Dan took a hard right down a hallway, his heavy boot falls echoing off the marble floors.

"Is it this way?" she heard Vlad's voice from somewhere further down, followed by further stomping from Dan.

"You have no right to be here!" Dan's voice rose, almost a scream. "This is a warrantless search!"

Dan made another sharp turn down another hallway, Mandy still jogging behind him. She stopped as he disappeared around a corner, catching her breath. No use tagging along to this ridiculous cat-and-mouse game. If Vlad was willing to go to such absurd lengths, there must be something worth finding. She threw one more glance down the hallway to make sure Dan hadn't doubled back and slipped off towards a door ahead of her.

This door opened on what Mandy guessed was once the nave of the abbey. Colonnades of pillars connected by graceful arches ran down both sides of the space, rising up to the vaulted ceiling. She guessed there had once been frescoes running along the walls and ceilings, but all those had been stripped away or plastered over and now all the surfaces gleamed a sterile white, crisscrossed with the dark browns of the exposed wooden beams. Before her, the pews had been cleared out and floors redone with a creamy marble that spilled out like a pool of milk.

There was the beginning of an art gallery and rows of statuary occupying the space, much of it still bearing the styrofoam casing of packing material. Mandy heard the tap of her boots on the marble fill the nave as she stepped gingerly toward the central display. As she closed in on the first uncovered statue, she was startled to find its face insectoid, a thousand bulbous eyes bubbling atop an otherwise classically rendered nude Olympian.

Turning she saw she was surrounded by a grotesquerie of avant-garde pieces. This was a circus masquerading as a gallery. She noticed the pieces were arranged in a concentric pattern, with two outer rings of statues surrounding a single large exhibition in the center which was covered by a tarp. She tiptoed to the center, taking one more look around for Dan and then lifted an edge of the tarp.

It was a large sculpture, composed of multiple pieces that gleamed dully in the thin sliver of light that snuck under the raised edge of the tarp. But it was still too dark to see. She gave the edge a pull, gently at first, worried that some fragile component of the piece might come loose and shatter on the ground. Nothing feeling awry, she gave it a firm tug and the whole tarp came free in her hand. She gasped.

There in front of her was the brass sculpture she had seen in miniature on Vlad's desk. In the portfolio it had seemed so small. Here it was disturbingly large and lifelike. Five brass heads were arrayed in a circle that gave the impression of a Satanic pentagram looking up to the enormous American eagle in their center. Up close, Mandy could see that the neckline of each severed head was ragged, as if cut with a serrated edge and sitting in a little brass pool of blood. The eagle, which was almost as big as she was, was lowering its cruel beak towards the head closest to her.

This was Van Helsing's handiwork. She was certain of it. It was as if someone had bronzed the victims' heads and put them on display. And the eagle - it even looked like Dan! Who but a psychopath would purchase something like this, much less make it the centerpiece of their home? It was a shrine... *A trophy case.*

She felt a desperate urge to cover the thing back up and run. She heard the sound of Dan's voice approaching from somewhere deep in the manor - *hurry up!* Her fingers fumbled with the tarp until at last she got a decent hold. But how to get it back on? She could barely reach the top of the eagle. She tried to whip the tarp up like a tablecloth, failing once and then twice and then at last getting the edge above the brass feathers.

Mandy skittered away, the pitter-patter of her feet against the marble so loud in her ears. She had just made the hallway when she saw Vlad coming towards her, waving his hands above his head apologetically. Dan was on his heels, his face contorted in anger, his teeth bared. Mandy blanched at the sight, panic telling her feet to run.

"Next time I'll just take a piss on the hydrangeas in the garden. I'm sure you won't mind that," Vlad's voice sounded irritated, but he shot Mandy a mischievous smile.

"There won't be a next time!" Dan's voice was nearly hysterical.

"Yeah, don't bet on it, pal."

Vlad turned and dug in his heels as Dan stopped abruptly in front of him. Mandy had a terrible feeling that Dan might reach out and strike him down then and there. But something in Vlad's manner calmed her.

There was Dan, the tall, hawk-faced terror, springing like a demonic caricature from one of her trashy vampire thrillers. He was taller than Vlad and broader too, but Vlad was uncowed. Standing with his arms crossed, his head cocked, staring with amused contempt at the demon glowering down at him. It was a showdown between Dracula and Phillip Marlowe.

Dan held his snarl for a moment and then relented. His lips uncurled into an unpleasant smile and a blank look descended over his face. Dracula had lost this round. Mandy felt a sigh escape her lips.

Vlad smirked and turned away, catching Mandy's elbow and pulling her along with him as he exited the way they had come in. Their pace quickened. Vlad was almost skipping. After they cleared the manor and reached the cars, he finally stopped and turned to her, his eyes ablaze.

"Did you see it? I couldn't find it."

"Yes." She was breathless. "It's awful to look at. Did he buy it from Russell?"

"Buy it? He made it. Russell wouldn't give me a name, but she did tell me it had been a vamp intern that had worked on it with her. I did a little digging and the only two vamps enrolled in her program at the time were Dan and Mikhail Andreanu."

The blood rushed to Mandy's brain. *Dan and Andreanu?* She opened her mouth to speak but Vlad shushed her.

"Let's get out of here before he starts getting paranoid."

They caravanned out of the foothills and hugged the river back towards midtown. Mandy's eyes stuck to the road as her mind raced. *Dan and Andreanu!* Had the Bat Pack turned on each other in an incestuous orgy of violence? Van Helsing, the letters, her "great cloud of witnesses" - all a ginned-up hysteria to distract them from some internecine war over drugs and money? And she'd fallen for it! Her embarrassment was soon overtaken by something more like elation. He was nearing their grasp at last! Vlad was ready to pounce!

They pulled into the keyed entrance of her building, descending into the shadows of the parking garage. Vlad was quizzical as he got out.

"Isn't this Dragescu's building?"

"The same," she chirped, summoning the elevator. "Wait until you see which apartment I got."

He shook his head in disbelief. "You wouldn't believe the deal I got on it! Besides, it helps keep me focused on the case."

He glanced down at the riding pants clinging so tightly to her legs as the elevator rose. "And you're wearing Nasturel's clothes. You must have a thing for dead vampires."

She reached out playfully to grab at the loose end of his polo. "Some of the living ones are alright too."

The elevator stopped with a jerk, toppling her against him. She rested there, feeling his heartbeat against his chest. The doors opened and she stepped out first, snagging Vlad's hand and pulling him along.

The door opened on a beautiful sunset filling the still empty space with a gorgeous crimson glow. The advantages of no blinds. She had a little loveseat propped in front of the view, but that was it for furnishings other than the mattress upstairs - everything else would have to wait until the next paycheck.

She pranced to the bar counter separating the kitchen from the rest of the room and snatched two glasses to go with the bottle of cheap Moscato she'd picked up the day before. She filled them both and handed one to Vlad. "To celebrate breaking the case."

He scoffed but took the drink. "We haven't broken anything. All we know is Dan has exceptionally bad taste." He wrinkled his nose at the sweetness of the wine. *I was on a budget!*

"Don't be so modest. I was thinking about it the whole way over and he fits perfectly. Your whole theory. He uses his buddies to build back his father's drug trade. Duma's chemists supply the product, Dan and Petricean move it, Dragescu launders the money. I don't see how Andreanu's involved, if he even is. Maybe he's just a user. But the rest of them: they all get rich."

"So what makes Dan decide to turn on his friends?" asked

Vlad, with the smile of a teacher enjoying his student's dawning realization. He took another sip of the Moscato, this time without disapproval.

"Can't just be the usual greed... There was plenty to go around." She emptied her glass and poured another. *Liquid intuition.* "Was he covering his tracks?"

"We put his father in jail on the testimony of his native confederates - who all got immunity," said Vlad, with a trace of regret. "The bloodbath with the Cottonmouths... I initially thought that was for turf, but now I think it could have been severing a link with the past. Then it continued with the intimates of his inner circle."

"But if he killed all of the people helping him, doesn't the money dry up?"

"Not if he already went legit. Dan's one of the biggest shareholders of Dumatech. Their legal drugs will make far more for him than the street stuff ever would."

"I think he was alluding to that when I asked him about his money today," she mused, remembering his forest speech. She stared down her freshly emptied glass and saw those ridiculous riding pants bending in its concave bottom. "You know I left my new dress over in his stables. Maybe I can use that as an excuse to go back and do some more digging."

"As if you'd need an excuse. He couldn't take his eyes off you." She thought she saw a flicker of jealousy in his eyes. It made her smile.

"He did invite me to his little fox hunt this weekend. I should go. There's a few things I could do to win his confidence. Just need a wire." She ran her hand down her stomach and down her hip, as if searching for a place to put it.

Vlad stepped closer to her. "You need to be careful. He knows he's a suspect. He'll know what you're doing. It wouldn't be safe."

She brought her hand up to rest on his chest, feeling his heartbeat hammering at her fingertips. "There's a lot of things that aren't safe. Doesn't mean we shouldn't do them." She looked up and his lips were on hers, his arms sliding around her waist and pulling her so tight she could hardly breathe. But she didn't want to breathe! She wanted to disappear into him, to feel every part of him become part of her.

A sudden shattering of glass separated them. She'd dropped her glass. Its shards had scattered over the floor, jagged edges pointing upward. Vlad looked briefly at them and then pushed back towards her. She held him off gently, gasping to catch her breath.

"Sweep those up for me, would you." She looked down, still catching her breath. "Give me a second to change out of this stupid outfit." *Don't say slip into something more comfortable.*

She gave him another gentle push and headed up the stairs to her loft, grabbing the rail to steady her quivering legs. She reached her loft and was embarrassed again by the state of it. A mattress on the floor - *you're not 19 years old anymore!* She staggered to her closet and rested her spinning head against its frame as her fingers flipped through its contents. All these fancy clothes and nothing to wear. But the clinging clothes were so hot and confining - she couldn't get them off fast enough.

She dropped the clothes on the floor like spent gloves and took a deep, ecstatic breath as the cool air swept over the glistening beads of sweat that covered her. Her eyes shifted from the clothes rack to the mirror on the inside of the door and took a look at herself. *You know he wouldn't mind if you came down just like this.* A little smile played on her lips and she pushed the door open wider to get a better look at herself.

She gasped as the face that stared back at her was Vlad's, standing with eyes wide behind her at the top of the stairs. She snatched the closest article to her - a thin satin robe - and covered herself as best as she could, turning to face him as she retreated backwards into the closet.

"What do you think you're doing?" she said, almost whispering. She felt her cheeks burning their brightest red as heat coursed through her.

"I'm sorry," he said, but he did not look away. "I was hoping you had something to wrap on this." He held out his hands, one clasped in the other, and Mandy gasped again. His right palm was gushing blood from a deep laceration.

"Stay right there," she ordered and turned into the closet, closing the door just enough to get her robe on properly. She dug into the back corner behind another box of clothes and unearthed her first aid kit. She emerged from the closet with a bandage and an antiseptic spray and gestured for him to come close.

"You realize you can get pretty sick if this blood gets anywhere in you," he said, holding back.

"Get over here before you bleed out!"

He gave her his hands and she pried them apart, the blood flowing freely over her hands and onto the floor.

"Sorry to bleed all over your floors. There's a lot more downstairs, too."

"It's alright. It's not like these floors haven't seen vampire blood before." He winced as she sprayed the wound and then pressed the bandage in place. "How did you manage to do this anyways?"

"Some sharp glass you had down there."

"Yeah, but I didn't think you'd impale yourself on it." She wrapped the gauze, tilting her head as she applied the clasp to hold it in place. Vlad leaned forward as she did, bringing his lips so close she felt them brush her ear.

"It was worth it just to see you," he whispered and his lips descended to her neck and he began to kiss her. She caught her breath and leaned into him - she couldn't help it. She couldn't move.

Then his unbandaged hand, still wet with blood, rose to caress her cheek as he continued to kiss her neck. His fingers traced a soft crimson line from her cheek, hugged the curve of her chin and then her neck until it reached the nape of her satin robe. His fingers pushed - so slowly, so gently - and the satin began to give, inching to her shoulder and then falling all at once, like a waterfall, onto the ground at her feet.

His hand followed the downward path of the satin, the heat of his fingers driving away the cool of the air and suffusing her with warmth. Her mind was gone. The intensity of feeling had overwhelmed her ability to think. She was weightless, electrified, a paralyzed conductor of his energy. Then, from some other dimension, came a sound. A rude, jarring sound that forced her brain to consider it and evaluate it and pull back from a total surrender to ecstasy. It was a knock on the door.

She nuzzled into Vlad's neck, burrowing away from the noise. His arms slipped around her and pulled her in close. The knocking ceased and her lips found Vlad's, and in them a portal back to that feeling!

BAM! BAM! BAM! The knock again, louder this time. Mandy sighed.

"Who do you think it is?" asked Vlad, his voice ragged and

breathless in her ear.

"I don't know. Maybe if we ignore them, they'll just go away."

Another set of bangs battered away at that hopeful notion.

"You'd better get it," whispered Vlad and Mandy nodded. She pulled away from him, covering herself shyly as she stooped down to pick up her robe. She put it back on and tied the rope belt this time, throwing one more look at Vlad as she did. His expression was unreadable in the dim light, but his eyes still glinted as they fixed on her.

"Wait here," she said as descended the stairs and headed for the knocking. She opened the door a crack, hiding herself and her skimpy little robe behind the door. Her stomach dropped as she saw the face. Angel.

He brightened at the sight of her. "Hey Mandy!" Like a little boy. "I brought some of the stuff you left behind at the apartment."

He gestured beside him and sure enough there was her old chest, an old suitcase and something else wrapped in a wrinkled old bed sheet. He stood next to it with a stupid look of pride. *Look how nice I am! Don't you wish we still lived together?*

"Thanks, Angel, but I was just about to jump in the shower," she said, glancing back towards the loft. "If you could just leave it out here in the hall, I'll grab it when I'm done."

"And let somebody steal it? Nah, I'll just put it inside for you." He didn't wait for permission, but pushed one of his broad shoulders through the door and dragged the chest and suitcase in behind him. He deposited them just inside the door and then lurched back out to grab whatever was in the bed sheet. He left a booted foot in the doorway, as if to keep Mandy from shutting it on his backside. *I would never.*

"Look what I brought for you," he said, coming back in with a big picture frame in both hands. It was her mall kiosk masterpiece - the surrealist painting he hated. He looked down at it, shaking his head. "You know I never like this thing, but this past week I've just been staring at it. Makes me think of you." He looked up at her now with a terrible tenderness in his eyes. Mandy couldn't help it - she looked away.

Angel's eyes narrowed on the red line traveling down her throat and then saw the blood on her hands. He grabbed at her hands impulsively and pulled her towards him.

"What happened? Are you okay?" That tenderness again. It used to be that whenever she dressed in something like this robe, Angel would paw at her like a piece of meat, almost drooling. But now, even with the satin parting in front of him like the red sea, he could only look at her hands, searching for a wound.

"I'm alright. You don't have to worry about me," she said softly, stopping before *it's not my blood*. "Just a little accident with a wine glass." She pulled back from him, crossing her arms over the robe.

He nodded, his eyes dropping to the ground, suddenly bashful. "I'm sorry for barging in on you like this. I've just been searching for any excuse to come see you. There's a few things I have to say to you."

His eyes flitted up to her now, not pleading but earnest. She met them apologetically. "I understand but now is really not a good time, maybe -"

"I'll be quick," he interrupted and dug both hands into his pockets to pull out a folded piece of paper and what looked disturbingly like a box for an engagement ring.

"I bought both of these a few weeks ago, right before everything went to hell. This..." he unfolded the paper and handed it to her. It was a real estate listing with a color picture of a squat little house behind a white picket fence.

"And then this..." He produced the velvet box and flipped it open. A diamond flashed out at Mandy and she backed away, shaking her head.

"Angel, let's not-"

"No, no!" Angel interjected. "I'm not proposing. I know I'm not the sharpest tool in the shed but I'm not completely blind. I know you don't want this..." He trailed off for a moment, looking down into the ring and then back at her. "But I wanted you to know that this is what I wanted."

Mandy squirmed and shot another glance up at the loft. Vlad was right there, perched on the banister like a hawk, just watching them. How did Angel not see him?

"I'm gonna go now," Angel continued, pocketing the ring. "If you ever need me, that's where I'll be." He nodded his head at the listing in her hand and then ducked out the door.

Mandy closed and locked it behind him. She leaned her forehead against the door and sighed. Vlad descended the stairs behind her and she turned to face him. The glint in his eye had dulled.

The daring "where were we" died on Mandy's lips - the energy was gone, blown away by whatever ill wind Angel had let in as he blundered around with his newfound emotions. And now Vlad was standing there like a beleaguered tourist ready for his vacation to be over so he could get out of here and back to the comforts of home.

She suddenly felt ridiculous standing in satin lingerie standing between her boss and the door. Like a bimbo flight attendant. *Your emergency exits are here, here and here.*

"I guess we have a lot of work to get to," she said ruefully. "So many distractions."

"Yes." Vlad was awfully quiet.

"I can finish getting dressed and then can gameplan some more on Dan... if you'd like."

"I would..." He looked almost sad as he continued. "But we should pick this up in the office tomorrow morning."

"That's probably best." Her shoulders slumped as she felt a miserable weight descend on them.

Vlad reached his hand out to take a hold of her drooping shoulder and she felt a little jolt of the earlier electricity. She straightened up.

"Thanks for the drink and the bandage," he said, flexing his palm under the gauze. "Make sure you get my blood off you. I'd hate for you to get sick." And with that he moved her gently out of his way and opened the door.

As he left her with his sad smile, the weight returned, this time heavier. She forced her way to the kitchen counter and the bottle of Moscato - *half-empty* - and grabbed it before succumbing to gravity and sliding all the way down to the floor. She stared vacantly out towards the glass door and the balcony view beyond. Like her, the sun had sunk to the edge of the horizon. The warm crimson glow burned faintly for only a few moments and then it disappeared, granting the descending blackness control of the sky.

19

Simion Codrescu noticed with some alarm that his foot was keeping time to this idiotic "hip-hop" beat pulsing from the radio. He forced it still, glancing at his driver to make sure he hadn't noticed. He sighed - even the slightest concession to his lower nature must be resisted. He hadn't reached this moment - the cusp of victory! - by giving into the seductive rhythms of the jungle!

Codrescu was not much for American culture, and certainly not for its vulgar tendency to glamorize seedy underground criminals and their environs. Gangsters! Thugs! Pimps! Still, he could not altogether deny their charm. After all, a similarly debased culture had produced as its antithesis a man such as Eliot Ness. A crusader! Purger of filth! Civilization's guardian angel! Codrescu had a picture of him hanging in his office, right next to his diploma from Yale.

If he'd followed his youthful ambition and gone into law enforcement instead of law school, perhaps he would have been another Untouchable. He would have stood proud and tall - as much as his twisted back would allow - above the morass of corruption and degradation that consumed every order of American society. He would have wielded his unflinching propriety like a whip to bring the American beast to heel. Garroting Capone with the red tape from the tax code - imagine it!

But going into law enforcement would have meant walking in the shadows of lowborn adventurers like Vlad Paler, rogues who sought the glory their birth had denied them by throwing off their natural station and going native. Of course, the path into law had not been without such contaminants - one had only to look up at the innumerable billboards for the odious Dacian Popa and his army of ambulance chasers to be reminded.

Nevertheless, Codrescu had persevered, plotting a path as tortuous and crooked as his spine to achieve his goal with his dignity intact. And here he was, a colonel at the head of his own little regiment, sallying forth to push the regressive Haggerty and his cult into the river. *Back to the swamps from which you came!*

He glanced from his driver back into the interior of the transport van. A dozen men in riot gear ready to his bidding. Two vans filled with more of the same followed behind, ready to spill out on the riverbank at his command. He admitted to himself a certain appeal to their dark figures, almost medieval in their black helmets and body armor. Like the knights commanded by his ancestors. If only his back had allowed him to don the armor and take his place at the front of the charge. Alas, his only armor was the immaculately tailored black suit he had donned for the occasion, his only weapon the rolled-up court order in his hand.

Codrescu felt the breath catch in his lungs as the van rolled up on the fringes of the park. The river was still out of sight, but they were already surrounded by the overflow of parked vehicles covering both sides of the road. There were so many! *Too many?* Codrescu felt beads of nervous sweat breaking out under his collar. Would this little riot squad be enough, or would they be chewed up and spit out by the torrent of retrograde humanity waiting for them at the river?

As they rounded the corner, the river came into view, or rather the swarm of people where the river used to be. Rising from their midst was the long black neck of a camera crane, a brontosaur emerging from the primordial swamp. The crane swung out over the crowd and fixed on a man approaching from the road. He wore a white robe with the cowl thrown back for the sun to set his red hair aglow like a heavenly crown. Codrescu didn't need to see the fleshy face or hear the voice thundering from his barrel chest to recognize Pastor Jim Haggerty. The crowd parted for him and the long retinue of white-robed elders that followed closely behind him. Elders... or were they armed security guards ready to bust some heads as soon as Codrescu made his move?

Behind him in the- van, the Lieutenant in charge of the riot

214

squad had pushed his head as far is it would go into the cabin to peer around Codrescu and take in the scene. Codrescu realized now it had not been mere wounded vanity when the man had been so irritated to cede "shotgun" - such a ridiculous term! - to him.

"We shoulda got him before he made it into the crowd. We're gonna get ourselves surrounded." Unspoken but understood was the rebuke from their earlier conversation - because of its location and the sheer numbers it attracted, Haggerty's mass baptism at the river made for an unpredictable and potentially disastrous theater for operations. They should have waited for the next weekend when Haggerty would be back and contained in his megachurch facility. There they would have clear paths for support if things got out of hand, a staging area for detaining any rowdies and exits less deadly than a raging river. Codrescu hadn't merely dismissed the Lieutenant's concerns - they were valid - but the man clearly had no eye for the bigger picture.

Now might be the last best chance to make a meaningful show of strength - a "splash" in native parlance - to the hatemongers. If Paler had any sense, any decency, any consideration for the community's long-term welfare, he wouldn't have rushed headlong into this lunatic conspiracy theory. A vampire detective pinning the greatest outbreak of anti-vamp hatred on a fellow countryman? And not just any countryman, but a lightning rod like Adrian Dan!

When word reached Codrescu that Paler was planning some sort of "sting" operation for Dan this weekend, he had done all his power to scuttle it. But Garrick had refused to go along - never trust a garlic-eater! - and Codrescu had no choice but to rush ahead with today's venture, however risky it appeared to the Lieutenant. To dither now would be to cede the narrative to the most hateful operators in the city, men like Haggerty. Thirty years of work would be undone. The community would be driven back into the shadows by the cross-wielding mob! *Never again!*

Seized again by the urgency of the moment, Codrescu cut off the Lieutenant - still blathering about tactics - and gave the order. He swung his door open and set his loafered foot to the graveled shoulder before the van had even stopped. He had to lead! He heard the rear doors open and the other vans jerk to a halt beside them. His men emerged, scrabbling about like beetles until they formed into a tight phalanx around him, riot shields facing the crowd. The crowd had turned to watch them with a bewilderment that was rapidly transforming into a buzz of alarm.

The corridor through the swarm that had opened for Haggerty and his vanguard was still open. Codrescu pointed a finger at it and turned to the Lieutenant who had pushed his way beside him. "There's our path. Let's go get him and then we can disperse the crowd."

The Lieutenant grimaced but barked the order and the phalanx marched into the gap, a shiny black bullet headed straight for its target. Even with his twisted spine, Codrescu stood almost a head taller than the men around him. They had exacerbated the difference by moving forward in a half-crouch, leaving Codrescu exposed like a tortoise's head extending out from the shell. But at least he could see and he saw that Haggerty and his men had reached the river and now turned to watch their approach. Haggerty stood waist deep in the brown waters of the river, flanked on either side by his men.

Suddenly Haggerty's voice rang out above the noise of the river and crowd with a clarity and resonance that shocked Codrescu. Where were the speakers? It wasn't humanly possible for a man to have a voice so naturally powerful.

"Folks! Let's give a nice warm welcome to our friends in law enforcement today." He opened his arms magnanimously towards the phalanx as the roar of the crowd surrounded them. As it subsided, his voice rang out again. "Y'all didn't come dressed for a baptism!"

A melodious laugh sounded from within his barrel chest and was echoed a thousandfold by the crowd. The noise pressed in on Codrescu from all sides; only the chink of the shields and the stomping of boots kept it at bay and gave him room to breathe. His phalanx continued to push forward until finally coming to a stop at the river's edge. Codrescu pushed to the front, shuddering as cold water lapped into his loafers. He glanced behind him and noted with a nervous thrill that the crane-mounted camera was directly on him. His moment would be televised live!

"Mr. Jim Haggerty," he shouted, disconcerted at how weak and muffled his voice sounded. He turned back and snapped his fingers impatiently. "Give me the bullhorn," he hissed into the phalanx. It was produced and he turned back to Haggerty, bullhorn to his lips and his free hand raised high to brandish the mighty paper.

"Mr. Jim Haggerty," he began again with impressive volume. "I have in my hand an injunction, ordering you to cease and desist all broadcasting on public channels, effective immediately."

A silence followed the declaration. Haggerty just stood there, his clean-shaven jowls frozen into a blank expression. As the silence lingered and Haggerty continued to stare, Codrescu began to worry he hadn't been heard. But he shouldn't have to repeat himself! They had plastered every front page, saturated every local media outlet with their announcement of the new ordinances banning any conduct that fostered a climate of hate and violence. Haggerty had to know they would be coming for him after all the bigotry he'd poured out in his last televised sermon. *Your day of reckoning is here! Why won't you say anything?*

At last Haggerty spoke, his face calm but his voice still so impossibly loud and commanding. "I see the paper in your hand. By whose authority do you make these orders?"

"By the Municipal Court of River City and my own as a duly elected representative of this city," he declared with conviction, only to realize he had forgotten to press down the trigger of the bullhorn and that his voice had floated off on the river. But Haggerty wasn't listening anyway, taking advantage of the pause to swell up his barrel chest. *A hot air balloon.*

"I recognize a higher authority," boomed Haggerty with theatrical gravitas, sliding his hand behind his white robe - Codrescu felt the Lieutenant flinch behind him - and into the pocket of his button-up to produce a slender blue-bound booklet with an American eagle embossed on the cover. "The Constitution!"

"Our forefathers had the foresight to protect us from our forked-tongued, fine-feathered friends in the government." His powerful voice rolled mellifluously over every 'f.' "In their wisdom, they guaranteed freedom of speech and freedom of assembly for all their posterity, and none shall infringe on those rights."

"You can take it up with your attorneys," Codrescu fired back, remembering to press the button this time. "But as of now you must immediately cease broadcasting and disperse this crowd or face -"

"But I appeal to a higher law still!" roared Haggerty, his stentorian baritone overwhelming even the bullhorn. In his right hand had appeared, apparently ex nihilo, an over-sized bible, which Haggerty now raised above his pocket Constitution. "And if

George Washington himself stepped out of his grave and commanded me to cease speaking the truths in this book, I would tell him…" The big chest swelled again, rearing up for a huge blast. "YOU'LL HAVE TO KILL ME FIRST, GEORGE!"

The crowd broke into a deafening chorus of hoots, hollers, chants and amens. And this time it did not dissipate, Haggerty waving his arms at them like a river shaman commanding the waters to roar. Codrescu retreated back into the phalanx, buffeted by the noise. The Lieutenant grabbed a hold of his shoulders and shouted in his ear.

"We need to get out of here!"

Codrescu shook himself fiercely, shedding the impertinent man's grasp. "Nonsense!" he shouted, his voice rising in a piercing shrillness that cut through the cacophony of the crowd. "Arrest him!"

The Lieutenant stared at him, incredulous. "Do it!" Codrescu screamed. The Lieutenant nodded reluctantly and adjusted his chin strap. On his command, the phalanx advanced another step into the muddy waters, their boots squelching. Codrescu couldn't help but be caught up in the line - to stay put would have meant facing the crowd alone.

As their black tide inched forward, the biggest of the white-robed men detached from Haggerty's side and blocked the path to Haggerty with his refrigerator-sized body. He crossed his arms, combining with the sharp angular lines of his crewcut to make him almost perfectly rectangular. The rest of the white robes line up alongside him.

"Get out of the way!" the Lieutenant growled into the megaphone he'd reclaimed from Codrescu. But the white robes stood motionless. Codrescu saw the Lieutenant draw his black wooden baton and raise it. The rest of the riot squad followed suit. They took another step forward and the rectangular giant suddenly sprang forward. He moved with frightening speed for a man half-submerged in water. His eyes blazed right through the cops to fix squarely on Codrescu. It was a look of intense hatred.

Codrescu quailed at the sight. He knew this man. Peter Dykstra. The savage, vamp-bashing brute he had helped to drive from the police department and only just fallen short of getting him thrown behind bars. And now only a few feet of river and a single line of police separated them. Codrescu moved to put another line of men between them, but his feet wouldn't move. He looked down with horror to see that his loafers were encased in mud that sucked at his ankles and clung to his feet.

Dykstra's gigantic rectangular form was on them now, his shoulder lowered. He hit the line and Codrescu could hear an "ooof" as the impact drove the air from his men's lungs. A sweep of the white-robed arm and the cop that bore the brunt of the initial collision, already bowed, was cast aside like a piece of driftwood. There he was, the native Goliath, face-to-face with the quivering vampire. Codrescu squirmed helplessly in the mud, his body tensing for a blow.

Codrescu gasped in relief as the Lieutenant shouldered his way in front of him and thrust the tip of his baton into Dykstra's midsection, a Roman legionary driving his gladius into the belly of a barbarian beast. The giant's eyes bulged as the air left his lungs and the Lieutenant followed up the strike with a fierce swing at his head. Instead of the crack of wood against bone, however, there was only a slap as the baton struck the palm of Dykstra's hand. Wrenching it free, Dykstra crumpled the Lieutenant with a blow to his helmet. Then, flinging the baton away, he wrapped both hands around Codrescu's neck and pushed him straight down into the muddy water.

Codrescu's arms beat weakly at the hands that drove him down. He felt the suction of the mud pulling the back of his head, then his ears and temples. He felt a strangled relief as he saw the rest of the riot squad surrounding them. Their batons descended on the giant's shoulder and back like a black rain. But the huge bigot didn't even seem to feel them. The hatred in his eyes grew only more intense and he pressed down all the harder.

As Codrescu slipped further into the river's mud his panic began to subside. Yes, it had reached his forehead and would soon climb his chin. But it was soft and cool to the touch. It extinguished the fiery nerves around his throat where the fingers continued to squeeze. It enveloped his misshapen back in a gentle embrace that bid painful gravity to depart. His mouth, which he had opened to scream and gasp for air, began to fill. It felt like pudding as it gurgled down his throat on its way to his lungs. He had ceased to breathe when the mud finally covered his eyes.

***

As much as Enoch cherished the 23rd Psalm, he had never cared for tending his herd animals and the chaos surrounding him now reminded him why. The Lord had blessed him with height - no Zacchaeus, he could almost always see above a crowd and had been looking forward to a good view of Pastor Haggerty baptizing these thousands. The preacher may have been too much of a holy roller for Enoch's comfort, but he couldn't shake his admiration for the way brought in the harvest. The swelling of the flock! And Angel among them!

There was a downside to Enoch's height, however, and his high center of gravity now rendered him helpless against the tides of stampeding sheep surrounding him. If the tide had been toward the open space of the road, Enoch would have been content to drift along with it, but the crowd was of two minds. One current pushed madly toward the road and escape, but the other, dragging at his calves like a mighty undertow, surged towards the bedlam on the river. Pulled in both directions at once, Enoch's balance had become precarious and he'd already come close to falling. If he did, he would not long survive the pounding of so many hooves.

Those immediately behind him seemed to favor a push to the river and so Enoch kept himself moving with them, his feet taking short, choppy steps as quickly as he could make them. His head still high, he could see where this tide was taking him and he prayed for a way to change course. He looked around desperately for Angel. They had been separated in the initial chaos and he could not see him in the maelstrom. Some twenty yards ahead but moving straight towards him was the angry black cloud of policemen.

As they moved, their batons swept out in front of them, cutting through the churning masses of believers like oars through the water. But so thick was the crowd that no matter how many fell or flew from the blows, fresh waves were pushed forward. Behind the baton-swingers, Enoch saw a second line with sinister metal canisters that sprayed a reddish mist into the crowd. The batons would drive some back, the spray would send others rolling to the side and then the police would move forward into the breach. Then there would be a fresh wave and the terrible cycle would begin again.

Enoch saw that it would soon be his turn to face this human buzzsaw. For the first time, he felt the panic of the stampeding herd, not as the external force pushing him forward, but as something inside. An overwhelming need to go somewhere, anywhere other than towards the pain ahead of him. His legs, crushed together by the force of the crowd, were helpless to carry out the manic demands of his nerves and so the panic traveled upward, causing his body to writhe, his arms to push, his hands to claw. A voice inside, deeper than the fear, pled with his mind not to give in to these bestial urges, but he couldn't stop. *Is this what the unrepentant sinner feels on his descent into hell?*

The man in front of Enoch now met the dreadful edge of the oncoming policemen. He too was manifesting the wild throes of panic but could not escape the impact. Enoch realized with horror that it was own hands that were pushing this man to the brink. There was an awful crack as a baton struck one of the man's flailing limbs, followed by a howl of pain. Then a black arm reached out from the cloud and flung the man to the side.

Enoch saw them now. Wide eyes full of fear and anger staring straight at him. Jaws set grimly. Enoch at last gained control of himself, folding his arms to stop their gyrations and focusing all of his strength to push back against the tide that forced him forward.

"Move!" barked one of the police, raising a black canister menacingly.

"I'm trying!" Enoch shouted back, hearing the anger in his voice.

Then another voice sounded from out of the crowd. "Enoch!" It was Angel.

Enoch turned his head and saw him. His stocky body knifed through the crowd with heartening speed, like a lifeguard cutting through the waves with powerful strokes of his arms. He broke through to Enoch's left, braving the edge of the saw to charge towards Enoch.

"Off-duty officer! Off-duty officer!" he shouted as he moved and the stinging batons pulled back. But the black canister did not. As Angel reached Enoch, the gloved black finger squeezed and a red spray gushed from the can. Angel's bulky frame acted like a shield, cutting an Enoch-sized hole in the mist.

"Off-duty officer!" Angel continued to shout, his voice choking on the spray. He pulled Enoch with him across the narrow slice between the cops into the crowd until they were at last free of the choking throng and running with a loose pack towards the river.

When they reached the water, Angel stumbled and fell to his knees.

"My eyes. Oh, God, my eyes!" Angel cried. Enoch knelt beside him and winced as he saw his face. His cheeks and eyelids were grotesquely swollen. The eyes that his fingers rubbed so desperately blazed a crimson red. Enoch placed a hand on Angel's head and pressed down gently, guiding his face towards the surface of the water. With his other hand, he cupped the cool water and brought it to his inflamed eyes. Angel let out a gasp that sounded like the hiss of steam.

"More!" he yelped. Enoch pushed his head under the water, watching its muddy swirls surround him as he almost disappeared. Then he pulled him back up as he spluttered.

"I know this wasn't the baptism you were expecting today," Enoch said sadly. "But John the Baptist did warn us that the Lord would baptize us with fire."

"Does this count?" Angel said through panting breaths, his eyes pinched shut as he tried to look at Enoch. "Am I baptized now?"

"In the name of the Father, the Son and the Holy Spirit," Enoch said, breaking out into a big smile. "So glad to have you in the family, brother."

Enoch leaned over to embrace him, clapping him heartily on the back. His eyes stung - it was probably the effects of the spray - but the pain was extinguished by the tears of joy that now welled in them. *Praise the Lord for this fine young man, for rescuing him from the darkness in time for him to rescue me!*

The two continued to embrace at the river's edge as Enoch's tearful eyes watched the pandemonium rage behind them. Joining the screams and shouts of the crowd were the *chunks* of tear gas launchers followed by thick clouds of white smoke rising from within the stampede. He praised the Lord again, this time for gusts of wind coming off the river that swept the gas up and away from them.

He turned to look out over the river before closing his eyes to pray. Just before his lids closed, a disturbing sight slipped through at the corner of his eye. A body floating motionless in the water, face down. His eyes blinked open and he searched for it. It was nowhere to be found. Sighing, Enoch closed his eyes again. *Lord have mercy!*

20

It was not an unusual sight to see the foothills half covered with the battered white work trucks and vans. Even on a weekend like this one, there were more than a few workers needed to keep the avalanche of new construction rolling. All the new money coming off the river or descending from towers down seemed to end up here in the hills. But if a hawk-eyed observer were to peer into the tinted windows of the white Econoline parked at the foot of the hill below the Dan estate, he would see not Mexican laborers but suspiciously white and clean-cut young men busy about the work of surveillance.

It was much too crowded inside the van for Mandy's liking. There were the techs at the recording bay, Valentine and Reese eating greasy hamburgers that stunk up the small space and Krause, the matronly female detective they'd taken on loan from Vice. Adding to Mandy's claustrophobia was the wire corset that Krause had rigged her up. It felt like an anaconda wrapped around her torso, crushing the life out of her. At least they had ditched the tight riding pants and given her one of those old-fashioned pairs with the poofy breeches to hide the rest of the recording equipment. She looked a little like a British cavalry officer, but it was a small price for a little breathing room somewhere on her body.

The one person she wished was here had taken a powder. She saw him through the tinted glass, leaning against the hood of the van, smoking a cigarette. Even in splattered overalls, he made a terribly unconvincing workman. His posture was too elegant, his hair too perfectly groomed. Even the way he smoked a cigarette - it looked like he had just plucked it from a silver cigarette case, not snatched it from a crumpled pack of Marlboros. He was a refugee from a GQ cover in a bad disguise.

But there was nothing phony about his broody silence. It's not that he had spoken to her. In the days since their little bedroom farce, they'd spoken exhaustively about today's operation. But it was always at an arm's length. If their hands so much as brushed against each other, he would pull away like she was a hot stove. And if she dared bring up anything outside of the scope of their work, he would find an excuse to disappear. Krause just lifting the hem of her shirt to trace the path of the wire had been enough to drive him from the van.

He stirred now and opened the van door. "It's time," he announced as he climbed in, a dullness in his voice.

Valentine hopped over to the driver's seat and started the engine. The sound woke the butterflies in Mandy's stomach. She tried to squash them with the same self-talk she'd rehearsed over the past several days. *This is just Vlad going overboard on his pet theory. We've got nothing on this guy. It isn't a crime not to have an alibi. Possible drug connections don't make you a murderer. No law against having a psychopath's taste in sculpture. This is a sting without any sting.*

But it didn't take this time. She felt her stomach lurch as Valentine put the van in gear and they rolled forward. Why had Vlad gone over escape routes so exhaustively, if there wasn't any real danger? Why had he insisted on code words to have them come running? This was no ordinary interview! This was a rendezvous with a possible serial killer. They'd be riding around in the darkness of the forest while her closest back-up would be several hundred yards away on the other side of a castle wall. Her only protection would be the tiny .380 she'd strapped to her right thigh - another reason to be thankful for these silly poofy pants.

The van stopped in front of the power substation tucked in between two hills. They'd hidden her car in the gravel drive behind it.

"Here we go," Mandy muttered to herself as Reese peeled the sliding side door open for her.

"Don't forget this!" shouted one of the techs. She turned to see him extending his arm to hold out a small black pocketknife. It wasn't for self-defense, though Mandy guessed it could help her in a pinch. Underneath the bezel that held the glossy RCPD emblem - the pocket knife was one of the staple items at the gift and gear shop near headquarters - was a miniature transmitter Vlad had asked the techs to install. He'd been enamored with the notion of GPS trackers since he'd seen them in Mrs. Petricean's house, and a little research showed them to be within the bureau's equipment budget. It was the only part of this operation that Mandy thought made sense, though she wondered at how it would work encased in all that metal. There was also the ridiculousness of handing the person of interest his tracker as a birthday present.

Mandy slipped the knife into one of the tiny pockets of her riding jacket and moved to the door. A hand caught her as she stepped down onto the gravel. It was Vlad. He pulled her close, whispering in her ear.

"Be very careful." The fearful urgency in his voice set her nerves a-flutter all over again. *Does he know something I don't? What am I walking into?*

She could still feel the heat of his hand on her arm as she drove out from behind the canopy of transformers and electrical wires and towards the Dan estate. The little *țăranii* village just past the gates had transformed from a sleeping medieval village into a crowded parking lot, filled with the incongruous combination of shiny sports cars and gigantic pick-up trucks pulling horse trailers. The crowd too was made up of repeating sets of odd groupings; tall, pale young men and women in spotless riding gear, surrounded by swarms of swarthy *țăranii* in their traditional peasant garb.

Mandy parked behind one of the horse trailers and stepped out of her car, uncertain what to do next. One of the *țăranii* swarms quickly surrounded her, their peculiarly downcast faces encircling her as they spoke in murmurs. Whether their language was Romanian or thickly accented English, she couldn't make out a word of it. Eventually they gave up and migrated to another freshly arrived car, leaving Mandy standing alone. Vlad had prepped her for everything but he'd somehow managed to omit the instruction for whatever this was.

"Wasn't expecting to see you here," a voice said from behind her. She turned to see the figure of a man above her, seated on a glistening black stallion. "Adrian doesn't usually invite the police to these sorts of things… Or are you undercover?"

Mandy smiled as she squinted to see his face with the morning sun blazing just behind his head. With a click of his tongue he nudged his horse forward and his face came into clear view: it was Mikhail Andreanu.

"I didn't think so, but maybe I am. I seem to be completely invisible to everyone but you."

"The *țăranii* aren't used to outsiders and everyone else wouldn't want to be seen with anyone wearing those pants."

"They're comfortable!" she protested lamely, checking again to make sure the outlines of the pistol and the recording equipment were not visible beneath them.

"A horse is also a traditional accessory to these functions, but I don't see yours."

"I was hoping to borrow one from Mr. Dan."

"Mr. Dan!" he scoffed. "He doesn't deserve your politeness. I'm guessing he brought you as his own personal fox."

"I guess I don't deserve politeness, either."

"I'm sorry. This place brings the worst out of me. Let me start over." He pulled on the bridle to bring his stallion abreast of her and dipped his head in a bow. "Mikhail Andreanu at your service. Would you do me the honor of allowing me to escort you to yonder dark castle?"

He pushed himself back on the saddle to make room and leaned over to offer her a hand. She hesitated, casting a glance at the steep rise of the hill and road leading up to Dan's house. This at least would be better than hoofing it up there on her own and sticking out even more like a sore thumb. She grasped his hand and caught her breath as he yanked her up with a single motion.

It was a snug fit for both of them in the saddle and Mandy spent the ride fretting over whether Andreanu could feel the bulky mic wire through the back of her shirt. *No big deal, just cuddling up with Dan's co-conspirator!*

"You do a lot of hunting with Dan?" she asked, feeling the nervousness in her chest, but not in her voice.

"Unfortunately," he said sourly. "It's a habit I'm trying to break."

"Being out here in the sun with the fresh air, getting exercise… Seems like a pretty healthy pastime to me."

"Now imagine it from the perspective of the fox."

"I don't have any sympathy for the fox. I've seen too many

chicken massacres."

"The man kills the fox, the fox kills the chicken, the chicken kills the worm, the worm eats the man. There's no escape from the circle of death." His voice was sharp with irony but the overwhelming gloominess came through. It was not hard to see him as one of the punk rockers who's theatrically despairing screams had been all the rage when she first moved to the city. *Melodramatic, but a killer too?*

Andreanu slowed his horse as they came to the edge of a crowd of riders near Dan's stable. He maneuvered around the group, keeping his distance, and brought her inside the stable. There stood Dan, stroking the neck of his white charger. He left the horse to one of his attendants and strode towards them, his eyes narrowing on Andreanu.

"I'm so glad you made it, Miss Parker." Without asking, he extended both hands to grab her about the waist - right on the wire! - and brought her gliding down to the ground. "If I'd known you were here, I would have come and fetched you myself... I could have spared you the clutches of the angel of death up there." He threw a venomous look at Andreanu.

"I thought you'd be happy I saved you the trouble and brought your birthday present to you," Andreanu said coldly.

"Forgive the crudeness of his mind and the rudeness of his manners, Miss Parker. There's an unfortunate streak of barbarism that runs in his bloodline and bursts out from time to time. Not unlike your man Paler. Makes him do things like show up to a man's house uninvited and insult his guests."

"You know I could never miss one of your hunts," Andreanu called out as Dan steered Mandy away, guiding her deeper into the stable.

"No matter how fine a man builds his stable, he can never be rid of the flies," Dan declared loudly as Andreanu rode off.

"I thought you two were friends," Mandy said, watching him go.

"Friends? Never. But I've never been rid of him. Since I was a child, he's been my shadow."

He looked away from Andreanu's retreating figure to take her in. His eyes were so penetrating, so invasive that she worried anew he would spot the secrets wrapping around each of the curves he seemed to enjoy so much. She put her hand in her pocket and felt the cool metal of the RCPD knife. *Now is as good a time as any.*

She pulled it out and thrust it toward him with more "back off, creep!" energy than she had intended. He stepped back instinctively, taking up what looked almost like a fencer's pose.

"Happy birthday," she said with meager enthusiasm, opening her palm to show it off. Dan laughed at the sight. "We had it made specially for you," she added, rubbing the glossy RCPD with her thumb.

"You guys put one of these into my father's back. Nice to get mine from the front." He snatched it out of her hand and held it up to the dim lights hanging from the vaulted ceiling of the stable. "I like it," he said finally, sliding into a pocket-slit in his skin-tight riding pants. "Maybe I'll even use it today."

Hopefully not on me. Dan placed a hand behind her back and led her towards a stall in the rear. Inside was a dazzling Arabian with a smoky gray coat that made it look like a storm cloud, quite the change from the plain brown mare she'd had her last time out. "We call this one Trouble. I saw how fine a rider you were, and I decided I could trust you with her."

Mandy felt another flare of nerves. *Assassination by horse.* But a look at the Arabian's big gentle eyes staring curiously at her set her at ease. "She's beautiful."

After the *ţăranii* attendants saddled Trouble, Dan and Mandy mounted up and joined the waiting throng. At the sight of Dan, the whole group set out for the wilderness beyond the gardens, trotting at a leisurely pace. Dan mingled widely, leaving Mandy to hang out at the fringes.

It was a much different crowd than the riding parties she used to comb the back country with. Tagging along with her older sisters, they'd ride around with all the teenagers from church, following dried up riverbeds and wandering through the spooky ruins of abandoned farms. They'd ride any creature they could get their hands on. Esther had a fine mare, but the rest of them settled for any old nag, pony or mule. Now she was surrounded by thoroughbreds, mounted by a different set of thoroughbreds, getting ready for a fox hunt. She felt like Eliza Doolittle gone to the races, a flower girl shanghaied into the upper classes.

Dan returned to her from his wanderings and together they moved to the head of the troop. As they crested the hill, she heard the yipping of dogs and looked downhill to see a bustling pack of black and tan terriers led ahead by yet more *ţăranii* servants. They pulled and yanked at their leashes in every direction, looking like helium balloons at a kid's birthday party.

"Have you ever been on a fox hunt before?" he asked.

"Does a foot pursuit count?"

He laughed. He pointed ahead to the brush that filled the V of the widening valley that led into the forest. "We're heading towards the covert where the fox is hiding. And by hiding I mean waiting in the cage where my keepers stashed him."

"Doesn't that take the romance out of it?"

"Yes, but when nature doesn't provide us with prey, we must make do for ourselves."

"Must we? If there are no more foxes to hunt, couldn't nature be telling us to evolve and choose a different pastime?"

"Such as?"

"Something less old-fashioned, less bloody. Didn't your friend Pavel Petricean enjoy tennis? Or how about boating like Alex Duma?"

"Or running like Dragescu?" There was a mocking lilt to his voice. Mandy shrugged. *So much for subtlety.*

"All of those men hunted with me whenever they had the chance," he continued. "A hunt is like a whetstone. It hones a man's instinct and smoothes the jagged edges of his animal nature. It readies him for higher calling of civilized life."

"Letting out Mr. Hyde to help Dr. Jekyll get through the day?"

"I don't understand the reference," Dan said, quickening his pace to pull ahead of her. Mandy gave Trouble a squeeze to catch up. They had reached the dogs and Dan dismounted to walk among them, handing his reins to one of the servants. The dogs surrounded him with slobbering tongues and eager paws that muddied his pristine clothes. He laughed. Mandy rode up alongside him, feeling Trouble tense in the presence of so many dogs.

He turned to her and looked up, a smile on his face. It was the only time she'd seen happiness in his face. "I know why you're here," he said, a hint of menace returning behind the smile.

She returned his look, innocently, but she felt herself tensing along with Trouble.

"I know what you saw in my gallery and I can only guess what theories Paler has been telling you about me," he continued, watching for her reaction. She did her best to keep her face blank.

"You police are just like dogs. Once they're on a trail, everything else disappears until they have the target in their jaws. It doesn't matter to them if it's the wrong trail."

"It matters to me."

"Then get Paler to call off the chase. He has the wrong man." His hawkish face hardened as his voice took on the tone of a command. "Those men were my companions, and Irina too. They were loyal to me. I would have no sooner harmed one of them than one of these dogs."

"I understand that, but..." she gulped, feeling for a moment like a fox facing the hunter and his hounds. "Do you understand what it looks like to have a piece like that in the center of your home?"

"A man should never have to explain anything he keeps in the privacy of his home."

"It would be in his best interest to do so when so much is at stake."

Dan's eyes took on an unpleasant intensity. Mandy shifted in the saddle and threw a glance behind. The sight of the rest of the party approaching set her at ease.

"It is none of your business, but I assure you it has nothing to do with the deaths of my friends. It was the product of a youthful passion that has long since cooled."

"Then why make it the centerpiece of your home?"

"There's much more to my home than the gallery," he reproached her. "But I will admit a fondness for it. I've devoted most of my years to the pursuit of wealth and pleasure and I aim to devote many more. But I like to have a reminder of what could have been if I would have continued in the arts." He looked down at his hands, as if marveling at their skill.

"And how do you explain the uncanny resemblance to the crime scenes left by Van Helsing?"

"I don't," he said with a coldness that unsettled her.

"Adrian!" came a shout from behind them. "Are you going to spend the whole morning flirting or are we going to hunt?" The rest of the party had clustered around them, the ground trembling under the impatient stamping of hooves. Dan smiled contemptuously at them and remounted. At his command, the dog keepers moved forward to the shrubs ahead.

As they approached, the dogs began to pull and strain at their leashes, wild with enthusiasm at the scent of something in the underbrush. Dan pulled something from a pocket in his jacket and dangled it in front of Mandy.

"This gadget opens the fox's cage. I like to give the prey a healthy head start." As he pressed a button on this remote, a sound of metal scraping against metal came from somewhere ahead of them and the dogs began to bay. The keepers, with as much as a dozen leashes to each, were almost swept from their feet.

Dan snapped his fingers and another attendant appeared. He handed him the remote in exchange for a slender brass horn. He brought it to his lips and gave it a blow. The noise made the hairs stand up on the back of Mandy's neck.

At the sound the dogs were unleashed and they took off at a dash, accompanied by a frenzied chorus of yips and barks. The party started off after them, Andreanu emerging from their midst on his gigantic black steed to lead them. Mandy gave Trouble a squeeze to follow but Adrian reached over to grab her reins and slow her.

"Best not to follow the crowd," he said casually, but his hand kept a tight hold on the reins. "Most of my dogs are incompetent. Bred for their pretty coats and their long legs, not their noses. The ones to watch are the twins." He pointed to a pair of terriers, smaller and squatter than the rest who had peeled off from the charging pack to meander towards the forest, noses to the ground.

Dan gave a click and his horse took off after the pair at a slow trot. Trouble, his reins still clutched in Dan's hand, rode abreast. In a few moments they were under the thick canopy of the oak forest, the rest of the party out of sight.

A cold sweat broke out under Mandy's corset. She straightened her back, hoping it would escape down the small of her back and her anxiety with it. *He doesn't mean to harm me.* All the same her hand snuck to the pistol hiding under riding breeches. *Let him try it.*

But still the sweat poured. *What did Andreanu mean when he said I was another fox for him? Was he trying to warn me?* She wanted to tell Dan that they had nothing on him but Vlad's hunches, an absence of alibis and his peculiar taste in artwork. Attacking her here in the darkness of the forest would only serve as a confirmation of these suspicions. The thought chilled her. *Am I just bait?*

"Over there!" Dan shouted, pointing ahead to a dip between a gnarled pair of oaks. As they came on it, the dip widened into a ditch, almost a ravine that plunged down toward a small creek.

Dan finally let go of her reins, but Trouble was already committed to the slope, following the breakneck pace of Dan's charger. Down they went, Mandy squeezing the saddle with all her strength to keep from tumbling headlong. She realized she had been holding her breath all the way down when she gasped for air as they reached the creek and the ground leveled out. But before she could gather herself, Dan and his charger had bolted off down another gully and Trouble followed without any prompting from her.

The brush grew thick around them, branches stretching across their path, pulling and scratching at Mandy as they hurtled on. Dan's stallion blazed ahead, heedless, Trouble insistent on following close on his heels. Mandy tugged on the reins, to no avail. Then, lifting her head to see where they would turn next, she saw a low hanging vine drooping directly in front of her. Before she could duck it had wrapped itself securely around her chest and yanked her bodily from the saddle.

She landed on her side with a crunch. Fortunately, the earth below her was soft, thanks to an abundance of moss and mud from what she guessed to be a little underground tributary of the creek behind her. She realized that the crunching sound must have come from the tape recorder on her thigh. She placed her hand over the poof in her pants and felt what must have been a hundred shards of plastic underneath. *Not like he said anything of value anyways.* She only hoped whatever radio transmitter connected her to the van hadn't been broken too.

She placed a palm against the damp ground to push herself upright, placing her weight gingerly on one leg and then the other. *Nothing broken but the recorder!* She felt her feet sinking unpleasantly into the muck and looked around for an escape to higher, drier ground. The gully was surrounded by thick covering of shrubs, their arching branches denuded of leaves by winter but so thickly intercrossed and heavy with dormant vines to shrink the space into a claustrophobic tunnel. What had Dan been thinking leading her into a place like this? Even if she had been an excellent rider, only someone familiar with the terrain could be expected to navigate these gullies without mishap.

Was it a trap? The speed, the sudden turns, the way he'd yanked the reins. She hadn't even seen the dogs once they'd entered the forest. Had he hoped her head would strike one of the thicker branches and knock her out cold? Would he circle back to finish the job?

The distant sound of hoofbeats from somewhere above her accentuated that last unhappy thought. Asthma attack! That was the code for mayday Vlad had given her and it now rang through her head, pressing against her lips in panic. No! She wouldn't give in to mindless fear. He had no reason to attack her. If he was circling back it would only be to help her after he saw Trouble riderless.

She pushed the words back down and pushed on. The gully only deepened as she went further, its sides climbing higher and the imposing thicket of shrubs still blocking any exit. The squelch of her feet in the mud was uncomfortably loud in her ears. Panic or not, she didn't want to be so easily heard. As the gully descended still further, she heard a trumpet blow. Dan's riding horn. It seemed close.

Another stab of wild paranoia told her the horn was for her. *I'm the fox! They're coming for me! Asthma attack!* She dismissed it but quickened her pace. After what felt like several minutes of running through the mud, the gully widened and the shafts of light broke through the canopy. Mandy stumbled out into this clearing, panting for breath.

Her eyes scanned the area as she bent over, hands on her knees. She startled at an unexpected sight. Plopped in the middle of the clearing was a large metal cage, so rusted it blended in with the dead leaves that carpeted the ground. She guessed it was one of Dan's hunting aids; it had a sliding rail for the door attached to an electric motor. But it was much too large for a fox. Mandy straightened up, realizing that the cage was a good match for her own dimensions.

The unmistakable snort of a horse sounded from above her, filling her anew with dread. She whirled around, searching the ridge that surrounded the clearing until she saw it. A huge black horse filling a gap in the brush, and atop it, Mikhail Andreanu staring down at her. The spears of light piercing the canopy struck his long black hair and gave it a preternatural glow that unsettled Mandy almost as much as his silence. She felt her breath catch in her chest.

"What happened to your horse?" he said finally. His voice was quiet, but it carried clearly through the silence of the forest.

"I got tangled in some vines. Just trying to find my way back."

"It's a long way on foot," came the quiet voice again. "And it's not safe to be out here alone." He started to move towards her, his face shadowed as he passed out of the light. Mandy felt a sudden urge to run but settled her hand on the .380 instead.

"What are you doing out this way picking up a straggler like me? I thought I saw you leading the pack."

"Not all of us are here to hunt a fox." He was within a few yards of her now, towering over her on the huge black horse, his face still hidden in the shadow. This time she couldn't stop herself - she took a step back.

Andreanu dismounted and took another step forward, walking into one of the spears of light. The sun cut away the shadows and with it the halo of menace that had accompanied him down the slope. His brow was furrowed and his eyes dark, but they were glistening with what looked to Mandy like genuine concern. She relaxed, her hand drifting from the .380. Andreanu's eyes scanned the foliage behind her, as if waiting for someone to pop out. She turned to follow his gaze, her eyes falling again on the big, rusted cage.

"This thing isn't for foxes, is it?"

He hesitated, his big brown eyes settling on her. "Adrian likes to offer his guests a variety of prey," he said, finally.

"What kind of prey are we talking about? Deer? Wild boars? People?" she tagged the last with a sly smile, but Andreanu didn't return it. He only studied her more intently.

"You wouldn't be here if you didn't know there was something deeply wrong with Adrian," he said, speaking slowly, as if considering each word carefully. "He doesn't believe morality, or the law, applies to him or his friends."

Mandy probed his brown eyes for whatever he was holding back. He seemed ripe for the prodding. "Do you think there might be circumstances that would ever lead him to hunt his friends?"

Now Andreanu laughed. An unhealthy laugh, soaked through with bitterness or spite, Mandy couldn't tell which.

"You think Adrian Dan is Van Helsing?"

"Is it so ridiculous?" Mandy tried to get a lock back on his eyes, now veiled as he lowered his head to chuckle derisively. "There's motive, opportunity, ability…"

"Do you really think he would have written those letters?

234

There's not a drop of moral sensibility in his blood." His eyes were back on her and alight with a new emotion. *Scorn? Passion?*

"Maybe he's got layers you don't know about. Did you know he used to be an artist? Have you seen the piece he's got in his gallery?"

Another laugh, this one more incredulous than the last. "He showed you the heads?" She nodded. "You know that whole idea was based on a joke. It was supposed to be satire. But Adrian was so obsessed with Theresa, he took it seriously and made it to try and impress her. And he couldn't even do that right. He had to pay the other interns to finish it after he made a mess of a beginning."

"So he doesn't have the sensibility of Van Helsing... Maybe he had an artsier accomplice... Weren't you one of Russell's interns as well?"

He smiled ruefully. "Every regret I have in my life has something to do with Adrian Dan. If I were ever to embark on a murder spree, I'd choose a different partner."

Mandy opened her mouth to give him another prod when rustling in the bushes overhead made them both turn. Andreanu took a step forward, as if to shield her. The rustling grew louder and multiplied, the sound of dead branches snapping under heavy feet. Then, from the corner of her eye she spied a dark figure breaching the edge of the clearing. It was a man in a black bulletproof vest with a black pistol clutched in his hand, held up at an angle to ward off the clinging vines.

"RCPD!" he shouted. "Back away from -" His command cut off as his boot struck a tree root jutting from the ridge and he came tumbling down the slope. He hit the bottom of the clearing with an "oof" and the gun flew from his hand. Mandy saw his red face staring bug-eyed at her and the gun that had tumbled all the way to Andreanu's feet and she immediately recognized him as Valentine.

Andreanu stooped to reach for the pistol, but Mandy caught his arm and pulled him back. "I wouldn't." She nodded her head towards the ridge where Valentine had just fallen. Standing there was Vlad, flanked by Reese and Krause, all with guns drawn and pointed at Andreanu.

"Step away from her!" Vlad barked, descending the slope with a surer step than Valentine, his gun still trained on Andreanu, his eyes flicking to Mandy in concern. Mandy gave him a bewildered look. Andreanu raised his hands away and stepped away from her, staring coolly down the barrel of the gun.

"I'm okay! He's fine. You can put away the guns," she shouted. Valentine scrambled up and snatched his gun off the ground and trudged back to his partners, head bowed as Reese stared at him with laughter in his eyes.

Vlad ignored Valentine and lowered his weapon, his eyes shifting back to Mandy. "Your transmitter cut out. We thought something had happened to you."

"Just had a fall from my horse." She stepped away from Andreanu, lowering her voice to speak to Vlad. "A little mishap and you come busting in like SWAT? I thought we were gonna go slow on this."

He avoids her studying gaze. "I wasn't going to take any chances. Dan is a dangerous man. Where is he?"

"He's off roaming his happy hunting grounds, I'm sure," declared Andreanu, the keenness of his hearing unnerving Mandy. On Vlad's nod, Reese and Valentine took him by both arms and led him further away.

"He just kept riding after I fell," Mandy began. "I was worried for a little while that he led me through those low-hanging branches on purpose and that he was going to circle back to finish me off. But that was just me being paranoid, right?"

Vlad didn't answer. But the relief in his eyes said no. He turned away and made a wrap it up gesture to the other detectives. "We're done here."

"Done?" Mandy felt her expression tighten, fighting a tug-of-war between irritation and confusion. "Shouldn't I at least try to reconnect with Dan?"

"He got the knife, right?" She nodded. "Hopefully we can track him that way. We can debrief back at the van."

He nodded for her to follow Reese and Valentine, who were guiding Andreanu down a path that Mandy guessed led back towards the road. Krause was guiding the big black horse. Vlad turned his back to her, staring at the cage in the clearing. She moved to leave, but then turned back.

"I'd like my debriefing now, if you don't mind."

He turned back to her, surprised. "Let's do this later. I'm trying to wrap my mind around something."

"What do you think I'm trying to do?" Mandy let a hint of a plea into her voice and Vlad softened.

"Help me understand what's been happening," she continued. "I thought we were playing a long game with Dan, not cutting things off at the first sign of trouble."

"It was too dangerous."

"Was it though? All we've got is hunches on him. For all we know he's just a sketchy playboy."

"You don't know all there is to know about Adrian Dan," he said, insistent. "I was not going to risk you."

"Then why send me in here in the first place?"

"Perhaps I shouldn't have."

"Perhaps there's a lot of things you shouldn't have done." Mandy heard a sharp bitterness cut into her voice. She saw a glowering frustration building around his eyes.

"We can discuss this later. I'll escort you back." He reached for her arm, but she yanked it away.

"I'm not going anywhere until you tell me what's going on with us."

"Not here," he hissed, his eyes drifting to her shirt.

"Are you worried about this?" She pulled her shirt up to expose the wire corset. "Because I can take it off if that's what's keeping you from speaking your mind." She curled her hands behind her back and began to yank at the strings that held it tight, her eyes never leaving his. The corset loosened and began to slip off her.

His eyes flashed in anger and he sprang towards her, his arms encircling her waist to catch her wrists. "Stop that," he hissed again.

"Why?" she replied, acid on her tongue, her eyes staring up at him with all the provocation she could muster. "It's not like we haven't done this before."

"That was my mistake, which I'm trying my best not to repeat."

His eyes were stern now and cold, adding to the pain of his words. He released her wrists and moved his hands to her shoulders, holding her at arm's length.

"I'm not your boyfriend. I'm your boss. And I'm telling you to drop this." He paused, tenderness breaking up his stony gaze. "For both our sakes."

Mandy wrenched from his grip, her body shaking with too many emotions to give a single name. She turned to follow the path of the detectives.

The light coming down in shafts fell on the ground before her, lighting up squares of earth like spaces on a chessboard. She had fancied herself a knight earlier, consorting with kings and queens, pivoting sharply and unpredictably away from the straight lines of the bishops. But now she was a pawn, pushing blindly forward, knobby head bowed, incapable of looking back, fit only to be sacrificed in a greater gambit she could not understand.

21

In his twenty years of experience as a supervisor, Colonel Ivy had found the best place to have a difficult conversation with an employee was a no-frills diner that served the kind of greasy slop that was steaming on the plate in front of him. Bernhardt's not only fit that description, but they always comped the meals, which was important when you had to have several of these conversations in a week. He also liked how spacious the seats were - half these places you could barely squeeze behind the table!

Of course, his wife didn't appreciate all these detours from the dietary regimen she had instituted with religious fervor after the bypass surgery last year. But she had to understand it came with the territory, being in upper management for a department as big and dysfunctional as RCPD. Bacon grease was the oil that kept the wheels of justice running smooth!

He looked at the empty bench across from him in the booth. He wondered for a moment if vampires liked hash brown casserole. He'd seen the blood sausage on the menu - this place really was German! - but he'd thought ordering it might seem like a joke. This would be his first time sharing a booth with a vampire. Not that he had avoided their company - he'd eat with anybody - but there were so few in the department and they never seemed to come in for discipline. This Paler guy especially. Spotless record. Even the occasion for today's meeting wasn't really an infraction. Though he was running late. The Colonel esteemed punctuality highly - imagine letting a plate of hash brown casserole go cold!

At last, the chime over the door sounded and Vlad Paler strode through the door looking ostentatiously formal in his dress blues. Colonel crunched his bacon in irritation - a veteran like Paler should have known this would be an informal reprimand and dressed accordingly. A sudden shock of memory hit the Colonel in the gut, unsettling the first helping of casserole that had begun its maneuvers down there. He was dressed for the funeral! How had he forgotten? He'd have to swing by the house and change after they wrapped up here. *Helen better have remembered to let out those pants!*

"Paler!" he declared warmly, a little burp escaping in his enthusiasm. "Take a seat!"

The vampire captain sat stiffly across from him, all sharp lines and angles except for the soft waves of his brown hair. For all his sharpness, he looked haggard, but his cheeks still glowed with a ruddiness that was unusual for a vampire.

"I took the liberty of ordering for you," burbled the Colonel, gesturing at the magnificent plate still steaming under Vlad's nose. He glanced at it with a disappointing coldness and then looked up at him.

"I appreciate you trying to soften the blow, Colonel, but I think it would be better if you could come right to the point."

"If you insist," said the Colonel, reluctantly setting down his own fork. "Though I must say it would serve you well to savor the little courtesies this job has to offer. The most direct path is not always the best one."

Vlad blinked, unmoved. "I'm assuming this is regarding Van Helsing."

"Good instincts!" The Colonel liked to splice in praise and positivity whenever he could, but Vlad's icy exterior could not be thawed. He sighed and plowed ahead. "As you know, this case is a big priority for the city."

"As it is for me."

"No one's denying that. But it does seem like you might be developing a case of tunnel vision."

The Colonel detected a bristle. *This one responds more to the knife than the fork!*

"I had to have a difficult conversation with the chief and his people the other day," he continued after glancing around to make sure there weren't any eavesdroppers. "I had to explain that on the day a vamp councilman was murdered by a religious extremist, I've got my best guys chasing a vamp around in the privacy of his own property."

"Adrian Dan is a legitimate person of interest. And I don't see how Van Helsing relates to the death of Councilman Codrescu."

"Another example of your vision becoming too narrow. From the council's view, they are inextricably related. Both flow from the same stream of hate and fear produced by men like Haggerty and his followers."

"That's political theater, not police work. I'm pursuing the only concrete leads I have, not chasing phantoms."

The Colonel leaned forward. "Aren't you? I haven't heard of any arrest warrants coming down for Dan. What exactly do you have on him?"

"We're still working on the P.C., but he's got multiple demonstrable ties to the narcotics trade, he's been implicated in the disappearances of several missing people in the past, and he's one of the only people out there with the motive and the opportunities to kill our victims."

"That sounds like an awful lot of conjecture and hand-waving for someone who only pursues concrete leads. How close are you to an actual arrest?"

"We have to locate him first. He gave us the slip on his property and no one has located him since." Vlad rubbed at the sharp point of his beard, mulling his words. "But we may be able to track him. Just a few technical difficulties with the satellite system to work out."

"Satellites!" The Colonel felt his eyes bulging and a bit of congealed sausage working its way back up his esophagus. "We're trying to put every resource we have into the Haggerty manhunt and you're bringing in NASA to chase someone who's not even a suspect!"

"That's not -"

"No!" the Colonel interrupted, feeling the heat under his collar. He hated to lose his temper at this type of sit-down - always seemed to lead to indigestion - but the man was simply out of control. "I wanted to give you the benefit of the doubt. Your obsession with the Dan family has reached an untenable level. One big arrest years ago and now you can't seem to think of anything else."

Vlad opened his mouth to interject, but the Colonel raised his hand to stop him. "I'm taking you off Van Helsing, effective immediately." He lifted a finger to still another outburst from Vlad. "Let me finish! I'm also taking you out of criminal investigation until you can get your head right. You're temporarily assigned to missing persons until further notice. You can report there tomorrow."

Vlad's face blanched across from him, at last taking on the pallor of a normal vampire. He stood, a little unsteady and gave the Colonel a curt nod before turning and leaving. The Colonel felt a sudden pang of doubt as he watched him go. Had he been too harsh? Had he spoken too sharply? Vlad was almost a celebrity among the vamps. *Is he gonna run crying to the bigwigs and get me in hot water?*

No. Deputy Chief Flannery, an old classmate and always the sharpest tool in the shed, had assured him that Vlad, while well-known in the vamp community, didn't have much in the way of pull. Despite his relatively rapid rise up the ranks and his close personal friendship with the late vamp big shot Dr. Duma, he was not a political animal. Rather he was a foot soldier who climbed the ranks without much in the way of schmoozing or backdoor maneuvering. He was a hard-nosed cop of the old school. A shame - the Colonel always hated coming down on the good ones. They could use his abilities if he had more political sense. Maybe this sojourn in the wilderness would be good for him. Hopefully it wouldn't be too awkward running into him at the funeral.

The funeral! The Colonel hastened to dislodge himself from the seat. Couldn't be late. Too many VIPs would be there and watching. He slid a five under his coffee mug for the waiter, his eyes resting again on Vlad's untouched plate. Still steaming - remarkable! He raised his hand to ask the waiter for a to-go box - this would make a nice surprise for the homeless lady that was always set up to beg at the highway off-ramp. But that was ten minutes away and it might be cold and congealed by then. No, this casserole had to be enjoyed hot. *The funeral will have to wait.*

***

It was unsettling for Mandy to stare at Vlad's windowed office and see it dark and shuttered. The new boss, some vamp from Missing Persons, hadn't even shown up yet and the space had been vacant for several days running. *Kind of like me.*

The whispers around the new boss were that he was an empty suit, who rarely even showed up to work. But that hadn't stopped him messing with Mandy from afar. The turkey-faced secretary who had trotted in to take over at Maggie's desk, Maggie having vacated to Missing Persons with Vlad, had summoned her as her first order of business. Not even looking up from her notepad, she had informed her, emotionless, that Acting Captain Rusu would be reassigning the Van Helsing case to Reese and Francis, the longest-tenured veterans of the bureau.

When the initial sting of it had faded into a dull ache, she had felt a passing wave of sympathy for old Francis. The hot potato had bounced through the whole department and found him again. Meanwhile Mandy was back on the O.D. brigade. The files had been stacking up in her inbox and she'd scarcely even flipped through them, too busy staring at Vlad's old office, wondering what could have been.

She had been about to select a random file to "investigate," her catch-all excuse to drive aimlessly around the city until she found a cafe or diner with a sufficiently moody view of the river, when her desk phone rang and the turkey-face's voice droned on the other end of the line. She was only a few yards away - Mandy could see her from her desk! - but God forbid she walk over to her.

"Detective Parker?" came the voice, shrill and needle-like. Mandy waved in greeting from the desk, but the secretary pretended not to notice her.

"Yep, it's me," said Mandy with a heavy sigh.

"I've got Councilman Garrick on the line for you," came the curt reply then a click as the call transferred.

"Hello?" Mandy spoke into the faint hiss on the other line. Her earlier enthusiasm about the special task force he'd dangled in front of her had already wilted, unwatered by any follow-up from the council and buried by the events of the past weeks.

Garrick's voice came across the line, effusive with energy and effervescence, like an expanding ball of hot gas. He swung effortlessly between apologizing for not calling her sooner and exultation over the possibilities of a hate-fighting task force. Mandy wasn't so depressed that she wasn't flattered by the attention of a city councilman, but the sheer amount of caffeinated charisma pouring through the receiver was overwhelming. By the time she'd agreed to meet him for coffee - as if he needed any more! - she felt tired and out of breath.

She slunk towards the elevators with the same heavy footsteps that had taken her past Vlad's empty office and down the elevator on the aimless wanderings of the last few days. But the embers of enthusiasm were not long dormant, and before she had reached her car the pep had begun to reinvigorate her step. *The councilman wants to meet with me!*

Garrick's chosen coffee spot was an old longshoreman's hangout attached to a little market on the wharf. It smelled strongly of fish. Garrick was sitting in a plastic chair at the edge of the outdoor eating area, staring at the huge, rusted barge that blocked all views of the river. There was a reason this place didn't attract tourists.

Garrick was wearing a shabby windbreaker and a weathered baseball cap as he sipped his coffee. Mandy guessed it was his incognito ensemble, but the effect was undercut by the sun's glint off the silver Rolex on his wrist and the gold-framed Ray-Ban's on his nose.   Not to mention the perfectly-coiffed blonde hairs pushing up against the too-lightly resting cap. He looked like a refugee from a yacht club. *But who was going to recognize a random city councilman on the docks anyway?*

"Mr. Garrick?" she asked and he startled, almost spilling his coffee. But the surprise quickly morphed into a huge smile of perfect white teeth as he sprang up to pull out a chair for her.

"I didn't know if you'd recognize me!" He took off his sunglasses to fix her with a gaze that made her feel like she was getting hit with high-beams. Everything about him crackled with energy. *Sunshine on a cloudy day.*

He wasted no time launching his charm offensive, praising her white paper exuberantly, talking up her future in the department. He threw all kinds of dazzling adjectives at her - fascinating, brilliant, sparkling, mesmerizing! On an intellectual level, she knew it was pure schmooze, the wagging of a silver tongue, but she humored him anyway; it felt nice to be wooed like a swing voter, especially by a sun-bronzed Ken doll with perfect teeth. He'd brought her a coffee, dosed heavily with cream and sugar, of course, and she sipped at it, basking for a while in the glow of his praise.

Sufficiently warmed, she finally brought him to the point. "Not that I don't want to hear all these nice things about myself, but I'm assuming there was something concrete you wanted to talk about."

He brightened even further, his engines roaring for this green light. "The task force!" he declared. "I need someone to head it up and I think you're the perfect person for the job."

"I just got booted from the Van Helsing case. I don't think I'm such a hot commodity anymore."

He shook his head and waved away the clouds with a dismissive hand.

"Nonsense." He began to rattle off her qualifications, counting them out with his fingers. "You might not believe it, but your name still has traction in the vamp community after that Liggins show." Up went the thumb. "And that white paper! You might be the only person in the department who could have dreamed up that vision, much less put it to paper." That was the index finger. "Plus, and yes, I did some digging, I love that you have a conservative, religious background. That gives you a finger on the pulse of the common man in this town that us silver-spoon sucking Ivy Leaguers in City Hall really need." That was the middle.

"Finally," he continued, the ring and the pinky springing up together. "And I hope you forgive me for being blunt and just saying it, but you're a very attractive young woman with a pleasant demeanor. You belong in front of the camera." He closed his outstretched fingers into a fist and gave it an enthusiastic pump. "I don't just want you for this, I need you."

Normally an onslaught like that would have made Mandy blush, or cringe, but there was a burning sincerity imbuing Garrick's manner that transcended the usual sexual energy behind such compliments. His eyes glowed, not with lust, but belief.

"I'm genuinely flattered but I'm not sure I quite share your vision..." she began. "I've been a detective for all of a couple months. I don't think anyone would take me seriously."

The fist broke into another dismissive wave. "You can't think like that. A few months ago, I was a nobody who rode into the city council on the Mayor's coattails. People called me boytoy *in my presence*. And look at me now - me and Vinea are effectively running the city now." There was no braggadocio in his voice. He seemed genuinely amazed at the development.

"The city is teetering right now," he continued, a fervent earnestness flowing through his words. "We are caught between two eras, between the solid conservatism of our past and the wild, almost frightening, possibilities of our future. We're swinging between these two poles, like a seesaw seeking its fulcrum."

"It is critical to the city's future that we find that fulcrum, that we establish that rock that allows us to pivot smoothly, gently into the future and stop the wild convulsions we're experiencing now."

"Is that what Councilman Codrescu was trying to do?" As much as she felt swept up in Garrick's zeal, Mandy couldn't resist the poke. He nodded and took it in stride.

"Poor old Slim. He was really trying. But he pushed too far forward, too hard and too fast. Look..." he gestured out towards the river, as if the intensity of his vision could burn through the rusted hull of the barge blocking their view. "The vamps are our future. The meetings I've had... If you could see what they're working on in medicine, in computer science, in genetic research... they're gonna open new worlds for all of us and probably run them too... But for now they're still living in our world and they need native schlubs like you and me in their corner. That's what Slim, may he rest in peace, could never come to terms with and it ended up costing him his life."

Mandy shook her head. "Wasn't my white paper saying everything Codrescu believed? Maybe I was pushing too hard. If we're pushing the same message, why shouldn't we expect a similar response?"

"Because the messenger matters more than the message. Putting a vampire at the head of the spear, especially one as antagonistic as Slim, was an act of provocation. It put everything on a war footing. But a beautiful young woman with a good head on her shoulders who knows how to talk to religious folks? They wouldn't be able to resist you!"

The way you talk me up, I can't even resist me! Mandy felt her reservations crumbling under the force of his enthusiasm. She scarcely noticed the buzzing of her pager on her hip, confusing it at first with the tingling of goosebumps on her arm. She stood up, revealing the pager apologetically. "That's work. I've got to go."

"Duty is calling!" he declared with another grin. Then he reached into his windbreaker and produced a business card with nothing on it but a phone number. He handed it to her. "That's my direct line. Call me when you're ready."

Hiding his mesmerizing gaze behind shades once again, he gave her a firm squeeze on the shoulder and then strode away. As he disappeared around the corner, Mandy felt her newfound energy dwindling, her shoulders sinking back down. The pager buzzed again.

She used the phone in the fish market, breathing in through her mouth to suppress the gag reflex as the phone rang. She was surprised to hear Maggie's cheery voice pick up on the other end.

"Mandy!" came the squeal. "I know it's against protocol since we're not working together anymore, but I just can't stand dealing with that battle-ax they put on my old desk!"

Mandy had a hard time resisting this invitation to gossip. She knew it would only take a little prompting to get Maggie to spill the tea. *Why did Vlad leave CID for a dead-end outpost like Missing Persons? Did he get in trouble? Or was he trying to get away from me?*

"So what kind of call do you have for me?"

"Christina Haggerty called for you! She says it's urgent."

Mandy felt a tingle travel up her spine, followed by a twinge of bitterness. "You're gonna want to send her to Reese or Francis. They're handling Van Helsing now."

"Oh, I heard about that. What on earth are they thinking upstairs?" Another invitation that Mandy declined with reluctant silence. "But she was insistent on talking to you, personally." Maggie gave her the address: it was Haggerty's mansion. Maggie warned her it was going to be a zoo with so many agencies camped out there waiting for her father or his goons to show up.

Mandy buckled up and felt a renewed vitality as her foot pressed down on the accelerator. There would be no keeping her on the sidelines. The universe would not leave her to toil in obscurity or even to sulk over a break-up. She was caught up again in the pulse of the city and wherever its beating heart was pounding, that's where she would be headed.

***

Andreanu didn't wear a helmet on the ride over. The wind in his hair felt good and he didn't care about getting pulled over today. He took the scenic route that skirted the county line around the foothills and then went off-road for a stretch on the old railroad tracks that cut between a long row of abandoned factories and mills.

It was a bumpy ride and more than a little dangerous taking the bike through the patchy gravel that filled the spaces between the rails, but Andreanu didn't mind. He loved the spectacle of these huge empty metal buildings. They were at once foreboding and inviting, with their mysterious, brooding smokestacks glowering down at Andreanu even as their profusion of ladders and slides and cranes bid him to climb and explore their funhouse nooks and crannies. That a jungle of vines now covered their walls and formed tenuous bridges across the canyons of their interiors only made them more enticing. But he did not stop to explore them on this day. He liked them as they were, the virginal space of his daydreams, and he would leave them that way.

He cleared the tracks and entered the decrepit old suburbs that were crumbling into a less romantic variety of ruins. The yards giving way to meadows were pleasant enough but the houses behind them exuded a miserable loneliness. There were no children playing jump-rope or hopscotch on the weed-choked sidewalks. No gray-haired grannies watching and waving from rocking chairs on the vacant porches. No teenage lovers holding hands as they walked under the colonnades of the beautiful old oaks and maples that lined the streets. Just row after row of relics, the memories boarded-up behind plywood, their epitaphs written in illegible graffiti.

He ended his ride at the old school, which in turn had been the old church before becoming just another abandoned building. It was an ugly edifice, just like pretty much every public building in the city. Concrete and plaster, rectangles and squares, a testament to a lack of imagination, not even a hint of a tower or vault or arch. But buried within this barren slab of cement were the very best moments of Andreanu's life. Here had been the revelation, the stirring of his soul, the breaking of the eclipse that had engulfed his life. He dismounted his bike, grabbing the bulky suitcase he had clipped to the rear storage compartment and heading for the double doors straight ahead of him.

The cheap padlock barring the main doors succumbed to a single blow from a stray chunk of cement and Andreanu was inside. He strode down the dark hallways, lit only by the pale beams of light streaming through the window panels on the door behind him. But he didn't need any light to navigate this place. His fingertips touched the concrete of the walls as he walked, reading their porous surfaces like braille.

He was passing the Sunday school rooms now. How eagerly

had he devoured the word of God there, dispensed in smiling mouthfuls by the deacons. How tightly he would squeeze Christina's hand as they surreptitiously reached for each other under the table. Ahead was the auditorium and gymnasium that they squeezed the huge congregation into when the weather was too bad to meet outside. He could hear Pastor Haggerty's voice filling the room and feeling the heartbeats of the congregants packed so tightly together that everyone had to raise their arms to testify. Beyond that was the aquatics center they had restored and repurposed as a giant baptismal to recreate on a micro-scale each week the annual Gathering at the river.

Andreanu remembered fondly the smooth feel of the fiberglass floor under his bare feet and the aroma of chlorine in his nostrils on the day of his baptism. But he had wondered what it would have been like to be washed in the ancient waters of the river, with tens of thousands watching... To stare up at the sky and see the clouds parting and a dove descending! Alas, it was not to be. Just one more beautiful sacrament forever tainted by the corrupting touch of his kind. Codrescu couldn't just leave them alone, could he? *And neither could I.*

He felt the sharp corner of the wall and turned to the right, plunging himself into the total darkness of the stairwell leading down to the basement. Here again he needed no guide but the rails and the memories of disco balls and fog machines leading the teens into the intoxicating mysteries of Christ. Here too were tucked away little rooms, not for Sunday school, but for spiritual warfare. Brother clasping brother, renouncing the works of the devil.

He wondered if the old furnace was still there in the boiler room. It had long ceased functioning even when the church was still going, but that didn't stop them from putting it to ceremonial use. Cast those dirty magazines into the fire, son, lest you be cast in along with them! Unwind those cassette tapes and drown those demonic lyrics in the crackle of the flames! Andreanu had felt a tremendous sense of relief hurling his own album into the simulated blaze - not that anyone had listened to it anyways. But he'd always envied the boys beside him. Theirs were external thorns that, no matter how difficult and painful, could be plucked from their bodies and burnt away. But his curse reached down into his DNA. Freedom for him could only come hurling himself into the inferno.

He had always longed for Christina's presence in those boys-only assemblies, and he felt her absence keenly now. She was a cool glass of water on a hot day. Her voice, always so calm and gentle, always carrying words of such comfort and grace, always untangled his perpetual angst like a masseuse's fingers working through knotted muscle. Her eyes, brimming with tender affection for him but ever-twinkling and eager for laughter. Her absence was an ache that wracked his entire body and doubled him over on the linoleum floor. He knew she would drop everything and come running if he called, but he couldn't. This was no place for the innocent.

He dropped his suitcase on the floor and unlatched it, feeling blindly into its interior. This would be difficult to do properly in such pitch blackness. A partner would be a huge help. But Andreanu was done entangling others in his schemes. He had always hoped for a purifying, redemptive effect to his work, but the work itself had turned out to be hopelessly corrupting. This final act would have to be a solo performance if it was to have any merit. A final dose of much-needed virtue for the virtuoso.

As his hand closed round the slender piece of wood in the suitcase, his body started at a sound. It was muffled and distant, like a stifled scream. Could it be Christina, running to his rescue one more time? The thought stirred a feverish hope in his chest and with it a sudden urge to run to her. To lose himself in her arms and let the tingling caresses of her fingers through his hair drive away all thoughts of the day of reckoning.

But what if it was the sound of someone else? Not Christina running through the hallways looking for him, but another young woman, a stranger, running away from him, her screams choked with panic. Down dark forest paths, where brambles snared her feet and sent her tumbling to the earth. There had been no postponing that day, no one to run to, nowhere to hide except the dust. And now it was time to resume the chase into that final refuge. *I am still pursuing you, little fox, but you have nothing to fear from me now.*

Everything was in place now. He groped for the plastic bag in the suitcase and opened it, instinctively reeling at the overpowering odor. He emptied the contents into his hand and held his breath before stuffing them into his mouth in a single motion. His gag reflex was immediate and intense, but he controlled it, driving it downward along with the terrible fear that was now making his legs shake. He reached into the suitcase for the final item - the letter - and rose unsteadily to his feet.

Another memory of the church fluttered into his mind as the blood drained down to his toes and left him light-headed. Very early in his time at the church, he had been herded into a room with the other young people and divided into pairs. The youth pastor lined them up like dominos, one behind the other, the one in front told to close his eyes and stand on tiptoes. The pastor and his assistants then walked between them, giving a gentle push to the one in front. Down he had gone, his arms flailing, his body clenching for the impact with the floor. But there was no pain, no crack of his head against the linoleum, only the "oof" of his partner catching his weight and the feel of the arms that caught him in a saving embrace.

"After the fall, we have no one to catch us but Jesus!" the pastor had declared as they fell about laughing with each other. "If you died today, would he be there to catch you?"

Andreanu stood on his tiptoes now. He did not need to close his eyes, it was so dark, but he did anyway. He felt saliva dripping from his lips and down his chin, and worse, down his throat, carrying with it the acrid taste of the garlic. His stomach rose in revulsion but he ignored it. *Groan all you want. Soon you will be quiet along with the rest of this corrupted flesh.*

Then he lifted his head to the ceiling and thought the prayer that his mouth could not utter. *Father, deliver me from this life that I might join you in the next!* Holding his breath, he rocked himself backwards on his heels and fell.

22

If the old office had been a captain's cabin in a magnificent pirate's galley, the new one was a dank corner of the brig on a man-o-war slowly sinking down to the bottom of Davy Jones' locker. Vlad chided himself for this bit of uncharacteristic self-pity, but it wasn't just sour grapes talking. The old building where Missing Persons and the other rubber rooms of the city bureaucracy had been abandoned by the higher-ups precisely because it was sinking, quite literally though very slowly, into the marshes where their panglossian predecessors had decided to build it. But with a shelf life of at least another decade, the same higher-ups had felt no urgency to send for the departmental detritus stashed in places like Missing Persons.

Vlad's square of this leaning tower was a corner office near the ground level - the upper levels had been left vacant as a precautionary measure. It was a cramped space with ancient metal furnishings, protected from rust by the heaps of dust that had accumulated over the past decades, and a single square window which allowed only a few narrow beams of light through the thick iron bars that guarded it from the denizens of the garbage-strewn alley outside. The space had only recently been vacated by his predecessor - and successor at CID - but, from the looks of it, this office hadn't been occupied in a generation. There was no place for Maggie either, at least not one she would have accepted for long, so he had finagled her a spot on the new building and relied on the old rotary phone as his one remaining connection to the city.

In truth, his new digs didn't bother him. It was a squalid, miserable office in a condemned building, but it suited the darkness of his mood. It was a doghouse, but he was a dog. He had faked it for a while, but everyone knew he wasn't fit for polite company. He followed his nose to force his way into forbidden closets, chewed at priceless furniture to keep his teeth sharp and lost his mind over an attractive female in heat. Sure, it was a kick in the nuts to be thrown out of the big house, but out here he'd at least be free to follow his instincts. And he was a loyal dog. However much he might growl, he would never actually bite the hand that fed and beat him.

Besides, what his masters meant for humiliation and correction may have just offered him a new avenue for misbehavior. If he was no longer allowed to pursue Adrian Dan as a homicide suspect, might he not continue the hunt from his new office now that Dan could be classified as a Missing Person? He had already started the file, using himself as the complainant, and had put in another call to the satellite tracking company. Any day now they were supposed to get a fix on the location of that knife Mandy had given him.

In the meantime, there was plenty of housekeeping to absorb his attention. The only pieces of furniture without a dust carpet were the three beige filing cabinets in the corner that someone had been stuffing with the neglected cases of the bureau. Vlad had cleared a table to pull them out and review them. He knew there were several detectives assigned to the bureau, but he'd yet to see one grace the office and recognized several names on the list as among the most notorious no-show deadweights in the department. As the only live body in the domain, Vlad would have to do all the heavy lifting until he could get some new blood transferred in.

He emptied a box of files on the table with a sigh, feeling keenly the absence of Mandy at his elbow. A partner, a friend, a light in the darkness to work beside… lost! All because he couldn't control himself. The thought of her did what his bosses could not with all their demotions: he felt the terrible sting of the exile, wandering alone, away from the tender comforts of hearth and home. For the first time, the sheer extent of the files felt overwhelming and Vlad wished he had his old chair to sink back into and the *Battle of Trafalgar* to carry him back into his daydreams.

No! He coughed away the encroaching despair and the dust

filling his lungs and stared anew at the files. Most had photos paperclipped to the front of a folder. Chosen for recency, not for nostalgia, these pictures formed a grim gallery of faces ravaged by exposure to the elements and the injection and ingestion of the street's favorite poisons. These were the kinds of faces that no one would recognize, the faces you turned away from when they accosted you at the gas station or passed by you on the sidewalk conversing with their demons. They were missing persons only in the technical sense - they were missed by no one, other than maybe a long-suffering mother or a bleeding heart like Bouchard.

Bouchard! Vlad wondered if the poor old preacher's daughter had been stuffed somewhere in these stacks, lost in the shuffle of druggies and derelicts that filled these cabinets. He switched on a task light and spread the files left and right until they covered the desk and much of the floor. Turned out she was an easy spot: a young pretty face, with only a patina of the street dulling her eyes, she sprung quickly to the surface of the sea of mummies and zombies staring up at him.

He felt again the pang of regret that he hadn't followed through on her case as he had promised. Here she had been, abandoned and neglected in a forgotten building while her body was trapped in the sand bar, a feast for the crabs. *Patricia Currington.* Vlad's chin jutted in resolution as he held up the file. Here was where he would begin his path out of exile and despair. He would right this old wrong, pluck the mystery of this poor girl's fate from the abyss, and, with her, put himself and the Missing Persons Bureau back on the map.

It was a slender file, consisting only of the information form that Bouchard himself had filled out and a single page of surprisingly detailed notes from a Detective Gore. Vlad recognized the name; like anyone with a pulse Gore had been plucked out of Missing Persons to work elsewhere. Bouchard had written that he suspected his daughter had gone into prostitution after clients told him they'd seen her hanging around the old Emporium, the heart of the red-light district. Gore had followed this lead and found several hookers who knew Patricia and could specify her last known whereabouts as a derelict parking garage on 4th Street.

The location immediately set neurons firing in Vlad's brain. They'd tracked Pavel Petricean's car to the same spot! He read on intently, according to the whores Gore canvased, Patricia was brand new to the trade and had been recruited by a drug dealer and pimp known only as "JJ." Here Gore had written in all caps "POSSIBLE VAMP TRAMP."

Vlad had never worked in Vice and he'd never indulged as a customer, but curiosity had made him familiar with the phenomenon. The younger, fresher hookers, though theoretically the most precious and valuable assets in a pimp's stable, were often given the most dangerous Johns. And vampires, because of the risk of disease transmission and their status as a symbol of fear and loathing for the underclasses, fit that bill. No matter how much money a vamp waved around, most of the more seasoned streetwalkers wouldn't bite. So the job fell to the youngest and the most naive initiates of the profession. In his first years on the force, Vlad had heard of many cases of such women showing up deathly ill to local hospitals or dying at the big abortion clinic downtown - each a potential tabloid headline and an embarrassment to the community.

But it had been more than a decade since he'd heard of one. Either vamps had become more disciplined and less desperate or the hookers stopped taking their money. *Or they stopped ending up in the hospital and started filling up cabinets like this one.* Could Dan and the Bat Pack have gotten mixed up in human trafficking along with the drugs? Had Patricia gotten into a car with the handsome Petricean to start the evening and finished the night at the bottom of the river?

Vlad frowned. *Wild conjecture. Your obsession with Dan is making you see things! Get a hold of yourself.* He could hear the Colonel's voice bleating in his head even if he didn't believe the accusations. But even there was something to the idea, the trail had gone cold a long time ago. They hadn't been able to muster even a single sighting of Petricean's kidnapper within a day of his death; what hope was there of getting anything of worth on a hooker who disappeared months ago? The painful irony was that the only one who could pull any info of value from that human junkyard was the man who had asked for his help in the first place: Bouchard.

Now that he thought about it, it was strange that Bouchard, who knew more about the streets of River City than the most seasoned beat cop and the most toothless junkie, had come to him, a CID captain, for help with a missing person. At the time, Vlad had assumed that he was just the first cop to come to the grieving man's delirious mind, or at least the highest-ranking one. But that couldn't be true. Bouchard knew plenty of beat cops and he had rubbed shoulders with men far higher up the food chain. The man had probably seen more of the brass at charity dinners than Vlad had in his whole career.

Wouldn't it be more likely that he had already done his own digging… that he had already found out what Gore did and more before he ever came to Vlad? That he was coming to Vlad not as a friend but as the man in charge of the homicide bureau? Had the old man already pieced it together? He tried to remember that meeting in more detail. He remembered the tears, the awkwardness, the haste he felt to get this weepy old relic out of his office and make his hopeless case someone else's problem…

The phone rang. It was Maggie.

"There's something big going down over here!" she said, her voice only slightly above a whisper. "You might want to come over."

Vlad hung up and grabbed his trenchcoat. He stopped at the door to realize Bouchard's daughter's file was still in his hand. He tossed it back to the table, and it slid face-down onto the pile, disappearing into the manila morass.

***

The Haggerty mansion didn't so much rise as sprawl, much like the huge megachurch it adjoined. It was a wide, low building, built in a Spanish Mission style, with shimmering white adobe walls topped by the dull reds of the clay roof tiles. Neither it nor the church were to Mandy's preference, but the size of it was undeniably impressive. Haggerty had carved himself out his own city-state. The whole campus was so big it was beyond the resources of RCPD to shut down, but that didn't mean they weren't trying.

There were squad cars posted at each entrance to the church parking lot and the long private road that led over a pleasant little creek and down to the mansion. Yellow crime scene tape stretched from the young trees that dotted the perimeter forming a flimsy barrier around the whole property. Mandy found Christina poking her head out of a little copse of trees next to the main road, just beyond the yellow perimeter. She was wearing jeans and a flannel shirt, her bright red hair put up under a baseball cap. She looked small and scared. *A little kid running away from home.*

Mandy pulled up beside her and leaned over to push the passenger door open. Christina got in and closed the door quickly, exhaling a sigh.

"You know I could have picked you up at your front door and saved you some trouble."

"The police wouldn't let me leave," she replied, placing her hand on her chest to slow her heartbeat.

"You'd be amazed at what they let me do with this thing." She brandished the gold detective badge dangling from her neck, but Christina didn't notice.

"I'm sorry to be rude, but can we hurry?"

Mandy shrugged and pulled off from the curb. "Grey Birch High School, right?" She nodded. "Any idea why he'd be hanging out at an abandoned school in the middle of nowhere?"

"It's where my dad's church used to meet when I first brought him there. It's always held a special place in his heart... And he wrote something in his letter that made me think he might be headed there."

"Yes, the letter. You think I could take a look at that now, while we're on our way?"

Christina's hand slipped to the pocket of her jeans, protectively. "I'd rather not. It's personal."

Another shrug from Mandy. She kept an eye on the road, but tried to sneak a study of Christina's profile through sidelong glances. She was a nervous wreck, her breathing just short of hyperventilation, her eyes puffy and bloodshot from crying, her hands wringing in her lap. *Was this all for Andreanu?* She tried another tack.

"All this going on with your father and your church must be weighing on you..."

She glanced at Mandy, almost confused, as if returning to the subject from somewhere far away. "I guess... Yes... I'm worried about my dad." Her eyes turned back to the window.

"But you're more concerned about Andreanu?" She didn't bite. Mandy continued: "Forgive me, but if my dad was the subject of a citywide manhunt, I wouldn't be stressing out over an old boyfriend."

Christina turned to Mandy with a flash of anger in her eyes. *That got her.*

"I love my father and I pray for him all the time. But I know he's okay-" she stopped herself. Maybe the glint of Mandy's badge reminded her she was riding with a cop. "I know all this nonsense the newspapers are talking about will go away in time and he'll be back at home like he always has…" She trailed off and then added in an icy tone: "And Andy is not my boyfriend."

"I'm sorry if I misunderstood."

"We were never together in the way you're thinking."

"So what you told us last time was a lie, then? He wasn't with you when Dragescu and Petricean were killed?"

Christina didn't respond and looked away again. Now it was Mandy's turn to be angry. She pulled onto the shoulder and slammed on the brakes.

"Enough. If you want a chauffeur, I can arrange one who will take you express downtown for obstructing justice. But if you want to continue to ride in my car, you're going to start talking. Which is it gonna be?"

Christina mustered a look of defiance that seemed to harden and then broke suddenly into tears. She doubled over and the tears gave way to sobs. "I'm sorry," she gasped.

Mandy was transported back to the time when Esther, with her freshly minted driver's license, had backed over Mandy's tabby in the driveway. There Esther had been, a puddle of tears and snot prostrate before her and it had fallen to Mandy to comfort her. Mandy's cat dead, smashed into a gruesome pancake when it was taking a nap in the sun, and she was the one doing the consoling. And here she was again, her hand reaching out mechanically to squeeze the shoulder of the bereaved. *I've got a vampire ex too, you know, and you don't see me in hysterics.*

"I've always tried to protect him," Christina began, the words gushing out with the tears. "He was fighting so hard… trying so hard to be rid of it."

Mandy started to drive again as Christina continued her confession. The story of her tortured relationship with Mikhail Andreanu spilled out of her. How they'd met at a punk rock concert in a trashy underground club downtown. She the pastor's daughter, a goodie-two-shoes out on a rare rebellious adventure with her bad influence best friend; he the lead singer for the opening act that was hopelessly overshadowed by the main event. How she'd seen him moping around the bar and left her wallflower cove to strike up a conversation with him. How that blossomed into an intense friendship, with Andy confiding in her all the inner torments that found voice in the screams of his songs.

Mandy listened closely, driving slowly to give Christina time to unload the whole story. But she felt her irritation mounting. The cliche of the squeaky clean church girl falling for the brooding bad boy would be irritating enough if it didn't so closely mirror her own teenage romance. It had felt so bold and thrilling at the time, like she was the heroine in the story that other girls would only ever dare to read about. But now to hear the same story playing out for someone else, in the same breathless tone of her own inner narrator, was to realize how ordinary and predictable her own drama had been.

Christina was so convinced she was special, the star of a cosmic tragedy, not just another silly girl falling headlong into an age-old trope. But even her delusion wasn't quite so embarrassing. The lead singer in the band. A rich kid, practically a prince. And a vampire! Christina's romance at least had the trappings of an epic. Mandy's bad boy had been a pony-tailed mortician's apprentice who collected Star Wars figurines. She shuddered involuntarily.

Christina had finally approached the present tense by the time they had reached the exit for the old mill district. She confirmed what Vlad had alluded to before: that Andreanu was a compulsive hypovolemic. He would go through prolonged periods where he would refuse to feed. Christina insisted that was religiously motivated - that the behavior had started after he had converted to Christianity and begun attending her father's church. But Vlad had believed it was a mental psychosis that had predated any religious impulse. A rare, but well-documented and recurring condition in the community. The "bloodfast" they called it.

Regardless of the origin of the behavior, there was no doubt that it had become more extreme over the past several months. He had taken to fasting for weeks at a time and with it came the most extreme symptoms of hypovolemia: wild emotional swings akin to manic depression, auditory and visual hallucinations and debilitating tremors. Then would come the concomitant "bloodfeast," an orgiastic spree of gluttony when the appetite broke through all resistance and he drank red until he passed out.

"He would always have his worst attacks just before his 'falls.' You know, when he would break the fast," Christina continued, the sniffles almost gone now. "He would climb the vines outside my room, push through the window and collapse on my floor."

"And that's where he was when Dragescu and Petricean were killed?"

Christina stared at the floor. "I don't know... He was there on those days but I don't know the exact times." She squirmed under Mandy's burning gaze. "I know I misled you and I'm sorry. But I genuinely believed he had nothing to do with those terrible killings. It's not like him. He's always been so gentle. Even the thought that he might have hurt someone made him distraught."

"If you thought he was innocent, why were you lying to protect him?"

She paused again. "I thought he might be dealing again," she said slowly. Mandy gave her a blank look. She didn't quite understand what she was referring to. *How does this choir girl know more about illicit vamp stuff than me!*

"He was doing it when I first met him," she continued, sensing Mandy's confusion. "He'd get drugs from his friends and trade it for... you know."

"For blood? Why not just buy it from a dispensary?"

"When they get really thirsty, they want it fresh..." Christina cringed as she spoke and Mandy felt herself joining. Discussing vampire appetites felt like talking dirty. And the mental image of the regal Andreanu slinking around back alleys, hunting for a good vein. Just another junkie...

"Did he ever... get it from you?" Mandy inquired suddenly, giving into an irresistible attack of curiosity.

"No, never! He never wanted to see me that way." Her hand rose involuntarily to her neck. *But maybe you wanted him to?*

"So that's what he was doing when they got killed? Leeching off hookers and crackheads?"

Christina looked at her sharply - couldn't talk about her precious Andy like that!

"I wouldn't put it in those terms, but, yes, that's what I was concerned about... But I'm not so sure now." Her hand left her neck to dig back into her pocket. She hesitated and then pulled out a letter. She held it out to Mandy with pained reluctance.

Mandy took it. It was a strange fold for a letter - down the middle with sharp angled creases along the sides. *A paper airplane!*

"He always send you letters like this?"

"He loves his little games," she said with a sad smile. "I never know when he's going to stop by so I leave my window open when the weather's nice. He's really like a little boy in a lot of ways."

Yeah, trading designer drugs for blood and getting mixed up with serial murder. Just like a little boy!

She unfolded the letter. It was written in pen with a flowing script. The excellence of the penmanship made it seem like a letter from the distant past. Mandy's curiosity was overpowering. She didn't want to pull over again, but she didn't want to wait to read it either, so she held it against the steering wheel, her eyes devouring it in furtive gulps.

> Dearest Christina…
>
> It is an ill wind that carries this letter to you and I am afraid that you will take its contents as ill tidings. But we both know that what the Devil intends for evil, the Lord works for good. That, I trust, will be the epilogue for my own story: born for trouble, destined for peace.
>
> I had hoped to deliver this message in person, but the weight of it was too great for my tongue and so I have resorted again to the pen. Knowing that my words will bring you grief, I have also arranged, selfishly, for you to receive it without any means of responding. I hope you can forgive me this little indulgence; my hope was to preserve my last memory of you smiling at me in the rearview mirror. It is that image I wish to take with me to eternity.
>
> There is much you will hear about me in the coming days and the worst of it will probably be true. I am ashamed to have hid so much from you, but I'm not ashamed of all that I have done. I kept my actions from you not because they were wrong, but because the perception of their righteousness will be late in the coming, and I feared you would try to stop me. Such is your power over me that I would not have been able to disappoint you, no matter how just my cause.
>
> No matter what you read or hear of me, I ask that you focus on your memory of me, for you knew me better than anyone ever has. Hold up anything said about me to this mirror of memory; if there is any disparity, discard it as a falsehood and be untroubled.

I leave you now to go to the place where my struggle began. I have faced many foes since then, some you know about and others you don't. Only one remains to be vanquished and he has always been the most daunting. He is the one enemy I will not survive, or if I do, it will be because he has beaten me again. But no matter the outcome of today's battle, the outcome of the war has already been determined. I will be rid of him in the end.

"Look out!" Christina's shout pulled Mandy's eyes from the crumpled paper. So much for darting glances - the letter had consumed her. Even with Christina yelling it was hard to rip her gaze from the words and back to the road. When she did she saw two squad cars, alarmingly large and close, hurtling towards her. No, they were stationary... she was flying towards them! She slammed on the brakes.

A patrolman emerged from one of the cars, his face red with anger, his arms gesticulating wildly. Mandy lowered her window and held her badge out to stop him in his tracks.

"Sorry!" she shouted out the window as he waved her through to the street behind them. The road was rough and full of potholes, with overgrown grass and weeds taking over the cracked sidewalks that ran on both sides. The old school was further ahead on a hill, like an old ruined castle without any of the romance.

Beside her, Christina had gone deathly pale.

"All these police... did you call them out here?"

Mandy shook her head. Christina began to sob again. As they pulled into the school parking lot, they saw the yellow crime scene tape stretching in a perimeter around the building. Christina's breath shortened and she began to hyperventilate. *Am I gonna need to get paramedics out here?*

She remembered the Colonel, who had scarcely spoken a word to her before, pulling her aside and telling her in his affable way that, going forward, she wasn't even to touch the Van Helsing case. And now she was pulling up on what had all the earmarks of another Van Helsing crime scene with a key witness in her car. She felt the surge of a panicky impulse: pull a U-turn and hightail it out of here. *Nobody saw you but a red-faced patrolman who didn't really see anything but your badge.*

But her curiosity was rising even faster than the panic. Another

Van Helsing strike? At an old garbage heap like this abandoned school? That didn't fit his M.O. But this letter... It read an awful lot like a confession. Had Andreanu been Van Helsing all along? Had he been working with Dan? Then there was the church angle... If Haggerty and Dykstra were responsible like Garrick and all the newspapers were saying, maybe they would strike at their old church. Maybe Andreanu was the latest of their victims. Maybe they lured him here, playing on his past and his guilt... Her head swirled with theories.

Out of the corner of her eye, she spotted a flash of red and familiar figure. It was Francis - yep, a Van Helsing scene all right! - toting the red tape they used for the inner perimeter on murder scenes.

"Oh boy," Mandy heard herself say as her eyes tracked Francis. Christina followed her gaze and saw the red tape with HOMICIDE emblazoned all over it. She gasped and Mandy heard the sudden unbuckling of a seatbelt and the click of the door. In a blink, Christina was out of the car and sprinting up the hill towards the doors behind the red tape. Mandy struggled out of her seat to give chase, but it was too late - Christina already had twenty yards on her.

"Francis, behind you!" she shouted. Francis turned in alarm to see the pint-sized redhead sprinting towards him. He snatched her up with one arm as she shrieked and clawed to get past him.

"Get a hold of her, would ya?" Francis shouted at Mandy. Mandy closed the distance and together they wrestled Christina back to her car, depositing her back into the backseat. Francis flipped on the child safety locks and slammed the door.

"Why did you have to go and bring her here?" Francis' aviators had come off in the struggle and his blue eyes had the fearful look she remembered from his last stint on the case. *Poor guy - he just couldn't escape this case.*

"She reached out to me for help and I didn't have anything better to do. I didn't know it was going to be a crime scene!"

"You should have known better than to poke your nose back into this thing. The Colonel's gonna pitch a fit if he finds out you were here."

"He doesn't have to know," she said, peering over Francis' shoulder at the doors behind the red tape. "What do you have here? Is it Andreanu?"

"Don't you have anything better to do than get yourself into hot water?" Francis' voice was exasperated, but she could already feel his energy and will to resist fading. "Word around the office was you were getting a plum spot on some cushy new task force."

"That's all on paper right now. And I can't just sit by if Van Helsing's still at work. This has got to be another one of his, right?" She took a step towards the tape.

"Parker." He meant it to come out firmly, but it just came out limp. *Tired old man. Used the last of his reserves fighting Haggerty's daughter.* He put his arm out to bar her way, but she pushed past it like it was a turnstile.

"Keep an eye on her for a second, please," she called back over her shoulder. She heard his weak protest and shook her head. "Don't worry about me. I'll only be a minute."

The doors behind the tape opened on stairs descending down into the darkness. She felt around her waist for a flashlight only to come up empty. *You're not a patrolman anymore.* But she saw the glow of someone else's light illuminating the edge of the hallway at the bottom of the stairs and headed down.

She moved slowly. Basements were already creepy and the near pitch blackness, plus the prospect of an unknown homicide lurking around the corner didn't make her any more comfortable. There was also a strange and pungent aroma that made her nose crinkle. *Garlic.* She missed the last step in the darkness, her foot landing heavily against the linoleum.

She heard a man's voice curse and got the blinding beam of the flashlight in her face.

"Parker?" came the voice. It sounded like Reese. "Jeez. A little warning next time. It's scary enough around here without you creeping around behind me."

"Sorry... What you got?"

"Nobody told you?" A malicious grin lit up his face along with the flashlight he raised under his chin. "Here, check it out." He beckoned her over and then pulled her by the crook of the elbow until she was positioned in the middle of an open doorway. "Look straight ahead," he said quietly and then flashed the light into the interior of the room.

Mandy shrieked. Only a few feet from her was a head, suspended upside down just above the ground, long black hair dangling down, mouth horribly ajar, dead black eyes staring right at her. It was Mikhail Andreanu.

Reese laughed. "Freaky, right? Imagine coming around the corner and having that staring at you with no one else around. I'm just glad I wore my brown pants today."

Mandy grabbed his flashlight and moved in closer. The smell of garlic was overpowering now. She peered closely into the half open mouth to see several pale lumps shoved in there. A few had fallen onto the ground. Garlic cloves.

She continued, treading carefully. His whole body was angled backwards, like a gymnast starting a backflip. A wooden stake rising from the floor pierced his back and poked through his chest. *A butterfly on a pin.* There was a tripod platform under the stake, holding it upright. From the looks of it, Andreanu set it up and then fell, tripped or got pushed backwards.

"How did you find him?" she asked. Basement of an abandoned building... From the looks of it, no janitor or maintenance man had stepped foot in this place for years.

"Charlie Grace got another letter. This time he was smart enough to let us know before he got the scoop himself. Guy had a lot of writing to do before he kicked it. Check out his hand."

She followed the right arm that hung limply from his body - rigor mortis must have come and went - to his hand, fingers just barely hanging on to a rolled up letter. The urge to reach out and grab it was almost irresistible.

"Bet you a million bucks that's our confession letter, right there. Could have wrapped it in a bow."

She turned back the flashlight on Reese to see him grinning. Could he be right? Was this it? Van Helsing a vamp? Done in by his own hand, in his own style? She felt a sudden rush of anger. Reese over there grinning like he solved this case. *I do all the legwork and you get to walk in when it's all wrapped up and act like you're Sherlock Holmes?*

"When's crime scene getting here? I've got to get a look at that letter."

"They should be here any minute now..." His face wrinkled. "So they put you back on the case?"

"No, not officially. I was just in the neighborhood."

His grin flipped into a scowl and he reached to grab her elbow again.

"Then what the f*** are you doing on our scene? You better

get out of here before the Colonel shows up or it's all of our hides." He pushed her roughly back into the dark hallway, deftly snatching the flashlight from her hands, and then blocked the door with his big frame.

Her protests failed to move him and so she crept her way back to the stairway and towards the faint light surrounding the doors to the outside. As she climbed the stairs, the fire of her curiosity began to dwindle and anxiety snuck back in. Would there be angry brass on the other side of the doors? She pushed them open with trepidation. *Nope, just Francis.*

"That Haggerty girl's making an awful racket in your car. Would you get her out of here?"

His panic was contagious. She moved briskly to the car, hearing Christina's wailing from the back seat grow louder. She slipped into the car and put it in reverse.

"Is he dead?" Christina blubbered.

"Yes," Mandy said quietly, bracing for another round of hysterics. Instead, the wails subsided into ragged breaths.

"How?"

Normally Mandy would have put up more resistance to a grieving party, but she was distracted by the unmarked car heading straight for them on her way back out. "A stake through his chest, a mouthful of garlic, just like the other Van Helsing victims."

Mandy tried to avert her gaze and hide her face as the car passed, but to no avail. There was no mistaking the jowls that turned to look at her. *The Colonel!*

"Are you saying he was murdered, like the others?"

Mandy let Christina stew, clenching her hands on the wheel as a powerful wave of irritation swept over her. Why did she have to slink around just to help out on a case that had been hers a few days ago? Now she was going to get chewed out, maybe even suspended, for following a lead. Not even one she pursued, but one that fell in her lap and one she'd been about to dump on Francis only to have her dumped right back.

She spied Christina in the rearview mirror, staring at her expectantly with her red, puffy eyes. Ready, even eager, to spill whatever was left in her guts on Andreanu. Maybe enough in there to bust the Van Helsing case wide open. But what was she going to do? Interview her on the sly, type it up and then give it to Francis and Reese? Let them take the victory laps, while she cooled her heels on ODs and hoped the Colonel wasn't so pissed he'd take her off Garrick's task force?

She looked over to the passenger seat in the desperate hope that Vlad would be there, his sharp eyes cutting through her uncertainty, his quick mind untangling her mess, his warm hands grasping her trembling shoulders... He would know what to do.

The gas station just before the interstate had a row of payphones that beckoned. A quarter in the slot and the wire would take her to Maggie and then a punch of her finger to his voice. *No. You're done dancing on that line. Just take her home and wait for Garrick.* She nodded at the sageness of this advice to herself as she pulled up in front of the payphones and stepped out of the car.

"Won't you please speak to me?" came Christina's plaintive cry from the backseat.

"Just a second," Mandy said as she closed the door and dialed. Maggie's cheerful voice filled the receiver.

"I'm guessing you're over there at the big scene at the old school?" Maggie asked after they waded through their usual small talk.

"Who told you that?" Mandy felt defensive and vulnerable all of a sudden. Just how many people knew she was here?

"This whole place has been buzzing. Everybody's there or on their way."

"Vlad too?"

"Of course. You know him. He couldn't resist something like this no matter who told him to stay away." She continued in a low voice, just above a whisper. "Is it true what they're saying? Did they finally get Van Helsing?"

Mandy's eyes drifted to the street where a familiar black Mercedes was heading eastbound, towards the school. *Vlad.*

"Sorry, gotta go," she said, leaving the receiver hanging and sprinting towards the road, waving her arms like a pant-suited cheerleader. Vlad saw her and slammed on the brakes, hopping out of the car, his eyes wide with alarm.

"What's the matter? Are you okay?" His eyes scanned the gas station parking lot for threats.

"I'm fine," she said, reddening. "You probably don't want to go all the way in - the scene is crawling with higher-ups by now."

"Did you see it?" he asked, his eyes narrowing on her with an intensity that made it hard to breathe. She gave him a quick recap of what she had seen, and what she hadn't - the letter clutched in Andreanu's hand.

Vlad moved in closer. "Could it have really been Andreanu this whole time? Was he working with Dan? Was Dan manipulating him? We've still got to find Dan…"

He trailed off, his eyes flicking to movement in the back of her car. He raised his eyebrows quizzically.

"Christina Haggerty!" Mandy heard her voice jump several octaves in excitement. His hands grasping her arms, his electricity pulsing through her. They were back on the case! They were going to solve it. "Her alibi for Andreanu was a lie. And I think she's ready to tell us the whole story on him."

"This is it, isn't it?" His eyes turned back to her with an almost childlike sparkle.

"I think so." Her voice was still high and breathless. "If we can just get her in front of a tape recorder we might be able to put the whole timeline together."

"I've got some equipment at home. If we can get something really concrete, something rock solid…"

They were so close now she could feel his breath. She looked up into his eyes, basking in their passionate intensity. But as soon as their eyes locked, a darkness swept over his forehead and over his eyes and he looked away. His demeanor changed with alarming suddenness, his shoulders drooping, his chest heaving in a pained sigh.

"What's the matter?"

"It's not going to work." He pulled away from her and looked back to his car. "I shouldn't have even come down here. I let my curiosity get the better of my judgment." He glanced at Christina in the car. "You should take her to the station and let them decide what they want with her. This case doesn't belong to us anymore."

The abrupt shift from the warmth of his gaze to the cold shoulder brought on a feeling of anger so visceral it felt like nausea. *I don't know if I should spit on him or throw up.*

"Is there something so wrong with me that you can't even bear the thought of working with me again?"

"There's nothing wrong with you," he said tersely, unwilling to look at her. "There are some roads you just don't walk down."

"That's ridiculous. You were willing to spit in the face of the whole department, the whole community on nothing more than a hunch." Mandy heard the anger in her voice rising, and her volume with it. But she couldn't rein it in. "But as soon as I enter the picture it's the company line all the way down. Why don't you just admit you can't stand to be with me?"

"That's not true and you know it."

"Then stop acting like I'm toxic." She lowered her voice, softening. "I just want my partner back. I want to finish what we started." She reached out to hold his hand.

He looked at her now, pain in his eyes. "You don't know what you're asking. You haven't been down this road before. I have. And I can't do it again." He shed her hand and strode to the car, not looking back.

Mandy felt tears escaping her eyes. She brushed them away roughly with her sleeve and turned back to her car. She saw Christina staring at her and looked at the ground. She got into the driver's seat and did her best not to slam the door.

"I can take you back now," she said sullenly.

"You're not going to tell me what you saw?" came the quiet voice from behind her.

"He's dead," Mandy blurted out. "I'm sorry, but he's dead and there's nothing more I can tell you."

Christina began to cry again, not the hysterics from before but a soft sniffling. Mandy felt like joining her and the realization irritated her. What a pathetic pair of caricatures they were, mooning over brooding vampire men who could never give them the time of day. But recognizing the cliche didn't make it hurt any less.

23

Infested. The word crawled into Enoch's brain and stayed there, wriggling and multiplying like the little white orbs clinging to the bottoms of the spring leaves in the orchard back home. Emily had told him the bad news the previous evening. The boys had spotted them and reported back to her that they were everywhere. *As if the blight wasn't enough?*

Hexbugs was what his mother had called them, not, she claimed, because they were a curse but because of the hexagonal shape of their bodies. That may have just been another of Mother's attempts to sanitize the petty pagan artifacts of her upbringing because the devastation wrought by the nasty little critters sure felt like a curse.

As soon as those eggs hatched, the tiny bugs would venture out like a Mongol horde, devouring every fruit in their path until they grew into insatiable monsters the size of Enoch's thumb, so full of acrid chemicals that even his chickens wouldn't eat them. The soft, fuzzy flesh of his baby peaches, punctured relentlessly by those miniature mandibles. Death by a thousand little bites.

It had been almost a decade since he'd had to deal with the horrid little things. It took weeks of painstaking pesticide application to the bottom of just about every leaf in the orchard to be rid of them. It was far less painful to prevent them by keeping the base of the trees mulched and free of weeds and other insect havens, but he'd let the landscaping slip when the new grandbaby came.

Emily hadn't come out and said it but they both knew the boys wouldn't be able to handle it on their own. They'd hardly been out of diapers the last time the bugs had been out in force and they didn't have the knowhow. Nor did they have the wiggle room to hire on an experienced hand to help them - Enoch had burned through the rainy day fund on this expedition, though he was making enough to send a little home now. The choice was inescapable: return home now or lose their biggest and most reliable cash crop of the year.

The thought of it dogged him for the whole day he'd been on the job. The new construction site was up in the hills, beyond the furthest limits of the city. Perhaps the air up that high was a little thinner, but the work had taken much more out of him. The work itself wasn't so unusual - just clearing and leveling the ground for an extension of what seemed to be a giant medical complex up there. But it was getting lonelier. Angel had come off his suspension and returned to police work, and many of the migrant laborers they had become close with had left to return home with their earnings. That left only a handful of familiar faces to go along with his only truly constant companions: the aches in his back, arms and legs. He felt only relief when he told the boss it was his last day and collected his final payment.

When he'd crossed the threshold of the Garden Inn that evening he'd kicked his boots on the door frame to dislodge the mud caked around the soles. *Shake the dust off your feet.* The thought had brought tears to his eyes. Was that what Mandy had been reduced to? Dust to dust, ashes to ashes. Was his little girl truly lost?

No! his mind shouted back into the void. She was not yet lost, not yet forsaken. Perhaps the Lord had sent him on this expedition for Angel. Perhaps he had something else in store for Amanda's rescue. *But the dreams...* Why had the Lord sent him those terrible dreams?

These anxious thoughts hammered at his head like an anvil chorus. He pulled the suitcase from the closet and began to pack, clicking on the TV. He had successfully resisted this Pandora's box of titillating vice for the duration of his stay, only turning it on for Pastor Haggerty's program. But tonight he needed some kind of noise without to combat the noise within.

Haggerty's program wasn't on TV anymore. In its place was a

vulgar display of young women wearing brightly colored skin-tight clothing and gyrating their hips provocatively, supposedly in the pursuit of fitness! He sighed and changed the channel to the local news program. A woman with hair dyed so blonde as to be almost white, her face hidden behind a mask of makeup, spoke in a strangely upbeat voice about the daily roll of murder and mayhem.

The screen cut to a shot of an old school building behind yellow crime scene tape. The chyron running at the bottom of the screen said "VAN HELSING STRIKES AGAIN?"

"Police have yet to release the victim's name and information, but sources within the department have told Channel 7 news that it is indeed another vampire and the scene has all the signatures of Van Helsing. If confirmed, this would be the fifth victim of the serial killer, all of them vampires."

The screen cut back to the female reporter with a picture of Pastor Haggerty and another man - Enoch thought he might be the big security guard who had always been hovering by the pastor's side.

"This news comes as the manhunt for River City televangelist Jim Haggerty and his head of security Peter Dykstra, intensifies. The two are wanted for the murder of city councilman and leading vampire statesman Simion Codrescu. Our sources also inform us that they are persons of interest in the Van Helsing investigation. Meanwhile the city continues its month of mourning for the fallen councilman, with a march of remembrance scheduled for tomorrow morning. Our reporter Chet Hainsley has the latest..."

Enoch sat heavily against the bed and its garish orange comforter as the reporter spoke in front of workers assembling a big red parade float. He leaned back and stared upwards, looking again for God in the cloudy tufts of the popcorn ceiling. Everything in River City seemed so upside down. A famous man of God as the prime suspect in a serial killer case! A vampire - an open practitioner of a Satanic cult! - elected to leadership of the city and held up as a martyr.

He wondered what the talking head with her electric blonde hair would say about him and his family and his little church back home. In his father's day, city folk had regarded them as the salt of the earth, envying the cleanliness of their air, the slow pace and simplicity of their daily life, and the sincerity of their faith. A place to visit to refresh their souls and send their children in the summers… But modern city-dwellers seemed to view their country cousins with suspicion and disdain. When it wasn't sneering at them as slow and backwards, the media painted them as gun-toting religious extremists and potential enemies of the state.

Enoch had left his guns back home, but this city did make him feel like an extremist where religion was concerned. It wasn't just the moral laxity and religious indifference of his immediate surroundings. No, there had been enough of that at home, though nowhere near as flagrant as it was here. It was the outright hostility to belief that he'd never encountered before. From the local newscasters to the mayor and her councilmen, when they spoke of religion it was as if the word itself was synonymous with hate and violence. They spoke of Pastor Haggerty, who struck Enoch as a sincere if perhaps too showmanly preacher, in tones couched with fear and horror.

But perhaps they were right to be afraid. A man of faith who spent any extended stretch of time in a place like this, where the highest authorities called good evil and evil good, would be stirred to a righteous anger that might look a lot like hatred to someone outside the faith. Enoch had felt similar stirrings in himself on his walks through town, and especially when he listened to the radio on the drives to the job sites, or flipped on the news as he had tonight.

One more reason to head home, before the mantle of Elijah slips onto my shoulders and I do something that gets me in hot water with these city folk. It could easily be his picture next to Haggerty's and that security man on the TV. He'd been there at the baptism when all hell broke loose. His amens had rung out in those pews when the pastor had railed against the crimson stain of vampirism in the city. His own off-the-cuff ramblings on the subject had been enough to make Mandy redden in embarrassment and check to see if anyone else in the little cafe had heard him.

He muted the TV in disgust and began to pile his clothes in his suitcase. A knock on the door roused him from his creeping lethargy. He checked his watch. It was about time for his neighbor's parade of gentlemen callers to commence. Several of these, probably the most drunk and distracted of the lot, would inevitably knock on Enoch's door. They were invariably shocked to see Enoch's skinny six feet and five inches filling the door frame instead of his neighbor's voluptuous five and two. Enoch unlatched his suitcase to fish out the tracts that he had been giving them and then reached the door in a single long stride.

He swung the door inward, shocked to see not another slump-shouldered, shifty-eyed john but his own daughter, her hands clasped behind her back, stabbing at the concrete floor of the motel patio with her toe.

"Mandy!" he shouted with unfeigned joyfulness and grabbed her in a hug. She hugged him back and lingered in his embrace, as if sucking up the warmth of his affection. From over his shoulder she spied his suitcase on the bed and pulled back from him, giving him a look. Was it reproach in her eyes? Did she not want him to leave now?

"Headed back home?" Yes, there was a strong undercurrent of disappointment in her voice.

"Hexbug infestation in the orchard."

"Oh… that's too bad." She chewed her lip. "I thought your truck was still in the shop?"

"The truck's been fixed for over a week now."

"Really? I'm surprised you stuck around, then. Mom and everybody else have to be missing you terribly."

"Your mother's been very patient with me. She knows I had important business to attend to here." Enoch reached out and grabbed her hands. She blushed and stared down at the ground, shyly.

"I'm sorry I ignored you. Leaving you alone in this terrible motel…"

"It's not so bad once you get used to the smell," he said with a smile.

She avoided his gaze to look around the motel, settling on the TV. "Since when did you start watching TV?" she asked in surprise.

"A man can resist only so much temptation."

She found the remote and turned on the sound, taking a seat on the bed.

"We go live now to Councilman Garrick, who has just begun to address the press regarding the latest Van Helsing slaying…"

The program cut to a handsome young man in mid-speech, his blue eyes boring holes in the screen in their emotional intensity.

"This reign of terror ends now. For far too long, our vampire community has been forced to live in fear of us, their neighbors. In spite of this fear, they have devoted their careers, their talents, their lives, to making our city a better place, to bring jobs and prosperity, to develop lifesaving medicines and technology... And how have we repaid them? By fostering a climate of envy and hatred based on the baseless superstitions and outright lies of our past."

"Our police continue to do their best to apprehend the individuals responsible for these terrible killings and for the murder of my colleague, and the city will continue to do its utmost to accomplish this. But this problem goes beyond a few rogue actors and beyond the powers of law enforcement. The deeper problem is within us, in our midst, lurking in our churches, our clubs, even our family gatherings... Until every citizen of River City decides to refuse sanctuary to the backward beliefs and intolerance that linger in our own communities, hatred and violence will continue to find safe harbor in our city."

Enoch glanced over at Mandy as she shook her head in disbelief. "Did he not see the crime scene? Why are they still banging this drum?"

Enoch reached forward and turned off the TV with the switch on the set.

"You didn't come over here to watch TV, did you?"

"No, of course not," she said slowly, staring at the ground again.

"Then let's talk. We've left too much unsaid and now I've got to go."

"I'm sorry it took me so long to come over. If I'm being completely honest, I just didn't want to face you." Her voice dropped just above a whisper. "I know you've got to be disappointed in me... in the choices I've made..."

"It's always hard on a parent when their child goes off into the world and has to make their own choices, but I have to admit you could have done a lot worse than Angel."

"We're not together anymore."

"Yes... but it might not hurt to give it another chance. I know he'd be willing. You've already built so much together, given each other so much..."

"You know he wasn't my first, right?" She gave him a look that looked a lot like pity.

"Ahh... the undertaker back home." Just the thought of that greasy-haired predator filled Enoch with pain. *The wolf loose among the flock.* How had they not seen the risk? How had he failed to protect her from a man ten years her senior?

"Now there was a mistake," she said with a sigh. "I was in a very dark place when all that fell apart and that's when I met Angel. He helped me get back on my feet when I was struggling and I'll always be grateful for that."

"He's a good man. The kind who can help you build something that lasts."

"I'm sure he is. But I think I'm better off taking a break from relationships for a little while. I don't want to keep making the same mistakes." She stared back at the ground, her toes dangling just above the carpet as she slung her legs over the sides of the tall bed.

"That sounds like good solid wisdom, sweetheart. The good news is no mistake has to be permanent." He studied her as she continued to stare at the ground. Could this be it? The moment he'd been praying for? She didn't say anything.

"I remember when you were first born, you were so small I could almost hold you in the palm of my hand..." He held out his palm and she looked up at it, smiling. "I haven't been able to hold you like that since, as much as I might want to. But Jesus has bigger hands than I do, and he says that no one will be able to snatch-"

"Dad." She interrupted him, a cold firmness in her voice. "I came over here to apologize and to talk but that doesn't mean I want to get preached at."

"I didn't mean to preach at you."

"I know you didn't. It just spills out of you." Her words came out of her like a sigh. "I want you to be a bigger part of my life, dad, but if all you can think about is the Bible, we're not going to have much to say to each other."

Enoch knew his face must have fallen because he saw a stronger version of the previous pity in her eyes. It was his turn to stare at the floor.

"You really don't believe in it anymore?" he said to the low-pile carpet.

"No, Dad. I'm not sure I ever did." Then, in a half-hearted attempt to staunch the wound. "But I still believe in you. You're a good person and a good dad and I don't want to lose you."

"You're never going to lose me, sweetheart."

They embraced again and she began to talk, pouring out her

frustrations with her job, her boss, the city. There was passion in her voice, so much so that she was almost trembling. Enoch did his best to listen and nod, but his mind and eyes kept straying to the sight of her slender frame sinking deeper and deeper into the orange comforter that surrounded her like the flames of hell.

***

Each time Vlad left the Missing Persons office, which was quite frequently now that the weather had turned so happily warm, he took a heaping of dust with him on his person. The knees of his pants bore the worst of it from him kneeling amidst the stacks of files, organizing, stacking, discarding. Trip after trip, he went to and fro, carrying with him the debris of a decade of neglect on the fibers of his clothing, a human feather duster. After a while, the dusty cloud that followed him on these journeys took on the aspect of a ghost, dogging his every step, silently demanding resolution.

Vlad had at least finagled a couple live bodies from headquarters, including his old whipping boy from Homicide, Valentine, to replace the institutional deadweight he had inherited. In doing so he had inadvertently created a new file for the bureau, as one of the detectives assigned to Missing Persons turned out to be a missing person himself, having gone several years without ever coming to the office or having any contact with the department. It took an afternoon of detective's work on Vlad's part to discover that someone was at least still cashing the detective's biweekly paycheck somewhere in the Caribbean.

The corruption and sheer incompetence that this little administrative detour had uncovered had gotten Vlad's dander up for a while. But after a circuitous series of journeys into the bureaucratic labyrinth of human resources and payroll in a fruitless attempt to stop payments to the erstwhile detective, Vlad's wrath was spent and replaced with a begrudging admiration. He still harbored the desire to track the man down, but now with a mind to join him. *What better destination for a Vampirate captain?*

But such daydreams succumbed to Vlad's irresistible instinct to set his dusty little fief into order. As soon as he had secured his new detectives, and cured them of their expectation of a life of ease and obscurity in the departmental glue factory, he had doubled down on the work of clearing the backlogged files and setting the bureau back on the straight and narrow. Having weighed down his reluctant workhorses with the cases that were most likely to be cleared with a few phone calls from the office, he reserved the hardest cases, those promising the most legwork, for himself. Foremost among these in his mind was Patricia Currington.

On this day, he was retracing Detective Gore's steps through the red light district. He hadn't known whether to expect that the same hookers would be working the same corners, but sure enough there were. *Who said there were no constants in this world?* He found them less forthcoming with him than they had been with Gore. Their faces, hard behind the soft cakes of make-up punctuated with smokey arcs of eye shadow and bursts of bright rouge, regarded him with suspicion and fear. Vlad could tell it wasn't the usual dead-eye stare they reserved for cops and it certainly wasn't the come-hither look for johns. He'd seen the same look in the eyes of old church ladies when he'd made scenes as a patrolman. It was the xenophobic dread of a vampire. But Vlad didn't know if these ladies of the night had a more legitimate basis for their fear than their Sunday morning sisters.

"Do I make you uncomfortable?" he asked the frizzy blonde, who stood a little ahead of the others.

"You aren't our type," she said flatly.

"What if someone like me was looking for someone to keep me company tonight?"

"You'd have to ask around. But none of the girls here would be interested."

"How about her?" he said, proffering the picture of Patricia. "Did she like guys like me?"

She looked at him coolly and shrugged.

"Is there anyone in particular that might have picked her up that night? Anyone you might recognize?" Vlad reached his hand around to his back pocket and thumbed the photo line-up that had Dan and the rest of the Bat Pack sandwiched between a variety of other vamps and pale-faced natives.

"No and like we told you before, we already told that other detective everything we know." She gave her blonde wig a flip to signify that the conversation was over and turned to walk away, the others following her lead.

Vlad gritted his teeth in frustration and grabbed her elbow before she could get out of reach. He felt a quiver pass through her body and saw her knees buckle. Her stiletto heels couldn't take the sudden shift of her weight and she fell to the ground. Vlad immediately regretted his roughness and stooped to help her. She turned to face him with eyes wide in terror, holding one hand to ward him off and pushing herself away with the other.

"I'm sorry," Vlad stammered. "I wanted to ask you one more question."

As he reached his hand out to help her up, she let out a shriek that made Vlad recoil. The girls around her pulled her to her feet and they trotted off as fast as their heels would take them. Vlad stood there feeling foolish as the passersby rolled down their windows to stare at him. Even the homeless man on the corner stopped his schizophrenic ranting to cast him a suspicious glare.

So much for that avenue. But her horror at his grasp spoke much louder than her silence. For a seasoned prostitute like this blonde, whose hard-lined face and dull eyes suggested many years of experience and abuse on the streets, to transform into a petrified damsel in distress at his mere touch... Her look was that of a prey animal staring into the face of her most dreaded predator.

Vlad watched the hookers still running, the sun setting in front of them, and felt the hairs rising on his neck. This was a vampire hunting ground. That was what Petricean was doing down here so many nights. Preying on the prostitutes and junkies that littered these streets. Luring the most desperate of them with those designer drugs and then dragging them back to the lion's den. Dan's estate. Those human-sized cages. These monsters were dragging the community back to the dark ages.

A honk sounded from behind him. He turned to see Valentine leaning out the window of an old Crown Vic.

"Why the long face, cap?" he grinned, nodding at the retreating hookers. "Ladies didn't want to ride the V-train?"

Vlad blinked away his thoughts to focus on the red-faced fool in front of him. "Ladies? Enough Adam's apples to fill an orchard. You can probably still catch them though."

Valentine's face fell at the surprise jab. "What are you doing here?" Vlad offered him as a reprieve.

"The satellite company says they finally got a preliminary signal from that tracker you gave Dan."

Vlad brightened, thoughts of Patricia Currington receding as the scent of the old prey wafted back into his path. "Where is he?"

"It's too early to tell. They need a few more readings I guess."

"And how long will that take?"

"A day?" he said, shrugging.

Vlad felt a sharp but familiar stab of irritation and remembered again why Valentine had been so easy to pluck away from Homicide. "You stopped work on all those cases I gave you just to drive out here and tell me we're a day away from maybe getting a fix on Dan?"

Another shrug and a dumb, vacant look. "I thought you'd want to know." Vlad glared at him in unveiled aggravation. Valentine's expression changed into something less idiotic and more pitiable. "Please don't send me back to that dungeon," he pleaded. "I'll suffocate if I have to spend another minute in there. Don't you have anything for me to do out here?"

They went back and forth for a few minutes before Vlad gave in; Valentine had a way of wearing him down.

"Fine. You win. Follow me down to the impound lot. There's an idea I want to test tonight."

The impound lot had been tucked into the shadows of gigantic overpasses where River City's two major freeways met. The city must have hoped that the huge concrete arches would hide this elephant's graveyard of rusted out, smashed up, dust covered wrecks. But the city proved too deadly to automobiles to keep within these limits and the lot had ineluctably broken out of its containment to turn the once idyllic meadow surrounding the freeways into an extension of the blighted wasteland.

Vlad and Valentine carefully navigated the narrow paths through the wreckage to arrive at the hangar where they kept the vehicles still under investigation as well as the few precious intact luxury vehicles that fell into the lot's hands. The jewel of the lot was Petricean's Rolls-Royce Phantom, which shone like a diamond in their eyes after the endless parade of junkers they endured to reach it.

It took some negotiating and cattle trading with the lot Lieutenant to pry this crown jewel of his collection out of his clutches. In the end it took Vlad's promise to get with his contacts on the Gleaner's Club board to make sure the Lieutenant's recently graduated spawn could get an interview at one of the big finance outfits downtown just to borrow the thing for a couple hours.

Vlad checked first to make sure there were no more secret compartments full of contraband and then they were off. The

Phantom was an intoxicating driving machine, so powerful it rocked Vlad back in his seat at the lightest touch of the accelerator but nimble enough to turn on a dime, and all of it whisper-quiet. It felt like he was leaving the lot on a magic carpet.

The thrills of driving such a car were diminished by Valentine's presence next to him. He was quieter than usual - maybe he was busy working out the best way to ask whether he could drive. Vlad enjoyed the silence but felt an unpleasant stab somewhere in his gut every time he saw something shifting in his peripheral vision and he turned to see Valentine's greasy red face instead of Mandy's perfect alabaster skin.

He distracted himself from these pangs by refocusing his mind on their little adventure. Driving Petricean's car along Petricean's old route - he still remembered the circuits traced by Mrs. Petricean's magic screens - might not accomplish anything concrete but it wasn't just a joyride. He hoped the sight of a vampire driving Petricean's car through his old haunt might trigger something new, just as his presence had broken through the hooker's opaque facade earlier that afternoon.

It was dark by the time they reached the decrepit parking garage downtown, its human wreckage spilling its bounds in an uncanny likeness to the creeping junk of the impound lot. They entered the labyrinth and began the spiral upwards to the fateful spot on the third floor.

The difference from his previous trek into this domain was immediate. The sallow faces of the homeless no longer stared lifelessly at him as they had when he'd driven through in his BMW. Instead, they sparked with interest and something close to excitement. Their arrival sent a ripple through the downtrodden masses, transforming their languorous repose into a buzz of activity.

Valentine shifted uneasily in his seat. It was one thing to ride in here running several squad cars deep. It was another to do so in a car worth six figures without a uniform in sight, especially when the crowd was stirring to agitated life instead of cowering in their tents.

"You remember any of these faces?" Vlad asked.

"Dunno," he said with a shrug. "After a while, all the toothless crackheads start to blend into each other in your mind."

"Any of them from that group that Bouchard brought by

headquarters to be interviewed?"

That set something ping-ponging around in that empty head of his. "Oh yeah… Yeah, definitely. A bunch of them."

"Did any of them say anything about recognizing this car or Petricean?"

"I don't think so."

As they rounded the corner to reach the second floor, the crowd began to push forward on both sides, arms outstretched, eyes wide. Several were pushed in front of them and Vlad slowed, honking the horn and inching forward in hopes that they would get out of the way. Valentine shifted again.

"It's like a zombie movie in here. Have you seen enough? Can we get out of here?"

Vlad ignored him, pushing forward slowly as the shuffling horde continued to cluster around the car. Their faces, startlingly full of life and desire, were so different from the dead stares he was accustomed to seeing from these derelicts. This car had been a vehicle of hope for them, carrying earthly delights far more coveted than the necessities in Bouchard's "homeless ice cream truck." It seemed to Vlad beyond doubt now that Dan's crew peddled their chemical wares here. But he had already known that or at least suspected it. What he wanted to find out now is what would be awaiting them on the third floor.

As the Phantom crested the ramp that brought them to the third floor, the surrounding scenery changed markedly. The clusters of tents were gone along with the masses of glassy-eyed and long-bearded homeless men that had swarmed out of them. In their place were rows of fifth wheel trailers, vans and other spacious vehicles, all showing varying degrees of dilapidation and decay, but most showing at least some signs of use and maintenance. The population, much less concentrated, was also overwhelmingly female; their cheap clothes, uniformly bright and skintight and some gleaming with rhinestones, made a dazzling contrast with the filthy rags a floor below. The handful of men were transvestites or leather-clad male prostitutes, though Vlad spied a few shadowy figures behind the campers that he guessed were pimps.

All eyes were on the Phantom as Vlad snaked towards the vacant spot at the north end of the floor where they had found it. As he parked, they saw the prostitutes moving slowly and cautiously toward them. Desire and fear mingled in their bright eyes. Valentine jumped in his seat as a sudden pounding came on his window - he had been too busy ogling the girls to see the approach. Vlad rolled the window down and a shadowy face peered in. He had none of the accoutrements associated with the profession - no fedora, cane or flashy jewelry - but the shark eyes and the way the women lingered expectantly behind him said "pimp" loud enough.

The pimp looked at Vlad first but his eyes lingered on Valentine. He shook his head.

"Looks like you boys made a wrong turn. There's nothing for you here."

"We're just looking for some company and conversation," Vlad said slowly.

He shook his head again. "You're looking in the wrong place. This is a rough neighborhood. You should leave before something bad happens." He delivered the threat flatly, his monotone harboring more than enough menace.

"We'll just be a minute," Vlad replied, opening his door and signaling Valentine to do the same. As Valentine popped the handle the pimp slammed it back in his face.

"I told you-" the pimp gasped in mid-sentence, the air in his body evacuated by Valentine's fist that had sped through the open window and directly into his solar plexus. Valentine popped the handle again, quickly, and this time kicked the door out with his leg, the frame catching the stunned pimp in the chin and knocking him backward. Leaping out of the vehicle, Valentine stomped savagely on the hand that was reaching towards the black handle of a gun poking from the pimp's exposed waistband. Valentine was about to reach for his own gun when Vlad stilled with a sharp command.

"Just hold him there. I want to talk to the girls."

The hookers shrank back slowly as he approached but there was something in his countenance that stilled them as his long strides closed the gap. They looked petrified. Vlad fished in his pocket to retrieve the picture of Patricia Currington and showed it to them.

"Do any of you know this woman?"

Their wide eyes glanced from the picture back to Vlad's face, but they said nothing.

"One of you had to have known her," he pleaded. "She was one of your own. She was working in this garage. I just want to know, was she picked up in a car like this by a man who looked like me?"

They look back at him with dumb stares, their mouths not budging.

"Did you know they found her body in the river? Her head missing... Her body half-eaten... No way to recognize her other than the serial number of the birth control device she had stuck up in the one place the fish and the crabs hadn't got to?"

Vlad's eyes darted to a younger, dark-haired member of the group who had gasped in horror. He zeroed in on her, the weakest of the herd. The other girls parted to clear his way to her.

"You knew her, didn't you?" he demanded. Her face held the blank look of the others, but betrayed hints of grief around the margins - a quiver around her cheek, a moistening at the corners of her eyes, the shortness of her breath. "You know who took her."

She shook her head and attempted an insolent sneer. "I don't know what you're talking about," she said, her tone petulant. But again, her face betrayed her, her lips trembling as if she was holding back a sob. But she didn't wither under Vlad's fearful glare.

He suddenly reached out to snatch her by the shoulders, simultaneously drawing himself up to his full height to scowl down at her. He bared his teeth in as savage a snarl as he could muster. The way she wilted in his grasp, he wondered if his canines had transformed into a proper set of tabloid fangs.

"You're going to open your mouth and tell me everything you know, whore, or I'm going to rip the truth out of your throat."

The ferocity of his speech surprised him. He hesitated for a moment, fearing he had gone too far. But no sooner had he drawn in his imaginary fangs than the girl's resistance broke and she dissolved into tears.

"Don't hurt me," she whimpered, sinking to the ground, her whole body shaking.

Vlad fought off a wave of sympathy and dug his fingers cruelly into her arms. "Tell me!"

"There was a car..." she began, struggling to speak, her voice barely a whisper. She was shaking so much, she seemed to be on the verge of convulsions. Vlad eased up, relaxing his grip but not releasing her. "Just like that one..." She trailed off, looking around at the other girls and beyond them to the row of campers.

"And?" He shook her again but she had clammed up. Vlad hesitated, then roughly yanked her to her feet and dragged her to the car, tossing her into the backseat. "Get in," he barked at Valentine.

Valentine snatched the pistol from the pimp's waistband and frisked his pant legs before pulling his foot off him.

"Give him his gun back," Vlad ordered, adding sharply: "And pay the man!" Valentine looked at him, incredulous. "We're taking his girl, he should have some compensation." Vlad turned to the pimp, still laying on his back. "Fifty should cover it." The pimp grunted.

Valentine, still shaking his head, reluctantly pulled the cash from his wallet, then field stripped the weapon and dropped the parts and the cash in a heap on the pimp's belly.

Vlad peeled out of the garage at a reckless speed, not giving the zombies on the lower floors a chance to swarm again. As he gunned it over the speed bumps at the exit, he caught Valentine staring at him, slack-jawed.

"What?" he snapped.

"We're not actually *hiring* that girl, are we?" he asked, Vlad detecting a note of hopefulness in his voice.

Vlad ignored him and pressed on the accelerator to rocket down 4th Street. He wanted to get this girl out of her usual territory as fast as possible. Somewhere that felt remote. Somewhere with some dark woods.

"That was pretty wild back there, cap," Valentine began and Vlad sighed internally. *Here comes the babbling.* "I mean I almost thought you were gonna bite the girl for a second. Some real Dracula sh**. No offense. But it was pretty bad-ass!"

"Just be quiet," Vlad snapped again, throwing him his most chilling Dracula look to shut him up. Valentine silenced, Vlad glanced at the rearview mirror to see the girl quivering again. *Good, let her be afraid.* He had just the place in mind.

There was a thick copse of trees next to the freeway that had been preserved from the manic building spree around downtown and now served primarily as a place for fleeing felons to lose cops in foot pursuits. It was usually too dense, swampy and bug-ridden to attract either the homeless or any yuppie hikers. That made it perfect for Vlad's purposes.

He pulled into the copse using an overgrown maintenance road that dead-ended under a canopy of overhanging branches and vines.

"Let her out," he told Valentine, watching for the girl's reactions in the rearview mirror. She was staring out the windows into the encroaching darkness at the moss-covered trunks. Her shakes intensified, bordering on convulsions.

Valentine handled her like she had leprosy, holding her out at arm's length, as she wriggled and squirmed and shook like an animal in its death throes. "Is she okay? You think we should call an ambulance?"

"Set her loose," Vlad said coolly. Valentine released her and she dropped like a ragdoll to the ground. But on Vlad's approach she pushed herself onto all fours and scrambled away. Vlad followed at a measured pace. Stumbling awkwardly to her feet, she shed her heels and took off running into the forest. Vlad followed her.

Valentine, like an eager puppy, took off at a sprint, but Vlad slung out an arm to catch him mid-stride.

"Stay back with the car. I'll handle this."

Valentine looked concerned but obeyed and Vlad resumed his pursuit. The girl would have made easy prey for either of them at a sprint; she was making pitifully slow progress, staggering and stumbling in her bare feet over the sticks, roots and brambles that choked the forest floor. Even the darkness of the forest canopy and the thick cover of the dense foliage would have afforded her little protection, so loud was her ragged breathing and the grunts of pain as pine cones and sharp rocks poked at her feet.

But Vlad kept his slow pace and chose his steps carefully, stealthily. He wanted the forest darkness to surround her, overwhelm her. He wanted his shadowy, silent presence to torment her in its absence. *A sick game, but not without its thrills.* He regretted the euphoric sensation that clouded his mind and did his best to subordinate it to his clinical purposes. But his heartbeat quickened all the same.

He heard a sharp cry of pain and a crunching of underbrush as she fell somewhere up ahead. He slowed his pace even further, choosing an upward slope that went above and to the right of where the sound had come. From this high ground he was able to peer down through the interlacing branches to see her prone on the ground. She must have sprained her ankle because she wasn't getting up. She army-crawled forward, her head constantly swinging back to look behind her. *Perfect.*

He pushed down the hill at a diagonal line, using his long strides to cover ground quickly but quietly. In only a few moments, he had placed himself directly in her path, though obscured by the rotting trunk of a huge dead tree. He waited until her gasping breaths grew so loud he could almost feel them and then he stepped suddenly out in front of her. She screamed at the sight of him, tall and motionless, his face cold and cruel.

She turned to crawl in the opposite direction and Vlad dropped down to snatch her ankle. From her yelp, Vlad guessed it was the sprained one. He grabbed the other and flipped her over onto her back. She screamed again, not a single scream, but a series of piercing shrieks. He advanced, wedging his knee against her thigh to pin her to the ground and then forcing her mouth shut with his hand in a vise grip around her jaw.

"Is this what he did to her?" he shouted, his fingers squeezing tighter around her jaw and pushing her head back to expose her neck. "Did he hunt her and catch her and suck the life out of her veins?"

She gurgled in his grip, unable to speak, her body wracked with convulsions of hysterical panic. Vlad held her for a minute of terrible silence until she fell still. *Did she pass out? Was she dead?* He released her suddenly and felt a rush of relief as she stirred to roll over and began to sob on the ground.

"What do you want with me?" she said at last, her voice hoarse and choppy through her tears.

"Tell me what happened to her."

She struggled to prop her heaving frame onto her elbows and stared up at him, her mascara drooling down across her cheeks in ghoulish lines as her face still quivered in gasping sniffles.

"They took us to their place."

"Who?" he demanded, moving angrily towards her again.

"I don't know!" she cried with another sob. "They were vamps, like you."

"We thought it was just going to be another party," she continued, her sobs abating as if she finally was convinced that Vlad wasn't going to feed on her then and there. "There were other girls who had gone with them before."

"Did they ever come back?"

"Yes! Me and Trish weren't stupid," she had pushed herself

from elbows to hands now and recovered enough to look offended. "They said these guys liked to play a little rough sometimes but they really paid well. And the place they took us to was really nice, like a mansion."

Vlad knelt slowly and softly, the fierceness gone from his eyes, his head cocked inquisitively. The predator turned confidante. She continued her tale, her voice smoothing and her pace increasing as her panic seemed to subside. She even shared her name: Cathy. The place Cathy described could have been none other than Dan's estate - as soon as she mentioned a stable, he had no further doubts. Her descriptions of the two men who picked her up were too sparse, but she was sure one of them had a nose like a hawk.

She remembered the "party" was much smaller than they expected, just a handful of men, which was a big red flag. The presence of another woman set Trish somewhat at ease, but Cathy got another bad feeling from the way the woman looked at them. "She looked at me like a man looks at me," she said with a shiver. She thought all of them, including the woman, were vampires.

These vampires all had horses, but Cathy and Trish didn't know how to ride, so two of the men lifted them up to ride with them. Here Cathy confessed to some excitement - a ride in the country in the arms of a handsome man wasn't usually what she got paid for. But Trish grew increasingly uncomfortable, squirming in the saddle.

The one with the hawk nose, who had Trish with him, dismounted when they came upon a pack of dogs held on leashes by strange little men in funny outfits who spoke in a language Cathy didn't recognize. Cathy's man set her down too and she ran over to play with the dogs. Trish snuck over to her and whispered in her ear: "This doesn't feel right. What kind of rough stuff are they looking for?" Cathy paused here to cry again.

"I told her it was all going to be fine. That we should relax and have fun because tomorrow we'd be back in the camper vans with truckers and teenagers." It took a few more sniffles and some gentle coaxing from Vlad before she could begin again.

While the two of them stood with the dogs, the vampires congregated together and spoke in the same strange language as the little men. Their discussion was animated, with the youngest of them seeming to argue with the others while they laughed back at him. At last, this young one detached from the group and approached them with a sullen look on his face and a backpack in his hand. He handed the backpack to Cathy. It was surprisingly heavy. He reached into it to produce a thin stack of cash along with... Cathy trailed off with instinctive reticence, but Vlad could guess from the track lines on her arms what other payments would entice them and did not prod her further.

The young one dangled the pay in front of them with one hand and then with the other held out two black strips of cloth. He said they could take their payment now if they were willing to have some fun and play a game. He said the first step in the game was to put on the blindfolds. It was Cathy's turn to be hesitant now, but the sight of the prize had cast out all of Trish's misgivings. She laid hold of the pack eagerly and accepted the bargain for them both. Once they had both been blindfolded, the young one led them to what Cathy guessed was some sort of golf cart which took them on a long and bumpy ride. When it stopped, he helped them down and she felt the crunch of twigs under her feet. They walked a few paces, then his hand detached from them and they heard a metal clang. They took off their blindfolds and saw that they were in a large metal cage. Cathy had screamed, but the young one had smiled reassuringly.

"This is all part of the game. When we begin, you'll hear a horn and the door to this cage will spring open. And then you run!"

When Cathy shrieked at this, he calmed them both with a generous hit from the bag and then gave them a more detailed explanation. They would run, his friends would chase and when - not if! - they were caught, they would roll around on the forest floor and have some fun. Don't make it too easy, he cautioned them. Some girls like to get caught, but it's best for everyone if they make his friends feel like they earned it. He then turned to leave in his golf cart.

They huddled together, Cathy near hysterical, but Trish calm as long as the pack was in her grasp. She reassured Cathy, saying that they would act scared and run and give them their fun and when it was over, they would split the contents of the pack. Then a buzzer sounded and the gate sprang open. They sat there paralyzed for several moments, but at the sound of the baying dogs and thundering hooves they took off like a shot.

Cathy ran so frantically she soon lost sight of Trish. The sound of the dogs grew fainter as she went, but there was still the sound of the horse. When she finally collapsed in exhaustion, a vampire on a black horse appeared twenty yards behind her. Before she could get up, he had dismounted his horse, and closed the distance between them with terrifying speed. He pounced on her, knocking her down and pinning her shoulders to the ground and drawing his face close to hers. Cathy shuddered at the recollection.

He had long black hair that fell down around her and framed a face so demonic it still haunted the back of her eyelids. She had seen men's lust in many shades, from bashful sidelong glances of the virginal youth to the savage glint of the hardcore pervert, but she had never seen anything like this face. His was a look of hunger and hatred, so intense she could remember a burning sensation as she wilted under his stare.

She had been certain for a moment that he would kill her, going for her neck and tearing at her flesh like a rabid pit bull. Instead, he had looked away, his hands clenching at her shoulders so powerfully that she thought her bones had fractured. And then, just as suddenly as he had pounded on her, he let go of her, standing up and pushing her away. Refusing to look at her, he told her in urgent tones that she had to get away as fast as she could and never return. His head still averted, he pointed a long finger off into the forest and told her there was a highway just beyond the forest.

Cathy felt certain that this was just a trick, a ruse to get her to run again so he could have another chase. A mouse freed from the cat's paw only to be trapped again... But she ran and after several terrified moments, she realized he had not followed. When she reached the highway, she caught a ride back into town.

She trailed off again and this time Vlad didn't push for more. As she had talked, a lightning storm of firing neurons had set his mind ablaze with questions and connections, so much so that he had a hard time standing still. He had an urge to ditch the girl with Valentine, snatch Mandy from that ridiculous task force and put the whole case down on paper.

He had it, he had it all! Dan and Andreanu, bookends of a murderous high society set that ran a fledgling drug empire by day and sated its bloodlust with human prey like poor Patricia Currington by night. All happening right out in the open as they rode around the city on their motorcycles and fancy cars. And they had been getting away with it, abetted by a city too full of the bright promises of its future to believe any of the darkness of its past could resurface. And too paralyzed by guilt for its xenophobic crimes and fear of killing the vampire golden goose to even think of policing these homicidal playboys.

No, the Bat Pack had been allowed to deal and kill with such impunity that their only real enemy was their own success. After hunting and slaughtering their only competition in the Copperhead gang, they had taken to preying on each other. Whether for greed, jealousy, fear of betrayal or perhaps even boredom, Vlad did not know. But he guessed that Dan and Andreanu had orchestrated this suicidal spiral. They were rivals in so much, perhaps it had even become a competition for them. That they had done it all under the ludicrous banner of Van Helsing and his anti-vamp screeds must have been some sort of joke for them.

His brain abuzz with anticipation, his eyes settled on Cathy in some surprise that she was still there. *A few more loose ends.*

"Did you know what had happened to Patricia?" he asked her suddenly.

She looked down at the ground before answering.

"I figured they did the same thing to her as they did me. Get their kicks and then let her go. And then when she didn't come back for the next few days, I got to thinking she'd found another place and was dodging me because she didn't want to share... It wasn't until her dad came around asking for her that I realized something really bad might have happened to her."

"The Reverend?" he asked, his ears perking up. "Did you tell him everything you told me?"

"Not everything, but I think he got the gist."

Vlad frowned, a faint but discordant twang upsetting the grand symphony his mind had almost finished. To this missed note was added the clamor of crunching twigs and snapping branches as Valentine came barreling out of the underbrush to join them. He stopped suddenly at the sight of them and stood there scratching at his hair, sheepish.

"Just wanted to make sure everybody was okay," he blurted out. *And that I didn't eat her, you forgot to add.* But neither Valentine nor the girl could occupy his thoughts anymore. He had the bird's eye view now. The whole landscape of the case now unfurled before him and all its gullies and shaded contours could not hide anything from him. His mind's-eye soared with the satellite and, with one more pass around the earth, together they would zero in on their man. There was only one last detail to attend to.

"Get a cab and take her wherever she wants to go," he told Valentine, producing a fifty from his wallet to snip his budding protest. "I've got to handle one more errand."

24

Bouchard always tried to give every soul that passed under his care a funeral, though there usually wasn't much in the way of pomp and circumstance. When a street person died, there was rarely anyone on hand to mourn, no one for him to console in their grief, no next of kin to take custody of the body. Indeed, if it hadn't been for his insistence, most of them would end up on a shelf in city storage, their incinerated remains encased in sterile plastic, unremembered and untended until the Second Coming. But he'd convinced the city to release these lost souls to him, and he made sure to give each and every one of them as close as he could get to a Christian burial.

To help him in this quest, a sympathetic city judge had pulled some strings and gotten an abandoned mortuary with a few green acres attached signed over to his ministry. It was in a leafy, mostly vacant part of the city, not far from where they'd found poor Andy. Normally, Bouchard enjoyed being out there, digging at the earth in the coolness of the shade, singing the spirituals his grandma had taught him as he worked. It's not that he took these funerals lightly, but that he found peace and tranquility in putting such troubled spirits to rest.

Today, however, he had three souls in his care - he'd never done a triple funeral - and each of them weighed heavily on him, so much so that he had to stop and rest every few minutes, leaning on his shovel like a weary shepherd on his staff. In his mind, he had told himself that every soul should have equal weight, but he couldn't help feeling differently about these three. No matter how much a man told himself all of mankind were his brothers, he could never bring himself to feel for them like he did for his own flesh and blood, his only begotten daughter.

There she sat on the little red wagon in her porcelain urn, looking almost regal in comparison to the two containers that beside her, one a gray plastic tub from the city morgue, the other a rusted metal bucket half-filled with ash. When Trish was a baby, sleeping peacefully in his arms in those few quiet moments when he and her mother weren't screaming at each other, he always wondered how such a beautiful creature could have come from him. She had never seemed like she belonged to his world - too smart, too graceful, too gentle - but something deep inside her had chained her to it, keeping her down no matter how hard he worked to push her above it. And now to lay her to rest besides these schizos and junkies who passed away with no one but the old Reverend to mourn them… the grief pierced him like a knife.

He turned from her to the gray plastic cylinder on her right. Here was her kindred spirit, though they'd only met once on the earth. He was the brother she'd never had, a son to him in his old age. Unlike Trish, he had the royal blood to go with his royal bearing, but like her he had been driven to the streets by a primeval, self-destructive urge. They were both his children, alright, fellow laborers in the same field, sufferers under the same curse, shedders of innocent blood. Bouchard by his hands, Trish by her needles and Andy by his teeth.

Even so, it was a miracle that Andy was there on the little red wagon and not up in hills where his family had wanted him. Bouchard had never seen such a mess of lawyers at the morgue before, but there they'd been, shouting and waving papers in the air, demanding the release of the body. But Andy had gone to great lengths to make sure his own paperwork was ironclad and, in the end, even this corrupt city had to submit to his final request: to be cremated and turned over to the care of his friend, the Reverend Bouchard. It had taken a week for the coroner to greenlight the cremation after the autopsy, but now it was done and Bouchard could lay his two children to rest.

The third soul on the wagon, piled unceremoniously in the rusted metal bucket, did not belong in the sense of kinship. Nor did anyone know he was here. His was an unauthorized funeral, a secret cremation, one that Bouchard had been forced to perform himself, reigniting the fires of the old mortuary's long dormant crematorium. It had kicked up an awful stink, releasing some fumes that had almost made him pass out. But Bouchard had stuck it out, relishing the sight of each part of the dismembered body entering the flames. *The flesh and bones will burn to ash in a few moments, but your soul will burn forever.* He had grinned at the thought before repenting and begging the Lord for forgiveness. *Am I not just like him?*

In another fit of malice, Bouchard had thought of scattering his ashes in the makeshift ditch he dug as a latrine for his visits out here. But he had repented of that too. This one too was a child of God, however misshapen and twisted by his curse. Would that he had fought against it as valiantly as Andy, but who was Bouchard to judge? Had he not indulged all of the most savage impulses of his youth, finding grace only when they had been restrained by the force of the state and tempered by age? Yes, his daughter had been the victim of this man, but how many fathers could visit him in wrath for the wounds and corruption he brought to their children? *Too many.* He sighed. This third soul was his child after all, the child of his wrath as the others were of his mercy.

He glanced down at the red wagon to see the handful of belongings he would lay to rest alongside their ashes. His daughter had been stripped of everything by the river's grasping waters, but she was not without property. Bouchard had treasured the little silver cross she'd left behind on the sink before her final departure. His gift to her on her 13th birthday. The only thing he'd given her that she hadn't lost or pawned. He liked to think that she left it for him intentionally to let him know where her heart truly lay.

Next to the tub that held Andy, he had a well-worn pocket Bible, a gift from his old friends at Rivers of Mercy. Over its tiny words, invisible to Bouchard's glassy eyes, they had huddled together in the depths of their grief. Inside the pages bore a thousand stripes of the red pen that had vented Andy's agonies and ecstasies in underlines and scribbled notes.

Bouchard flipped the Bible closed and turned at last to the bucket. He knew of no precious mementos to bury with this man. All he had was the contents of his jacket pocket: a little plastic remote and a pocket knife with an eagle and some letters embossed on the handle. Bouchard didn't know if the items had any special significance to the man, but they would lay down with him all the same.

The sound of tires on gravel came suddenly to his ears from around the bend. It was so still and peaceful here, and Bouchard's ears had grown so keen from the decline of his eyes, that he knew the vehicle was still a ways off, just at the beginning of the winding path that led from the road to the mortuary. Tired though he was, his mind prepared his old legs to run. He was only a few yards away from his van. He should be able to load up the wagon and be off down the exit road before this mystery vehicle made it around the long bend.

But something deeper than his mind bid him be still. *You've fought the good fight, you've finished your race.* And so his legs shook off their brief burst of adrenaline and he leaned heavily against the shovel, watching for who should appear.

***

The view from Mandy's new office was even more spectacular than the one from her penthouse balcony. There were none of the docked barges to clutter up the breathtaking expanse of the river, only the occasional stately yacht drifting leisurely by. She could see the Babylon Bridge, its black steel beams rising up from the water like the legs of leviathan, its arches rolling along its back like spiny fins, its massive body pushing into the thick fog that obscured its terminus. *A bridge to nowhere.*

The view and the office that went with it had lost much of its romance, though it did at least offer a distraction from the surprising tedium of her new job. A special assignment to a new task force with its own dedicated space in a highrise! The ear of the biggest mover and shaker on the city council! A chance to work side-by-side with the best people from every major agency in town! What a load that had turned out to be.

The job was really just glorified secretarial work. Listen to talk radio. Watch the local religious programming. Jot down any comments that could be construed as incitements to violence and enter it into the new tracking database. There wasn't even any field work: who needed to leave the office when they put a radio and a TV right in your office? After a few days of dutiful slogging, she'd decided to bring her concerns to Garrick. *Weren't there going to be others assigned to the task force that could handle some of the paperwork side of things? Wouldn't she be better suited consulting on the still open Van Helsing investigation?* But all these and a hundred other questions and requests died on the pencil-necked barricade that barred her every attempt to gain Garrick's attention.

Garrick's assistant Wennington, a stick-skinny twerp with a huge mouth and lispy Southern drawl, was utterly impassable. She had tried everything - the small talk and gossip that had won Maggie to her did nothing to break his big, fake smile. *How interesting, but, no I'm sorry, the councilman will not be available to meet with you today.* Flirting had even less of an effect. Her last desperately imperious attempt at invoking "serious police business" had completely failed to impress him, leaving her to retreat in humiliation to her talk radio and televangelists.

But then, unprompted and unrequested, Garrick's head poked into her office like the sunrise, and, for a moment, all of her initial excitement and enthusiasm returned to her.

"How's my army of one doing?" he asked with a rueful grin.

"Awaiting reinforcements!"

"Rest assured; they are on their way. I just got off the phone with - wow, that's quite a view!" he said in sudden wonder, taking up a position in front of the floor to ceiling glass.

"I was wondering," Mandy began as he continued to stare out the window. "Maybe I could put some of this paperwork on hold until we get some more bodies in here and I could go back out into the field."

"The field?" He turned to her, surprised. "Why on earth would you want to do that?"

So much for enthusiasm. She proceeded cautiously. "There's much out there to be done on Van Helsing. Haggerty's still at large. So is Adrian Dan. And there's still so many questions about the Andreanu suicide."

"Suicide? Don't tell me you're on that again," he cut in sharply. She bit her tongue, remembering how firmly he had touted the ridiculous company line that Andreanu was just another Van Helsing victim. In the few conversations she'd been allowed with Garrick, she'd encountered hints of a rigid dogmatism that stifled any inquiries that might lead away from the conclusions he'd already reached. It wasn't like talking to Vlad.

"See, I do need to get out of this office," she said with a smile. "All this time cooped up in here listening to all this talk radio has got my head full of conspiracy theories."

He looked at her curiously and then smiled. "Maybe you should get out of here for a while... But don't go near that Van Helsing case. The Department's already on it and we don't want to give the impression that the city council is trying to meddle." He nodded sympathetically at the disappointment she failed to hide from her face.

"Hey now," he said, tilting her chin up with his hand. "Don't lose heart on me. And don't feel you need to hold back either. I'm a big boy. I can handle it if you think I'm off-base."

She looked up in his blue eyes and found the dogmatism softened into a startling tenderness. She couldn't resist - before she could think better of it, the words she'd kept back started to spill out.

"I just can't help but think that maybe this whole task force is misguided. You didn't see that crime scene. I'm telling you; it looks like Andreanu was our guy. Maybe Dan too... How can we go around crusading against vampire hate if the whole Van Helsing spree was cooked up by a couple of vamp playboys?"

She braced for a rebuke, but it never came. Instead, Garrick sighed, his blue eyes oozing sympathy and understanding.

"I feel terrible letting you soldier through this alone with these types of questions in your mind. I don't know how much consolation it will be to hear this but know that you are not the only one to voice these concerns. They are completely valid and you are right to have them..."

His hand dropped from her chin to rest on her desk as he leaned closer. "I wish I could address them all right now, but there are few sensitive items I'm not at liberty to share just yet. What I can tell you is that the toxic forces we're dealing with here..." - he gestured to her radio and TV - "... are so powerful that even vamps aren't immune. I wish I could give you more detail, but for the moment, I'm asking you to trust me and know that our purpose here is as important as ever."

He stepped back from the desk and gestured out the window at the gorgeous view. "It might not seem like it right now, buried in all these data points, but if you could see the big picture, you'd know how vital the work you're doing is. We're on the precipice of greatness. We're almost ready to make an extraordinary leap. But if we can't put some of our baggage behind us, we're going to sink like a stone. That's where I'm depending on you." His eyes descended to the river bank and he stepped back from the window, as if conscious of the office's height for the first time.

A set of bony white knuckles rapped at the door and Wennington's nasal voice said something Mandy couldn't make out. Garrick sighed and took a step for the exit, stopping to look back at her.

"Are we good here?" he said, his eyes glancing at her apologetically. She released him with a thumbs up. But as soon as he was gone, all the positive energy in the room went with him, leaving her with her yellow notepad, her radio, her TV and her growing frustration. She leapt when the phone rang, snatching up the receiver eagerly.

It was Valentine, as happy as ever to waste time in vulgar banter. She indulged him for longer than usual, until even the droning of talk radio seemed preferable to letting him finish his story about the hooker he'd driven around town the previous night.

"So what do you need, Val?" she asked, cutting him off.

"Yeah, I was wondering if you'd seen the Cap today." Just the mention of him released butterflies into Mandy's stomach. *Vlad? Was he coming here?*

"No, why?"

"I've got some info he was waiting on and I can't seem to find him." Mandy's ears perked up.

"When did you last hear from him?" There was an urgency building in her voice.

"When he left me with that whore yesterday. Man, when I tell you he was acting strange. I spent half the night worrying he'd gone feral and that he was gonna make me accessory after the fact to a tabloid murder."

"Has anyone else heard from him? Did you get a patrol car back out to where you left him to check the area?"

"Geez... I didn't mean for you to freak out on me. I'm sure he's fine. This is what he does all the time now. He's been AWOL almost every day since he dragged me over to missing persons. I was just wondering if you'd seen him, not trying to start a search party..."

She let him prattle on a while and then cut in.

"So if he does decide to stop by, is there something you wanted me to tell him?"

"Yeah, tell him the satellite people got a fix on that tracker you gave Dan."

Mandy felt a thrill travel up her spine. "Oh… if you give me the coordinates, I can tell them to the Captain if I see him first."

"Sure," he said, a sound of crinkling paper coming from his end. "It's gonna be on the corner of Kiss and My Ass."

"Val!" Her voice rose in irritation.

"Like I'm gonna let you scoop this one. Cap would have my hide."

It took some more coaxing and wheedling but eventually she got them out of him. It helped that Valentine remained under the impression that she and Vlad were still thick as thieves, and that if anyone should be allowed in on the goods, it would be her. Valentine also passed along the tidbit that the tracker's signal had been coming from the same location for at least six hours.

After hanging up on Valentine, Mandy grabbed her purse and skipped out of the office without so much as a second look at her view. She cast a glance down the hall to see Wennington's desk untended and breathed a sigh of relief. Her gaze lingered for a moment on Garrick's closed door. *He did say I should get out of here for a while.* Of course, he'd also said not to go near Van Helsing, but wasn't the company line that Dan had nothing to do with that? That would at least be her rationale if she got caught, she told herself as she took the long elevator ride down.

When she got to her car, she popped the trunk to unload the huge road atlas she'd nicked from a squad car. She wasn't much for latitude and longitude, but after a bit of fumbling and backtracking, her finger arrived on what she figured was the position indicated by the satellite coordinates. She frowned: she was pointing in the middle of a green patch well off any main road, out in the mostly abandoned eastern quadrant of the city. Not a place she would have pegged for someone like Adrian Dan to hide out. Indeed, it looked more like a spot for a landfill. Had Dan just chucked the pocket-knife in the garbage and it had ended up on some garbage heap in the middle of nowhere? It was always the most likely outcome.

But it was too late to return to the office now. She had set her foot to the chase and there was no looking back. She hopped into the driver's seat and headed for the interstate. Worst-case scenario, it would just be a long drive on a nice, sunny day, with a pit stop at a scenic landfill, before returning for another afternoon in front of the yellow notepad. *Or, really worst-case, Dan springs from his hidey-hole and slits my throat with the RCPD penknife.*

***

Vlad's eyes blinked open and there was nothing there. Nothing but a dark blurriness, a blue haze just short of pitch blackness. A dull hum sounded around him. He blinked again and awoke a sharp pain that had been slumbering with him. An angry bruise throbbed somewhere on the back of his head, reaching deep into his skull, sending screaming demands for relief that felt like stab wounds.

Vlad reached to massage the swelling, but his arm did not obey. Had it fallen asleep too? He tried the other with the same result. Was this all some sort of waking dream? Sleep paralysis. He shook his head gingerly, yelping involuntarily as the pain in his head rose suddenly to sweep over him. He lay stiffly with his eyes shut tightly waiting for what seemed like hours for that terrible pain to subside. When at last it did, he opened his eyes again and the blurriness had lessened.

He could make out thin lines of light tracing a rectangle in the darkness. His eyes followed their slender pale rays back to himself and he saw himself on what appeared to be a gurney. His wrists and ankles were fastened to the gurney's cold metal rails with zip ties, each pulled so tight that they had cut off his circulation and rendered his limbs insensate. He struggled now against the ties and felt the first pin-pricks of their return to life. Ceasing his weak thrashing, he looked around him.

Was he in a hospital? Perhaps the nurses had needed to restrain him? There was a sink and cabinet across from him that had the look of a hospital room, and there was the faint odor of bleach he associated with a trauma ward. But everything seemed so small and narrow, like the walls were pressing in on him. Maybe that was just an illusion produced by his reeling senses. But he didn't feel like a patient. He was a prisoner.

He lay still again and closed his eyes, hoping for his brain to settle enough so he could probe it for the memory of how he got here. He had remembered driving the Rolls-Royce on the interstate. He'd been trained after the adventure in the forest but had neglected to pick up some red. Perhaps he had zoned out and had an accident? No... he had made it off the interstate and onto

301

the old, bumpy roads of the eastside. What had he been doing all the way out there? That's right. He'd been in midtown first. At Bouchard's church… One of the neighbors there had told him the Reverend had gone to do a funeral at the old mortuary on the East Side.

Yes, he'd reached the mortuary after sundown. Bouchard had been there alone, drenched in sweat, those old foggy eyes wet with tears. A one man burial crew, digging the graves and administering the ceremony for some poor chump without anyone else to grieve for him. Vlad had tried to spark up a conversation with the old man about Trish, but he had been unusually taciturn, continually lifting the shovel as if ready to begin digging and then resting against it again with a sigh. *Had he just been too tired to talk or was he hiding something?*

Then Vlad had turned to the little red wagon beside Bouchard and examined its strange contents: a plastic bin, a ceramic urn and a rusted metal bucket. Ashes. He'd queried Bouchard as to the identities of this odd trio, but received only a grunt in reply. Then the bright gleam of moonlight reflecting off something at the base of the bucket had caught his eye. He'd reached for it and then… *What then?* Another shake of his head failed to summon anything but pain.

He stretched uncomfortably in the gurney as he felt sensation return to his arms and all the way down to his fingertips. He felt something under his right hand buried in the cloth of his pocket. It was small and hard… it felt like metal. And then he remembered. The knife! The RCPD knife! All that work to get the tracker working and he'd just stumbled on to it in a jumble of ashes in Bouchard's potter's field. He must have snatched it and put in his pocket before-

The sound of a door shutting from somewhere outside snapped Vlad's eyes open again. He heard heavy footfalls, faint at first. They were growing louder. Someone was approaching. He saw a shadow pass over the outline of light at the door frame and then the whole room shook. Vlad realized then that he was not in a room but a vehicle, and someone had just stepped onto the tailgate.

Vlad tensed as he heard the click of the door. He decided to lean back, close his eyes and pretend to be unconscious. It was all he could do to keep his breaths low and regular as he heard the creak of the door and the sound of a booted foot clomping on the metal floor of the vehicle. He felt a warm, rough hand grab his wrist. *Feeling for a pulse.* Then there was a shuffling. Someone was rustling through one of the drawers.

Vlad's eyes rolled under his lids. He desperately wanted to steal a glance at his captor beside him. He couldn't resist - he cracked a lid to see a hulking figure backlit by the moonlight streaming through the open doors. The figure held up something to the light, turning toward Vlad as he did and Vlad snapped his eye shut.

It was Bouchard! His mind reeled. The old man must have clobbered him with his shovel as he was leaning over to pocket the knife... Adrian Dan's knife. Had those been Adrian Dan's ashes? Vlad's feverish thoughts cut short as he felt Bouchard's breath on his cheek. He was so close! He felt the hand grab his wrist again. Vlad couldn't help it - the muscles in his arms tensed.

"You can stop pretending now, Captain." Bouchard's low rumbling voice sounded as warm and kindly as ever, if a little more tired than usual. Vlad kept his eyes shot for another moment - perhaps it was just a test. But he could feel the old man hovering, unmoved, waiting for him. He relented and blinked open his eyes to see Bouchard staring back at him, his eyes two vacant orbs of gray mist. They betrayed neither malice nor mercy.

What menace was missing from Bouchard's gaze, Vlad found in the glinting tip of a syringe in his hand.

"What are you going to do with me?" Vlad said, his eyes on the syringe. His voice struggled out of his throat in a croak. He was overcome with a sudden thirst.

"Don't you worry about this," Bouchard said holding up the syringe before discarding it into the sink behind him and pushing back an IV tower. "I was just worried about your fluids. But now that you're up, we can take care of you the old-fashioned way."

He pushed himself back from the gurney - he was sitting on a rolling chair - and towards a small fridge by the sink. He produced a handful of plastic tubes from the fridge and rolled back over to Vlad's side. He displayed the tubes in both hands, like a waiter holding out a menu.

"Let's see what we got here... Type O negative... Got this off a crackhead yesterday... Oh, and look here, three vials of AB negative. You don't see that everyday. Let's go with that..."

He popped the top off one of the tubes and held it up to Vlad's mouth. Just the sight of the dark crimson surging forward to the lip of the bottle was enough to make his mouth water, to make his bones ache, but he turned his head away.

"Tell me why you're doing this," he croaked again, the words barely audible.

"How are we supposed to have a conversation with that frog in your throat? Just drink this and we'll have a long talk."

He pushed the vial to Vlad's lips again and this time Vlad couldn't resist. The red flowed into his mouth and down his throat. It was cold, but it spread like fire from his stomach to every extremity. Even the throbbing pain at the back of his skull melted under this volcanic eruption of vitality. His back straightened at the rush and for a moment he felt he could flex his forearms and break free of his ties with one powerful burst. But realism set in as the euphoria ebbed and he sat back instead, regarding Bouchard again with a wary clarity.

"There we go," said Bouchard. "Before I begin, I ought to apologize for that knot you got on the back of your head. I think I must have panicked and before I could think better of it, you were under my shovel."

"What about me coming to visit you caused you to panic?" Vlad asked, evenly.

"Wasn't quite ready to face the facts," Bouchard said with a sigh. "When you got so close to Mr. Dan, something just came over me and - whack! - down you went."

"Adrian Dan? Those were his ashes?"

Bouchard nodded. "I guessed he was the reason you came around. Some of my people said you were asking around about Trish. But I didn't count on you figuring things out so fast."

Vlad stared into his eyes but couldn't pierce their cloudy surface. *Figure out what?* Had this old man really tracked down and murdered a ruthless killer like Adrian Dan? A half-blind preacher beat all of RCPD to the punch?

"Dan was a very evil man," Vlad said slowly. "I've been after him for a very long time. If you had anything to do with him ending up in that little bucket, this whole city would owe you a debt of gratitude... if it wasn't for these restraints, I might even shake your hand."

Bouchard chuckled. "And then you'd clap irons on me for the rest of what I've done..."

"I don't know anything about that," Vlad said quickly. "All I know is you were burying some people out here. No crime in that... And you should know that there are judges that have ruled that a man can't be prosecuted for things done in a state of extreme grief. A man who lost a child under terrible circumstances is held to a different standard."

"Oh, I've been watching the news. A Bible thumper like me shedding vampire blood? Plus what I've done in my past... I know what kind of standard they'll hold me to," said Bouchard, looking away to the light streaming in from the rear doors. "But that doesn't matter. I'm ready to face the consequences when the time comes. You coming here almost makes me think that time is now."

Almost? Vlad did his best not to gulp. "Nobody's going to push you into that meat grinder. You know me. You know I'm a straight shooter. You've got a lot of friends in our community who will go to bat for you. We know you're not just a hater. We know you're not one of those fundamentalist bomb-throwers like Haggerty and his gang."

Bouchard's chuckle rumbled into a bitter laugh. "You're painting the wrong picture, Captain, but maybe I haven't given you all the colors. Don't you realize who you're talking to?"

Vlad looked at him, his mind blank. His thoughts were too paralyzed by fear, too hamstrung by pain, to make whatever leap Bouchard was asking from it. What wasn't he seeing?

"I guess Andy's fancy words did the trick," he said, shaking his head. "It was his pen that proclaimed the deed, but it was my hands that did the work."

Behind Vlad's blank stare, a terrible epiphany struck that sent him sinking back into the gurney. Could it be that none of this had been about drugs or rivalries or a cover-up? Could it have been so simple after all? Dan and his Bat Pack had strung out the man's daughter and killed her in one of their twisted games and he had taken his revenge. On all of them... including Andreanu?

Vlad knew it was smarter to play dumb, to do anything he could not to remind Bouchard that he was directing this confession to a cop. *I'm not Captain Paler anymore; just think of me as your clueless chum, too stupid and too loyal to connect any of the dots you keep setting out for me.* But the detective in him was too strong and his curiosity overrode even his instinct for self-preservation.

"Why?" The word burst out of him.

Bouchard sat pensively beside him, slow to speak, mulling it over. Vlad again spoke compulsively.

"Was it all for what they did to Trish?"

At the mention of her name, a spasm of anger contorted Bouchard's face, twisting his placid countenance into an animal snarl. But it passed as quickly as it came and Bouchard shook his head.

"There is an evil in me that wanted to hurt them, yes. To take from their flesh what they took from her... from me... I can't deny that darkness had a hand in what I did... what we did to them boys... But in my heart I tried to forgive them just like I forgave Andy. And I do. I forgive them for what they did."

Vlad studied Bouchard's face. His words sounded insane, but his face was placid, his voice measured and somber.

"Andreanu was helping you?"

"He was the one that convinced me to do it!" Bouchard exclaimed. "Don't misunderstand me now. I'm not trying to shift any blame. But it was his vision from the beginning." The pace of Bouchard's speech picked up, his hands gesticulating. He spoke with the rushed, gushing cadence of someone who had been waiting to speak for too long.

"He came to me a few months ago after he saw one of the missing posters I'd put out for Trish," Bouchard continued.

"He told me that he'd been with the people that did it. No, first he said he was the one that did it. I didn't believe him, but I'm guessing the poor kid was hoping I'd strangle him right there on the spot. When he didn't get the fight he was looking for, he dissolved into a big puddle of tears and told me the whole story."

"He felt guilty?"

"He felt everything. He was carrying so much weight on his shoulders, he couldn't help but break. It wasn't just Trish. He told me she was the tip of the iceberg. He said his group had done the same to dozens just like her."

"Surely, he was exaggerating," Vlad protested, his arms pulling against their bonds. "There's no way they could disappear that many people without us noticing, not even in a city this big."

Bouchard turned the big gray clouds onto Vlad, pensive.

"Andy said the community wouldn't let them get caught - he said they'd have him institutionalized if he even breathed a word about it. He said the whole community was in on it in one way or another. That people like me were just livestock to people like you."

Vlad felt a shiver at the transition from 'they' to 'you' but he still couldn't see any malice in those eyes. "You of all people should know that's not true. You've been working with the community for years. You've seen the money and time and care we've given to the poorest people in the city. All that stuff he was saying he must have picked up from the tabloids or that garbage that Haggerty was spewing…"

Bouchard nodded. "That's what I told him. But Andy said all that kindness and generosity was just the flip side of the same coin. He said there were some like Dan that like wild game to hunt and kill. The others seemed nicer and kinder, but that was because they like domesticated animals, to feed and milk and fatten up for the slaughter."

Vlad scoffed bitterly, unable to control his disgust for Andreanu. *That silver spoon sucking brat. Growing up with everything handed to him, growing tall, strong and handsome on the toil and sacrifice of his ancestors only to turn on them, spitting the most vicious lies and slanders ever concocted by their enemies.* "I knew he was troubled, but I didn't know he'd sunk that far…" He turned again to Bouchard, searching his face for some clue to his inner thoughts. "Did you believe him?"

Another pause. Vlad's heartbeat quickened. "No," Bouchard. Another pause. "Not at first. And you were one of the main reasons why. You had always been a help to me and you never seemed to ask or expect anything in return. I always felt you had a real heart for the city and a real passion for justice."

"I do!" yelped Vlad, too eagerly. His composure had frayed almost to the breaking point.

"I told Andy that he was delirious. That his bloodfast was making him crazy. That he was letting his guilt over Trish run away with him. I told him about all my friends in high places. That they'd help me out. That they wouldn't let a few savages with important last names get away with murder. I got him to agree to not do anything foolish while I went about it my way…"

A sinking feeling began in Vlad's stomach as Bouchard continued.

"He told me to be careful. That if Dan found out Andy had betrayed him… that we were going to report him… he'd have us both killed. So I agreed to be cautious…"

The big clouds were fixed on Vlad now and for the first time an intensity seemed to pierce the haze, a single sharp beam of white light emerging to cut Vlad to the quick.

"You were the first person I came to..." The words crushed Vlad like an anvil. The old man had known everything when he came to his office months ago brandishing Trish's photo and pleading for help. He'd been offering Vlad a chance to step up to the plate. He'd been giving him a test. *A test I failed.*

"I remember and I'm truly sorry I didn't take it over personally. If you'd only told me what you knew..." Vlad tried to keep the accusatory tone out of his voice. The new piercing quality in Bouchard's eyes flickered, the clouds returning and he was again opaque and unreadable.

"I understand. I wish I had been more forthcoming with you. But you weren't the only one I spoke to. I worked with that man you sent me to in missing persons. I went to everyone I knew with any kind of power. My councilman. Mr. Ryan. The mayor. They all met with me. They all told me how much they were concerned. They all told me they would see that it was handled properly. They convinced me."

He leaned back in his rolling chair. "But it didn't convince Andy. He told me that as soon as the first clue of any connection between Trish and Dan and his friends and they'd all drop it. He said if I kept pushing, then they'd start putting the squeeze on me. I didn't believe him. I told him these people knew me and respected me. But everything he said turned out to be true."

Vlad felt the force of Andreanu's dark theories descending over him, a storm cloud that rumbled with the invisible threat of a sudden bolt of wrath to strike him down where he lay. "I understand the frustration. The bureaucracy strangles anything it touches. But that doesn't mean there was a conspiracy..." He trailed off, feeling pathetic as Bouchard just stared at him, politely waiting for him to finish.

"I thought the same things. I gave them weeks. Then, when I called to check in, they stopped taking my phone calls. When I showed up at their offices, they wouldn't see me. When I wrote them letters, they sent me form letters back saying they hadn't had the chance to read it but they appreciated me taking the time..."

Vlad tried to pipe in, but Bouchard pushed through, his voice rumbling, the preacher getting into his rhythm. "So I pushed

308

harder. I met with the party leadership to ask why a devoted community servant who had rallied the vote so many times couldn't get the time of day. I called up the big newspapers asking why no one in power cared about people disappearing and dying. I did everything a political operator has to do in this town. And what did I get for it, a big mover and shaker like me? A black eye and a punch in the gut."

"The day after I called the newspaper, a reporter calls me. Did he want to know more about Trish? No. He wanted to know if I had any comment about the allegation that my ministry was a front for the drug trade. That Sunday detectives came to my church with a search warrant and turned the place upside down. Then a lady from the Ryan Foundation calls me and tells me that there's a discrepancy in my last grant report and that my funding was frozen until further notice. Then a city inspector tells me my building's not up to code and hands me a list of items to fix in the next two weeks or it will be condemned."

Vlad wanted to interject, but he was speechless. He'd known the corruption of the city in gangster heyday when Dan's father was openly buying political favors. But he'd been at the tip of the spear that broke his organization. It was dead and buried. And even at its peak it never could have orchestrated anything like Bouchard was describing. Was Bouchard lying? Wouldn't Vlad have known if he was the target of a drug investigation? Maybe Bouchard was just crazy after dealing with so much grief and spending too much time with schizophrenics. Vlad dared to dispute.

"But your ministry is still here. You've got your funding. You're not in jail."

"That's because I caved on everything. I sent every signal I could that I was done stirring the pot, that I'd let my depression over Trish lead me into wild delusions. I apologized to everyone I had asked for justice…" He stared at the wall behind Vlad, his tone icy. "They took the squeeze off me, and I played nice from then on. But my heart was overcome. I had so much anger. I was ready to do whatever it took… And Andy had a plan."

"He wanted to help you get justice for Trish?"

"He wanted a lot more than that. He wanted to bring the whole temple of power down on itself, like Samson and the Philistines."

"And he wanted you to be the Samson?" Vlad knew his Bible well enough to remember the suicidal strongman.

"Andy was always afraid of what would happen if he let his darkness out. He spent his whole life fighting those urges. He needed someone who could do the dirty work without losing control. And he knew I had learned to leash the dog in me a long time ago."

"Did he take any part in the killings?" For a moment, Vlad had forgotten that he was the one bound and slipped into his usual interrogation rhythm.

"Andy would tell me their routines. Or he'd set up a meeting and lead me right to them. After the deed was done, he'd take back over. All that stuff with the bodies and the letters was his work."

"Like putting Dragescu's head on that silver platter?" Bouchard nodded. "What was the idea behind the Dracula business with the bodies - the garlic and the stakes and all that?"

"Andy said he was trying to tap into the old myths to awaken the cultural memory... He would have explained it better than I ever could. But it was all his way of trying to alert people to the dangers..."

"Of people like me and him?"

"Yessir," Bouchard nodded again. "Though Andy never had a bad word to say about you. He said the vampires like you were just cogs in the machine, caught up in something bigger than them."

"And what did his vision have in store for these cogs?"

"We had some disagreements on that. Andy was convinced that even the taste for blood defiled a man. That as long as he had the need to feed on his fellow man, he would always be a tool of the devil. I told him that as long as a man can know the difference between good and evil and choose the good, there's still hope for him. But Andy was a hard man to shake - you saw what he did to himself."

"Are you still of the same mind?" Vlad asked, nodding his head towards the ties on his wrist. "Is there still hope for me?"

"If I didn't think so, you'd be in the ground with Dan and Andy and Trish right now. It's what Andy would have done, as highly as he thought of you." Vlad shivered again. "He wanted the work to go on, no matter what."

"And you don't?"

Bouchard heaved a heavy sigh. "I'm an old man and I'm tired. I don't have Andy's vision. I don't have his certainty. I don't want any more blood on my hands. Everything in me wants to throw in the towel…"

But? Vlad tensed. He knew there had to be a 'but' coming or he'd already be a free man by now.

"But I promised Andy I would be faithful to complete the work we began. There's too much at stake. It doesn't matter how I feel about it, the work has to go on."

Vlad leaned forward. This was his moment, his last chance.

"Then let me carry it on for you. I'm not going to lie and pretend I approve of Andy's methods. And I'm not sure the conspiracy runs as deep as he claimed. But you said yourself I have a heart for justice, and I can assure you, it is burning at the corruption that forced you to take matters into your own hands…" Vlad took a deep breath and assessed Bouchard's reaction. The old man was still inscrutable, but he at least seemed to be listening.

"I have resources that neither of you had. And with your cooperation, we'd have the leverage to break open these smoke-filled rooms once and for all. In custody, I could protect you. I could make sure everything that you've seen, everything that's done makes it into the light of day… You were right to come to me first, I was just too oblivious and preoccupied to realize what you were showing me. But my eyes are open now. Give me another chance."

Bouchard hesitated and then rolled himself backwards in the chair towards the sink and cabinet. Vlad held his breath as he rummaged through the drawers again. *Not another syringe.* He let his breath release as Bouchard's hand emerged from the drawer with a small pair of silver bandage scissors.

"Let's get you out of those," he said, rolling back toward Vlad and entwining his big fingers into the little holes of the scissor handles to cut at the air. The metallic rasp of their little *snip snip* sounded like chains breaking. He was almost free of this nightmare! But then another sound reached them, fainter at first then the snip-snip but growing steadily louder. The sound of tires on gravel.

Bouchard pulled back and with him the scissors, so tantalizingly close to the plastic on Vlad's wrists. He stuck his head out the back of the van, and then turned to Vlad.

"Is that your back-up arriving?"

Vlad shook his head vigorously. "No one even knows I'm here!" He felt his stomach sink at that admission, but it was too late to pull it back. "Don't you think you should let me out of these ties? If someone saw me bound up back here, it would be pretty hard to explain."

Bouchard brought a finger to his lips to shush Vlad. Turning he let himself down from the tailgate and closed the double doors behind him. Vlad was immersed in darkness again, his blinking eyes searching the slender lines around the door frame for any hint of a silver lining.

25

Mandy winced with every jolt and crunch of the big, jagged hunks of gravel pushing up from under her tires. This little rabbit trail had already gone on for far too long - her misread of the map had already added an extra half hour to the now hour-long trek. She knew that pencil-neck Wennington would be poking his head into her office and glancing at his watch. *That's a long breath of fresh air.*

This winding path to nowhere wasn't doing much for her nerves either. Every turn seemed to be hiding some new gully or ditch, just waiting to ensnare her car and leave her stranded out here. The smell wafting in through the vents wasn't helping either. Someone had been burning something that wasn't wood, though it was strangely familiar to her nose. Maybe some type of garbage? *A landfill. I came all the way out here to go digging through a garbage heap.* For at least the tenth time since she started out, she considered turning around and going back.

She soldiered on, gingerly pressing down on the accelerator to keep the bumpy ride going forward. At last, the bend in the path up ahead opened up on some daylight and she saw the glint of a bumper. She stomped on the brakes. It wasn't just any bumper, but the spectacularly shiny chrome on the back of a Rolls-Royce. *Pavel Petricean's car.* She felt a momentary shiver that stilled as soon as she remembered Val talking about them taking it out of the impound lot. Vlad was here!

She stepped out of the car eagerly, the handle of her Beretta catching on the seatbelt. The thought of encountering Dan solo had been enough to override her usual inclination to shirk policy by leaving the big gun and its bulky, uncomfortable holster behind on long road trips. It was a needless encumbrance now that Vlad was here. How had he gotten here? Val must have found him after she left. And while she was driving around in a circle like a fool, he must have beaten her to the punch.

Her heartbeat quickened as she stepped out into the clearing. The Rolls-Royce was empty. She turned around, shielding her eyes from the sun to survey the scene. She was surprised to see not a landfill but a pretty little field of flowers and gravestones riding a gentle slope up a grassy hill. At the crest of the hill was a pleasant little brick building with a strangely large smoke stack emerging from behind it. The cemetery gave it away, but she would have recognized it anyway: it was a mortuary.

The roof was in disrepair and the long dark windows that covered its front were coated with thick crusts of dust and mineral deposits. But it didn't look abandoned - the grounds were kept, there were fresh tire tracks leading up and behind the parking lot in front of the building. And then there was the lingering odor of smoke that suggested recent use. *Of course. That wasn't garbage burning, it was flesh.* The smell transported Mandy back into her memories with an almost violent force.

She was a teenager again, wide-eyed and full of wonder as she approached the house of the dead. Her first real job, if you didn't count selling peaches by the roadside. What grotesque marvels would await her inside? Slabs of the town's dead, their cavernous eyes staring blankly at the vaulted ceilings, each of them waiting for her to don the aluminized apron and push them into the flaming furnace of the crematorium.

Mandy blinked and she was back, standing alone in front of the crumbling mortuary, her mind again returning to the mystery at hand. Where could Vlad be? And how on earth had Dan or his tracker ended up here? A cemetery in the middle of nowhere... Was this where he stashed his victims? She was chilled by a sudden disturbing thought. Had he sprung a trap for Vlad here? Was Vlad now buried under one of those headstones sprawling across the fields behind her? She had noticed the upturned soil of what looked like new burials on her walk up. She shook her head. *No way could Dan get the drop on Vlad.* All the same she resisted the urge to call out to him.

Ahead she noticed the front door to the mortuary was slightly ajar and she moved towards it cautiously. The door opened soundlessly, and she poked her head inside. The lobby the door opened on was dimly lit by the few rays of the afternoon sun that had struggled to make it through the thick film of dust and grime on the windows. The hallway leading from the lobby into the interior was almost completely dark.

The floor beneath her feet resounded at the tap of her rubber soles. No cheap linoleum - only marble made a sound like that. She remembered the floors of Dan's mansion and shuddered, making sure to tiptoe into her next step. As the door closed behind her, the light grew even more faint and she strained her eyes to search for any figures or shapes lurking in the dark. *Why here?* The thought echoed with her footsteps.

She pulled a little penlight from her jacket and flipped it on. Its thin beam pushed forward weakly a few feet into the dark. She stepped forward. The now unmistakable smell of cremated flesh grew stronger the further she ventured into the interior. It was an odor unique to these older funeral homes, where the furnaces kicked up such a powerful aroma, unsettlingly familiar to barbeque, that cities forced them into forest hideaways like this one. Old Man Rawley's place back in Copper Springs had been pushed out all the way onto the fringes of town - which had made her forbidden encounters with Brad all the easier to hide from the prying eyes of the small town.

The hallway quickly grew too dark, the long shadows too foreboding to continue the walk down memory lane. Mandy's ears pricked up for any sound, her free hand clinging tightly to her still-holstered Beretta. *Someone burnt a body here.* Who would come to a derelict old furnace to burn a body other than someone with something to hide?

She imagined a phantasmic Vlad walking before her, his flashlight on, his pistol drawn... Then a shadow slinking behind him, stalking him, waiting to pounce, to knock him out cold, to push his unconscious body into the waiting ovens... She slowed and took a deep breath, drawing her pistol and hugging the wall with her back, her heading flitting forward and backward along the corridor. No one was going to sneak up on her.

Her little light glinted off a small metal sign hung on a door ahead, leading off from the hallway. Crematorium. With another deep breath, she mustered enough momentum to push herself off the wall and tiptoe towards it. It was unlocked and the door swung inward. It was pitch black inside. She stepped in.

The pale beam of her penlight reflected off the dull metal wall across the room, where she could make out the faint outline of two archways: portals into the furnace. Scattered between her and these ominous arches were the rolling tables that carried the coffin-like boxes into the flames. One of these carts was set on grooves in the floor that led right to one of the furnaces. A rollercoaster to hell. She approached, her fingers searching for the release that would spring the coffin lid.

There was a sudden click behind her - the door! Hearing herself yelp in surprise, Mandy swung round, struggling with the release on her holster, shining her little light into the darkness behind her. The door was shut and someone was in the room with her.

***

Darkness didn't bother the Reverend Bouchard. He'd been shrouded in it since his eyes first started to cloud over. He could work in it, move in it, as quiet as a church mouse, as deadly as a spider.

It was the darkness in his heart that bothered him. How easily his hands had slipped to the work of killing after so many years. The thrill he'd felt as he'd stalked Dragescu into his apartment. When he'd pounced on Petricean in the shadows of the parking garage. When he'd chased Duma through the wetlands beside the river after dispatching his lover. And most of all when he'd hunted Dan in his own hunting grounds.

He'd been able to justify those deeds, repenting of his pleasure in the acts but clinging to the demands of justice, to his belief in the Lord's inspiration of Andy's vision and the fundamental decency of Andy's purposes. But the Lord's voice had been silent in his own heart. Or perhaps He had been hardening it like Pharaoh's in order to bring down the judgments of His righteous wrath.

Now that Andy had sent himself off to glory, Bouchard was alone with his heart of stone and his blood-covered hands. How was he to continue the work without Andy's prophetic voice to guide him? How could he know if it was his flesh or the Spirit directing his hands? Was it a selfish fear or commitment to the work that led him to strike and bind Captain Paler? Was it humility and faith or cowardly resignation that had produced the impulse to release him?

He was stalking again now. Whether he was right or wrong, he didn't know. With no clear direction, he had been reduced to instinct. A mere beast. Balaam's ass, or a lion seeking whom he may devour. He was aware of an undercurrent of anger running through him, causing his fists to clench as he crept after the figure creeping forward in the mortuary with a flashlight in hand. From the light splashing back to outline her frame, he guessed it was a woman and the way her hand clutched at something near her hip, he felt sure she was carrying a gun. Paler had lied to him. And if he had lied to him about back-up then everything else he'd promised had probably been false as well.

Bouchard was an optimistic, amiable man by nature; he wanted to see the best in people. But again and again Andy's prophecies of doom had proven true, crushing his hopeful outlook and causing a black gloom to descend over him like a pall.

The woman stopped suddenly and pressed herself back against one of the walls of the hallway. Bouchard instinctively slid behind the receptionist's desk and knelt down. He saw the light from her flashlight illuminate the wall behind him and he remained still, trusting that he had not been detected. The darkness made people paranoid, made them see and hear things that weren't there. In a moment she would be satisfied again that she was alone and would proceed and he could resume his hunt.

But what would he do with her when he caught her? It had been easy to hunt the other predators, knowing on whom they had preyed. But this was a woman. From the litheness of her step and the lightness of her frame, she looked to be a girl not much older than Trish. Nor could he know if she was a killer like that fearsome Irina creature who had fought him so fiercely in the back of that Range Rover. For all Bouchard knew, this was just a policewoman in search of her partner. She could not deserve the fate his hands were preparing to visit on her.

No man, having put his hand to the plough, and looking back, is fit for the kingdom of God. The verse rang out in Bouchard's head in Andy's voice. How he needed that young man with him now. He was an old man and though his flesh retained its strength his spirit had grown tired. Without Andy's vitality, how was he supposed to sustain this terrible, exhausting work? A note of bitterness echoed in response to Andy's voice. *You checked out when you couldn't take anymore. Why must I then continue?*

He chided himself for the thought. Andy had been given a weightier cross to bear and had borne it his whole life. Bouchard could not begrudge him for succumbing after so long a struggle. He had fought the good fight and now his burden fell onto Bouchard's big, broad shoulders like the mantle of Elijah. The Lord had made him strong; he could carry this mantle on for as long as was required, and as far as was necessary.

His resolve returning, he rose to look over the lip of the desk and saw the hallway empty. Moving quickly, he stole back into the open to recover her trail. He could still hear the light tap of her soles against the floor, but fainter. She had gone into one of the rooms. As he closed the distance, he saw the door to the crematorium ajar and entered, glancing first to make sure her flashlight was not pointed in his direction.

As he stepped through, pushing gently on the door, he must have released some hydraulic pressure in the rusted old door mechanism above him and the door closed behind him with a hiss and then a loud click. He dove behind a stack of cremation coffins as her light whirled round to probe the darkness around the doorway.

He heard the snap of her holster release and the scrape of her gun as it slid out. Her breathing was elevated and loud, so loud it would be no problem locating her in the dark. It would be easy to creep up behind her and break her neck. But when he told his legs to move, nothing happened. His knee had frozen, locked in the curled position he'd assumed behind the coffins. Putting weight on it now, he felt the tendons around his kneecap thrum, as if just one more ounce of weight would cause them to snap in two. He was no longer the apex predator, at home in the shadows, but an old cripple who had fallen and could not get up.

"I know you're there!" Her voice cried out into the stillness, shrill and shaking, like a slender reed in a gale. It was a familiar voice but Bouchard could not quite place it. But he could almost taste the sweat beading on her trigger finger. Yet he could not move - his knee refused the weight.

"Show. me your hands right now or so help me I'm going to blow you away," her voice came again and Bouchard remembered

318

it. Little Miss Mandy Parker with her shy eyes and big words and those willowy arms that swished at her sides as she walked. Just like Trish. His heart sank. There would be no killing this one. He couldn't do it.

The tap of her soles began again and her light glowed at the edge of the coffins. She was making her way round. If Bouchard didn't move now, he'd be a sitting duck. Was this it? Was a little girl and a bad knee going to be the end of him? No. Setting his jaw to absorb the pain, he threw the bulk of his shoulders forward and pushed off with all the strength he had. He sprung forward as the lock in his joint gave way with a pop that sent a bolt of searing pain shooting across his nervous system.

He couldn't help it - he groaned. A guttural sound that rumbled in his chest and forced its way out of his throat like a roar. With it came a BANG and new pain. A sharp, stabbing sensation in his side. She'd shot him. The little girl had shot him! But he'd cleared the coffins, and even with every nerve in his body screaming, he was moving again, prowling behind the carts.

He heard her feet tapping behind him, the pace picking up. She was chasing him now. The blood gushing from his side would lead her right to him, no matter what shadowy corner he could find. As she sped up, he was slowing down, his head swimming, his knee buckling under his weight. *This is the end; I am poured out as a drink offering.* He could lay down here and bleed out. His race was done.

He stumbled forward, colliding heavily with something hard and flat. He leaned against it to keep himself upright, feeling knobs pressing into his heaving chest. It was the control panel to the furnace. The support of the giant machine steadied his head and his mind. He felt at his side. The bullet had gone in and out. More than a graze but it didn't seem so bad. He wasn't going to bleed out. Even his knee wasn't beyond hope. He could still rotate it, albeit with pain. There was more of him to pour out after all.

He felt his blood revive in him, the pain focusing his mind afresh. He knew what to do. He clicked on the furnace and slid open the grate before ducking down behind the gigantic metal pipes that rose from the floor to ceiling. The orange flames of the crematory burst to life and cast a demonic glow throughout the room.

From his hiding place behind the pipes, he saw her rush forward and then come to a dead stop in front of the furnace. She stared into the fire, mesmerized by the display, or paralyzed by fear. This was Bouchard's chance. His hand stretched out from behind the pipe towards the furnace, his fingers at last grasping cool iron. It was one of the long hooked pokers used to push and pull the coffins into the furnace, as he had just done with Dan. He grabbed it, the iron dragging against the floor with a loud and heavy scrape.

She jumped at the sound, casting about wildly with her gun and her flashlight, looking for a target, any target. She seemed to be looking right at him. But Bouchard knew she couldn't see anything. After staring at the flames, she wouldn't be able to see anything in the darkness, even if it was headed straight for her, as he was now.

Raising the iron rod over his head, he charged. His knee buckled at his first lunge and he nearly tumbled to the ground, and he was forced to bring the rod back down to the floor to steady himself. She startled at the clang of the iron against the marble and the gun and flashlight swung to point directly at him. With a roar, Bouchard swung his rod, over his head and then down, smashing her forearm as the gun fired into the ground.

She screamed in pain, her forearm shattered under the weight of the rod, the gun slipping from her insensate fingers. Bouchard bent his knees for one final spring, but he could only fall into her, knocking them both to the ground, the rod falling beside them with a clang.

He pinned her with one arm, using the other to push himself off the ground. Her eyes, wide with terror, blinked in stunned recognition as the orange glow illuminated his face. She didn't speak, but screamed in anger and pain as she struck at him with her one good arm and writhed under the immovable weight of his body. He could scarcely even feel her blows; it was not so different from the terrible tantrums Trish had when she was a young girl and how he'd held her down, waiting until her manic energy drained into the ground.

But what was he to do with this girl when she stopped hitting and thrashing? Hug her and let her know it would all be okay? Or put his hand around that long white neck and squeeze the life out of her? Just the thought of it sent a terrible throbbing ache into his core and he looked away. Perhaps if he just didn't look, he could imagine her as one of the gang that hunted and killed Trish. Was it so different? Wasn't she fighting him to uphold the same government, the same society that was feeding on the helpless and the innocent? *No, she is helpless and innocent.*

"It's alright, it's alright. I'm not going to hurt you." The voice came rumbling out of his chest, thick with fatigue and sincerity. He felt himself easing the hold he had on her, the hand that pinned her to the floor shifting to her shoulder.

But his words had no calming effect on her. She thrashed like a wild animal, immediately working to free herself from his weakening hold, wriggling wildly, still unable to get up, but inching out from under him with each gyration. Her free arm gave up its impotent strikes and began to stretch across the floor. He followed it and saw she was reaching for her gun where it had skidded to the base of the furnace, a few feet away.

Bouchard felt some dull ring of alarm that bid his fingers to tighten, to stop her before she ended him and the work they had begun. But he gave it no sense of urgency. He would not listen to any voice that told him to hurt this broken little bird in his grasp. It could not be the Lord's will. Or was that just his weakness and cowardice speaking again? Could not the devil work as well through a pretty young face as through the cruel twisted face of man like Dan? If he let her go, would she not gun him down? Would the work end simply because he couldn't face the little girl who was trying to kill him?

With a frustrated grunt, his grip tightened around her shoulder and his free hand grasped about her waist. Still, she clawed for the gun, her eyes rabid with desperate desire to have it, to use it, to kill him. Was that the devil inside her? Why couldn't she just look at him like a human being? Why was she making it so difficult? But still she thrashed. Gritting his teeth, Bouchard lifted her bodily from the floor. She writhed in his arms like a snake and screamed.

"Let me go!"

Real human words! Had that been so hard? His knee was throbbing underneath him, his whole body sending off alarms. He needed to find someplace to put her before he collapsed in a heap. The coffin on the cart behind her beckoned. That would scare some sense into her. He slung her up into the air to get over the lip of the coffin and bumped off the lid with his hip. She hardly weighed anything but the way she was struggling and the exhaustion that wracked his whole frame made his usually reliable muscles spasm in rebellion. That made him drop her into the coffin more roughly than she had intended, the impact knocking the breath from her lungs, which mercifully stopped the screaming.

As she lay there stunned, he took a moment to catch his breath, propping himself up with one hand on each side of the coffin, his big shoulders heaving. "Now will you stop fighting me for a minute and listen?"

She nodded. At last, a civilized gesture! He breathed a big sigh. His head reeled, as if all the blood had drained from it. Was his wound worse than he thought?

"This isn't the way I want to talk to anybody, but it might be the only way to get you to understand," he began, still panting. "I never wanted to go back to being a man of violence, but nobody would listen any other way. The whole city going to hell and no one starts caring until you put their skin in the game..."

She stared at him, blinking, wordless. He worried for a moment he had damaged her the way he'd thrown her in there. She was such a little thing. Had he given her a concussion? But there were bigger things to worry about. If only he could force his mind to focus.

"You've got to know when you're on the wrong path, that you're on the way to hell," he continued, taking a hold of the cart. "Is that where you want to go?" He gestured his head toward the flames licking the air inside the furnace and pushed the cart towards the rectangular opening. She arched her neck to follow his gaze - the walls of the coffin blocked her view, but from the terror that flooded her eyes, he could see she guessed the general idea. She shook her head no.

"Right now, that's the path you're headed on. The people you're working for. That's where they're going to lead you. But there's another path that leads out of this terrible place and into the light." He gestured back towards the door. Bathed in the orange light, he could see that it was slightly ajar. Hadn't he closed it? The thought rang dully in his mind but it faded as he sought to regain his train of thought. *The light. Lead her to the light.*

He pushed her closer to the orange glow, the proximity of the heat bringing sweat to his brow. He stopped. Where was he going? He was beginning to feel delirious. The rise in temperature had combined with his exhaustion to drain whatever was left of his energy reserves and now left him tottering, barely able to organize his thoughts. And was he still bleeding? He couldn't tell. He strained to focus on her. She was still staring at him, wide-eyed.

"It's up to you and the Captain. You two are the only ones who can carry on the work. I'm too tired to do it all alone. But I've got to be able to trust you."

She seemed to be mouthing something, but there was a ringing in his ears that kept growing louder and he couldn't make out what she was saying. He shook the cobwebs from his head and the volume of the ringing lowered. He leaned in closer.

"You can trust me," she was saying. "I'll help you." He felt a cooling sense of relief wash over him. He had brought her to the edge of the lake of fire and she had seen the light. The skepticism that had dogged him when the Captain spoke had receded, submerged under the heat and sweat. He wanted to believe. He wanted to set down his plow. He wanted to sleep.

"Thank you," he heard himself saying and one hand released the support of the coffin wall to scoop her out. To rescue her from the flames. As he pulled her closer, he saw her eyes flit behind him, spark, and then return to his. He looked over his shoulder reflexively and saw nothing, though his vision had grown so cloudy that he could scarcely be sure. He looked back at her. Had it been a trick? Was she trying to distract him? Did she have some other weapon on her? Whatever doubts he had dissolved when he looked back at her face. Such fear! Such innocence! A child's face. Trish's face… after she had run in from the rain after falling from her bicycle, tears falling along with the rain drops…

But then he heard it. A dull sound that vibrated underneath the ringing and into his mind. Footsteps. Coming up rapidly behind him. He swung round to see a figure sprinting towards him, pale face aglow, teeth bared, eyes cold and cruel. Captain Paler. In his outstretched hand, Bouchard saw something glinting, cutting through the air, heading straight for his chest.

And then it was inside him and he felt the air hiss from his lungs as a short blade passed between his ribs, slicing like a butcher's cleaver through his muscle. He stared down in shock and the brass handle shined back at him, sticking out of him like a bulging tick, swollen with his blood.

The Captain yanked at the handle, struggling to pull it free. The pain was enormous but Bouchard could not scream. He gaped and gurgled but no air could escape his lungs.

"Kill him! Kill him!" he heard her shriek behind him. He turned to see her face transformed, her doe-like eyes turned black and merciless, her porcelain cheeks red with fury. The angel of innocence vanished and a demon in her place. A devil behind him, a devil before, the flames of hell all around them... They'd lied to him! Satan had laid a trap for him and his weakness and cowardice he had stumbled right into it. He had to get out. He had to breathe.

Paler yanked again at the knife and this time it came free. The pain that had paralyzed Bouchard eased and he felt a last rush of strength to his limbs. Paler struck again with the knife but this time Bouchard was ready. He swung both arms with the speed and ferocity of the old streetfighter, the first blow catching Paler's forearm and knocking it off target and the the next catching him on the chin, rocking his head back. Another right hook to the jaw and he tumbled backwards onto the floor.

Bouchard knelt and grabbed the great iron rod from the floor and used it to push himself off the floor, his knee now immobile. His lungs felt as if they had swollen and popped inside him, his ragged breaths sucking uselessly at the air. But he was still moving. The Lord was with him. He raised the rod above his head once again, ready to drive it through Paler's chest as he lay dazed on the floor.

He heard her screams behind him as he staggered forward. Then he felt a weight on his back. The little banshee had jumped on him! He felt her slender arm hook round his neck and squeeze, her other arm - the one he'd snapped almost in two - dangling uselessly over his shoulder. All of her little strength was focused on choking out the passage of air to his ravaged lungs.

A blackness started at the edge of his vision and flooded towards the center. He felt his arms holding the rod slack and he heard it thud on the ground, his tingling fingers losing their grip. He felt his good leg go numb beneath him and he sensed that he was beginning to sink towards the floor. His consciousness was falling like a shroud, the veil was tearing. Soon he would be on the other side. *But not yet.*

With the last of his strength, he raised the rod. His eyes had gone black, but he struck down with all his might at the place where Paler had been. Then, pushing against the rod he flung himself backwards towards the open mouth of the furnace. The last sound he heard was her scream.

26

Mandy blinked and saw nothing. Another blink and she became aware of a glow, not the orange glow of her nightmare, but a soft, yellowy white, like a sheer curtain draped over the face of the morning sun. With the glow came a hot pain that spread all over her back and up her neck, but stayed low and dull, like something or someone was holding it down, pushing it under the surface.

She stirred and began to stretch, but some internal voice warned her not to, some vague sensation of confinement. She moved slowly, feeling the gentle resistance of a soft, yielding fabric that nevertheless held her in place.

"Lie still." It was an unfamiliar voice. Feminine but authoritative. Like her own if it still worked. She tried it now, expanding her lungs and putting tentative pressure on her vocal cords. Her voice came weakly, her tongue heavy, laboring to push out a single mouthful of words.

"Where am I?"

"St. Anthony's," the other voice replied. "Now be quiet and go back to sleep. Your body needs to rest."

The hospital! The thought pierced her sluggish mind, triggering a powerful impulse to leap upright and cast off whatever this fabric cocoon was that encased her. But the muscle impulse died under an equally sudden wave of fatigue that crushed her back down onto her hospital bed. Her mind kicked and fought against the wave, struggling to breach the surface as the undertow dragged her back down towards unconsciousness.

What happened to me? Her mouth couldn't say it but her mind screamed it with such force the nurse must have heard it for she sensed her moving closer.

"Mandy." It was not the nurse's voice. It was deeper and softer and familiar. She felt hands touch gently at her hip and shoulder, fingers pressing through the dense webs of fabric. For a moment she felt as if those hands would lift her from this bed.

Then, with a terrible shudder, she remembered the other hands that grasped her and thrown her into a coffin. Had she ever left? Was she fading from a dream? Would she awake back in the flames? Her whole body began to shake.

The nurse's voice cut into her mind again. She couldn't make out the words, but she took comfort in their reality. This was no dream. She was insulated, medicated, but she was here. If she could only break through the gauze and see.

"You can't be here. You need to leave. It's not safe!" The nurse's strident commands echoed in her skull, meeting the mumbled replies of the man whose hands had left throbbing imprints at her sides. She strained her neck, lifting the head that weighed a thousand pounds and squinting her eyes.

There he was, a dark outline in the soft glow, reaching towards her as the smaller form of the nurse pushed him back and away from her. His hands were outstretched and for a brief second she could feel them on her again. Grabbing, yanking, tearing, pulling with feverish intensity, crying out desperately. *Hold on. Hold on!* Rescuing her from the flames.

She blinked again and he was gone, the door closing, and she felt the weight again and she was slipping back towards the bed, back to the heat. Back to sleep.

***

Enoch stood in front of the vending machine, surprised by his appearance reflected in the glass. The flesh of his face, normally so lean and sharp, hung off him in jowls. It wasn't just his face - every part of him seemed to be drooping towards the floor. He hadn't slept or changed in two days, not since the phone call.

There had been no dreams that night, no visions, no warnings. Only the bone-deep sleep of an exhausted man on his first night back in his own bed with his wife. The phone had woken them in the middle of the night. Enoch had sprung out of bed and hadn't stopped moving since. He'd told Emily to stay behind with the boys. He'd send for them later. And then he had driven through the night, pushing the old truck back to its breaking point to reach River City and St. Anthony's just after dawn.

He'd tried to bust right in and see her, but the nurses had barred his way. Third-degree burns over a third of her body. Too much risk of infection! As if the hands that had cradled her since she was a newborn could ever hurt her! But his pleading fell on deaf ears and cold shoulders. He'd been pushed to the waiting room, separated from her by doors and shrouds and surrounded by the well-wishing police officers and dignitaries that had swarmed in and out of the place, day and night.

They had been kind and thoughtful and gracious. *Where are you staying? The Garden Inn? Nonsense, we've reserved a suite at the Hilton for you and the whole family.* He had thanked them warmly, but his only bed would be the plastic chairs by the trauma wing doors. *Does that smoking wreck parked out front belong to you? Let it burn, we've got a limousine waiting to take you wherever you need to go.* But he didn't need to go anywhere but through those doors. *Hungry? Take your pick from these hot meals prepared by the best chefs in the city.* No thanks, no appetite. All he needed was a little caffeine from the $.50 coffee that burbled out of the vending machine in the corner.

"Mr. Parker?" A voice called to him out of the clouds. He blinked and realized the coffee was already in his hands. How long had he been staring blankly at his reflection?

Behind him stood the tall golden-haired young man who had been responsible for most of the back-patting he'd received. Enoch couldn't remember his name, but he knew he was some kind of big shot the way people ran and jumped for him.

"I want you to meet somebody."

He gestured behind him and a nurse appeared pushing a wheelchair. Seated was a pale-faced, long-legged man in a hospital gown, his sloppily-combed black hair drooping over his eyes. Both of his hands were buried under the same heavy white gauze they'd wrapped Mandy in. The man looked up at Enoch, his eyes weak with pain and fatigue.

"Mr. Parker, this is Captain Vladimir Paler. This is the man who pulled your daughter from the fire."

Enoch fell to his knees, driven by a weight of emotion he had not anticipated. He grasped at the sides of the wheelchair when he wanted to grab the man's hands. He bowed his head, his "thank you" too choked by feeling to be audible.

"Please, stand up," said the Captain, his voice soft, with a hint of sheepishness. Enoch did not stand but he raised his head, exposing the tears that streamed down his cheeks.

"I owe you my life for what you've done for me. Why am I only meeting you today?"

"They have a separate ward for us vampires. They wouldn't let me out until they were sure they had me all wrapped up."

Enoch stared at him in shock. This was a vampire? This handsome young man, too shy… too well-mannered to hold eye contact with the man sobbing in front of him… Enoch stared at him, too bewildered to remember his own manners. He was a little on the pale side, though with an Irish ruddiness around his cheeks. A little sharper in the nose and cheekbones perhaps, but with a little more sun he could have passed for any of the low country farm boys Enoch had grown up around.

Enoch continued to gape at him, knowing how rude he must seem, but unable to muster any words or change in his expression. He could scarcely even move. The Captain looked up from him to the big shot.

"Can we see her now? I think we've both waited long enough."

"That's gonna be up to the doc."

On cue, Doctor Bremer appeared, trailed by his white-coated posse. All of the glad-handers had assured Enoch that Mandy was in the best hands in River City with Bremer. But Enoch had been less than satisfied with this gloomy and elusive physician. "Not out of the woods yet," he would say in his faint Dutch accent, almost always in passing, as he and his attendants rushed back behind the forbidding trauma doors. Enoch wondered if he had only appeared now because of the big shot with them.

"Councilman Garrick, always a pleasure," Bremer said in his mincing way. He nodded at Enoch, his eyes barely acknowledging him before they leapt to the Captain. "And if it isn't our favorite patient, the irrepressible Captain. I hope you've secured him to the chair," he added to the nurse with a cold smile.

The Captain pushed himself up from the wheelchair, defiant, as Bremer shook his head.

"We want to see her," he declared, wobbling on his feet.

"Sadly, that is out of the question," Bremer clucked, still

shaking his head. "She's not out of the woods, yet. We must minimize any chance of contamination and any distractions that will keep her from getting the rest her body needs to repair itself. Nor is it good for you to be stomping around and arguing with all the meds you are on."

Bremer's eyes remained on Captain Paler, regarding him with a coolness that bordered on disdain. It made a remarkable contrast with the warmth with which he'd greeted Garrick and even the vague indifference that had characterized his interactions with Enoch. Enoch wondered what sort of bad blood existed between them. For the moment, he was just glad the vampire was standing up to the doc and trying to get them past those doors.

"Keeping her in total isolation is more dangerous than any miniscule chance of infection," retorted the Captain, with an edge in his voice that suggested that they'd had this conversation before. Bremer simply folded his arms and stayed put, as if to say his words were final.

"Come on, Mr. Parker," the Captain said, waving Enoch along as he took a long step towards the trauma doors. Bremer sidestepped to block their path.

"I cannot allow it," Bremer snapped, his voice rising an octave. "All visitors must remain in the lobby or they will be forced to leave the premises."

The Captain stuck a forearm into Bremer's chest. The doctor recoiled in horror as the vampire pushed at him with the giant clump of gauze at the end of his arm, apparently immune to the pain.

"I'm going in there. If you're not gonna stop me yourself, you can call the cops." He gave Bremer a gentle shove and the doctor stumbled backward, protesting violently. He looked to the councilman for support, but Garrick could only shrug. The Captain pushed the trauma doors open, this time unable to hide the pain as he did. He waved again to Enoch with a gauzy stump. Enoch hesitated.

"Come on, pops, you coming or what?"

Braving Bremer's withering gaze and stuffing the misgivings they'd planted in his head over the previous day, he followed. On the other side of the doors, the Captain took a step down the hallway, his leg shaking. Another step and he crumpled towards the floor. Enoch leapt forward to catch him.

"Should I get the wheelchair?" Enoch asked.

"No, just give me an arm. Careful!" He gasped as Enoch grasped too close to the edge of the bandaging. Pulling his hands back to the Captain's elbows, Enoch lifted him back to his feet and guided him toward Mandy's room. A pair of nurses moved to intercept them, but they retreated at the Captain's ferocious scowl.

Enoch opened the door to Mandy's room and ushered the Captain in. As soon as they crossed the threshold, the Captain caught sight of her. His legs failed him again and this time Enoch couldn't catch him. He had fallen to his knees, his hands catching the hem of Mandy's bedsheet. From the gasping of his breaths and the heave of his shoulders, Enoch knew that he was crying.

So heavily wrapped and still on the bed, she looked like the prey of some huge spider, paralyzed and tied up in silk and just waiting for the spider to return and finish her meal, sucking the juice out of her from the plastic tubes snaking out from every opening in the gauzy sac. She was covered from head to toe, so thickly that Enoch couldn't see her chest rise or fall. The only sign she was alive was the dull steady beeping of the electronic heart monitor beside her bed. The sight had nearly destroyed Enoch yesterday, and it was only the numbness brought on by his extended anguish and sleep deprivation that prevented him from collapsing next to the Captain.

What had moved this man so? Enoch knew little of vampires, but enough to know that they were not given to emotional displays. This was not the grief of a co-worker or even a friend. This man cared for Mandy with an intensity that radiated from him like a morning star. What could reduce a man to this helpless state… could lead a man to thrust both hands into a furnace? What else but love? This man, *this vampire*, was in love with his daughter.

But Enoch could not ponder this bewildering matter further. Though he found himself avoiding the sight of her, Mandy's presence crowded his thoughts to the exclusion of anything else. She had stirred the first time he'd come in, filling him with hope and with anger towards the hospital staff that had pushed him out and then kept him at bay. But now she seemed so still, so lifeless, like an empty cocoon after the butterfly had taken wing.

Beneath him, the Captain had recovered and pushed himself up, hiding his face as he used his club-like hands to wipe away unseen tears.

"We've got to get her out of here."

"But where? The doctor says it's too dangerous to move her."

"That's because he's a small-minded little coward. He would rather let her die in the safety of the hospital if trying to save her came with the slightest risk of him taking the blame." Now he was looking at Enoch, his eyes searching. "My people could save her. We have the best physicians in the world, the best medicines… We can override Bremer. He's not a god. We can get her transferred to the Duma Sanatorium."

They both turned as the door opened behind them. It was Bremer, his eyes bulging with outrage.

"I understand your eagerness to be with the patient," he hissed. "But you must think of her needs now, and not your own." He held the door open behind him and two massive security guards squeezed through, eyeing Enoch and the Captain pitilessly.

"Please don't jeopardize her health further by causing a scene. We can continue this conversation in my office."

The Captain stared down Bremer's goons with another fierce scowl, apparently ready to tussle with them right on the spot to call their master's bluff. But Enoch pulled gently at his elbow. "Come on, Captain," Enoch said softly. "We can talk outside."

As soon as they'd all been escorted back to the lobby, the Captain had regained some of his composure and spoke again.

"I've already talked to the staff at Duma. They have a bed ready for her and a burn specialist in residence. They'll be faxing over transfer paperwork today."

Bremer's eyes bulged again. "Out of the question!" he spluttered. "We're not even close to a point where I could possibly sign off on a transfer."

The Captain waved his arms derisively. "I've seen it done a dozen times for vamps in conditions just as critical as Mandy's. And Duma saved them all."

"Yes, and all of them were members of your community. But the hemotypical constitution is more delicate than yours," Bremer retorted, acid on his tongue. "We cannot be so cavalier to the risks in Miss Parker's case."

"If you're worried about the liability, I'm sure Mr. Parker will sign any release forms." The Captain turned to Enoch, suddenly bashful. "I'm sorry. I shouldn't have spoken for you. But you can ask the doctor. There's no better place than Duma for her."

Enoch turned to Bremer with questioning eyes. Bremer sighed heavily. "I cannot deny that the Duma Sanatorium has a remarkable record, one that any hospital would envy. But I can assure you, St. Anthony's is up to the task of caring for your daughter and we will resist any effort to remove her from our care and exposing her to unnecessary risks."

The Captain leaned in close, blocking Enoch's view of the diminutive doctor with his shoulder. "We've both seen her. She's got burns over half her body... She needs more than this hospital can give her, not just to live but to have a life... She needs the state of the art. Only Duma can give her that. And we don't have much time. He can't say no to you."

Enoch glanced between the two of them, feeling helpless. The conversation overwhelmed him. He'd spent his life avoiding hospitals. He hadn't been inside of one since his mother passed and the memories of that terrible day only filled him with foreboding at the thought of Mandy staying in that bed.

"I... I don't know. Is there somewhere I can go to think about this... to pray?"

The Captain turned away from Enoch in exasperation, but Bremer nodded. He summoned one of the nurses with a hook of his finger. "Show Mr. Parker to the chapel."

The chapel was tucked away in a corner after what felt like a mile walk down the main hallway. It hid behind one of the beige-painted doors Enoch had come to loathe in this place. But inside was a marvel of soft light infused with rich colors and a powerful sweet aroma, so different from the humming fluorescent lights and overpowering odor of pine-scented cleaning products that dominated every other space in this wretched hospital.

The walls on both sides were illuminated with dazzling stained glass, depicting a halo-capped man pleading with a thousand silver fish glowing in a shimmering blue sea. Enoch was too tired to guess at its meaning but felt comforted by the warmth of the light that streamed through its panes. Bathed in this light, a row of prettily carved pews lead up to an altar backed by a huge and gory crucifix, its bloody Jesus staring with drooping eyes at Enoch as he made his approach.

Good Baptist that he was, Enoch would have normally felt uncomfortable with all these graven images, but today he was too exhausted to register any theological complaints. Instead he was grateful for a physical form of the Savior to welcome him, arms outstretched, beckoning him to come nearer… To throw his own fatigue, his crippling fears, his daughter's terrible burns onto the back of Jesus, where they could disappear into his wounds…

He tumbled to his knees before the altar, the weight of his worries pushing him all the way to the floor. He attempted to lift his eyes to Jesus, but his head felt so heavy and the carpet so soft underneath his palms. He had so much to ask the Lord. He needed so much wisdom. He would close his eyes and lift the whole matter into his hands. And so he closed his eyes and rested his head against the carpeted stairs and fell into a deep sleep.

***

Patrolmen are always the last to know. Angel had been so eager to get back in the city's good graces. They'd given him the worst beat in the Pit and stripped him of all the perks he'd accumulated with what little seniority he had. But he never complained. Indeed, he'd devoted himself to the job with more energy and enthusiasm than he'd had fresh out of the academy. Now that he had no one to come home too and a mortgage to pay, he'd started working doubles whenever they were available. And as bad as the Pit was, they were always available.

With his nose to the grindstone, however, he was even later than the rest of his partners in picking up on the Van Helsing news as it made its slow trickle downhill. So when it came over the radio that Haggerty and his murderous bodyguard Dykstra had been spotted in an abandoned building in the North Precinct, he was quick, too quick, to show himself en route. He'd be the man that caught Van Helsing!

Somebody got a tip that the pair of them were holed up in an old bowling alley. Angel had joined the blue horde that flooded in after they exits had been secured. They'd found the preacher and his giant huddled together over a meal of crackers and condiments. The foot chase that ensued had them all slipping and sliding over the lanes as Haggerty and Dykstra fled to the hallway behind the pinsetters where the back exit was. Finding that exit blocked, Dykstra had decided to make his stand, waiting in the narrow hall for anyone with the balls to come around the corner and face him.

The fool in front had gotten spooked hearing Dykstra's voice hurtling taunts and decided to unleash blindly with the pepper spray without looking round the corner, emptying the can. The spray had stopped well short of Dykstra's position, but it did leave a dense cloud of burning mist for every cop to run through. Worse, the hall was so narrow, they had to move in single file, which not only made progress through the pepper spray cloud agonizingly slow but spit them out one at a time at the end half-blind and flailing into the punishing fists of the enormous bodyguard.

After the first few of them to make it had been sent back bruised and battered into the line, where the pain of the spray had spread from their eyes to their lungs, with Dykstra's disembodied jeers echoing out of the fog, panic had begun to set in. A scramble for the other end of the hall had begun. Angel was proud that he had been one of the handful towards the back that had kept their heads, vaulting over their retreating fellows with jaws set, teeth gritting and batons drawn. It had taken some time and another wave of reinforcements, but eventually Dykstra had succumbed and they'd dragged both of them out of the hallway from hell in cuffs.

The encounter with Dykstra's iron fists had left several of them in bad shape, and the sudden shooting pain that followed Angel's whoop of triumph had let him know he was one. He'd ended up in a hospital bed with a doctor poking and prodding him to tell him he had a cracked rib and they'd be keeping him overnight for observation. Nobody liked staying in the hospital, especially not here at City Hospital South - the rat-infested dive that served as the dumping grounds for all the violent tweakers and gangbangers that everyone hoped wouldn't survive their injuries. But Angel at least had been comforted by the prospect of a big city welcome wagon of higher ups coming by to shake his hand and congratulate him and maybe pin a medal on his chest where his intact rib used to be. Here's one of those valiant wounded warriors that brought down the mighty Van Helsing in brutal hand-to-hand combat!

But no one had come other than a few of his partners and classmates and a single flunky from a city councilman's office. They brought tepid praise, stale donuts and the belated word that Van Helsing had at last been caught. Not by Angel, but by Mandy and her vamp wonder, Captain Vlad, who were both convalescing across town at posh St. Anthony's. Angel couldn't help but fume at the news. His ex and her new flame, the toast of the city. Now she would be bound to this new man with ties stronger than the mere casual attraction and comfortable co-existence that had kept her with him. And together she and this superman would ride to the top of the department, heroes, while old Angel would still be just another patrolman, nursing busted ribs that hurt like wounded pride.

He wished Enoch were back here with him. That old man would shake him out of this pity party and set his sights back on the higher things. Then another partner showed up and told him that Mandy's dad was in town and, *oh, by the way, did you hear that Mandy's in a bad way. Burnt up all over. Like toast. Say didn't you guys used to go together?*

Angel sprang up at the news. Like toast. He snatched his buddy's coat and slung it over his hospital gown, a brutal pain stabbing from his ribs as he stretched. He winced, but he relished the sensation. Every throb pushed away the ugly bitterness and resentfulness that he'd been wallowing in on that hospital bed. *Imagine whining over your ex getting all the good press while you're sitting watching soaps on TV and she's got third-degree burns from head to toe.* His Mandy!

It was easy enough to discharge himself from the hospital. The nurses didn't even look from chatting at the desk to see him running towards the doors in bare feet with his gown sticking out from under the coat, his partner jogging behind. He looked like just another junkie making his break.

They made it to St. Anthony's in a few minutes, Angel weaving in and out of traffic as his partner cringed. There were some raised eyebrows when he stormed through the emergency room in his gown, but his partner's badge got him past the nursing station and into trauma. There in the family waiting area, he saw Enoch sitting on a bench, his long legs bowed out, his head in his hands.

"Where is she?" cried Angel, surprised at the emotion in his voice. Enoch looked up. There was a faint sparkle of recognition in his eyes that was barely perceptible under the drooping skin of his haggard face. Even lifting his head seemed to tax him. Angel had never seen him look so tired, so weak, so old.

"She's going to a better place," Enoch wheezed. "They just left." He seemed as if he wanted to say more, but his head collapsed back onto his hands.

Angel gathered up the old man, snatching his arm to sling it over his neck and then reaching behind his back to grab his belt and pull him to his feet. The effort re-awoke all the pain in Angel's chest and the shock of it made him stumble. As he regained his feet, he heard a voice behind him.

"Just where do you think you're going?"

He turned to see a pretty nurse with her hand on her hip, staring at him with eyebrows raised.

"I was going to get him home." He followed her gaze down to the gown sticking out like a dress below his jacket, hovering over his bare feet.

"And by home, do you mean the psych ward?" Her arm still cut its sharp inquisitorial angle from her hip, but he detected a smile on her lips.

"I'm a cop, honest. Just got out of the hospital, myself. See there's my partner coming now."

The smile finally broke out. "That's good." She stepped forward, placing a hand softly on Enoch's shoulder. "We've been worried about him since his daughter got transferred. He wouldn't sleep and wouldn't let him drive. We've been waiting for someone to come and take him home."

"We'll take care of him. By the way, do you happen to know where they took his daughter?"

"Duma Sanatorium..." She lowered her voice and leaned in closer. "It's the vamp hospital up in the foothills..."

"Vamp hospital? Why would they take her there?"

"I wish I could tell you. They don't even let us travel nurses in there. But they say it's the best facility in the state. I've heard a few stories of vamps getting transferred out of the v-wing here as vegetables and coming back from Duma right as rain a few weeks later."

"And was Mandy... his daughter... was she like a vegetable too?"

The nurse softened, seeing Angel's eyes go so wide and hearing the tremble in his voice. "Oh, honey, I'm sure she'll be alright. She had some bad burns, but it looks like she's got friends in high places who are doing whatever it takes to get her better again."

Angel nodded, feeling Enoch slumping next to him, sleeping on his feet. The downward weight was making his ribcage scream in protest but he gritted his teeth and bore it.

"I almost forgot," the nurse said, producing a business card from the pocket of her scrubs. "This is Dr. Bremer's card. He had to go home, but he wanted Mr. Parker to call him once he got situated. He said it was important." She held out the card and then retracted it suddenly, scribbling something on the back of the card and then handing it to Angel. "That's my personal number on the back. If you need anything, just let me know."

Angel nodded again, lingering for a moment in the warmth of her smiling gaze, before turning to lug Enoch back to the car.

27

Mandy awoke to the sensation of rocking. She was swinging from left to right. She felt a weightlessness in her gut, like she was suspended in air. Or over an abyss. She fought the fatigue that descended on her as soon as she tensed the muscles to open her eyes. But it came on, nonetheless, pushing her down, shoving her towards the abyss.

She opened her mouth to shout at whatever was pressing her down. *Stop! Let me live! I want to live!* But no words came out. Not even a croak. Just a rasping sound. The heaviness came on again and she almost succumbed. She tried to twist away from it, to break from its grasp. As soon as she moved, a pain ripped across her back and neck like a sudden burst of flame. She wanted to scream but again her throat failed.

She ceased her writhing, but the pain did not stop. It only intensified and spread, reaching to the back of her head and the small of her back, a searing heat that triggered an explosion at the nerve centers at the base of her spine and brain that sent scorching agony rocketing through her body and mind like Roman Candles. The pain burned through the heavy blanket of fatigue and forced her eyes wide open. Immediately she wished for a return of sleep and its cool, suffocating embrace.

The world around her was bright, painfully bright, but her eyes would not close. She could move her neck or head but she could swivel her eyes in their sockets, seeking any gap in the gauzy blur. She found it just to her left. A hole into another world, away from the pools of deathly blackness and the licking flames. She saw cabinets full of open boxes, out of which hung plastic tubes and tourniquets and white gloves dangling like severed hands.

Then something blocked her view, something big and blurry that breathed hot, moist air that smelled like anise and tooth decay. What demon was this? Then her eyes adjusted and a face came into focus. A small, sallow face, with dark eyes sunken in cavernous sockets, staring dully at her. She heard a voice, but it seemed so much farther away than the face, though the lips were moving. The voice was muffled and incomprehensible, as if it spoke in another language. She could only decipher one word - morphine - and the sound of it made her want to scream. *Give it to me! Kill the pain! Kill it!* But, again, there were only rasps that left her throat.

Then another voice cut in, wonderfully familiar and strong and clear. *Vlad! He's here!* The thought so excited her that she forgot what he'd said, only that he was there and he was close. She struggled to move her arms to reach for him. Her bridge back to life! She remembered his face, appearing out of the fire. His hands reaching in, pulling her away, bringing her back to where it was cool, where her lungs could expel the burning, poisonous air, where the flames could not reach.

She clung to his voice as another wave of oblivion washed over her, the searing pain hissing under its cooling expanse. The big sleep was coming for her again, but this time she had something to hold on to and she gripped it as she once again slipped under.

***

Vlad shifted uncomfortably on the bench as the *țăranii* paramedics squeezed past him, heads bowed, to open the ambulance's rear doors. The whole ride out here, he'd been unable to shake the memory of Bouchard's murder-mobile. It was bad enough to see Mandy lying there comatose, wrapped up like a mummy, without getting flashbacks of his own zip-tied imprisonment. His bandaged hand slipped to his pocket. The pain of the pressure was worth it to feel the bump of the knife. It was useless to him with what was left of his fingers still incarcerated in gauze, but he had vowed never to let it leave his side again. It had saved both their lives, that little knife, first by cutting his bonds, then by finding its way between Bouchard's ribs. Something like that you didn't leave to burn in the furnace.

Just knowing it was there comforted him, gave him strength for what was ahead. The ambulance had stopped, but the bumpy ride was just beginning. Just as he'd feared, the vamp doc was waiting on the other side of the doors, his arms crossed, his body blocking Mandy's entrance to the hospital. Flanking him were a pair of deputies, jaws jutting under their black sunglasses.

"Looks like you boys got off at the wrong wing. Infirmary's on the other side of the complex," the doctor said, an edge underneath his cheery tone. Alarmed enough to raise their heads, the paramedics glanced between Vlad and the doctor in confusion. They probably couldn't figure out which of them outranked the other in the complex vamp social hierarchy. It would have been easier in the old country, when the size of a man's estate, the finery of his clothes, or, in truly close calls, the ornateness of the filagree on the hilt of his saber could be used to determine his station. But now that everyone wore the non-descript uniforms of the American professions, the pecking order was beyond the ken of most *ţăranii*.

Vlad, however, saw the glint of the ruby on the doctor's signet ring, the haughty tilt of his aristocratic chin and the way the deputies looked to him. Vlad didn't know the doctor by name, but these were all the clues a vampire needed to know for certain that he was a scion of one of the Twenty Families and in good standing. A mere constable like Vlad Paler, no matter his civilian status in the city, had no footing to challenge any one from such bloodlines. Up here in the foothills, Vlad was more of a peer to the deputies that stood by like heavies awaiting their beating orders.

But he wasn't going to back down. The stakes were too high. No social niceties would stand in the way of Mandy's well-being. He stepped down from the ambulance, hiding both bandaged hands behind his back and raised himself to his full height to stare down the doctor.

"This is a special case. This is the woman who brought down Van Helsing."

"We know who she is. But our admissions protocol doesn't make exceptions for heroism. She'll receive perfectly adequate care at the Infirmary." The doctor nodded at the paramedics, who, having at last discerned the power dynamics, pushed Mandy's cart back towards the ambulance.

"Wait," Vlad cried, blocking the paramedics. Not the Infirmary.

What was that place but a glorified veterinarian's clinic to tend to the vamp barons' *țărani*? Better to call it the Glue Factory.

He felt a rising sense of desperation. He'd hoped he could have at least gotten her in the facility before beginning the inevitable fight with the administration. The battle had turned into a siege, and he had neither the pull nor the time to win that fight. Really, he had only one real card to play, but he dare not play that too soon.

"You can't take her to the Infirmary. Her injuries are too severe. She needs this facility."

The doctor's eyes narrowed, his patience wearing thin, his arms crossing tighter over his chest. "There's no magic in this hospital, Captain. She will receive all the care and attention we can provide at the appropriate facility. Our own staff can facilitate it if it would make you feel better. But we shouldn't delay any longer."

Picking up their cues from the doctor's changing body language, the deputies both took a step forward. If Vlad didn't move out of the paramedics' way, they would make him. He took a deep breath. *No other choice.*

"She doesn't need your staff. She needs a transfusion." The word stunned the doctor so much that he appeared to stagger backward. The deputies stopped dead in their tracks, gaping at him. Vlad himself felt his body tense, as if it too was shocked that he had dared bring up the idea. Only the paramedics seemed unfazed, standing there dumbly waiting for whatever this standoff was to be resolved.

At last, the doctor regained enough composure to address Vlad again, this time with a patronizing look. "I understand you too were seriously injured in the incident, Captain," he said, his voice now velvety and accommodating. "I think it would be best if you checked in here to be examined. Sometimes injuries to our extremities can cause unexpected effects in the rest of our systems. Sometimes the pain and trauma can bring on temporary delirium…"

"I'm not delirious. I know what I said and I stand by it. I am formally requesting a transfusion."

The word alone was enough to stun the doctor again. "You don't know what you're asking!" He spluttered.

"I do." It was Vlad's turn to fold his arms across his chest.

"But you don't have the authority!"

"We both know who does." Vlad watched the doctor's eyes

widen and his face redden.

"Absolutely not! Impossible!" The words came out like a gurgle. Vlad's words had reduced him to a shaking pillar of incredulous outrage. Vlad knew his demands bordered on insanity, violating every rule of propriety and decorum that the community had beaten into him since his birth. Any respectable vamp, which would be any vamp in authority, would react the same way. But he had no other choice. Could he let Mandy die? *No!*

He took a deep breath and said it.

"Wake him."

***

The light of the descending afternoon sun came through the slats of the plantation shutters and joined with the doorbell to wake Enoch from a nightmare. He struggled upright, his legs cramping from being bunched up on Angel's loveseat. He stared, bleary-eyed, at his watch until the hands finally came into view. Five o'clock! It had been one when he'd said goodbye to Em and the kids and then crumbled, exhausted, onto the sole item of furniture in Angel's living room.

Now he stumbled towards the door, trying to shake away the dream fragments clinging to his mind. He opened the door to see Doctor Bremer standing on the porch, looking prim and proper in a gray suit, his spectacled eyes just reaching Enoch's shoulders. Without his white coat, he looked more like an accountant than a doctor. Enoch ushered him in, feeling strange playing the host in a house he scarcely recognized.

"Thank you for taking the time to meet with me," Bremer said, in his delicate European voice. Enoch nodded, gesturing for him to sit before realizing there was nowhere other than the tattered loveseat that still bore the impression of Enoch's sleeping body. Bremer sat, shrinking down even closer to the floor as Enoch stood there awkwardly, holding back the yawn that tugged at his jaw and trying to remember where he was and why the doctor had come.

"I understand you signed the transfer papers for your daughter."

Enoch didn't understand much at all. The past few days had become a blur, as unreal as the nightmares that poisoned his fitful sleep. He had remembered a nurse waking him in the hospital chapel after who knows how many hours of sleep. She had guided him, like a sleepwalker, to an office where the Captain and a gaggle of unfamiliar faces floating atop white coats stared at him expectedly. They'd shoved a ream of paperwork in front of him and the Captain had given him an impassioned speech that Enoch could no longer remember. But he had remembered the tears in his eyes and his burning conviction that Mandy needed a special intervention if she was going to have any kind of life worth living. He had described in excruciating detail the crippling pain and disfiguring scarring Mandy would have to deal with if they didn't get her to the Duma specialists right away.

The doctors in the room had clung to the periphery of the room, refusing to commit to any of the hard, concrete answers that Enoch had so desperately sought, but also failing to counter any of the Captain's claims. Enoch had signed.

"He said it was the only way to save her, to give her her life back."

"Did he tell you how they would do that?" The little man's eye took on a piercing glint as they studied Enoch.

"I don't remember. But I'm not a medical man, doctor. I wouldn't have understood even if they did tell me." Enoch squatted down to get at the doctor's eye level and relieve the cramping of his legs.

"Have you been to see your daughter in the new facility yet?"

"No," murmured Enoch, a spasm of anger driving away some of the fatigue. "They have a strict no visitors policy." They had turned the whole family away at the gates. Poor Em had been so distraught. Angel had offered to put them all up at his place while they waited on news, but the farm had needed tending back home and now they were back in the same situation of Enoch waiting on Mandy while his family did without.

"That's a shame. I'm worried about your daughter, Mr. Parker. I won't deny the Duma is an excellent hospital with a remarkable track record. But I'm worried about the course of treatment I suspect Captain Paler may have had in mind when he was so adamant about a transfer."

"I don't know the Captain very well, doctor, but I believe he loves Mandy and wouldn't recommend anything to do her harm. He's the one that saved her." *While I was leaving the city in the rear-view mirror. She was screaming for help and I wasn't there.*

"It's not so much about harm… but…" The doctor trailed off, mincing his words. "It's difficult to find the right way to phrase this. How much do you know about vampires, Mr. Parker?"

"Not much. We don't have any back home. I'd always believed that they were a sort of a cult, but Mandy told me it was nothing more than a genetic mutation. Something about their mitochondria."

"Yes, they have a specialized organelle the rest of us don't, a sort of mitochondrial mutation. It allows their cells to metabolize erythrocytes for proteins that can delay the onset of apoptosis and to reduce entropic loss brought on by the typical mitotic cycle. Especially relevant to your daughter's case, it also aids in the rapid reconstruction of any integumentary damage."

Enoch felt his eyes glazing over. "As I said, doc, I'm not a medical man on the best of days and I haven't been getting much sleep lately. I'm not sure I understand what you're saying."

"I apologize for getting off in the weeds. I completed my residency in Bucharest before the Soviets took back control and I spent a lot of my spare time in the vampire records room. Vampire medicine has been a minor obsession for me ever since… In layman's terms, I'm saying that the vampiric mutation, the one that is carried in their blood, has enormously potent healing restorative properties, which I believe that Captain is depending on to bring your daughter back to good health."

"Isn't that good?" asked Enoch, still confused. His curiosity about vampires had never been particularly strong until the Captain had entered Mandy's life and most of his knowledge of them was based on half-remembered sermons his pastor had delivered on the wickedness of the age, connecting vampirism to pagan cults from Biblical times. Everything else he knew about them had come from the public service announcements he'd seen on the rare occasions he'd been around a television, urging citizens to donate blood and reject intolerance.

"The potential for good is there," continued the doctor. "But every clinical trial that has attempted to introduce the vampiric mitochondria to hemotypical patients has resulted in a violent immune response. You see, despite its many beneficial properties, the vampiric mitochondria act similarly to an invasive parasite, very much like malaria, and a patient's body will treat it as such."

"That's what the Captain wants to do? Give her malaria?"

Enoch's mind reeled. It couldn't be. He cared for her. He wouldn't do such a thing. Had he gone mad? *Why did I sign? Oh, Lord, why did I sign?*

The doctor seemed to pick up on the note of hysteria in Enoch's voice and raised his hands in a calming gesture. "No, I don't think so. But I do believe he may be pushing into treatment territory that represents... a gray area, scientifically and ethically." He paused, gathering his thoughts, while Enoch continued to stare, bewildered.

"In theory, when the vampiric mitochondria reaches a critical mass in the subject's bloodstream, the immune response will cease and the mitochondria will be free to spread throughout the body and begin its healing work. Again, in theory, this could be achieved by a massive transfusion from a vampiric subject to a hemotypical one."

"You keep saying theory. Has no one ever tried?"

"The contamination protocols in America are far too strict, even in lab settings, to allow it. But some of my old colleagues in Bucharest, who had worked under the Soviet bloc, told me of experiments where the critical mass had been achieved." Here Bremer paused again and looked around, as if to make sure they weren't being overheard. "My American colleagues dismissed this as conspiracy theory and crackpot science and chided me for being so credulous, but I have never been fully dissuaded. And when I saw the look of conviction in the Captain's eyes as he - a layman! - told me and my entire staff that our prognosis for your daughter was faulty and that he knew of methods that would guarantee her complete recovery... all of those old conversations came back to me. I tell you, I am certain he was thinking of a transfusion."

Enoch scratched his head, his stomach still roiling in panic as his brain tried desperately to track with the doctor's speech. "So you're saying that the place he's taken her to will do this transfusion... that is illegal... but that it will work? Mandy will recover?"

Bremer scratched his chin, looking carefully into Enoch's eyes before he spoke. "What I'm saying, and I'm going to be completely frank, Mr. Parker... what I'm saying is that I believe she would recover, but into something different than she is today. I think the Captain is going to turn your daughter into a vampire."

28

They were going to let Vlad wait in suspense. He was sitting in the courtyard at the rear of the Sanatorium, with its gorgeous views of the foothills where they broke into canyons and opened onto a spectacular vista of the alluvial floodplains below. This was where Dr. Duma had tended to the ills of River City's richest and most powerful citizens in the era when vampirism was still a closely guarded secret. Back then Dr. Duma was one of the brave handful who had worked so tirelessly to bring their people out of the shadows and to carve out a new home for his people in the new world.

Vlad paced, restless, unmoved by the views, his eyes studying his feet as he made the same circuit through the courtyard again and again. His bold gambit had gotten her past the hospital doors and him an escort to this place. But that had been days ago, and everyone at the Sanatorium had maintained their taciturn silence. The doctors had tended to his own damaged hands silently, ignoring his every demand for more information. And now that he had been discharged, his only company was those two deputies, who stood like gargoyles at the door, stone-faced, as they watched his every move.

He glanced at his watch. *How much longer?* He felt a twist in his stomach again as the terrible thought recurred in his mind. They were dragging things out, hoping that she'd die before he'd had a chance to make his case. He balled his fists in anger, flashing a look at the deputies. They had no right to treat him this way. This was not the old country! Not here in the seat of the new world that Dr. Duma had made, where every vampire could partake in the good life. While he was alive, the doctor had made sure no one in the community withheld anything from Vlad on account of his lonely station.

Since he'd passed, however, the old ways and hierarchies had begun to reassert themselves. Just like these aristocrats in their white lab coats with their men-at-arms barring the gates. They were trying to transform this wide-open garden of Eden into another exclusive domain, where the few hoarded the great gifts and left the rest of mankind to thrash about in oblivious darkness.

Then the doors opened, so suddenly that the deputies jumped along with Vlad, and out streamed a procession of doctors marching like a color guard on both sides of a *țăran* nurse pushing a tiny old man in a wheelchair. Vlad gasped at the sight.

Could it be? It had only been a decade since he'd seen him last, a fading shadow on his deathbed. The figure before him looked like a mummy, shrunken and shriveled into miniature, a raisin where a man had once been. But it was unquestionably him and he was unquestionably alive: twinkling within their cavernous sockets were those unmistakable eyes, like two great fountains of vitality gushing out over his warped and withered frame. It was Doctor Duma, awake and alive!

The sight was exhilarating, filling Vlad with a quivering sensation akin to spiritual ecstasy. The great secret of their people stripped of the cloak of centuries of subterfuge and superstition and manifested before his eyes. The great veil torn asunder. He had always believed, of course, but it had been the subconscious sort of belief, unconsidered and unappreciated, buried under so many layers of mundane concerns that it scarcely registered. Dreaming of the great beyond was for little children and the old men. But now he was a witness to a faith made flesh, a power to terrible to behold with his casual cynicism intact.

Before he was even conscious of his actions, Vlad had cast himself on the ground, his hands grasping Duma's bare feet, his tears wetting the coarse skin that stretched so thinly over his protruding bones. This was not just the joy of regaining his old and dear friend, but the groveling prostration of a mortal at the foot of a god.

A hoarse clucking sounded from above him and then Vlad

heard a voice, so faint it sounded like a ghost whispering from beyond the void.

"It's good to see you too, Connie." The voice was so warm and rich in Vlad's memory that his tears flowed all the freer. From any other lips, "Connie" would have been an insult, a derisive reminder of his days as a lowly constable back in the old country, but from Duma, it had always been a term of endearment. How Vlad had missed this great man! He felt a tug at his shoulder, so light it might have been the breeze. Duma was plucking at his sleeve, signaling for him to stand up. Vlad did, but kept his head bowed in awe. His downcast eyes darted to the lab coats flanking him on either side, and he was shocked to see glazed countenances. *They were bored! Even irritated!*

"Behold the magic of our people, Connie," Duma rasped. "Isn't it marvelous? I've been told I'm the picture of health and vitality."

Vlad risked a quick glance upward and saw a ghoulish smile on Duma's shriveled lips. Other than his sparkling eyes, he had the look of a lifeless shrunken head dangling from the belt of an Amazonian headhunter. It was unnerving to look at him. *Was this the magic of immortality or a carnival freak?*

"You look so old, sir," he said in low tones, staring back at the ground. Brutal honesty had always been the best policy with Duma and besides, what could he hide from a man risen from the grave?

Duma cackled. "You hear that, you vultures?" he crowed to their audience, who looked on blankly, as if inured to the abuse. "He says I look terrible! He's right. I look like a petrified cat turd. And it's all because you lot can never let a man get his beauty sleep. Always some new crisis that has you running to wake the dead because no one in this younger generation has the gumption to make bold decisions…"

Vlad kept his gaze at the ground as his jaw hung open. In his mind, waking an elder, like demanding a transfusion, was a sacred rite, awesome and terrible, recourse to be taken only as an extreme measure. *The nuclear option.* Further, he'd believed the practice had been so rarely resorted to that the tradition had receded into the mythic range of the community's cultural memory. When Vlad had made the request, he'd half-expected to be laughed at, like a child demanding to speak to Santa Clause. And now it appeared he was just one of a thousand callers, his request no more momentous than asking to speak to a supervisor at a retail sales counter. His mind was completing a rollercoaster circuit from religious epiphany back to world-weary ennui.

"I apologize, sir. It's my doing that you've been woken."

"Well, I'm glad you did. I have long wished to see you again, old friend. I hope at least that you've brought me good tidings. All these buzzards have done is steal my peace to bring me heartache..." A strong current of bitterness overtook the warmth in Duma's voice and with it his energy seemed to fade. "I wished so badly to have you at my side when they brought me news of Alex."

Two wizened hands reached out and squeezed Vlad's - it should have hurt, so recently had they finished the work on his own grafts. But the hands felt tiny and weak in his palms, like a pair of chicken feet, their hollow bones light and fragile in his grip. He squeezed them ever so gently back. If he squeezed too hard, maybe the old man would explode into a cloud of dust and the magic of his reappearance would be dispelled.

"I know I let you down. I wasn't able to save him."

He couldn't look the old man in the eyes but he felt another squeeze from his hands.

"He was lost to me long before those butchers took him." Duma's voice rose from a whisper to a hiss of disgust. "A son of mine running around like a lost pup after that hoodlum Dann and his crowd. My only consolation is that they all received the same bitter medicine... And that you and your little lady friend took care of the wretched creature that gave it to them."

Vlad looked up to see the grateful twinkle lighting up the shrunken face. Here was his chance.

"That's the matter I asked them to wake you for. She's in an awful bad way, sir. And she's done so much for the community. If anyone deserves a special intervention, it's her."

Duma held his gaze, his lips pursed. "Still pining for native girls after all these years, Connie?"

"I won't deny my feelings for her, but I'm not asking for myself." Vlad took a deep breath as he gathered himself. "You always told me that the community had to be about something higher than just self-preservation at any cost. That here in America it could be so much more than what it was back home. You said we could build something together out of the best that human society had to offer. And, sir, I think she's it."

Duma leaned back in his chair, thoughtful, a tiny hand detaching from Vlad to comb through the ghostly wisps of white hair across his mottled scalp.

"If you'd seen what I've seen over the last months, you'd know I'm not speaking out of some flight of passion or lust... This kid gave her all for this case. She lived it and breathed it. She took on her own kind without even a moment's hesitation when they were trying to turn the people against us. And she laid down her life to get justice for Dan and those reprobates while these... gentlemen..." Vlad gestured at their audience who continued to regard the little scene with cool detachment. "... never bothered to descend from their castles in the hills. And now they say she's got to just lie there, half the skin burned off her body..." The lump swelling in Vlad's throat choked off his voice and forced his eyes shut. He took another deep breath. "I know I'm making an extraordinary request-"

"Nonsense!" interjected Duma, energy crackling back into his voice. Vlad looked up at him in alarm. Had he misjudged his old benefactor? Was he just a reactionary like the rest of them, too mired in the past to see Mandy's worth? To see what an asset she could be to the community? Despair washed over him for a terrible moment as Duma twisted in his chair looking at his attendants.

"There's nothing extraordinary about it! And if my esteemed colleagues here have given you that impression, shame on them. They've been dangling transfusions as carrots to anyone they want to lead around by the nose. Every time I wake up, this place stinks of money and garlic. Why just this past month they had some golden-haired nobody up here for the preliminary tests. He looked like he'd just started shaving a few weeks ago and they were ready to treat him to the fountain of youth. Every time I go back to sleep, they go back to treating this place like a candy store." He threw up his hands in disgust.

Vlad steadied himself on the waves of relief, his despair draining away, but uncertainty still on his lips. "Did you approve any of these transfusions?"

"No!" cried Duma. "Membership in our great society is not a political bargaining chip. It's a precious birthright, a sacred responsibility. We are its stewards, not its pimps." He cast another withering glare around him, but then softened and spoke again in his low, weakened voice. "But how can I blame them when my own son was gallivanting around the town, opening his mouth and his veins to his billionaire buddies, acting like this place was his own private club?"

Duma shook his head, then turned again to Vlad. "But don't you worry, Connie, your young lady is different. Pending the tests and the interviews, I will be approving her transfusion." He tut-tutted Vlad's breathless thank yous. "This is not a favor to you, though you are not undeserving. I want to make you and your Miss Parker an example of what our community should be building here. We are to be a people of heroism and devotion, of vigor and vitality. We will merit the crown that chance and chaos placed on our brow and we will rise above it, pulling the whole human race along with it." He exhaled, pleased with his speech and too spent to continue it.

"Come, escort me back to my chambers," he said, dismissing his nurse with a dry snap of his fingers. Vlad took over and pushed Duma forward down a trellised path that led out of the courtyard and into the grounds. Dense honey-suckle vines covered the trellises, shading them from the sun, their white and golden trumpets hanging down to blast the air with their sickly-sweet symphony. The old man kept quiet as Vlad pushed along slowly, his hands trembling at the handles of the chair, a spirit of euphoria rushing through him.

"You honor me, sir," Vlad said at last.

"It's about time somebody did. You're the salt of the earth, Connie. You're what I always wanted my son to be... But don't let my words go to your head. I need those feet of yours planted on the ground. There's so much work to be done and I can't be the one to do it. I know I complain about being awakened so much, but the truth is, I demanded it. I couldn't trust those blighters with any big decision. Every one of them another Codrescu..." He sighed and they emerged from under the trellises onto the grounds, where the long boughs of the encircling cedars took over the job of shading them from the honeysuckle.

"Though I suppose they did at least wake me. Their parents' generation would have left me in the tomb and locked the door for a thousand years. I would have stumbled out into the light with nothing to my name, just another poor peddler hawking his wares... But eventually I will have to submit to the long sleep and trust my legacy to your generation until the grand day arrives at last." He reached back and grasped Vlad's hand on the handle of the chair. "I believe in you, Connie. Big things are in store for you; I've arranged them. Your responsibilities will grow in the coming weeks, and with them the weight on your shoulders. But you cannot falter. Our future is too important."

Vlad felt his hands begin to tremble again. They had reached the mausoleum row of the grounds. Here on both sides of the widening path sat the resting places of the greatest houses to ever spring from the earth: the Twenty Families. Often he had walked here as a pilgrim, awed by the grandeur of these gothic edifices, recreations in miniature of the awesome castles that had studded the hills of the old country like jewels in a gigantic crown. And now here was Dr. Duma, the wanderer and outcast from a great house who had risen to outstrip them all, building a mausoleum that dwarfed the rest, a veritable fortress looming at the end of the row, welcoming him into its midst. Entrusting him with the keys to the kingdom!

"I cherish your faith in me, sir," Vlad began, his voice trembling with his hands. "But I'm still just a police captain. I have a hard enough time dealing with my colonels. I can't even imagine wrestling with the leaders of the community."

Duma chuckled. "That's not what I've heard. You've stepped on more than a few hornet's nests while I've been asleep and acquitted yourself pretty well. And that was without my help, or at least any help you knew about. No, all you need to do is keep that fighting spirit hot, keep those ideals of yours bright. I'll take care of the rest. You're a conquering hero now, a man of the people and a champion of the community. Your elevation will feel natural, right, inevitable because it will be... Do you understand?"

Vlad nodded and came to a stop in front of the towering doors of the great Duma mausoleum, its sheer marble facade rising sharply in front of them, its simple classical beauty free of the gargoyles and medieval reliefs that covered every surface of its smaller rivals on the row.

"I'm ready to shoulder any burden the community needs me to bear."

"Good. I will sleep that much better, knowing you are representing me here. But ready yourself. It's a hard road ahead, and a lonely one. You will not find many allies among the old families. They have been working to undermine me and my vision since they got here. What support you will have will come from the travelers and vagabonds like ourselves and whatever new blood you deem appropriate to introduce." Here he paused to look pointedly at Vlad. "Have you spoken to your native friend about your plans for her?"

"Not in so many words. But I know her well, sir. She has none of the impediments that would have given me pause... She's as free-thinking a woman as I've ever encountered."

"And no attachments that will give us trouble?"

"An old boyfriend, but she's already cut ties with him. I have some concerns about her family. They are very religious and her father is quite tenacious."

"What sort of man is he?"

"A farmer. Lives several hundred miles away and has a big family back home, but he's left them behind to be with her. They've already had to turn him away at the gates multiple times."

"Hmmm..." Duma turned his head to look past the cedars and toward the unseen road that led back to the city. "It might be best for all involved to sever those entanglements and give her a fresh start, at least in the short term. Do you think she would be amenable?"

"With time, yes. She had to make a hard break with her family to come to the city in the first place."

"Make sure of it... I may sound cavalier regarding the old ways but I know you don't misunderstand me. We must respect the caution of the ancients and set aside any personal passions that might lead us astray."

Vlad nodded gravely, bowing his head under the old man's watchful eyes. In front of them, the doors to the mausoleum opened with a creak, and a pair of *ţăranii* in pale blue smocks and surgical masks stood, statuesque and expressionless like the gargoyles missing from the exterior. Behind them, the interior of the mausoleum was hidden in an inky blackness that defied Vlad's curious probing.

"We must part here and leave at least some shroud of mystery covering the secrets of the ancient ways," Duma said, a smile twitching at the end of those tiny lips. "I hate to wake, but I was so glad to see you. Do not hesitate to wake me again if you need me."

Vlad could scarcely say goodbye before the nurses whisked Duma out of his hands and rolled him into the darkness, the doors closing behind them. He stood at the threshold for several moments, resting his head against its walls, feeling the coolness of the marble against the hot flush in his cheeks. In a moment, he would turn and begin the short walk back to the Sanatorium, brimming with the intoxicating sensation of so many dreams fulfilled. He just needed a few minutes to let it spill over him, to saturate the cracks and crevices that had opened over the course of his long sojourn in the wilderness. He was a man coming down from the mountaintop. He was a man whose moment had come.

***

Beep... Beep... Mandy didn't know how long she had been hearing that sound. When her mind searched its origin, it pictured an infinite line vanishing into the horizon of her memory. But she was awake and knew that was a recent development. She pivoted her head and - miracle of miracles! - it moved! And no pain! She peeled her eyes open, feeling a disgusting layer of crust crumble away. Her vision was blurry but the gauze was gone.

"That did the trick," came a voice. "You'll want to be quick though; this stuff wears off pretty quick."

A different voice from the other side of Mandy's head mumbled something and then she felt something warm at her hand. It felt like a man's hand, but she couldn't be sure. There was something that felt vaguely like parchment paper separating them. She heard it crinkle as whoever it was squeezed her gently.

"Mandy?"

Vlad! She squeezed his hand in return.

"Where am I?" She felt her voice pour out of her throat smooth and clear. Had she really recovered. Then why was it still so hard to see and why did it feel like her whole body was encased in paper?

"You're in a new hospital. A better hospital. We're going to get you all better."

"I feel so much better already." Excitement was bubbling from her voice. She squeezed his hand tighter and used it to pull herself upright.

"Be careful. You've got a lot of new skin on you and you don't want to put too much strain on it. And you don't want to do anything that's going to hurt once this new drug wears off."

A thousand cuts of phantom pain lit up Mandy's back and she gasped. A drug? "You mean I'm not really better?" She began to cry and as she did, she felt his arms wrap around her, pressing gently against the crinkling paper on her back. The phantom pain disappeared in his embrace.

"Oh, Mandy, don't cry. You are going to get better. Better than you ever were. You've just got to be patient." She felt his lips touch her forehead. There was no paper there to keep her from his touch! She wished he would squeeze her tighter. She wished her lips could escape her parchment prison to find his. *You've got to be patient... I've got to be a patient.*

"I know what you did for me," she whispered into his ear. "I'll never forget it."

"There's something very important I need to ask you," she heard him whisper back. She felt his embrace tighten around her, securing her like a bullet-proof vest against the world and the pain and all the fears that had tormented her sleeping mind. In these arms, she felt invincible, completely and totally insulated against the flames.

"Anything," she said, pressing against his cheek. She didn't know if it was the drug, loosening what was left of her reserve and making her cling to him, but she felt that she could hold nothing back from him. He walked through fire for her, she would walk through fire with him.

"To get you all the way better, we need to give you some of my blood."

She snuggled into his neck, feeling a wave of sleep rising and with it a sense of lightness that bordered on silliness. Was this the drug? "That sounds good," she said, a giggle tickling at her throat. "I already know you're my type."

He pulled back from her, holding her shoulders with his hands. She imagined him staring her deeply in the eyes, but she still saw only a blur.

"This is important, Mandy. This wouldn't be like any other transfusion. There's a power in our blood. It has the power to heal, but not without cost. It will change you. It will make demands of you. You will never be the same."

There's power in the blood! The old hymn stirred in Mandy's memory, at first faintly and growing as Vlad spoke until it was a thundering chorus ringing in her ears. She was a little girl again, her head not yet above the church pew, and was tugging at her mother's skirt, asking if she could go outside. A sharp tsk-tsk from her mother and with it a command to join in. *Would you o'er evil a victory win? There's wonderful power in the blood!*

Mandy felt a spasm of unease and with it another wave of pricks along her spine, the phantom pain threatening its return. Couldn't Vlad just hold her again? Why must they do all this talking?

"Is it dangerous?" she asked at last.

"There's risk, yes. But once you come through on the other side... I don't know how to explain it, but it will be like your eyes are open for the first time..."

Mandy shivered in apprehension. "Will you be there with me?"

He leaned in close to her, bending his forehead to touch hers. "If you take my blood, you'd be one of us. You and I would be bound together forever, across all the ages of time. I would never leave your side."

"Yes!" The word came out like a gasp and her arms rose to wrap around his unseen neck, her lips searching for him. His hand cupped her chin and peeled the paper from over her mouth and there he was, kissing her with so much force she felt their teeth collide. His breath, hot and sweet, poured into her like mulled wine.

And then he pulled away, leaving her grasping at the air.

"There's one more thing," he said. *More talking!* She didn't want to talk. She wanted to disappear into him. But she could only nod and hunt for his face in the blur, her head beginning to feel heavy.

"It's about your family." The word landed like a mallet, dropping her head to her chest. She was back in church, caught between the pews, the tall timber of her parents' legs rising to block one exit and the mass of siblings closing off the other. No escape. "There are some things that are going to be difficult to explain to them..."

A fog had begun to descend on Mandy's mind, and it was rapidly growing thicker than the clouds that blurred her vision. She could hardly understand what Vlad was trying to explain to her. How would her parents understand? *Vampire blood in my veins? A vampire man in my bed?* There were no good answers and the thoughts swirled so chaotically through her brain that she felt dizzy and fell back towards the bed.

Vlad's hands were there to catch her, his arms enveloping her again.

"I'm okay," she said, but her voice was growing weaker. She flexed at her core to pull herself upright again, but her muscles ignored her commands and she could only fall back into his arms. "What were you saying?" she asked. Or she thought she did. A ringing was growing in her ears and she couldn't be sure the words had come out.

"It might be best if your family were to believe the worst for a little while…" Vlad's voice continued, as soft and gentle as velvet in her ear but she could no longer hear it for the ringing. She knew she was fading. She was back at the church again, but this time Vlad was there, holding her. The congregation was still singing, but it was growing fainter and she realized they were floating, the two of them, up and out of the pew, drifting ever further. She squinted and she could see her family was still singing, their eyes closed, their arms outstretched. Were they reaching for her or were they reaching for God?

Vlad was whispering in her ear. "Would you leave them for me?"

She snuggled into him, wrapping him around her like a dark blanket. "Yes," she whispered back and then she was gone.

29

The urn felt so light in Enoch's hands. Too light. He set it down on the table and then sat down heavily into one of the black leather chairs that surrounded the great mahogany table. The urn was fashioned from some expensive ceramic, its surface a swirling cloud of deep, rich colors that entrapped the eye. It made a pretty table setting in this upper level conference room where everything looked and felt expensive, except for Enoch in his faded button-up and tweed slacks and the brown penny loafers with all the scuffs on the toes.

A lawyer's office. A strange place to summon him to receive the worst news of his life. Were they worried he would sue? Were they covering something up? *You wouldn't know it from their faces.*

The men across from him, and there were so many of them, were the picture of gravity and sympathy. Only a pair of them were vampires - Enoch was getting better at spotting them - one a doctor from the Sanatorium and the other a suit, Enoch guessed some kind of big shot from where he was seated at the table. Enoch only recognized one of the rest: Garrick, the boyish councilman who'd glad-handed him up and down those first few days at the hospital. He seemed to have the most gravity in the room, as everyone else would look to him for approval every few moments, but it was the doctor who started the talking.

"I'm sure you'll have questions, but I'd like to reiterate that the staff at the Sanatorium did all we could to help your daughter. Ultimately, she was beyond the reach of medicine. I know it is small comfort, but she passed peacefully."

Enoch did not respond, his eyes lost in the whirling purples and blacks of the urn. It was Garrick's turn to talk now.

"This should go without saying, but the city is going to cover any and all funeral costs. And with your family's permission, we'd like to go all out and give her the hero's funeral she so richly deserves."

Enoch still didn't speak. He had an urge to reach out and grab the urn and feel the weight of it in his hands. *Just too light! A human being ought to weigh more than that.*

"Let's not forget the line of duty benefit." This time it was one of the suits that Enoch had never seen before speaking. He had coke bottle glasses that lured his eyes away from the urn but only for a moment. "Your family's entitled to a $300,000 payout per city policy. Miss Parker listed you and your wife as her primary beneficiaries on her paperwork." He paused, but seeing no reaction from Enoch, continued on. "That full amount won't be available until the insurance companies finish their inquiries, but the city had authorized me to present you with a check for half that today. The rest will come just as soon as the insurance comes through."

Enoch's eyes flitted to the coke bottle man once again. The man wore a friendly, encouraging expression as if to say "Congratulations! This is life-changing money!" *Now you can go dump that dusty ensemble and buy yourself a nice black suit!*

A moment of silence fell over the whole room. They needed some kind of reaction from him. A hysterical sob. A dignified thank you. An angry tirade. Anything other than the awkward silence. At last, Enoch spoke, his voice so steady and calm it surprised himself.

"Why would you cremate her?"

"That is the Sanatorium's protocol for all those who pass away in our facility," said the vampire doctor, his face blank. "The release was on the transfer paperwork you signed."

Again the papers. They had been staring up at Enoch in his nightmares, his hand spilling the ink that signed her soul away to the devil.

"No!" he cried, his fist pounding against the table. None of them stirred. This was the emotional outburst they had been waiting for. He had finally met, or sunk down to, their expectations for this meeting. "He rescued her from the fire. He wouldn't let her be thrown back in!" His voice sounded hysterical in his own ears.

"We all understand this is a difficult time for -" It was another suit speaking. A lawyer from the looks of him from the smugness of his expression. But Enoch was through listening. He cut him off.

"Where is Captain Vladimir Paler? He's the man I trusted my daughter to. He's the man who promised me she would be alright."

"Captain Paler is still at the Sanatorium receiving treatment for his own injuries," said the doctor. "He expressed his regrets for not being able to offer his condolences in person."

"Then he's a coward!" bellowed Enoch, rising to his feet and towering over the whole crowd of them, scorching them all with fire in his eyes. Only Garrick rose to meet his gaze.

"Don't let your grief make you slander a good man," he said, his voice level but commanding, his youthful eyes unblinking under Enoch's baleful glare. "Captain Paler is a hero, and I can personally assure you, no one worked harder to save your daughter's life. He was with her at the end."

"He lied to me!" Enoch roared, his voice cracking under the strain of his fury. He felt himself shaking, his knee trembling with sudden weakness. Garrick continued to regard him, his jutting chin relaxing in pity.

"If you'll excuse us, gentleman, I think this conference has reached its conclusion." With a little bow to the assembly, Garrick moved towards Enoch, placing a firm hand at his elbow and indicating the door to the hallway with a nod of his head. Enoch hesitated. He wanted to say more to these onlookers, but his wrath was spent. Instead, he reached for the urn, his hands trembling. What had been so light now felt terribly heavy in his shaking palms and for one horrible moment he thought he might drop her and spill her ashes across the mahogany table.

"May I?" Garrick asked, extending his hands, which hung in the air, strong and steady. Enoch handed her over, cautiously, and together they exited the conference room. They trudged down the hallways, their every footstep embraced by its soft oriental carpet. Garrick's stiff gait loosened into a carefree amble and he tucked the urn into a football hold under one arm so he could sling the other over Enoch's shoulder.

"I've never had a child, so I can't put myself in your shoes, but I had the chance to get to know your daughter pretty well over the last month," he said softly, his sincerity oozing into Enoch's ear. "She was a special little lady and this whole city is going to feel her loss."

Enoch continued forward, resisting the impulse to shrug the man's arm off his shoulder. He didn't know what the man expected him to say, so he remained silent. The elevator was waiting and at last the overly familiar arm slipped off him. Enoch turned to Garrick, his no longer trembling hands open to receive the urn again.

"Thank you for walking me out. I remember the way from here."

But Garrick waved him off and patted the urn like it was a bongo drum, smiling big and stepping into the elevator. "I insist," he said.

They rode down together, Enoch maintaining his confused silence, wondering how to get the urn back, how to be rid of this clingy city councilman. Garrick eyed him and rubbed at his lips, as if he was keeping a lid over his mouth. It was a long ride down and the silence didn't last.

"You're a man of faith, aren't you?" Garrick blurted out.

"Yes," Enoch said, surprised, a glimmer of an evangelical impulse percolating underneath the clouds that blanketed his mind. "Are you?"

Garrick smirked. "Officially, I'm an Episcopalian and I'll remain so as long as I'm in the running for higher office... but, off the record, I'm sort of between faiths at the moment."

"Do you know where you'd go if this elevator cable snapped and we fell the last ten floors?" Enoch's voice crackled with newfound energy. The Lord had brought this young man to him even on a day such as this. *Even in the depths of despair, I can serve Him!*

"Probably straight on down to the fiery pit with my rap sheet," he exclaimed with a smile that belied his words. "But I've got a lot of different pokers in the fire, so to speak, and I hope one of them works out for me."

"There's only one way to be sure," began Enoch, but Garrick raised his hand to cut him off.

"I get it, and I don't want to stop you mid-pitch, but my own personal eternity isn't what I wanted to talk about..." He stopped to give Enoch a judicious look, his lips churning as he chose his next words carefully. "Do you believe you'll see your daughter again?"

The question hit Enoch right in the solar plexus, driving his newfound enthusiasm right out of him along with the air in his lungs. It was the question he had been running from since the phone call last night.

"I don't know," was all he could choke out.

Garrick reached out his free hand and gave Enoch's arm an encouraging squeeze. "Take it from me. I don't have a lot of faith in hardly anything, but I feel very confident you'll see your daughter again." He smiled cryptically as Enoch looked up at him in surprise. "What do they say about God? He works in mysterious ways? Well, so do some of the people around here."

The elevator ding sounded and Garrick broke off his grip. The doors slid open on the grand lobby.

"I don't understand what you're saying," Enoch said as he stepped out of the elevator. But Garrick stayed put, the cryptic smile still hovering on his lips.

"I've got to get back to the war council up there; I trust you can find your way from here... Oh, and don't forget this!" Rolling the urn out from under his arm he tossed it into the air towards Enoch. Gasping in horror, Enoch lurched forward to catch it in mid-air. Before he could say anything, the doors had closed on Garrick, leaving Enoch to stand alone and trembling on the glistening marble floors of the lobby.

He walked out of the lobby and onto the downtown sidewalk in a daze. Angel was outside standing in front of his car, parked directly in front of the building, arguing with a meter maid as she leaned out of her cart. Angel abruptly broke off the debate to rush to Enoch's side, supporting his elbow with an outstretched hand.

"Are you alright?" he asked. Enoch nodded and stumbled towards the passenger door, dropping heavily into the seat after Angel opened the door. Angel ran to the other side, ignoring the meter maid as she slipped an envelope onto his windshield and beat a hasty retreat to her cart. He started up the engine and turned to Enoch, his eyes wide as he stared at the urn in his lap.

"Is that... Mandy?"

Enoch mumbled something incoherent back, unable to muster the energy to unwind the impossible knots twisting in his mind. He looked down at the urn, tilting precariously between his legs angling towards the floor. Was this pile of dust and ashes his little girl? Or had Garrick been trying to tell him differently with his bizarre behavior in the elevator? Enoch stared into the dazzling surface of the ceramic, as if its fractalized patterns held the secrets of the will of God.

***

If his was anything to go by, coronations were a lot less glamorous than Vlad had expected. It was just a lot of paperwork in a sitting room as an emotionless bureaucratic functionary looked on and droned out instructions. Even the act of dipping the signet ring into the hot wax and putting the official seal on the documents, once so rich with mystery and romance in Vlad's excitable mind, had become as dull and rote as signing off on payroll back at the office.

But at least the venue was nice, or was in the process of becoming so. Included in the mountains of papers he had already sealed was a document granting him a perpetual lease to the new manor Duma was constructing on the ridge of the canyon to the west of the Sanatorium. The huge home was only half finished, with not even a window in place - the sitting room was the only spot in the house where winds sweeping up from the canyon wouldn't obliterate the stack of papers - but that just made the views more spectacular, more immediate.

Vlad had taken to sleeping on the third floor on a makeshift sleeping bag made from purloined hospital pillows and linens. There the roof was still open to the vast night sky and Vlad could roll up to the very edge of the rail-less balcony, alternating his gaze between the eternity of space above him and the abyss below. The last few nights had been marvelous. The pain in his hands had faded to a dull ache that could easily be swept away on the exciting currents of his imagination. He was on the precipice of a whole new life, one with awesome new responsibilities and powers. A voting seat on Duma's board of governors... A fast-track to Colonel on the upcoming promotional exams... and then Chief! And then there was this new home here at the nexus of community power... All that was missing was someone to share in this feeling of exultation that filled him like new wine, bursting from the ruptured seams of his worn out old skin.

Mandy. He had imagined her by his side under the stars. More than that, he had felt her beside him, her presence so tangible he would sometimes roll onto his side to declare some epiphany only to stare at the empty space in crushing disappointment. But soon she would take up her place, filled with the blood from his veins, restored to him in all her beauty and quiet strength, born again from the ashes of Van Helsing's fire. Then they would fill this house with their children and take their place at the head of a bright new dynasty that would shame the twisted darkness of the great families of old!

But he was getting ahead of himself. His name had yet to ascend anything bigger than the tall stack of papers on the desk in front of him. Even the signet ring weighing so heavily on his finger was not his own crest - he was but one of a number of stewards of the great Duma name. And he was terribly alone - even the bureaucrat had gone. The only human sound around him was the clamor of the saws and hammers of the workers outside.

He had tried to send for Maria to bring some sense of home to the new place, but there was no place to put her. The Sanatorium staff had absolutely refused to allow another garlic-eater on the grounds - they were still smarting over Mandy - and Maria wasn't about to stay in the seedy rooming house with the *țăranii*. *Țăranii!* He had forgotten how many of them there were up here... How they scurried out of their little village at daybreak like rodents, clinging to the dark corners of the landscape, always with their heads down, always with their eyes dancing furtively. Vlad didn't like to be disgusted with any human being, but he couldn't stomach the whole lot of these.

The recent sights and sounds of a native work crew, brought in after the board of governors finally grew frustrated with the glacial pace of the *țăranii* crews, had felt like fresh air blowing up from the city, carrying away some of the old world stench left by the *țăranii*. The way they stood straight up and looked him in the eye. The way they laughed as they worked and sang along to the mariachi music that blared from their cheap stereos. This was the life and vitality that these highborn gatekeepers were so anxious to keep out of their precious foothills.

All that was going to change. He stepped out of the sitting room and into the foyer, where the big open spaces where walls and windows would be gave him a clear view of the native workmen digging a trench for the new sewer line. They worked with a carefree air, swinging their picks and spearing the earth with their shovels in an easy rhythm. Their sweat flowed freely from their brows to spill over the newly upturned dirt. They were blissfully unaware that the eyes watching them from the distant Sanatorium and the plantation houses beyond would be flashing with anger at this contamination of sacred ground. Vlad smiled. *Keep at it, my friends.* The time had come to mingle these separate channels of blood, sweat and tears that had plowed parallel courses through the rocky landscape of human history. Now they would meet to form a great river, so mighty that the whole earth would be left transformed in its wake.

***

The calluses on Angel's hands had just started to wear off and here he was again, putting on a fresh new coat of blisters. The work itself wasn't so unpleasant; he had come to appreciate the therapeutic qualities of a day's worth of back-breaking manual labor. Lord knows, he needed something to keep his mind off Mandy.

But there was a dark undercurrent to this return to the trenches. It wasn't that he was burning vacation days to work under-the-table for half of what he could get for a couple hours of overtime. More disturbing was whatever was going on in Enoch's mind and whatever he was about to get Angel mixed up in. In the two months Angel had known him, Enoch had never been anything less than an emotional rock, completely unmoved by the chaos around them, always ready with an encouraging word or a helping hand, always steering those around him to some Bible verse or prayer. That Enoch was still there in glimpses, but the old rock had fractured, and a new manic energy had overtaken him.

All this was more than understandable given what had happened to Mandy, but it didn't make it any less disconcerting to be caught up in the gathering tornado that surrounded him. The common sense warnings that sounded in Angel's mind, in the faint but heavily accented voices of his mother and uncles, had warned him to keep his distance, to let Enoch spiral down his own path. But ever since that first ride-along, Angel had never quite been able to say no to him.

So when Enoch asked Angel if he knew any forensic guys who could run tests on Mandy's ashes, Angel had said "sure," instead of telling him to get lost or go find a grief counselor like he would have with anyone else. When the test had come back negative, he had explained to Enoch what the tech had explained to him: that tests on properly cremated ashes rarely come back with any hits on DNA. But when Enoch dismissed all these caveats to spin off into wild conspiracy theories, Angel hadn't broken off and kept his distance. No, he had listened patiently as Enoch talked himself into the lunatic idea that Mandy was alive and being held hostage by the vampires in the foothills, instead of pouring cold water over his head and telling him to wake up to reality.

Worst of all, he had somehow allowed Enoch to talk him into joining him on this vigilante expedition with almost no knowledge of what the lanky preacher was planning. He had only told him that he signed on with Tom Layman again for a new job near the Sanatorium and would he be so kind as to come along and back him up. Angel had said yes, of course, telling himself he had to go just to keep Enoch from doing something truly insane. But there was something deeper inside of him that almost believed the old man was right, that Mandy really was alive. *Insanity is contagious.*

The first day the work had been so exhausting for the both of them that there was no time for whatever cock-eyed scheme Enoch had cooked up. Angel had even started to hope that the hard work was having its therapeutic effect and Enoch might be coming down from his feverish state. That night they'd driven back and hardly spoken two words to each other before Enoch fell asleep in the cab. But the next morning, his eyes had glowed with that manic intensity that had accompanied his wildest notions. On their way back up, he'd whispered to Angel that today might be the day.

They'd made it all through the morning and through lunch without Enoch making any sudden breaks, and Angel hoped the work was wearing him down to earth again. But he still felt uneasy. Layman had split them up after lunch to put them at the head of different teams; and Angel had to strain to keep his eyes on them as their projects diverged. He saw that Enoch had worked them at a terrific speed, so much so that they had earned a siesta under a solitary oak in the distance while Angel's men were still hacking away.

The crunch of tires on terrain turned Angel around. Tom Layman had rolled up in his truck and he burst out of the cab, red in the face.

"Have you seen Enoch? Is he with you?" He was shouting,

wiping sweat from his brow as he moved in closer, eyes searching through Angel's crew.

"He isn't over there under the tree?" Angel pointed, his stomach sinking as he realized he hadn't actually laid eyes on Enoch since a little after lunch. Had he made his move?

"No. They haven't seen him in an hour." Layman shook his head in frustration. "How many times have I told you guys? Can't leave a job site unsupervised around here. These Romanians will walk off with anything that isn't nailed down... I'm gonna bring Enoch's guys over here with you guys to finish the trench. When he shows back up, tell him I need to talk to him."

Layman stormed back to his truck and roared off. Angel scanned the horizon, looking for Enoch's long silhouette in the sunbaked prairie that stretched between the job site and the white walls of the Sanatorium in the distance. There was nothing, just gently undulating waves of golden grass.

Angel lowered his head and began to pray as best he could. In his short span as a man of faith, he had relied wholly on Enoch for leadership, but now he would have to take his first few baby steps on his own. The words fumbled from his lips as he tried to mimic the structure of the prayers he'd heard. *Dear Jesus... I don't know what to say or how to ask, but please help my friend Enoch. Please keep him from doing anything foolish that would take him away from his family... or from me. Please bring him back.... Amen.*

He looked around, sheepish, to see if any of the men had seen or heard him. None of them had noticed. He sighed and gripped the handle of his shovel. For at least a couple more hours he would lose himself in the earth.

It was dusk when the trench was finished and the pipes were in the ground, and Angel and the rest trudged back to the truck beds. His head down, his mind already ready for the familiar comfort of the sleep that would come when he was packed like a sardine and jostled out of his cares on the bumpy ride home. So Enoch's voice in his ear came like a thunderclap.

"I found a way in," he said, with whispered urgency. Angel turned to see Enoch hunched next to him, matching his pace as they moved towards the trucks. "There's a chute in the back that the laundry trucks back up into. It's a little tricky but it's climbable. Now's my chance."

Angel pulled him aside, out of the stream of workers. "Don't do this," he blurted out. "It's crazy. If they catch you in there, you'll go to jail."

"But Mandy's in there!"

"No, she's not. She's dead, Enoch! Why can't you admit it? Why can't you just let her go?" Angel felt his voice choking in his throat and his eyes welling up.

Enoch looked at him with surprise and then placed a hand on Angel's shoulder. A little of the paternal gentleness returned to his gaze, pushing out the manic intensity that had overtaken him. "Don't you see, Angel? I don't have any other choice. The Lord trusted Mandy to me and I can't let her go until He tells me to."

"How do you know it's Him talking and not... something else?"

"My sheep hear my voice, and I know them and they follow me," Enoch said, with that glow that came over him whenever he quoted the Bible. "I've been listening a long time, Angel. I know His voice."

"Then why can't I hear it?" Angel's voice was clouded with despair. "Everything inside me is telling me you're losing it... and to take you back before you get yourself into real trouble."

Enoch's hand squeezed Angel's shoulder tighter and pulled him closer.

"The Lord has a different path for all of us. We don't all have the same callings. This may be something he's asking from me alone."

Angel wiped at his face with his sleeve, embarrassed at the tears that had begun to fall. "I can't leave you here."

"Don't worry about me. The creator of the universe has my back. Just as He'll have yours when the time comes. Listen for His voice and be ready."

A harsh cry came from behind them. "Mount up, boys. This wagon train's leaving with or without you." It was Layman. Everyone else was already piled into the truck beds.

Enoch pulled Angel in for an embrace. "Goodbye, son. Thank you for all that you've done for me. You were a light to me when everything went dark."

Angel buried his head in the shoulder of Enoch's leather jacket. Enoch gave a final squeeze and then slithered free, waving as his long strides carried him quickly across the plain towards the hazy white outline of the Sanatorium on the horizon.

"Where the hell does he think he's going? He better not be expecting us to wait around for him." barked Layman as Angel clambered aboard the truck. Angel didn't respond as he slid into his place in the sardine can. The engine roared to life and they rumbled over the uneven terrain, heading down a slope towards the main road. Angel searched for Enoch's lanky silhouette in the distance. For a moment, he thought he saw him, a long black stick shimmering in the haze of the setting sun. But then he blinked and he was gone.

30

Doctor Sinescu arched his back and sighed as the crunch rippled up his spine. A lot of tension could build up over the course of a shift. Only one more consult and he'd be free for the next three days. He closed his eyes and took a deep breath as he resumed his walk through the halls. If he squeezed his lids tight enough to shut out the piercing brightness of the fluorescent light and breathed in through his mouth, he could imagine he was back home already, his feet treading the soft earth of his vineyards. His fingers outstretched, the ceramic wall tiles leading towards his office became the spring buds of the new pinot grigio vines his men had put in the ground this winter.

The vision left him suddenly, broken by the painful collision of a bony shoulder into the soft space just below his clavicle. His eyes blinked open to see another white coat rushing past him down the hall, long strides carrying him around the corner and out of sight before Sinescu could give voice to his outrage. Not even an apology! Must have been one of the new residents. Always in a hurry! So eager to slap the finishing touches on their resumes so they could make their millions for one of the giant pharmaceuticals in the city.

Sinescu sighed again and resumed his walk, hoping to summon the comforting sensations of his estate again without having to close his eyes. This new generation of vampire professionals cannonballing through these halls had no appreciation for the old country ways, the traditions that could only be savored through a real connection with the land. Yes, Sinescu was a professional like they were. He too had been a striver, toiling with abstractions and technological wizardry of modern medicine to make his mark here in the new world. But it had always been in service of recreating the life his fathers had led. The mighty Sinescus had a heritage that demanded preservation.

He felt a twinge of guilt at the irony of his situation as the door to his office came into sight. The esteemed Doctor Sinescu, lord of the one of the greatest plantations in the foothills, laboriously reconstructed according to the old styles and run in strict accordance with the old ways, on his way to facilitate the violation of the oldest and greatest of the community's laws. He hesitated at the door, his hand resting on the handle. If he kept straight on towards the staff parking lot and headed out for his long weekend, the odious job would fall to one of the junior staffers. Let one of those big city hotshots galloping down the hallways dirty their hands with this work.

The door opened with a click and he forced himself to step through. The lion of tradition did not run from anything. He reminded himself of what he'd said when the order first came down through Duma; if the terrible deed should be done, he would do it.

"Doctor Sinescu."

Sinescu turned with a start to see Vladimir Paler sitting on a stool in the corner, spinning himself idly like a bored child.

"Captain Paler." It was difficult to keep the scorn out of his voice. He'd despised this man ever since he showed up on his doorstep with his ambulance and that slab of human contraband. His manners, already bad on his arrival, had become outright offensive since Dr. Duma had inexplicably given him his blessing. Here he was, staring Sinescu straight in the eye, not even a hint of deference in his posture, extending his hand for a vulgar American handshake without even bothering to get up from the stool!

Sinescu bit his lip and forced himself to shake the proffered hand, feeling the cool imprint of gold sliding over his palm. He looked down and the sight of Duma's signet ring on Paler's finger filled him with a fresh wave of revulsion. Wearing a priceless heirloom around like some gaudy trinket! *This interloper, this bastard prince rubbing his ill-gotten favor in our faces!*

Sinescu turned away to hide the look of disgust on his face. He sat behind his desk, using the distance to regard Paler more critically. He had done some digging on this social climbing police captain after his advent at the Sanatorium. Paler was an unfamiliar name, but after a few days of research, the Archivist had traced it to a traveling clan that had blended with the gypsy caravans for centuries. From all accounts, Vladimir's father was typical of that breed, a bounder and vagabond, notable only for his seduction of the daughter of Radu Duma, cousin to the Sanatorium's founder and patriarch of that once great family, then fallen but now restored.

Young Vladimir had obviously taken after his father, who, as the old country rumors went, abandoned his mother, leaving that fine lady with no recourse but suicide. There were other tales of young Vladimir taking up with a garlic-eater, a gypsy girl they said, who met a fate similar to that of his mother. The episode was enough to bring shame even to as shameless a man as his father, leading to his being packed off to America under the patronage of his generous second cousin. What Dr. Duma had seen in him and still saw in him, Sinescu could not guess. By all appearances, he had inherited all the worst aspects of his mixed heritage and now seemed intent on further mongrelizing his blood to propagate its basest tendencies.

Paler didn't seem to mind this lengthy examination from across the room. He matched Sinescu's gaze with a look that suggested he knew he had been probed and had no shame for what had been uncovered. Sinescu broke the silence by clearing his throat and raised his hand to summon Paler to join him, momentarily dreading the possibility that he would refuse in some sort of ridiculous power play. Thankfully, he came and took his seat, though not without a smirk that made Sinescu's eyes twitch.

"So clue me in, Doc. I don't really know what to expect over the next couple days."

"I'm afraid I can't dispel all your uncertainty over the matter, Captain Paler," Sinescu said in clipped tones. "It's a fluid, dynamic procedure that requires a great deal of flexibility on the part of the medical staff."

Paler raised his brow with a skeptical, almost contemptuous look, as if Sinescu was his 'perp' and this office was his interrogation room. In the old country, the constables never behaved with the sort of reckless disregard for hierarchy that typified American police detectives. Back home, they were the upholders of the social order, not its interrogators. And they certainly didn't go around flaunting the signet rings of their betters!

"Just give me a rough outline of what to expect before I go under. I don't like to be in the dark."

"I can assure you there is nothing to be concerned about during the first phase of the procedure. It's simply a matter of lowering the metabolic level to the threshold required for a safe transfusion. As you know, the subject -"

"You mean Mandy," Paler interjected. Sinescu frowned to keep himself from snarling. This puerile infatuation had swung like a wrecking ball through his halls and Paler seemed intent on keeping it moving with all destructive force. He would leave no tradition undisturbed, no taboo unviolated.

"- Miss Parker," Sinescu muttered through pursed lips. "She will be medically induced into a comatose-like state to facilitate her body's acceptance of the transfusion. It's important that your metabolic rate and blood-sugar levels be lowered to within an acceptable range. We won't be inducing a coma in your case, but you will be heavily sedated."

Paler shifted uncomfortably in his seat. "I don't understand why it's got to be so complicated. If it was dangerous, how were we doing this hundreds of years ago without any of this fancy medical technology. The stories about neck-biting and wrist-binding had to come from somewhere, right?"

Now Sinescu had to suppress a smile. The usurper's ignorance was showing. "Our medical literature on the subject is lacking, but from what we do know, the vast majority of recipients in earlier eras died shortly after transmission. The evidence points to hypercytokinemia - a massive immune response of the body attacking itself to rid itself of an invader - as the most likely cause of death."

Paler looked unconvinced but remained silent.

"As is so often the case," continued Sinescu, his mood improving, "the taboos passed down by the elders turn out to have a solid basis in medical fact. We break them at our own risk."

"You've made your feelings pretty clear on that subject," Paler replied, his smirk curling into a sneer. "I know there are risks. I just hope the staff here aren't adding to those risks by playing the avenging angel of the past."

Sinescu sprang to his feet, bristling with indignant fury. "You will not besmirch the character of my staff!"

"Or what?" Paler asked as he too rose to his feet, so contemptuous he was almost spitting. "When I'm passed out and prone on a gurney, will one of them come to reclaim their honor? You think I don't know how I'm viewed around here? That I don't see the looks of hatred and disgust whenever your doctors check in on Mandy?"

"Whatever I and my staff may or may not feel about you and the subject on a personal level," Sinescu seethed, "I can assure you, no harm will befall you or her from our hands. No matter how obscene your speech or behavior, you can only expect the most conscientious care from all of us."

"Good," Paler said flatly, the spite that had contorted his face unfurrowing with his brows. "What time do we begin?"

"You will check in first thing tomorrow morning. I will be away, but Doctor Angelho will be monitoring you both. By the time you awake, I will have returned and I will personally supervise the transfusion."

Paler nodded and extended his hand again. Sinescu weathered the overwhelming impulse to slap it away and shook it briefly. "Remember, you must fast tonight. Your system needs to be clear when we sedate you."

He turned away to signal the conference was over and was gratified to hear Paler's footsteps and the click of the door as he exited. Sinescu sighed, the tension releasing from his shoulders, the scorn from his lips, and his thoughts winged their way back to his vineyards. Only a few more hours now and he would be walking the rows, feeling the first fruits setting from the spring flowers. It was only a matter of time now before they would grow plump and dark and ripe for the plucking. How sweet it would be on the days of harvest, when they would all be gathered together and crushed under the feet of his *țăranii*, and all would be right in the world again.

***

The rolling laundry bins were just large enough, and cushioned by enough linens, for Enoch to curl his long legs to his chest and fall asleep. But a few hours were all he could manage. His body was coming to reject sleep as an alien experience, something reserved for others. His nights were to be spent thinking and rethinking the same terrible thoughts, feeling the same aches and pains, navigating the same waking dream. *Mandy.* She was the one thread that held together the disjointed ramblings of his mind. Even as his consciousness frayed, picked apart by the jabs of his now ever-present migraine, he only had to think of her and a semblance of clarity returned.

Despite the ongoing breakdown of his body and mind, he never succumbed to doubt. He was not crazy. This was no fool's errand. He knew she was here, somewhere. And he knew it because he felt the hand of the Lord constantly about him. How else to explain how he had been able to wander freely through this huge facility undetected, unquestioned?

It certainly hadn't been on the strength of his disguise. He'd found a single white coat buried among the scrubs and gowns in the bins. It was clean enough and just broad enough for his shoulders, and there was a large pocket in front to store the one item he had brought along. But the arms were several inches too short, riding up to expose his sun-burnt and weather-beaten forearms to any who care to look. He looked more like the swarthy people that pushed the gurneys and carried the mops through the hallways than the lily-white vampire doctors.

And yet he had been free to roam, unbothered and unnoticed. The vampire doctors were few and far between and even when he bumped into one coming suddenly round a corner he had been able to make a quick getaway before the surprised man could even utter a word. The more numerous darker-complexioned workers were harder to avoid, but they were so uniformly reluctant to make eye contact that Enoch had ceased to shy away from them and now walked by and among them with confidence.

Still, what good was all this freedom to move with no idea of where to go? The facility was vast but surreally homogeneous in appearance. Several times already, Enoch's eyelids had grown heavy and he had fallen into a somnambulist's trance. When his eyes fluttered open again, he couldn't tell if he was in another wing of the place or the same hallway, whether he had dozed for a few seconds or a few hours. He was sure that he must have walked several miles over the past day, but he still had no clear sense of where he was in the complex. It didn't help that every sign was written in a foreign tongue.

The one landmark he had come to recognize was a small cafeteria frequented by the staff in scrubs. He'd come to depend on the coffee cart for sustenance. It was tucked away in a dark corner of the cafeteria where he could lean back against the wall in shadows, sipping at the black brew in styrofoam cups while the workers spoke to each other in hushed tones. Invariably, they spoke in their own language. Enoch would strain to listen anyways, hoping and praying for a miraculous intervention, for the gift of tongues to fall on him like the Apostles at Pentecost and grant him understanding. Frustrated, he would then resume his prowling of the halls, squinting through sleep-blurred eyes for any hint, any sign of her.

Enoch realized suddenly that he was walking again. When he had left his improvised bed in the laundry room he did not know. He wasn't entirely sure that he had ever laid down at all; perhaps it was just a wishful fantasy of his deteriorating consciousness. He thrust his hand down the front pocket of his coat to see if he was truly awake. He immediately felt the cool of the metal barrel against his fingers. He slipped his hand further down to the wood handle and gripped it.

A stab of guilt joined the sensations traveling from his fingertips to his brain. He hadn't stolen anything in his life, at least not since he was a boy. But he'd stolen this, sneaking into Angel's duffel bags while he'd been sleeping to find the little snub nose revolver that he now gripped in his hand. But he'd told himself Angel would understand, that he'd return it when the time came. He just couldn't risk asking and being told no. The time was too short. The stakes were too great.

But just what was he going to do with this ill-gotten gain? He'd wanted to be ready for whatever the dark denizens of this unholy place would throw at him, once they discovered his business. He'd told himself he was prepared to do anything to bring Mandy back. And that included pointing that barrel and squeezing that trigger at anyone who tried to stop him. *Thou shalt not kill... Thou shalt not steal... Thou shalt not bear false witness.* He squeezed at the wooden handle to push away the doubts. He was no rogue, no vigilante, no avenger of blood. He was nothing more, and nothing less, than the Lord's vessel, now and always.

The cafeteria was coming up in front of him and with it the murmur of accented voices. He let the revolver slip from his clutches into the bottom of the pocket and staggered towards the corner where the soft red lights of the coffee canisters beckoned. He grasped the styrofoam cup and filled it quickly, his fingertips searching out the microscopic contours of the foam, finding comfort in its softness. It was a welcome contrast from the cold weight of the gun. From its mouth poured life and energy and solace, not pain and death.

He had ceased even to taste the bitter swill, his tongue willing to suffer anything for sustenance, but this cup was so wretched, a gag reflex stirred in chest. It was unsettlingly thick and viscous, and unpleasantly lukewarm - they must have left it overnight in the tank. But Enoch forced himself to gulp it down, waiting for that ever-weaker surge of caffeine that would lighten his eyelids and return feeling to his extremities. But this time there was no energy, only a wave of nausea and with it a terrible sensation of vertigo.

He had to cling to the edge of the coffee cart with both hands to keep from keeling over. His stomach convulsed and he felt its rejected contents spilling from the corners of his mouth. He wiped it away and then stared blankly at the streak of dark crimson against the freckled white of his exposed wrist. He staggered away from the cart as the realization penetrated the fog of his mind. In his stupor, he had stumbled to the wrong cart, not the coffee station but the table in the opposite corner, reserved for the white coats. *Not coffee, but...*

He reeled on his feet, his defiled innards lurching to purge this filth from his body. He clung to the end of a table, certain that he was about to fall. Would this be his end - curling into a ball and vomiting his guts out onto the low-pile cafeteria carpet? The inhabitants of this wretched nightmare world could hardly mistake him for one of their own then. Another wave of nausea rolled over him and this time his knees buckled and bright spots appeared suddenly all over the backsides of his clenched eyelids. One more and there would be nothing to hold him upright and he would be down. A whispered prayer escaped his lips as he braced for the final wave.

"Please, Lord. Help me."

And then he heard it. Not his word, but another that was chained to it, one that would lead him to her. *Paler.*

He swung his head round to search for the source. He was dimly aware of a pair of nurses seated at the table behind him who had been hunched over bowls when he had stumbled past them. A third nurse now stood in front of him, a medical chart in his hand. He dropped the chart on their table and as he spoke the word came again: Paler! That single word thrown to him like a life preserver.

It was enough. The waves of nausea still came but their power had been muted, suppressed. A new clarity emerged at the top of his mind, a beam of moonlight piercing the dark clouds. Enoch straightened up and cast his eye on the hand that lifted the chart from the table.

It was a dark hand of olive complexion, tipped with black nail polish that had begun to chip from the edges. It belonged to a matronly woman who rose from the table with the chart in hand, murmuring her goodbyes in that exotic tongue and then stepping away from the table and toward the hall. Enoch moved to follow, waiting until she had disappeared around the corner and then hurrying to regain sight of her. She was scarcely five feet in front of him when he burst into the hall and he froze, fearing that his heavy steps would startle her and give up the game.

But she did not turn around, continuing forward with a lethargic gait that seemed universal to this strange people. It made for an awkward pursuit, as each of Enoch's long strides brought him perilously close to her, forcing him to zig and zag from wall to wall to keep a steady distance behind her. He was certain it would make a bizarre sight to any passerby, and he made a show of peering through the small glass rectangles on each door in the hall, as if he was a supervisor making his rounds.

Glancing at her chart, the nurse stopped in front of one of these doors and then entered. Enoch lingered in the hallway, unsure of what to do. He was about to peek inside when the door opened again and the nurse's wide behind backed its way through the opening. She was pulling a gurney. Enoch's heart skipped a beat. Was this Captain Paler?

The nurse angled as she backed further, until the gurney cleared the door. Enoch pushed himself against the wall, pretending to inspect a fire extinguisher. The nurse did not seem to notice him and pressed forward, her broad frame blocking Enoch's view of the patient in front of her. He resumed his pursuit.

The nurse took a right down another hall that led to double-doors under a sign with words in big red letters that Enoch could not read. She pushed through them, Enoch following, and her feet slowed to a snail's pace as she looked down at the chart. Enoch was forced to stop to keep from walking right into her. With no doors nearby to examine, his only option was to stand in the corner and lean against the wall. At last, she seemed to get her bearings and made a beeline for another corridor.

This corridor fed them into a wide open space, like a lobby though it didn't open to the outside. In the center was what looked like a temporary operating theater, with black walls on rollers pushed together to form an opaque square. For such a huge area, it was amazingly empty. Perhaps it was more of a quarantine zone than a lobby. Enoch and his nurse and whoever was on the gurney appeared to be the only two people in the area. It was disconcerting - there was nowhere to hide.

The nurse headed straight for the square, pushing the gurney through a thick plastic curtain that served as both its front wall and its entrance. It closed behind her and she disappeared from view. Enoch squinted as he approached, but the plastic was so thick it was nearly as opaque as the black walls. He could only make out the faintest outline of the nurse on the other side.

He paused before taking another step forward, as an epiphany struck his delirious mind. This was no mere medical tent. It was the tabernacle, straight out of the pages of Exodus! All that was missing was the gold embroidery of the fiery angels. Enoch felt a twinge of nausea in his gut. All in black, draped with these ghostly, unnatural plastics, this edifice was like a Satanic parody of the old house of the Lord of Hosts. Was this the place where they planned to usher his Mandy into their demonic cult? He shuddered in fury and took a final step forward, pushing his ear to the surface of the plastic curtain.

He heard muffled voices, the first especially quiet and feminine. The nurse. The second was stronger and sharper, cutting through the curtain to reach Enoch's ear and fill him with an irrational fear. A vampire doctor. Enoch pushed at the heavy curtain to peek inside the unholy tabernacle.

It took a moment for Enoch's eyes to adjust from the bright white light around him to the dimly lit interior of the square. After a few blinks he could discern a white coat with his back to him, and the nurse at his side. They stood inside a staging area illuminated by a single pale bulb, a large black curtain behind them swallowing up its meager light and cordoning off the rest of the square. The doctor made a sweeping gesture with his right hand and Enoch followed it to the gurney where for the first time he could see a body, its face out of view. As the doctor spoke, the nurse grabbed the gurney's railing and pulled it from the wall, the angle offering Enoch a split-second glimpse of the body's profile. It was Captain Paler! He was sure of it. His heart leapt in his chest.

The nurse maneuvered the gurney and began to push it toward the black curtain when a sharp cry made Enoch jump. It was the doctor. He snatched the nurse's arm and yanked her back savagely, the little round woman flailing like a rag doll in his powerful grasp. Enoch's body tensed as the doctor raised his right hand to strike her. But the raised hand stopped in mid-air and the doctor turned his head away, pushing her backwards with his left. She staggered backwards, crashing into a tray full of vials and knocking them to the ground. Several of the vials shattered on contact, spilling their contents into a crimson pool that spread across the floor. Enoch shuddered at the sight.

The nurse pushed herself upright again, only to bow low before the doctor in what looked like an apology. He spoke sharply again and then took the gurney himself, pushing it to the black curtain. He stopped as he reached it to look at the nurse and cast a finger towards the plastic curtain, right where Enoch's face was poking through. Enoch pulled away from the plastic and crept to the corner to hide himself by the adjoining black wall. He still felt exposed in this huge open room, but at least the nurse couldn't see him as she exited and walked in her slow, halting way towards the hallway from which they had come. Her head seemed to hang lower than before and Enoch thought he saw her limbs trembling.

When she vanished into the hallway, he thought of taking another peek. But he dared not attempt it again. If that ferocious doctor spotted him, the game would be up. So he clung to the wall and waited, listening for any sound but hearing nothing. Then came the squeak of wheels and he peered out from around the corner to see the nurse returning with a janitor's cart with mop poking out of it. Her head remained downcast, oblivious to Enoch's spying eyes.

She entered the tabernacle again and Enoch could hear the sloshing of the mop from within and then that sharp voice again. The doctor must have emerged from the inner sanctum. Another moment and the doctor had pushed past the plastic curtain and stepped into the open. He stopped one more time to bark something into the interior and then the nurse emerged behind him, pushing the little cart. The two of them proceeded to the hallway, the doctor stopping his long strides periodically to allow the nurse to catch up, like a man waiting for a chastened puppy. And then, finally, they were gone.

Enoch tip-toed back to the plastic curtain and pulled it open quickly to slip inside. The sudden jump from bright to dim again played havoc with his eyes. He could make out only a few splotches of what he guessed to be medical cabinets as he blinked and squinted to try to speed the adjustment. The space where the gurney had been seemed to be empty. Still mostly blind, he stepped towards where he thought the black curtain hung. His hand slipped into his pocket again and grasped the revolver.

Another step and something caught his foot and he fell forward onto the ground. He heard a loud crack and a pain shot up his shin. Had he worn himself so thin that a little fall had shattered his leg? He groped for his shin in the darkness and felt moisture. Blood? His searching fingers discovered something wooden on the ground and pricked against a jagged broken tip. Lifting it up he felt something cold and wet brush against his leg. A mop! The nurse must have left it behind.

Enoch used the broken mop handle to push himself up from the ground, feeling all sixty of his years at once, plus the extra decades he's tacked on over the past week. The jolt of pain had at least helped clear up the blotches from his vision and he could see the black curtain just in front of him, its velvety folds full of shadows from the incandescent bulb hanging behind him. He held his breath and reached his arm forward.

He hesitated, his hand trembling. Whatever was behind this curtain had been sensitive enough to make that doctor thrash that poor nurse for even thinking of pushing the Captain through it. Was this the unholy of unholies? What sort of Satanic presence might be awaiting him on the other side? Whatever there was, he was certain Mandy was trapped somewhere inside. He exhaled slowly and pushed through, holding the revolver close.

It was still darker behind this curtain, the only light coming from fiber-optic cables that stretched from floor to the tented ceiling and cast a ghostly pale glow over the room. The beep-beep of an electrocardiogram machine and the soft hum filled his ears, but all of his attention was now focused on the two gurneys in front of him. The one on the right he already knew to be Paler. The one on the left lay under a shroud.

The form underneath the thin linen shroud was smaller than Paler's and feminine in aspect. Enoch tugged at its hem with bated breath. It slipped to the floor and there she was. Mandy. As still and silent and stiff as a porcelain doll laid out on the table - too pristine and perfect for someone who had so recently been plucked from the fire. They had said she was dead and he hadn't believed them but he almost did now. She looked so lifeless... But she was breathing. *Praise God, she's breathing!*

But still she seemed different. Her skin was a hue so pale she was nearly translucent, blue veins coursing over her like spreading cracks in a windshield. And her hair... There was something strange about her hair. He stretched his hand out to touch it. It was finer and straighter than he remembered - her hair had always been so coarse, so full of little curls. It's not hers! But of course it wasn't hers. Hers had been burnt off the back of her scalp along with most of the scalp itself. This was a wig. This-too pale skin must not be hers either.

He reached for her cheek to wake her. Her skin was cool to the touch, but soft. There was life buried somewhere deep in there. He just had to get her out. She was attached to the room, not just by the wired nodes from the EKG machine but by a network of tubes, two traveling to IV towers, but the others disappearing down behind the bed and into the darkness where Enoch couldn't see. How was he supposed to untangle from this mess? Were these fluids they were pumping into her keeping her alive? He had to wake her.

"Honey," he said softly, leaning down close to her ear. "Can you hear me?" There was no response.

He looked around, worried that the doctor might reappear at any moment. Dare he speak louder? He tried calling her name, at first softly, and then gradually raising his voice until he felt like he was screaming. Her pretty porcelain face remained deathly still; not a twitch, not a flicker of recognition at the sound of his voice. Enoch's voice at last choked in his throat and he sank to his knees. He cried out to God for help, hoping against hope that he would be heard in this unholy place.

And then he heard an answer.

***

The sedative had wrapped around Vlad's mind like a blanket. His eyes had succumbed almost immediately, his lids descending to offer his thoughts a projector screen to cast their frenetic imaginations. *Mandy!* They'd finally let him see her: only a glimpse, but that's all he needed. What artistry! It had taken his breath away. That poor shriveled creature he'd dug out of searing heat and flame, her charred flesh crumbling away like ash in his arms. That image that had haunted him had finally been replaced with this medical miracle. She was like new! Not a scratch, not a seam on her! And all she needed was his blood to complete the process.

The peace that exuded from that perfect face had done what a thousand comforting admonitions from this new doctor could not and stilled the anxiety in his chest. His dreams the night before had been horrific; they had been since that day at the mortuary and the fast hadn't helped. He was running, exhausted, chased by some tall faceless apparition - an angel of death. It kept its distance so long as he was upright, but as soon as he sank to his knees, it would close the gap with terrifying speed, raising an awful blade to drive into his heart.

He had woken in a sweat, terror still gripping him, and had spent that morning dreading what dreams might come during the long sleep these sedatives would bring on him. But the sight of her had driven away flames and faceless nightmares and thirst like a gust of cleansing wind. The paranoia that had taken control of his mind after speaking with Dr. Sinescu had lost much of its paralyzing force, too. He felt comfortable with Dr. Angelho, who at the very least did a much better job of hiding any feelings of jealousy or aristocratic disdain. The way he smiled and the gentleness of his manners had put Vlad at near-perfect ease. He didn't seem the type to "accidentally" pull the plug or mix some poisonous drug cocktail in the IV.

Vlad was almost completely out by the time the nurse wheeled him into the tent. His mind's eye was already fixed on the imagination of Mandy's hand stretching across the darkness to grab his. The sensations from his extremities had long since faded - he was floating as far as he could tell. Only the muted sounds, the beeps and whirs, maintained a stubborn hold of his conscious mind, and even these were slowly loosening their grasp. Another moment and they would release him into what he knew would be a serene sleep, one that he would awake from in the arms of his beloved. The two of them - King and Queen of the new world, the mighty river unfolding before their feet like a red carpet.

But he did not drift off just then. There was a new set of sounds, of an angry voice and of shattered glass. They were faint, but they had the tenor of reality and gave renewed strength to the restless portion of his mind that still resisted surrender. When these at last faded, Vlad welcomed a return of the sinking momentum, but again there was a jarring noise, this time a sound of snapping and muffled cry of pain.

But Vlad would not suffer these disruptions any access to his mind. He deepened his focus on the image of Mandy's hand grasping his. He felt the softness of her skin. The glossy edge of her fingernails. The rhythm of her pulse. And then he heard her name. Not in his voice, but a stranger's. It started out quietly, a whisper, and rose steadily, until the name and the voice hammered at his ear drums.

"MANDY!"

Vlad's consciousness rose slowly from the abysmal pool and his eyes blinked open, pressing back the great weights that the sedative had laid on them. For a single moment, his mind brought him back to Bouchard's van and panic overtook him. But then his eyes followed the glowing sinews of the fiber optic tables and he remembered where he was.

"MANDY!" the voice cried again. Vlad arched his neck and saw a man in a white coat dropping to his knees and then bowing his head in dejection. Surely this wasn't Dr. Angelho. No vampire would descend to such histrionics and certainly not one of the doctors at the Sanatorium. Was this the angel of death of his nightmares? Vlad struggled to push himself up from the gurney, his arms as heavy as his eyelids.

"What's going on?" he croaked.

The man in the white coat whirled around at the sound of his voice and Vlad fell back in shock. It was Enoch Parker. It must be a dream.

Enoch looked like he had aged 20 years. The flesh of his face hung in drooping folds, revealing skeletal cheekbones and hollow caverns for bloodshot eyes to spill out of. His mouth hung open as he stared at Vlad. Suddenly he stretched his arm out and Vlad saw a snub nose revolver in his hand, its short barrel pointed right at Vlad's chest. The sight was enough to clear the cobwebs from Vlad's mind.

"Look at her!" he cried, his voice hoarse. "What have you done with her?"

Vlad tried to push himself back from the barrel of the gun, conscious of a debilitating weakness in all of his limbs. Whatever sedative they'd given him wasn't giving up without a fight. His eyes darted from Enoch's wild visage to the curtain separating them from the rest of the facility. He had no idea what the old man was planning to do, but no good possibilities were springing to his mind. If he just took off running... Enoch didn't look to be in any shape to chase anyone or hit any kind of moving target with that little revolver. But that was assuming his own sedated legs would last more than a few strides. And it would mean leaving Mandy. Not that Enoch would intentionally hurt his own daughter, but there was no telling what he might do unintentionally in this state.

"Our doctors saved her," Vlad said at last. He needed to feel him out before he decided on a course of action. Maybe he could be talked down. "She's alive thanks to them."

"Then why did they tell me she was dead? Whose ashes did they give me?" Enoch's voice was loud and hysterical and he kept the revolver trained on Vlad. Vlad wondered if his cries were loud enough to carry out into the hallways and bring the deputies down on Enoch's head.

"I understand you have a lot of questions. I would too, in your shoes. It might be impossible to believe right now, but I promise you there's a good reason."

"Why should I believe you?" Enoch's voice was angry and accusatory, but his eyes were weak and desperate. He wanted - no, he needed someone to believe. Vlad felt a burst of pity for him. This poor idiot. He had no clue what he was stumbling into or what was in store for him. Even with a gun pointed at him, Vlad almost wanted to protect this man, to steer him out of danger. Mandy would want it, of course, but he too had a sort of affection for the man. If only he could get the stubborn old billy goat to understand.

"You know that I love your daughter. That I'd do anything for her." That took some of the anger out of Enoch's posture. He nodded and leaned back against Mandy's bed, the gun lowered to his side. "And that's exactly what I am doing. I can't go into all the details now, but there's a procedure that she needs to finish her treatment... To bring her all the way back. To keep her from having to live disfigured and in pain for the rest of her life. It's not something we're supposed to do. That's why they told you all those lies. But it's something she needs."

"But you said they saved her. What more could she need? Why can't I just take her home now?"

Vlad stood up, stabilizing himself against the bed as his head spun. How was he going to pull this off with half his brain tied behind his back?

"Don't you want Mandy to have the best life she can have? The life she wants?" Vlad's voice took on a pleading tone. "I can give her that and more. I'm going to do it. I've put my whole career - my whole life - on the line to do it. But I'm asking you... I'm begging you... For her sake if not for your own... You have to let her go. Get away from here before you're discovered."

Enoch gave him those desperate eyes again. He was on the precipice. He was so tired. So defeated. So ready to give up the struggle. Just one more nudge.

Vlad's voice rose with passionate sincerity. "Mandy is on the verge of something that any father would want for his child. Health, longevity, strength, vitality... She stands to gain the whole world."

Vlad realized immediately he'd said something wrong. The desperate look in Enoch's eyes disappeared, replaced by something cold and hard. His wobbling legs straightened and he stood to his full height, staring down at Vlad.

"I'm taking her home now," he said, his voice still hoarse and weak, but the hard line of his jaw set against any more deliberation. Vlad felt a sinking feeling in his gut.

Enoch turned to Mandy's body, slipping the revolver into a pocket in his coat. He reached for the tubes and wires that attached her to the bed and then disconnected them one by one. Vlad leaned against his own bed, what little strength he had draining from his limbs. He understood stubbornness, but this was madness he was up against. Why wouldn't he listen to reason?

"Why?" he choked out. "Why won't you trust me?"

"I will always be grateful for what you did for my daughter," he replied quietly, still plucking methodically at the tubes. "But just because you saved her body, doesn't mean I'm going to let you take her soul."

"Her soul?"

"What you're doing here is demonic... Satanic," Enoch said, his voice still quiet, but dripping with conviction. "You're evil."

Vlad stood speechless. Could he really be such a simpleton? Just another religious nutjob... an ignorant bigot? He trembled with a sudden rush of anger. How had Mandy - so sensitive, so thoughtful, so open-minded - sprung from this mindless torch-and-pitchfork waving zombie? Disgust welled from Vlad's gut, twisting his lips into a snarl and returning some energy to his legs.

He knew the smartest move at this point was to go and get help. Let the deputies deal with this cretin. But he couldn't stomach the thought of leaving Mandy with him. And he couldn't risk a showdown between a gun-waving Enoch and those trigger-happy deputies with Mandy caught in-between. He would have to handle this himself.

Enoch's attention was wholly focused on extricating Mandy from the bed. Vlad could see the bulge of the revolver in his pocket. Vlad took a breath, gauging his strength. He still felt weak and light-headed and that was standing still with the bed as support. If he lunged suddenly for the gun he might pass out at Enoch's feet. He felt for his knife - it had already tasted the blood of the last bigot that stood between him and Mandy. But it was gone, stripped away with the clothes the nurses had replaced with this billowing hospital gown.

Vlad cursed under his breath and crouched down slowly, testing the spring in his legs. Enoch didn't seem to notice. Then out of the corner of his eye he saw something on the ground. A long wooden stick broken in two, the longer of the two with a terrifically sharp end. It was a stake, as deadly as the ones Bouchard and Andreanu had used to dispatch their victims.

This was Vlad's chance. He sprung forward, snatching the stake and lurching back. Enoch turned his head to look down at him, his eyes watchful but showing no signs of alarm. Down on the ground, Vlad felt like a pathetic little gremlin, poking his stick up at this giant. Raising an arm to the bed, he pulled himself up, pointing the stick at Enoch, his eyes darting from Enoch's face to the outline of the gun in his pocket.

"You can't take her. I won't let you."

Enoch stared at him with an appraising gaze. Could he see how Vlad's arm was shaking even under the meager weight of the stake? Could he see how tightly his other hand gripped the railing of the gurney to hold himself up? A quick draw and he'd be done for.

"There is nothing you can do to stop me," he said matter-of-factly. "The Lord is my strength and my shield." Then, sparing one last look at the end of the stake pointed at him, he turned his back to Vlad.

A feeling of helplessness fell over Vlad, weakening his outstretched arm still further. Why not drop the stake, crawl back into the bed and let sleep take hold? This could just be a drug-induced hallucination. A good dose of shuteye might cure all his ills, banish Enoch back to the backwater hole from whence he came and keep Mandy in her bed, a Sleeping Beauty waiting for him on the other side of the pillow.

But then he saw Enoch scoop Mandy from the bed, saw her gowned arm draped over his shoulder, saw him turn towards the black curtain… This was no dream. This was a real man taking her away from him. The helplessness receded and anger surged to take its place, to raise his arm again. Vlad pricked his finger against the point of the stake. It was real and sharp, and blood flowed freely from the wound. *Nothing I can do?*

"Set her down!" he commanded, grabbing the stake with both hands and raising it to strike. Enoch shook his head and took a step towards the curtain, again giving Vlad his back.

There was no divine aura protecting him. Only a flimsy white coat. He was a fool, a madman, a menace. A cross-addled garlic-eater. He had to be stopped. There was no other choice. Vlad gritted his teeth and thrust. He felt the stake pierce the cloth and he heard the squelch as it entered Enoch's flesh and struck bone. But there was no cry of pain, only a grunt. A splotch of red spread in a circle around the point where the stake had entered Enoch's back, a few inches shy of his spine. But the puncture was shallow, the stake blunted by his ribcage. With a single shake of Enoch's shoulders, it was dislodged. And still he would not turn.

"Don't make me kill you!" Vlad shrieked. But Enoch only took another step, slow and deliberate. Vlad hissed in fury. He gripped the stake again and aimed at the small of Enoch's back where no ribs would block its path. He kept his eyes open this time and struck with all his might.

Again the wound was shallow, the dulled edge of the stake repulsed by a thick knot of muscle tissue that his weak arms could not push past. But Vlad gave it a twist as he thrust and the point embedded deep enough to stick. This time, Enoch cried in pain and faltered, his legs giving way. Vlad felt a brief thrill of sadistic vindication. *That's right. Down on your knees, you stupid bastard.* He saw Mandy slipping from his arms and onto the floor.

Vlad left the stake protruding from Enoch's back and pounced, both hands reaching for the pocket and the gun inside. His finger reached the handle and he gave a yank. But Enoch's hand fell on Vlad's wrist, squeezing with surprising strength. Vlad yanked again, but it wouldn't budge. Enoch's hand slipped lower, his long fingers surrounding Vlad's and locking the gun in place. Vlad thought of squeezing off a shot to summon the deputies, but he couldn't with Mandy in the line of fire. He felt his energy sapping. He had to get this gun quickly and end this before it was all gone.

Vlad pulled one hand free and used it to twist the stake still protruding from Enoch's back. Enoch hissed in pain but the lock on Vlad's gun hand only tightened. He gave it another twist and this time an elbow came swinging and struck his jaw with a rattling force, sending him reeling towards the floor, held up only by his grip on the gun. Then Enoch spun violently in the other direction, bending Vlad's wrist backwards at an impossible angle.

Vlad bellowed and felt his fingers spring involuntarily from the handle to release his wrist from the agonizing pain. And then Enoch was on him, his forearm shoving his face into the ground, as their hands wrestled in the darkness for a grip on the revolver. Vlad reached desperately around him, grasping for the stake as his other hand groped blindly for the gun. Panic consumed his mind as his fingertips began to lose their sensation and he took the only course left to him. He sank his teeth into Enoch's forearm, clamping down until he could feel the tips of his canines puncturing the skin.

Blood flowed into Vlad's mouth and down his throat, hot and metallic against its palate. For a moment all other thoughts ceased and he was only aware of a marvelous sensation. This, the nectar of the gods, flowing into his belly. He clamped down harder and sucked it in, euphoria waking the limbs that had lost their feeling and driving away all pain and fatigue. Enoch's scream only made it taste sweeter. In all his days, he had never felt as alive and awake as in that moment.

A terrific flood of strength rushed to his arms and he lifted Enoch off him in a single motion, holding him above him at arm's length, wriggling and writhing like a screaming child. A sense of exhilaration crackled through his nerves. His body was coiled like a whip and a mere flex of his abdomen was sufficient to launch him from the ground and turn the tables.

In a flash, Vlad slammed Enoch against the ground. The old man was stunned, his eyes wide in fear, his hands fumbling in his pocket. Vlad towered above him, rage and elation swirling together in his mind. With blood dripping from his lips he must have appeared to Enoch as a demon incarnate - all of his most insane religious delusions coming true before his eyes! Vlad wanted to laugh - the thrill was coursing through his body and it was growing more intense by the moment. Enoch lay prone, wide open, helpless, his long pale neck inviting the kill. What need did Vlad have for a gun when in his mouth gleamed the most ancient and deadly weapons of his people?

The thrill raced from his head to the base of his spine as he gave himself wholly to instinct for the first time in his life. He plunged, mouth open, teeth bared, his eyes fixed on the pulsing line of Enoch's carotid artery. He was so close when he heard it. The unmistakable bang of a .38 revolver. The gun he'd trained on as a recruit so many years ago, aiming right for the heart of a thousand paper dummies. He never missed.

But this time the hole was in him. He could feel the blood pouring out of him. He could feel his heart shuddering. He landed heavily on Enoch, his teeth falling dull and harmless on his neck. He felt the old man sloughing him off to the ground. His hands reached for him, but it was too late. Enoch was on his feet and lifting Mandy, loading her on the gurney, taking her away. Her head rolled from the pillow, dangling over the bed, her eyes opening. They were blank and uncomprehending, blinking at him across a black chasm that widened between them. He was losing her... Vlad gave one last snarl, one last lunge, one last grasp for her before all went dark.

31

Enoch leaned heavily against the gurney, pushing as fast as he dared, as fast as his legs would allow, breaking through the plastic curtain into the clear. His lungs still burned from the exertion of lifting Mandy from the ground to put her back on the bed and his shoulders heaved with deep ragged breaths.

If anyone came close to him, they would know right away. He knew his face must be bright red, but it was the red all over the rest of him that would give him away. He had so many holes in him. The blood from his forearm had gushed down his left sleeve and turned it crimson and he could still feel something trickling from the punctures in his back. At least his neck was intact.

He knew he didn't have much time. The gunshot would have the whole hospital descending on that Satanic tabernacle in moments. He had to get out of the open. An open door jutting out into the hallway in front of him beckoned. He swerved the gurney inside, and without even checking to make sure it was clear, he swung the door closed behind him.

He looked around and breathed in relief; it was a janitor's supply room, probably the one the nurse had fetched the mop from. Enoch quickly stripped off the white lab coat and saw the blood dripping down to its hem. He looked below him in a sudden fit of panic to see if he'd left a trail. He couldn't see anything. And from the sounds coming down the hallway outside he knew it was too late to go back out and check. He exhaled a quiet prayer and turned to Mandy.

Her eyes were open! But there was no twinkle of recognition in them. They were glossy and empty, like a doll's eyes. Enoch's heart sank and he lowered his ear to her chest. Her breathing was still low but regular. *Thank the Lord!* Whatever drugs he had disconnected her from had at least not been necessary to keep her alive. It had been a terrible risk, but what other option had there been? To leave her there with that demon? How had he ever trusted that... thing... with his daughter? He shuddered involuntarily, remembering the terrible, inhuman look in the Captain's eyes... before he shot him.

The gun! Enoch scrambled for the white coat he'd discarded. It felt light - too light. The pocket was empty. Where was it? He groaned as he remembered; he'd dropped it when he picked up Mandy and, in his haste, he'd never picked it up. There was nothing to protect her with now. *Nothing but the blood of Jesus.*

Enoch took a deep breath and ran a hand through the wisps of his hair. He'd hoped to make a quick and peaceful getaway - the gun had only ever been a last resort. He'd never had a plan for getting out of this kind of mess. The white coat that had cloaked him so effectively was useless: it looked more like a butcher's apron now. And how was he supposed to get Mandy out now? They'd certainly be on the lookout for the missing gurney.

His eyes swept the janitor's closet as he heard the stomping of feet and the shouting of orders outside the door. He had to hurry. Rows of metal shelves filled with cleaning supplies stood before him, offering him no help. There was a roll of paper towels which he used to wrap around his forearms and torsos to stem the blood that still flowed from his wounds. There was a box of surgical masks - he slipped one on.

Then his eyes spied a rack of sky-blue coveralls tucked at the end of the shelves, hanging over one of the laundry bins. He snatched one of the coveralls and pulled it on; it was again too small and this time the legs came down to just below his knee, leaving his dirty work pants exposed. The bin however was spacious. He lifted Mandy gently from the gurney, grunting as his back spasmed in pain, and stripped the bed, pulling the mattress and dumping it into the bin. He then laid Mandy down on the cushioning, feeling for her pulse one more time. It was strong... stronger than before.

"I'm going to get you out of here sweetheart," he whispered

and then covered her with the linens. The gurney he shoved as far back into the shadows of the supply closet as he could and tipped on its side to keep it out of easy view. Then, pulling the bin with him, he pressed his ear to the door and listened. There were voices, but they sounded distant. He sucked in a breath and pushed out, praying for a clear path.

He exhaled. There was no one in the hallway. Then turning to the right, he saw, standing in front of the black-curtained tabernacle, a pair of deputies, tall and menacing with long-barreled silver revolvers drawn and dangling at their sides. They were looking away from Enoch, towards the hallways to the left and right of the open square, but at the squeaking of the bin's wheels, they both turned in Enoch's direction.

Enoch froze for a moment, sure that he was undone, flinching for the loud verbal commands, waiting for those long barrels to rise and point at him. But there was a voice from inside the tent and both deputies turned to poke their heads through the thick plastic curtain. Enoch pivoted quickly and pushed the bin at a rapid pace away from them, taking the first right to get out of their line of sight.

He picked up speed traveling down the long corridor before him, casting glances back at the corner behind, dreading the appearance of the deputies. Surely their suspicions had been raised - what was a janitor doing emerging from a supply closet five minutes after a shooting? They'd investigate, follow him and call out to him in their alien tongue and see how he'd respond. He looked back again, still no -

A sharp cry sounded suddenly in front of Enoch and he snapped his head forward. It was the doctor he'd seen roughing up the nurse - he must have come running down the adjoining corridor. Enoch had run the steel rim of the bin directly into his midsection and he was now doubled over in front of him, gasping for breath.

Enoch suppressed the urge to apologize and then the flight instinct that came after. Instead he lowered his head and slumped his shoulders in the manner of the nurses and janitors he'd spent so many hours following.

The doctor caught enough of his breath to straighten up and bark abuse at him in that foreign language. Enoch bowed his head lower and bent his knees to sink further towards the ground, daring not to make eye contact with the man. He hoped a swift tongue lashing would satisfy the doctor and then he'd presumably continue on his hurried way, probably to Captain Paler's body.

But the doctor was not satisfied with words and Enoch felt a stinging blow land against the back of his head. He lowered his head still further, until he was almost leaning into the bin. Still hurling unintelligible insults, the doctor grabbed Enoch by the forearm and yanked at him savagely, his long fingernails piercing the flimsy plastic of the coverall and the paper towels beneath to dig into the throbbing punctures left by Captain Paler's bite. Enoch couldn't bear it - he cried out in pain.

The sound of anguish apparently satisfied the doctor, for he released Enoch's forearm quickly and ceased his harangue. Enoch staggered forward, clutching at his forearm, trying to hold the paper towel in place. But the wounds had begun to gush afresh and he could feel the blood saturating the thin paper barrier and drip down his arm. He looked down and saw that it had already begun to trickle on the floor between his feet.

There was nothing he could do to stop the bleeding. He could only push forward and hope.

There was a shout from behind him. It was the doctor's voice again, he was sure. This time it sounded less like an insult than a command. But Enoch could not take the risk of waiting to find out. He bolted, pushing the bin forward as fast as he could. He heard another shout from behind him, but it sounded distant - the doctor was not giving chase.

Enoch was sprinting forward now, hurtling down the hallway, blindly trusting that there would be an exit somewhere in front of him. Every corridor he turned seemed to be part of an unending labyrinth, the walls always displaying the same colored lines and geometric patterns but never leading anywhere. There was the occasional nurse that stopped to stare as he rocketed past them, but no one barred his path. Though he heard no calls or stomping feet behind him, he could not shake the feeling that he was being pursued... that someone was following the trail of blood he left behind.

At the sight of another nurse he turned sharply onto a broad hallway that dead-ended into a pair of doors with no handles. He stopped, exhausted, when they resisted the shove he gave them. He panted and at last looked behind him. No one appeared around the corner. He took in his surroundings. This place was at least new. There was a metal disk on the wall beside him. He pressed it and the doors swung slowly open.

Brightness and warmth poured through the widening gaps, filling Enoch's eyes with hope. For the first time in so many hours he was seeing daylight. It was at the other end of yet another long hallway, streaming in through sliding glass doors. A dozen silhouettes stood between him and this long-awaited exit, his eyes taking several moments to strip away the black shadows around their forms to see the dark blues and reds of their uniforms. They were paramedics, idling and chatting, some leaning against the wall and smoking, others standing over gurneys with groaning patients.

"STOP!" The shout sounded clear and loud and Enoch's ears, in unmistakable English. He turned to see a man behind him on the other side of the mechanical doors, some 30 yards away. In his hand was a silver revolver. Enoch sprang into motion, hunkering down against the bin and speeding towards the light.

The paramedics all stopped what they were doing to watch this strange man wearing blue plastic coveralls pushing a laundry bin at so recklessly. Then came the crack of a gunshot and the mad scramble began. Enoch swerved from left to right, cutting a serpentine path as men leapt and dove around him, seeking any kind of cover in the open hallway.

BANG! BANG! BANG! The shots rang out. Enoch saw a paramedic fall in front of him, bleeding from his temple. He felt the sickening bump as he pushed the bin over his lifeless arm. More shots thundered from behind him and he saw the glass doors shatter in front of him.

He burst through the doors and he felt the rush of warm air pour into his lungs. So much sun and open space. Nowhere to hide. Nowhere to run... Except for the row of ambulances parked in front of him, one with a ramp lowered invitingly onto the pavement. He propelled the bin forward flying up the ramp and into the ambulance. He slammed the rear doors closed.

A narrow passage led up to the cabin and Enoch squeezed through, throwing one worried glance back at the bin. He desperately wanted to check Mandy again, to make sure none of those wild shots had found her, but there was no time. The keys were in the ignition and he jumped into the driver's seat. He stomped on the gas and the ambulance took off, dragging the ramp behind with a terrible noise. He swerved sharply and it detached with a clang. His bleeding body ached and cried with every bump in the pavement but he gritted his teeth and pressed down harder on the gas.

The Sanatorium parking lot was big but empty and Enoch saw a clear path to the familiar highway that wove back down the hills to the city. He glanced in his side mirror. There was a chaotic scramble of bodies spilling out of the doors he'd just left. But as yet, no squad cars in pursuit. He eased up on the gas as he hung a sharp left onto the highway, flinching as he heard the bin careening wildly behind him.

"Just hold on, sweetheart. I'm going to get you home," he shouted over his shoulder. How he was going to accomplish that, he didn't know. There was no way he was going to be able to drive this ambulance all the way to Copper Springs. And he was certain every cop in a twenty mile radius would be swooping down on him as soon as the word got out. His only hope was Angel. Angel could hide them at least long enough for them to find a way out of town. But how to reach him? Just drive up to his house and hope no one noticed?

Enoch checked the clock on the dashboard. It was five o'clock. Angel would be at work.by now. There was a radio receiver dangling from a cord next to the clock. Angel had let him help with the car radio on their many ride-alongs and Enoch had learned how to use it. He only hoped that the ambulance radio had access to the police channels. He cast another glance behind him - still no blue lights. Keeping an eye on the twisting road in the front of him, he fiddled with the radio.

A click of the knob and he heard the familiar back-and-forth of the squad cars and the dispatcher. He paused before keying up. Though he knew Angel's call sign - five-fifty-alpha - he knew that a strange voice piping up on the main police channel would only set off alarms. But there was a sub-channel he remembered Angel and his partners using when they wanted to chat outside of the dispatcher's hearing. As Enoch scanned the radio controls to find the right one, he heard a siren.

It was distant but unmistakable. There was no sign of them in the mirror, but with so many winds in the road, they could be close behind. Fumbling with the radio, he at last found the button to switch to the sub-channel.

"Five-fifty-alpha, you on here?" Enoch spoke into the radio, doing his best to keep the panic out of his voice. "This is Baptist." That was the codename Angel had given him to use on the radio so his partners would know when a civilian was communicating on their channel. Enoch clutched the radio, waiting for a reply, his eyes fixed on the mirror, waiting for the deputies to come speeding round the last bend.

There was only silence. Enoch repeated his transmission, fretting that Angel was not on the sub-channel. He and his partners had used it infrequently, switching over when there was some juicy bit of gossip to circulate or when it was time to sneak off somewhere to find something to eat or take a nap.

Then a voice came crackling over the radio. "Hang on there, Baptist. I think I know where he is. I'll see if I can get him on here for you."

A blue glow in the cloud of dust behind him drew Enoch's eyes back to the mirror. They'd caught up. He floored the accelerator, adding to the downhill momentum to make every turn down the winding highway a threat to send him and his precious cargo cannonballing off the road and down the hillside. But there was no slowing down. Let one of those deputies close enough and he was sure they would ram him and send the ambulance careening to the same rocky fate.

Enoch held his breath as he saw the yellow sign warning of a sharp turn ahead and remembered the long sickle the highway cut around the hill from the previous treks in the back of the pick-up. It had been enough to turn his stomach going 35 in a pick-up, and now he was doing 70 in a top-heavy ambulance that would tumble if he turned the wheel even a little too sharply.

And then he saw it: a dirt path cutting off from the highway at the beginning of the sickle, heading straight down the hill. He took it instinctively, bracing for the transition from the smooth asphalt to the dust and gravel. It was worse than he anticipated. Everything shook and groaned under the unending tremors, from the medical equipment rattling off the shelves, the bones vibrating in Enoch's body to the teeth chattering so loudly in his head that he couldn't hear anything else. The wounds on his body sang their fury at every jolt.

The terrible shaking went on for what felt like several minutes and then the path flattened out and took a sudden sharp cut to the left that spit Enoch out on a new path heading straight for a little creek. Enoch slammed on the brakes. The creek wasn't nearly as big or dark as the one back home; it couldn't have been more than 10 feet wide. Still, there was no telling how deep it was or whether the ambulance could ford it. There was no turning back, however - he could hear the sirens behind him.

He sped forward, the cab dipping suddenly forward as the ambulance crested the bank and hit the water with a splash. Muddy water began to gush in through the gaps in the door frame - it was deeper than he'd thought. The front wheels sank still further, spinning free in the mud. Enoch thanked the Lord for four-wheel drive as the the rear wheels propelled the chassis onward until the front wheels gained purchase on the opposite bank and he was across.

He stomped on the accelerator again and he was off down the new path. He saw the squad cars swerving wildly on the other side of the creek. He'd crossed the Jordan. They were free!

***

Consciousness came slowly to Mandy. First came the creeping awareness that she was awake and had been for some time. Whether minutes or hours or even days, she couldn't tell. Nor could she see or hear or move; she could only feel faint tremors. She felt like she was encased in a slab of marble and that someone was pounding away at the outside with a hammer and chisel, liberating her chip by chip.

Imprisoned in stillness, her mind struggled to conjure up a concrete memory, something to wrap her missing sensations around and reassure herself that she was still real and alive. Vlad's voice in her ear, whispering promises of their future together. His hand squeezing hers. His warmth enveloping her cold fingers, giving her permission to go to sleep. But when she searched for that warmth, it wasn't there, only something cold and dark. Something coming for her...

Another thump of the hammer and a ringing sounded in her ears. Then her eyes snapped open. But she could see nothing but shadow and darkness. Something was covering her. She commanded her hands to clear a path for her eyes, but there was no response. Her legs, too, ignored her demands that they stretch and feel out the borders of her prison. But her eyelids worked and she blinked them as hard as she could, hoping the impact would snap some life into the rest of her body.

Her jaw. She could feel it moving and she began to work it back and forth. The ringing in her ears gave way to a rumbling. The sound of an engine. This was no hospital.

Then she heard a voice, distorted and slightly mechanical. A radio.

"Go for five-fifty-alpha."

Then came another voice, this one natural, clear and close by, but strained, like a pipe about to burst.

"This is Baptist, five-fifty-alpha. I need your help." She knew this voice. It was a voice she had heard a thousand times, but the words did not fit the memories. She was able to crane her neck very slightly towards the sound.

"Advise your location," came the radio voice and that too sounded familiar. Angel. Her mind leapt at the recognition, the excitement surging down into her neck and shoulders. She could feel a twitch in her lower back now and with the return of sensation came a rush of thoughts. Five-fifty alpha was Angel's call sign... *Am I in a squad car? Then why can't I see? Did someone throw me in the trunk?*

"I don't know exactly. I'm coming up on the city from the hills but it's not a public road." No, that voice was too clear. She couldn't be in a trunk. And that voice wasn't any cop she knew.

"Describe what you see," came Angel over the radio again.

"There's warehouses coming up ahead of me. A lot of them. Past them is some kind of industrial complex on the left. It looks like a chemical plant."

"The plant... does it have a triple smokestack?"

"Yes."

"I'm not that far away from you. Pull up behind the stacks so you're out of sight. I'll be there as quick as I can."

All went quiet again but the rumble of the engine and Mandy found that she could now wiggle her fingers and toes. She could almost raise her hand. Then the rumbling too stopped and with it the lurching that she hadn't noticed until it ceased. There was a shuffling and she sensed the shadows above her shifting. Then, in a single motion, they rolled from her face like a drawn curtain and she saw her father's face, framed by a golden halo of light.

"Dad?" she said, and just getting out the sound was exhausting.

"Mandy!" he exclaimed. "You're awake!" He reached down to scoop her up. She realized then that she was draped in linens, like a baby in swaddling clothes. Her head drooped pathetically backwards along with her limbs as he lifted her up. She strained to lift her head.

"It's alright, sweetheart. Don't overwork yourself. I've got you."

Her head lolled back against his wrist and her eyes open to the dusky light pouring in through an open door. Enoch was stepping down and they emerged out into an open sky. Huge metal structures loomed over her, painted a dull yellow that made them look like part of a cosmically oversized construction playset. Enoch brought her under the shadow of one of these monsters and sat down slowly on a concrete step, cradling her gently but wincing as he did.

She felt his stomach rise underneath her as he let out a long sigh. For several moments he sat silently, staring out into the shadows with brows furrowed, his mind working out some unspoken dilemma. He lifted a hand to run through his hair and she saw his forearm was coated with blood, only just drying out. A sick feeling twisted her stomach.

"What happened, Dad?" she said, her throat too weak to speak louder than a whisper, but her mind racing. "Where are we?" Her voice was so quiet she couldn't even be sure she had spoken, but Enoch seemed to hear her.

"I don't know," he said, looking around them before looking down at her. His face was tired, with far more lines than she ever remembered. *How long was I out?* "But we're almost safe now."

Safe from what? She wanted to shout it, but her lungs would not cooperate. Instead she breathed out the words one by one.

"Don't worry about that, now. We've just to focus on getting you out of the city and back home." He looked away from her, craning his neck around and watching the path they'd just come with a fearful look.

This is my home! She wanted to shout again. Her emotions had been dulled along with her senses, but they were returning in force. She felt a terrible burst of panic and with it an urge to run that she knew she was incapable of carrying out. But then a voice, her own voice, spoke from within her. *Don't worry. It's a dream. It will pass.*

She rolled her head to look around, seeing only a slit of red sky between the hard contours of the metal structure. An ache of loneliness spread from inside her chest as the voice receded. *Where's Vlad?* A black figure suddenly crept up from her memory, crawling towards her, filling her with dread. She shuddered and cast about for a flesh and blood image of him. His hands, his face, his smile... But there was nothing there.

She felt Enoch stir behind her, and he eased her out of his arms and onto the concrete, where she lay limp and helpless. Enoch cocked his head skyward, his eyes widening. Mandy listened, struggling to hear what he was hearing, but there was only a residual ringing in her ears. But then she heard it. It was the distinct chopping whir of a helicopter and it was growing steadily louder.

Seeing Enoch standing now, his eyes glued to the patch of sky between the structures, she sensed the helicopter was looking for them both. Wrapped in strange blue plastic with blood oozing from his arm, he looked like an escapee from the mental hospital. She forced her head up to see her own get-up: a hospital gown. Her head fell heavily back against the concrete again as her neck's strength gave out and the blow to her skull did nothing to help her mind put together these jumbled pieces. Nor did it wake her from the dream. Tears welled in her eyes.

The helicopter was close now and from the sounds of it, it was circling. They would probably be spotted before long. It would only be a matter of time before squad cars converged on them. Sure enough, there was the sound of tires and an engine. Someone had pulled on the scene.

"Stay right there, sweetheart. I'll be right back." came Enoch's voice, and she heard his feet crunch a path away from her. She tried to push herself up, but the strength wasn't there and she could only lay there, focusing all of her mind on the sounds traveling to her ears. When she closed her eyes, she imagined Enoch running around the corner into a bristling line of shotgun-wielding cops posted up behind squad cars and she could almost hear the salvo of shots and see him falling lifeless to the ground. Again the tears welled.

But there were no shots. Only a series of exclamations, too distant for her to make out, and then the sound of two sets of footsteps making their way back to her.

Then she heard that familiar voice, growing louder as it drew nearer. "Sorry, it took me longer than I thought." It was Angel. "I had to get my car from the precinct. I don't know what you did up there, but every cop in the county is looking -"

His voice cut off suddenly along with footsteps.

"Yes, it's her," came Enoch's voice. "She can hardly move, but she's alive!"

"Mandy!" Angel cried and before she could roll her head over to him, she felt his hands slipping under her back and legs and then she was in his arms. *A ragdoll to be passed around.*

His face came into view. It was the same brown face she remembered, with the same broad, flat nose and the eyebrows as thick as hedges, all of it framed by the protruding jaw and Aztec cheekbones. His eyes, always so soft and tender and now moist with tears, were fixed on her, drinking her up.

"I thought you were dead," he said, his voice trembling. She didn't know how to respond and could only blink in return. He said something else but the helicopter banked in so close, she couldn't hear him over the noise.

Enoch moved in close, putting a hand on Angel's shoulder.

"It's time to leave."

"I'll get her in the car."

"No," said Enoch, with a finality that made Mandy twist her neck to look at him. "I want you to stay here with her."

Angel stayed silent, uncomprehending.

"If they don't find me in that ambulance, they won't stop looking for her. I can drive it away from here and you'll have a clear path to take her back home."

"That's not such a good idea. They think you killed somebody. They were saying you're armed and dangerous." The notion of her father as armed and dangerous was so ridiculous that Mandy's first instinct was to laugh. But even if her body could have sustained a laugh, it would have died on her lips as the rest of Angel's words settled in her mind. *Killed someone?* The black shadow crept up again. She closed her eyes and nestled her face into Angel's shoulder.

Feeling her shivering, Angel clutched her tighter. "We should get Mandy to a hospital."

"No, take her to Doc Quinn in Copper Springs. If you have to take her somewhere in the city, find Bremer. He's the only one we can trust."

"Fine, but let me take you into a police station so we can get all this nonsense sorted out without you having to risk running into one of those sheriffs. Those guys shoot first and ask questions later."

"You don't have to worry about me. I'll be fine. I didn't do anything wrong, only what I had to do to protect her."

Protect me? Her nerves fired and her body jerked at the sudden sound of a gunshot. A memory… She burrowed deeper into Angel, trying to push the sound away, trying to force herself back to sleep. But the black figure would be waiting for her there.

She felt something warm against her cheek. A hand. She turned into her father's palm to see him staring down at her. There was no halo around him this time, just shadows and a dull red glow from the setting sun.

"Let me take her to the car." Mandy flopped from Angel's to Enoch's arms. He walked slowly and she felt his arms shaking beneath her. His breathing was labored. *You're an old man. I'm a grown woman. You shouldn't have to carry me anymore.* But where was the energy to set things back in order?

"When you get home," he began, his voice low and distant. "Have your mother make you some of her lentil soup. It'll get you back up on your feet. Then, when you're feeling strong enough, maybe you can do something for me."

She looked up at him, and after a deep breath she had enough strength to respond. "What is it?"

He smiled broadly at the sound of her voice, the deepening lines in his face making him look just like grandma for a brief moment.

"Go back to church."

Her lungs twinged, not just from shortness of breath but a rising exasperation. Always the same few thoughts and ideas rattling through his brain, the same record on endless repeat for her entire life. What a stupid thing to bring up with so much swirling in the air! But what could she do but say yes? *Ragdolls who can't move their arms don't get to say no.* Besides, what did it matter? It was a dream.

She breathed an "alright." She couldn't see his face but she could feel his smile.

Enoch shifted her in his arms to free up a hand. She heard a car door open and he set her down. She slumped in the seat and felt herself toppling over but Enoch caught her and pressed her back against the seat, pulling a seatbelt across her chest and securing her in place with a click.

He leaned over to tighten the belt and then deposited a kiss on her forehead. His lips lingered for several moments, leaving an imprint of heat when he finally detached. "Goodbye, sweetheart," he said and then the door closed and he was gone. She tried to follow him with her eyes, but her neck gave out. Her view was the dashboard, a flat black surface, its only adornment Angel's police radio. She could hear muffled voices from outside. Angel and her dad talking. Deciding her fate. She shut her eyes and tried to will herself the strength to lift her head again.

She must have drifted off for a few minutes because when she opened her eyes again, Angel was sitting next to her, cutting on the engine. The micro-nap must have returned some of her strength because when she tried to speak, words came out.

"Tell me what's going on."

Angel looked over at her in surprise. "I'm still trying to figure that out..." He trailed off, staring at her with wide eyes. The intensity of his stare drained her and her slumped back down. "They told me you were dead... I believed them. I thought you were gone. But your dad, he never did. He was convinced... I thought he'd gone crazy!"

Mandy marshaled her strength again, this time not bothering to waste any energy looking at Angel. "Who said I was dead?"

"The city... the department... the newspaper... Everybody! They were about to run a funeral procession through downtown for you!"

The thought numbed her. Maybe she was dead and this nonsense world was the afterlife. Nothing made sense. Back in the hospital with Vlad, she'd felt so good... Miraculously good. And he'd spoken with so much excitement and enthusiasm about her future.. our future... How could anyone have written her off as dead?

She closed her eyes and probed her memory for answers. But there was nothing to glean from the sweet nothings that Vlad had whispered in her ear. They existed in her mind only as the shadows of meaning, the feelings without the substance. When she reached for the space that Vlad had filled, there was only a frightening void in the shape of a man.

"Why?" was all she could mutter.

"Your dad thought they were trying to turn you into... one of them." Angel reached over and squeezed her hand.

His blood in her veins. A vampire like them. Together with him forever. With the flood of memories came a wave of desire so intense that she gasped. She wanted it so badly. She wanted to close her eyes and wake up next to *him*, to have *his* hand clutching hers, not Angel's. She pulled weakly at her hand, unable to break Angel's grip.

"He was right, wasn't he?" Angel continued. "I should have believed him. I should have helped him get out of there. God knows what he's got himself into now."

Why couldn't he have let me be? The tide of desire had peaked and now ebbed, leaving pain and fatigue in its place. Mandy desperately wanted to be free of the seatbelt that held her upright, so she could curl into a ball and return to unconsciousness, return to the cocoon that Vlad had made for her... To finish what they started... *Why couldn't he have just left us alone? Vlad!*

"We better get going." There was a hint of reluctance in Angel's voice. He shifted the car into drive. As they slowly rolled forward, he switched on the radio. There was a crackle, but no chatter. There was silence for several minutes, interspersed with routine checks and updates from the dispatcher. Then, a voice cut in, taut with excitement.

"Three-forty-delta, I just had an ambulance fly by me with Tigris County cars right behind it going southbound on Wellington. I'm behind them."

Angel sucked in his breath. "That's him."

"Nine-hundred-delta," came another voice over the radio. A lieutenant's call-sign. "Keep your distance, three-forty-delta. This is the county's pursuit."

Her dad in an ambulance, leading cops on a chase. If that wasn't proof this was all some sort of medication-induced hallucination... But the radio continued to spit out updates until her mind was forced to grant the absurd notion the dimensions of reality.

"Just blew through the red at Halloran. They're going at least 90."

90! On road trips when she was a kid, her dad would break into sweats if he went 5 over the limit and now he was doing 90 on a main thoroughfare like Halloran? *Impossible.*

"Ambulance just took out a stop sign on Sweeney. Rear passenger tire flat."

"County's gonna try to PIT him... They got him! Ambulance just wrecked out!"

Mandy felt a tightness in her gut. She saw Angel's knuckle go white as they gripped the steering wheel tightly.

"Nine-hundred-delta. All cars keep your distance and set up a perimeter. Do not engage the suspect."

"We can't even get close, lieu. There must be twenty county cars out here. Looks like they've got him surrounded. He's coming out!"

Mandy closed her eyes and held her breath. None of this was real. This whole chain of events was impossible from the beginning. Her dad couldn't have done any of it. Not a straight arrow like Enoch Parker the Third. A man like that - a pillar of the community - wouldn't have snuck into the hospital like a thief in the night and stolen her away. The man who prayed over the livestock before he shot them with his old Boy Scout rifle couldn't have shot a man. He couldn't have squeezed the trigger on a .38 revolver and made that other man, the one that looked so much like the man she loved. He couldn't have made him crumple to the floor.

No! She pushed these shadowy images back to the nightmare realm where they belonged. These things hadn't happened. She hadn't woken and seen them. She'd only dreamed them and now she was sending them back.

"Shots fired! Shots fired!" Hysterical shouts burst out into the silence, forcing Mandy's eyes open and onto the radio. From the blackness behind the wire mesh of the speaker came the crackling of gunfire.

"The suspect is down! He's down... Multiple gunshot wounds... He's not responsive... Start an ambulance..."

Angel howled suddenly in anguish, slamming the palm of his hand against the radio and pulling the car over. He slumped over the steering wheel and began to cry. Mandy just watched. She'd never seen him cry before.

Not looking up, he reached his hand out to grab hers and squeeze it.

"I'm so sorry," he said, his voice a deep groan. "I never should have let him go."

She couldn't have pulled her hand away if she wanted, but this time she didn't want to. Though she didn't feel what he was feeling

- even the sensation of his fingers against her hand was so dull it was nearly imperceptible - there was something like a twinge of sympathy in her chest. *Poor fool. He thinks this is real.*

They sat in the car for several minutes as Angel stopped crying but continued to hold Mandy's hand. Then he released her, bringing his arm up first to wipe his nose and then his eyes with his sleeve. There was a lurch and the car was moving again. She let the rocking of the car numb her until she couldn't tell how much time had passed.

Then something changed in her gut. They were moving upward at a steep grade, like a rollercoaster car beginning its ascent. She flopped her head back against the seat and lowered her eyes to gaze out the front window. Ahead of them, the red crest of the sun poured through the black metal lines of the Babylon Bridge. They were leaving the city.

"You can sleep now," he said. *But I'm already asleep.* "I promised your dad I'd get you home safe."

She cast a sleepy eye in his direction. He was watching the rear-view mirror warily as traffic slowed in front of them, his brow furrowed. The muscles in his forearms were tense and he was angled over the steering wheel, as if he was poised to make a sudden break. She wanted to reach out her hands and massage the stress from his shoulders, to tell him it would be alright. That she wasn't his responsibility. That all of this would slip back into the dark pools of memory where all nightmares eventually receded. He would wake up in his cute little house with its white picket fence and she in her hospital bed with Vlad at her side.

Traffic cleared in front of them and Angel eased back in his seat, pressing down on the accelerator. The *chunk-chunk-chunk* of the bridge's surface under the tires vibrated the seats underneath them, a gentle rattling that shook some of the feeling back into Mandy's limbs. It was a familiar sensation, not from the last time she'd gone over the bridge - that had been years ago. No, this was much more recent...

The wheels of the gurney against the hospital floor... She was being pushed... Floating in and out of consciousness... And then they had turned suddenly and her neck had rolled to one side and her eyes had opened and she had seen him. The black shadow. He was lying on his back, his head rolling to face her. His eyes were wide and mouth was open, teeth bared in a horrible snarl, blood dripping from his lips. This was not the man she loved, not a man at all. It was a ghoul. One hand reached towards her, fingers outstretched like twisted claws, grasping for her. And then a thick curtain swung closed between them and he disappeared.

Mandy began to shake uncontrollably. She clung to the seat with what little grip she had to steady herself. She stared out the window, desperate for another image to fill her mind. The cables of the bridge fanned out on either side of her. They hung from the thin strands of wire that undulated in waves as Angel sped across. From such slender threads, the whole bridge was dangling from the sky, suspended over the wide and bottomless span of the rushing river. How easily could they be torn asunder, casting them all into the depths below.

She closed her eyes and imagined the waters swirling around her, and slowly rising to engulf her. It was a pleasant sensation, her body lightening, the water cool and caressing. Her shaking eased and she lay still, languishing in the water's embrace. It began to push at her nose and into her mouth, gently prodding at first, repulsed by the air bubbles that escaped from her throat, tickling as they left her. But the pressure grew ever more insistent until it surrounded her like a vice and then, at last, overwhelmed her, rushing in to fill her lungs until they burst.

She gasped and her body startled awake. Angel had taken his eyes off the road to stare at her. The *chunk-chunk-chunk* below her had smoothed into the steady hum of tires on asphalt. The vertical lines of bridge cables had given way to wide open skies, where the dim light of the evening stars competed to be seen against the radiating glow of the city lights. They were over the bridge and the city was fading behind them.

"Are you okay?" Angel asked, reaching over to squeeze her hand again.

"No," she said. And this time she squeezed his hand in return.

EPILOGUE

Emily Parker raised her hand to shield her eyes from the noonday sun as she scanned the billowing dust cloud on the horizon where the long dirt road from the house met the highway. There had been much coming and going on this road in the past several weeks, and each time the dust rose, she felt the same uneasy mix of trepidation and anticipation. The foolish, girlish part of her would always spring with the impossible hope that the outline of Enoch's truck would emerge from the haze. She pushed the thought and the fresh stabs of grief that came with it into the dull ache that rested permanently in her chest. *I will go to him, but he will not return to me.*

She felt it would be too soon to be Angel Mendoza's car, though she would have welcomed the sight with all her heart. That young man had first rolled into town like a storm cloud, bringing the dark tidings that cast a pall over their entire world, for several terrible moments, inundated Emily with a sadness that penetrated to the marrow of her bones. But he'd also brought the answer to the prayer she'd prayed so fervently every day for the last five years.

Angel had returned several times since, and each time he was more and more like a summer breeze, breaking up and blowing away the clouds that had first followed him. He was a help on the farm, cheerfully shouldering Enoch's routines and winnowing down the backlog of maintenance that had built up in his absence. The boys had taken to him immediately, shaking from the heavy melancholy that had held them down like entangling vines. The sounds of the three of them laughing and wrestling in the grass a few days before had brought a smile to her lips for the first time since that day.

She only hoped he could have a similar effect on Mandy. When he'd first carried her over the threshold, she was scarcely conscious. Emily had installed her in the girls' old bedroom, hoping that wonderfully cozy place with all its quilts and cushions and happy memories would restore some warmth to her ghostly countenance. But the big bed seemed so wide and Mandy would disappear into its center, sinking down into the silent despair that consumed her. Too weak to get up or say more than a few words at a time, she was fading away.

Emily had been so disturbed to find something pale and translucent that fell in sheaths from her bed sheets to the floor when she changed the bedding. When she stooped to pick them up, they crumbled into flakes in her fingers. It was dead skin. Mandy had been shedding it in great swaths, sloughing it off her back and neck and shoulders with her endless tossing and turning. Each night, more and more of it would come off, and with each vanishing layer, the mottled ridges and valleys of her scar tissue pushed closer to the surface.

Emily had taken to leaving her own too-wide bed to curl up alongside her in hopes, applying creams to the angry red landscape that stretched from Mandy's scalp to the small of her back, cooing and praying as her daughter whimpered. It had been sleepless agony for them both.

It had been Angel that turned the tide. He had returned from the city with a case full of medicated ointment he'd received from a doctor there. He would apply the ointment to Mandy's skin himself, his fingers tracing over her burns with the utmost tenderness. Then he'd sit by her side as the medication took its effect, reading whatever he could find on the bookshelf. The old Jane Austen novels had sounded silly at first in his low, halting voice, but he'd persisted, reading for hours at a time until she'd fallen asleep. It had done wonders for Mandy.

After another trip back to the city, Angel returned with a painting, a weird mishmash of strange shapes. At the sight of it, Mandy had begun to cough and Emily had rushed to her side only to discover it was laughter. After the passage of a few more days, Mandy had gotten out of bed and took to moving around the house using the furniture to steady her. When Angel visited, she would lean on his arm and they'd take short walks through the orchard. The previous Sunday she'd even borrowed a dress and gone to church. Then she'd lent a trembling hand in the kitchen when they'd made dinner afterwards. That week had passed like a parade of cheer, drumming hope into Emily's beleaguered soul. Until Sheriff McKenzie had driven up and brought the darkness back.

McKenzie had come by on the pretense of recruiting Angel for the department. But as soon as he had concluded that bit of business, he had pulled Angel and Emily aside, away from the family, and shared a disturbing tale in whispered tones.

On the morning before his visit, McKenzie had stopped for his usual coffee at Bob Forrester's donut shop off the highway when Bob told him of a strange visitor that had walked in just as he'd unlocked the door. He was a tall pale man who ordered a plate to go without sitting down and then promptly dropped a $20 tip on top of his bill.

He told Bob he was a buyer's agent from Apolleon, the industrial farming outfit from upstate, and that he was trying to locate a list of farming properties to put offers on. His problem, he said with a rueful smile, was that the map Apolleon gave him didn't match the territory. Would Bob do him a solid and help him find a couple of these? He pushed the list forward and sure enough, there was a heap of farm addresses on there... among them the Parker farm off Black Creek. Bob, a wily old sort, protested he had no head for direction - "that's why I built so close to the highway: so I'd never forget where I was!" But if the man would just wait a few minutes for Sheriff McKenzie to come in for his breakfast and he'd surely be happy to show him around; the Sheriff knew every backroad and hunting trail in the whole county.

The Apolleon man promptly left, driving off in a sleek black Mercedes that looked like it had accumulated several days' worth of dust. As it happened, Bob knew a fellow from Apolleon who had left a business card a year ago when he'd come through town. Bob called him up to ask if they were looking to buy in the area again. Turned out the company had consolidated its operations into its soy and corn crops and had no more interest in hill country like Copper Springs.

McKenzie, troubled, did some further digging. The official maps of the area did have a Black Creek Road, but it was in the barren west end of the country where there was hardly anything but shrubs, weeds and goat farmers. Sure enough, the farmers out there had seen a foreign car driving around the previous day and had stopped to ask them if they knew where the Parker farm was. The farmers out in the west county weren't big church folk, so they hadn't known the Parkers well, though they probably wouldn't have told the pale stranger even if they had. Sheriff McKenzie seemed confident that the man had thus far had found no success in determining their whereabouts.

But the presence of the mystery man so close to the farm had filled Emily with terror, and in every spare moment since, her eyes had been glued to the spot on the horizon where the road first turned off the highway. When Enoch had last spoken to her, a whispered phone conversation that ran continuously through her brain, he'd promised that Mandy wasn't dead and that he was going to bring her home. But he'd also worried that men would come looking for her. Powerful men that would be angry that he had taken her from them and desperate to steal her back.

Emily had shared her fears with the Sheriff early on, and he'd done his best to mobilize the town in the family's defense. Her own daughters and their families had already practically moved in. And the church had been so generous with their support since Enoch's passing. They brought home enormous quantities of food every Sunday and Emily only had to mention something that needed fixing on the farm and someone would show up the next day to repair it free of charge. It was only her stubborn pride that kept them from coming round every day.

But after the appearance of the stranger, nothing could have kept her people at bay. They'd taken to sending men to every roadway into town to keep a watch on everyone coming and going. Her phone rang off the hook from the wives' brigade asking if they needed to send their men by. It was all an encouragement, a great big security blanket surrounding her to suffocate her anxiety.

Still, she worried. What could simple country people do against these men of the world with all their power? What would stop them from ending up like her Enoch? In her nightmares, she saw an endless caravan of black vehicles with tinted windows coming down the road and none could stand in their way. Each time she woke and prayed, prayed for strength to resist, for faith to believe that it wasn't hopeless. And each time the pit of despair re-emerged, an ever-widening abyss that consumed all hope.

Her anxiety had grown more acute since Angel had left them suddenly, with great haste. He'd said only that he'd heard something from a friend in the city and that he had to go there to make sure. Emily had begged him not to go. She wanted him here. More importantly, Mandy needed him. But he had insisted and left, promising that he would return.

And so she watched the cloud on the horizon, certain despite herself that this was the precipice of doom, that they were coming to rip her daughter from her arms, to make vain her husband's sacrifice and to trample over any that stood in their way. Her body jolted at a sound behind her: a creak of the warped wooden floorboards of the porch. It was Mandy, so thin and frail, her pale skin almost luminescent. A will-o'-wisp flitting between the worlds.

"Oh, Amanda, you shouldn't be out here. It's not safe."

Mandy shook her head and stepped towards her, gingerly, one hand seeking the stability of the porch railing and the other holding out a mug of coffee.

"Here," she said, handing Emily the mug and leaning beside her to look out at the road. "It takes the edge off when you're staring into the void."

Mandy followed Emily's gaze to the cloud of dust. "It's probably just another big rig on the highway, mom."

"I don't think so," she replied, setting aside the coffee and wrapping an arm around Mandy to clutch her close, being careful to reach below the burn line on her back. "It's been moving towards us."

Mandy said nothing, only looking. Emily turned and watched her, the same question forming on her lips that had haunted her since Mandy's return. But this time she would not swallow it.

"If they come for you... Would you want to go back?"

Mandy was quiet for several moments.

"No," she said finally. "There's nothing there for me anymore."

Emily did not reply, but a warmth radiated from her heart and shrunk the pit in her stomach. She raised her eyes above the dust and stared gratefully into the white clouds that spread across the blue sky like heavenly continents. These were the words she had hoped and prayed to hear since the day she returned, and the painful years prior to that. Her daughter was home again. Enoch had kept his promise and brought her back, body and soul. She could forgive him for breaking his other promise: that he'd come home, too.

"Mom, look."

She followed Mandy's finger back downward to the road where an outline of a vehicle was emerging from the dusty haze. Emily's heart sank. It was not Sheriff McKenzie's car nor one of the old pick-ups of the church folk, but a black sedan. As the road curved, however, she could see that this was no ordinary car, nor was it the Mercedes of her fears. It was a hearse.

As the curve widened, they saw a caravan behind it, a line of cars that stretched beyond the horizon. These were the vehicles of the townspeople and not just some of them. The whole town seemed to be behind the hearse: pick-ups, tractors, threshers, everything. And there were her boys hopping down from the bed of a truck, running towards her. There were Esther and Hannah, babies on their hips, coming right behind them. And there was Sheriff McKenzie's squad car! And Angel!

The caravan came to a stop just short of the porch and the people began to emerge from their vehicles to approach Emily and Mandy. If this was a funeral procession, no one was dressed for it. There was brother Bob in his overalls and Doc Quinn in his duck hunting gear. It was as if they'd all stopped whatever it was they'd been doing to follow the hearse, which, as Emily later learned, was exactly what had happened.

Angel came running up to the front of the crowd, his face lit up with hope. Sheriff McKenzie trotted behind, wearing the same expression.

"They released him!" Angel shouted, pointing at the hearse behind him. "We brought Enoch home!"

Emily stared, her knees weakening. She was suddenly conscious of a presence behind the curtains of the hearse, a black hole pulling her eyes and thoughts into it and binding them to itself. But a voice of warning sounded in her mind and, with great difficulty, she shifted her eyes back to the horizon.

"But we're not being careful," she said, a note of panic rising in her voice. "We'll lead them right to the farm." She moved back towards the door, tugging at Mandy. She had to hide her!

But Angel was at her side now and held her still.

"No, Mrs. P, it's okay!"

"He's right, Em," said McKenzie from behind. "Tell her,

Angel."

Angel began to speak excitedly in words that Emily could scarcely understand, her mind being so rattled and her thoughts constantly seeking the contents of the hearse over his shoulder. But she was able to gather that there had been some sort of big change in the city... That a city politician had turned on the people that had chased Enoch and were looking for Mandy... That these people had so many problems now, they couldn't afford to go chasing after her... That she was safe.

"I don't understand," she said when he had finished. "But I trust you." She turned to Mandy - he was speaking her words, city words. She should understand. "Are you going to be okay?"

"Yeah, mom. It sounds like we're in the clear."

Nodding, she gave one arm to Mandy and the other to Angel and together they walked to the hearse. The townsfolk gathered around them, quiet. Her family took up their places alongside her. The hearse's rear door swung and there it was: a casket, metal from the looks of it. A simple coffin, just as Enoch would have wanted.

The driver of the hearse joined them at the door. It was Mr. Hanson, Copper Springs' new mortician, 'new' meaning he'd only been in town for five years. He twisted his hands nervously.

"I apologize for the irregularity of all this, ma'am. Very unusual circumstances. I didn't know such a whole lot of people would start following me. I hope I haven't caused you any distress."

Emily couldn't look at him - her eyes were fixed on the coffin - and she couldn't get out any words, but she reached out blindly to give his nervous hands a reassuring squeeze.

"If you'd like, we can continue on to the funeral parlor and arrange for a proper visitation and funeral."

"No," she said, her voice airy and weak, but still full of conviction. And then, pulling Mandy close, she whispered her instructions into her ear. Mandy nodded and turned to the crowd. She spoke in cool, measured tones, standing like a pillar of strength, the ghostly waif that had hovered at death's door become flesh again.

The men would take the casket down the wooded path where the hearse could not go, down towards the creek and the maple grove and the little spot where Enoch's mother and father had been laid to rest. Then they would dig a grave alongside it, just ahead of his father's, careful to leave another space just in front of his mother. Someone would also have to go and fetch Preacher, who was just about the only man in town who wasn't already there, so that he could say a prayer and conduct a little service. And then they would lay Enoch to rest.

It was all done just as Mandy said and then some. While the men attended to the hoisting and the digging, the women descended on Emily's pantry or ran back to their own to pour out the bounty of early summer into a feast. They would celebrate Enoch's life and Mandy's return with all the extravagance of a fifty-year jubilee. The excitement was like electricity in the air as they finished the work and Preacher concluded his message.

"The Lord Jesus himself told us that in his Father's house... in our Father's house... are many mansions. He went to go and prepare a place for us, that where He is, we might be also. Brothers and sisters, Enoch has entered into our Father's house in the place that our Lord Jesus has prepared for him. Now let us rejoice and be glad in this... And if we yet weep and grieve let it be because we must wait a little longer before we can join him."

There were shouts of "hallelujah!" as the tearful, hungry crowd dispersed and headed back towards the house. Emily remained where she had been throughout the ceremonies, kneeling beside the grave. Mandy leaned down beside her and gently tugged at her arm.

"It's time to go, mom."

Emily stood and joined the herd, clinging to Mandy's arm for support and choosing her steps carefully through the brambles that choked the ground. The brambles then gave way to a narrow but well-beaten path, a path that had been cleared and kept smooth by the daily tread of a long-legged farmer's boots as he went forth and then back again to fetch his lost sheep.

THE END

FURTHER READING

If you enjoyed this book, please be so kind as to say so on Amazon, Goodreads and anywhere else books are discussed. This book is the first in what will hopefully become a series delving into the secret history of vampires in America.